"Something's wrong."

"Not all kids have a curfew," I said.

"That's not it. I'm getting no emotions off of her," said Mandi.

Then I felt the slightest tingle on the back of my neck. My time as a possessed left me with the ability to sense different types of magic. Those involving Hell or demons I'm most sensitive to. If the girl was a demon or possessed herself, I would have known she was coming long before we could see her.

"I think it's a dead girl walking," I said.

The demon also enhanced my eyesight. As soon as the girl in the pink dress passed beneath a streetlight, my heart skipped a beat.

"It's Winnie. The bastard raised her daughter," I said, getting out of the car. A rage that wasn't entirely this sicko's fault took me over.

"Karver, get back in here. The raiser could be anywhere. We don't want to give away our position," said Mandi.

I was beyond listening. One of my dead was walking, and I had to stop Winnie before her mother saw her, or the emotional damage to Lucy would be something I couldn't imagine.

When I got close enough to the zombie child, I realized I didn't have a plan. Protocol dictates the best way to stop a zombie is to dismember it and separate the pieces. I had already sliced up this little girl once. I carried two blades under the back of my coat, but I couldn't bring myself to use them on her – not again.

<u>Praise for The DMA Casefiles:</u>

"As much as I wanted to hide my eyes behind my hands, peeking through the slits of my fingers, I could not help but continue reading... Thomas mixes ancient lore with what I like to call keyhole terror. The effect is a breakneck ride through established myths with full-bodied characters, while glimpsing the effects of horror through a keyhole, not in your face blood and gore, but the hint of its occurrence. Just enough scare to set the scene, the reader assumes the rest. The effect is one hell of a ride... Recommended for readers who like dark fantasy with a subtle twist of terror."   - Rae Bryant, The Fix

"Then Terror Came ... left me wanting more stories about the same "Men in Black"-type Agency that deals with the dangerously supernatural." -Bill Bodden, Flamesrising.com

AGENTS OF THE ABYSS
FRANKENSTEIN: MONSTERS OF THE ABYSS - STARING INTO THE ABYSS
DETECTIVES OF THE ABYSS - THE ABYSS STARES BACK

MYSTIC INVESTIGATORS™ SERIES
MYSTIC INVESTIGATORS   -   MEAN STREETS
ONCE MORE IN CRIME omnibus *Patrick Thomas & Diane Raetz*
SHADOWS & BRIMSTONES omnibus *Patrick Thomas & John L. French*

Other Padwolf books by John L. French & Patrick Thomas
RITES OF PASSAGE: *A DMA Casefile of Agent Karver & Detective Bianca Jones*
CAMELOT 13 *(editors)*

Other books by John L. French & Patrick Thomas
THE ASSASSAINS' BALL - THE SANTA HEIST

Other Padwolf books by John L. French
BIANCA JONES SERIES
HERE BE MONSTERS - MONSTERS AMONG US - THE LAST MONSTER

PADWOLF PULP
THE DEVIL OF HARBOR CITY - THE GREY MONK: SOULS ON FIRE
THE NIGHTMARE STRIKES - PAST SINS - MORTAL SINS

THE MAGIC OF SIMON TOMBS - BAD COP, NO DONUT (editor) - MERMAIDS 13 (editor)

Other Padwolf books by Patrick Thomas
AS THE GEARS TURN: *Tales of Steamworld* - EXILE & ENTRANCE - NEW BLOOD (co-editor)
THE WILDSIDHE CHRONICLES OMNIBUS (contributing author)

THE MURPHY'S LORE™ SERIES
TALES FROM BULFINCHE'S PUB - FOOLS' DAY - THROUGH THE DRINKING GLASS
- SHADOW OF THE WOLF - REDEMPTION ROAD - BARTENDER OF THE GODS -
NIGHTCAPS   -   EMPTY GRAVES   -   THE MUG LIFE

THE MURPHY'S LORE AFTER HOURS™ UNIVERSE
FAIRY WITH A GUN - FAIRY RIDES THE LIGHTNING - TERRORBELL THE
UNCONQUERED
DEAD TO RITES - LORE & DYSORDER - SOUL FOR HIRE: GREATEST HITS
BY DARKNESS CURSED   -   BY INVOCATION ONLY

MURPHY'S LORE STARTENDERS™
STARTENDERS   -   CONSTELLATION PRIZE

DEAR CTHULHU™ Series
HAVE A DARK DAY - GOOD ADVICE FOR BAD PEOPLE - CTHULHU KNOWS BEST
WHAT WOULD CTHULHU DO? - CTHULHU HAPPENS - CTHULHU EXPLAINS IT ALL
CTHULHU TAKE THEWHEEL

BIKINI JONES VS. THE BRAINNAPPERS FROM OUTER SPACE
BIKINI JONES VS. THE SEA MONSTERS

Patrick Thomas
John L. French

PADWOLF PUBLISHING INC
WWW.PADWOLF.COM
WWW.PATTHOMAS.NET
WWW.MURPHYS-LORE.COM

DARK RITES
An Agent Karver Omnibus
cover by Patrick Thomas
© 2024
includes

RITES OF PASSAGE

© 2013 Patrick Thomas and John L. French
Book edited by Alycia J. Mellgren
Cover by Patrick Thomas and Roy Maurtisen
Cover Design by Roy Maurtisen

DEAD TO RITES:
The DMA Casefiles Of Agent Karver
© 2010 Patrick Thomas
except
The Ties That Bind © Patrick Thomas & C.J. Henderson
Tag Team Match From Hell
© Patrick Thomas, C.J. Henderson, & John L.French
Cover Art © Rowena Morill
Book Edited by Alycia Mellgren
Special Thanks to Dr. Howard Margolin who found what others did not.

DMA, The Department of Mystic Affairs, Agent Karver, Murphy's Lore,
Mystic Investigators, and all related characters © &™ Patrick Thomas
Lai Wan © &™ C.J. Henderson
Bianca Jones and all related characters are © & ™ John L. French

13 digit ISBN 978-1-958310-06-9
Printed in the USA
First Printing

From the D M A casefiles of
Agent Karver & Detective Bianca Jones

rites of passage

From the pages of
MURPHY'S LORE™

John L. French
Patrick Thomas

To Roy Mauritsen
For his generosity in making my work look so much better.
PT

To Vince Sneed,
Bianca's first and biggest fan.
JLF

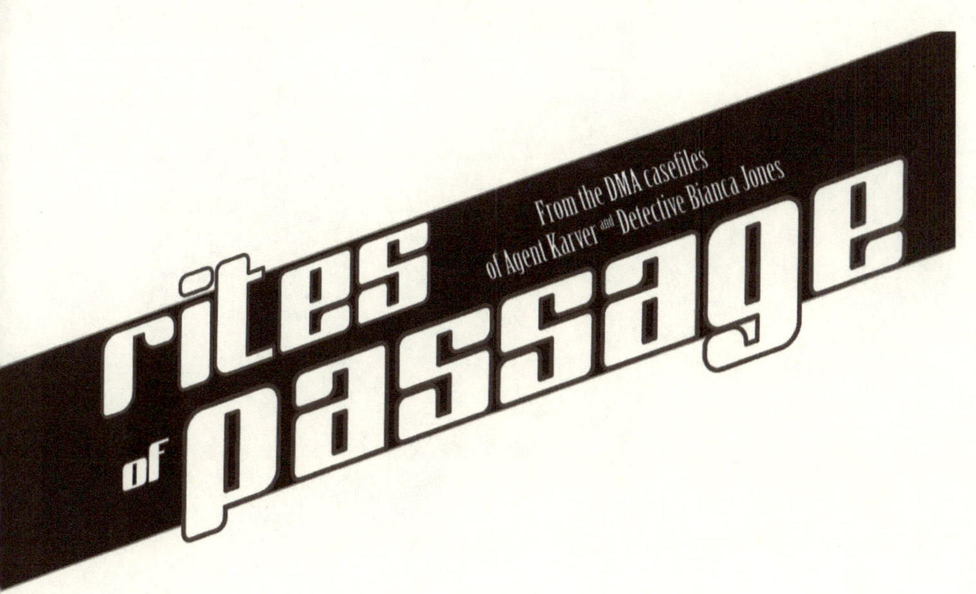

Patrick Thomas
John L. French

"Sometimes I envy the dead."
– Karver, former demon possessed serial killer

The memories of my dead haunt me. They have every right. All sixty-four of them suffered heinously before finally being murdered by the demon who hijacked my body.

Families were always the worst, especially the first. The seriál demon that possessed me seemed to get even more enjoyment from the horror and heartbreak of people watching their loved ones tortured and murdered than the actual deeds themselves. I know he enjoyed my anger and helplessness almost as much as the things he made my body do. The demon's joy was a dark and scary thing, so intense and pure that it made most human emotions pale by comparison and he absolutely reveled in destroying the lives of the innocent.

That may be why he chose that first family in Baltimore. Their last name was Innocent. There were four Innocents who died that night. The mother and father were Rich and Jane. Their teenage daughter was Lucy. The baby…

The little guy's name was Jimmy.

My demon puppeteer slid me through the darkness as silent as a shadow, using my hands to turn their house into a deathtrap, nailing and duct taping all the doors and windows shut so no one could get out. The demon had strengthened my body to the point where I could push the nails in without a hammer. That way there was no noise to wake anyone up. The final step was to lock the front door and nail that shut like a coffin in an old western.

The Innocents slept through all of this, which was a minor blessing. Waking earlier would have just lengthened their torment, which wasn't brief by any means.

Our first stop was the nursery. Later in other homes it would be the last, bringing the child to the other victims and forcing them to watch. The seriál found that it enjoyed the slaughter of infants above all else, especially when it could be done in front of those that loved them.

Little Jimmy had just woken up and he smiled and cooed when he saw me. His chubby little fingers reached up and grabbed hold of my thumb. I fought as hard as I could with everything I had to stop the seriál inside of me, to make him spare the baby and move on. The demon inhabited my brain in such a way that we shared thoughts and feelings. The demon wanted to turn its knife on the infant. I wanted to jump screaming through the window onto the hard cement below. My hand froze halfway to the knife.

I'd won the battle of wills. Or so I was foolish enough to believe. That's the bad part about belief. You can believe with all your heart, with every part of your soul and it won't be enough to make something true.

Lucy walked in. Brave kid, threw herself at me, even though I had sixty pounds and seven inches on her, all to try to save her little brother.

The seriál turned his attentions to her. I fought to hold my hands back, to save this brave girl, but it was like an ant trying to stop a herd of elephants.

It was a while before we got back to the baby and Lucy screamed for most of it. Her screams brought Rich and Jane running in. They were quickly subdued and tied up, their eyelids ripped off so they had no choice but to watch.

What the demon made me do to the Innocents still makes me sick.

"There are days I think I have the best job in the world. There are others where I know I also have the worst."
—Detective Bianca Jones, Baltimore Police Department

The sight was sickening. It was disgusting. It was the worst thing she'd seen in her career as a Baltimore City cop. It was something she knew would haunt her dreams for the rest of her life.

Rookie detective Bianca Jones forced herself not to turn away.

Short and thin, in the right light Bianca Jones could pass for a teenager. She was one of the youngest women to make detective in the BPD, and while an outsider might respect her for that accomplishment, cops are a funny bunch. They see horrors on the job that regular people did not and should not see, so they let off steam whenever they could. That included razzing the new guy, or in this case girl. The rank of detective wasn't an all-boys club, but was close enough that sometimes Bianca couldn't tell the difference.

"Hey, I thought the newbie was on this case. Shouldn't she be here by now?" said Detective Earl Beasley, despite the fact that she was standing five feet in front of him. When she didn't rise to the bait, Beasley made a big show of looking down and laughing. "Oh, there you are, Jones. I didn't see you down there."

Bianca looked around the crime scene, hoping to find something Beasley and the uniforms who had answered the call screwed up so she could blast them for it. They hadn't, so she had to hit below the belt.

"I guess that beer gut blocks a lot from view, huh? I'm amazed you can even go pee by yourself. I heard you need tweezers and a magnifying glass. I guess you just let loose in the general direction and hope to get somewhere near the bowl," Bianca said, never one to take an insult without giving back better than she got.

Still, she had to give Beasley credit. Other than her and a

crime scene tech, he was the only one who didn't look ready to blow chunks and contaminate the scene. Whoever killed this family was a sick bastard. The father had been gutted and dismembered. The wife looked like she had suffered indignities no woman should before the same happened to her. The killer hadn't just violated her natural openings; he had branched out and used ones he had made. The baby was the worst of them; a blade had been used on him repeatedly before his little head was smashed open on the wall.

Lastly was the girl. Not really a girl, an adolescent on the verge of womanhood. She had been abused almost as badly as her mother. Her blood was everywhere, leaking from wounds and orifices. Other fluids were as well, Bianca noted as she cataloged the girl's injuries.

Movement. Movement so subtle that had Bianca not been looking in the right place at the right time she would have missed it. The girl's chest, slowing rising and falling. She was breathing.

"The girl's still alive!" Bianca said, taking off her blazer and using it to staunch the blood flowing from the abdominal wounds. "Get that ambo crew back in here. She needs to get to Shock Trauma now!"

Beasley may have been an ass, but he got down with Bianca, providing first aid, putting pressure on the girl's wounds until paramedics arrived to rush her to the trauma unit.

"So, little girl, why don't you follow the medics down to University?"

Bianca let Beasley's "little girl" crack slide. There'd be time to fight that battle later. "I'd rather stay here and work the scene."

"No, I think you should go follow those buttholes and rip them a new one for not thoroughly checking the victims over. They failed that kid. Then get what you can from the docs. This," Beasley waved his arms to indicate the scene, "will still be here when you get back."

Lucy Innocent was in surgery for over twenty hours.

The girl lived, beating her killer.

"I hear people say things like law enforcement is a family and we should all work together. These people never had someone else come in and trample all over their cases."
– Detective Bianca Jones, BPD

More than anything, cops hate it when a bad guy gets away with a crime. Bianca Jones hated it more than most. It was her belief that every crime must be paid for, that every victim deserved justice. This was especially true when the crime was murder, when the investigator must act as an advocate for the deceased, sometimes the only advocate.

"We work for God," was a sign that Bianca had seen on the desks of several Homicide detectives. That she wasn't sure of, but she did work for the people of the City of Baltimore and she was not going to let any of them down.

Bianca was still on new detective rotation – three months each in Robbery, Burglary, Sex Crimes and now Homicide. When her detail ended she would either be offered a permanent assignment in one of them or sent back to patrol. *With my attitude I'll probably be sent back down,* she thought. She was determined to spend what time she had left in the unit looking for a monster.

When not out on DOAs or assisting other detectives, Bianca researched crimes similar to that of the Innocents. According to the Medical Examiner, the knife strikes the killer used were too precise, too practiced for this to be his first time out. So there might be similar open cases somewhere else. She was overwhelmed when she found several, most of which had been attributed to a serial killer called The Carver, a bloodthirsty bastard who always used a knife somewhere in the course of the killing. Unlike many serial killers, this Carver didn't have a favorite method of murder. He liked mixing things up.

Bianca spent an unpaid overtime shift making phone calls to the police departments where the other killings took place, talking with the detectives, having them fax her their reports. Few had any more on the killer than she did. Hell, if it wasn't for the semen and other DNA evidence left behind, she wouldn't even be sure she was looking for a man. It was more like a killing machine. He was so good that he didn't leave behind any witnesses. As a matter of fact, other than the biological evidence, the only thing that linked the crimes was a small design carved into each of the victims. Bianca searched in vain for what it was.

Eventually, Bianca's diligent search was red flagged by a government office in D.C.

Bianca knew nothing of this until two agents showed up at her desk the next morning.

"Detective Jones?" said a man who appeared to be one coiled muscle, with hair covering him everywhere. She knew detectives that had to shave twice a day. This guy looked like he had to do it twice an hour. The other agent was a blonde woman with Polynesian features.

"Who wants to know?" Bianca said.

"I'm Agent Buck of the Department of Mystic Affairs. This is my partner, Agent Mox Monroe."

The woman smiled and nodded. "Charmed I'm sure."

Bianca wasn't. "So how can I help the DMA? What kind of crackpot hoax has brought you to my city? Has Bigfoot been spotted in Druid Hill Park? Or have aliens landed in Canton?"

The tone in Bianca's statement made it clear that she didn't think agents from a fluff government agency were real cops by any means.

"Aliens are investigated by a different agency, Detective. The DMA is more interested in three murders and an assault by the serial killer known as The Carver," Mox said.

"So am I," Bianca replied.

"We'll need copies of all your case files – evidence, photographs, DNA results, pretty much everything – please." The delay made it clear that Buck didn't really mean the please.

Bianca was a team player. Given her recent activity she had no problem sharing with others. But she didn't like being told what to do, especially not by pretend cops spending their time chasing things that didn't exist.

"Well sure. I should be able to have it for you no later than a week from Tuesday," Bianca said, smiling with strained politeness.

Buck smiled back, but his smile was real although Bianca couldn't help think how much it made him look like a predator staring at prey.

"No problem. I'll wait," Grabbing a chair, Buck pulled it up close to Bianca's cubicle. Then he put his feet up on her desk.

As Bianca stepped forward to forcibly remove the Fed, she could have sworn she saw the stubble on his face grow longer. His partner's hands seemed to glow.

"Jones!" shouted Lieutenant Pompey Fredericks, the Homicide Unit's shift commander. "Come here."

Fredericks was Bianca's physical opposite. Large where Bianca was small, her skin was as dark as Bianca's was white. The only thing the two women had in common was a bad attitude generated by years of being overlooked and underestimated by the men they worked with. Bianca didn't like the lieutenant much, but she did respect her.

"Yes, Lieutenant?" Bianca said.

Fredericks walked the detective out of the hearing of the DMA Agents. "Is it my understanding that you are refusing to cooperate with a federal law enforcement agency?" she asked. "Or worse, start a brawl?"

"Lieutenant …"

"Save it, Jones. I don't like Buck's attitude any more than you do. And personally I'd like to see you try to take him down. It might teach both of you something. But the DMA is a good agency, despite anything you've heard. Kick the case to them. The Carver has never struck twice in the same city. That bastard is gone. Let the Feds chase him. I need you to deal with cases in our city, not running around the country on a wild goose chase."

Bianca begrudgingly nodded, acknowledging the order, then gave the DMA Agents copies of her files, but she was not about to stop investigating the case. The sheer brutality of the killings had touched her deep inside. Bianca knew she was a good cop, but she realized that she would have to become even better to deal with a monster like The Carver and others like him.

Even after being permanently assigned to the Sex Offense Unit, Bianca kept investigating the murders. She came up empty. Most did, except for an FBI profiler named Pine. Of course Bianca had some things against her, not realizing she had to factor in the supernatural and a seriál demon. After all, she didn't believe in magic.

She didn't know how soon that viewpoint would change and with it her life.

It was years later when Bianca saw the newspaper article that Bart Andrew Higgins, the serial killer known as The Carver, had been put to death in the electric chair.

The detective smiled, disappointed that she hadn't been the one to end his reign of murder but happy that FBI Special Agent Pine had brought him to justice. She had followed the trial; surprised that Higgins had refused more than the mandatory appeal.

What she didn't know was that someone had taken his place in the chair and that the DMA had recruited the former killer into their ranks. It was probably for the best. Had she known, very little in Heaven or Earth would have stopped her from bringing The Carver to the justice she felt he deserved.

And oddly enough, Bart Andrew Higgins would have welcomed that death with a smile and open arms, but he was about to find out that Death wasn't that cheap a date.

"Some people don't deserve to be able to draw breath. I just happen to be one of them."
– Karver, former demon possessed serial killer, DMA Cadet

I got called on the carpet, a carpet I had no right to be standing on when sixty-four people had died because of me. I worked my damnedest to get the seriál caught and both of us sent to the electric chair and what do I get for my trouble? Rescued and the demon exorcised.

I got a new chance at life. Yippee. What did my dead get? Nada, except maybe the chance to roll over in their graves. It wasn't right, it wasn't fair and there wasn't a damn thing I could do about it.

Well there was one thing. I wouldn't have to do that if they'd just let me ride Old Sparky like I was supposed to. Problem was I'd made a promise in a moment of weakness to Father Sundry, the priest who had given the seriál demon that had made me a killer his walking papers. He'd asked me not to. Said it was a sin and any life, even mine, was worth living. I told him my living had gotten sixty-four people dead, so his math was wrong. Besides, what difference would one more sin piled on top of all the others really make? Sundry told me his sins were legion, then told me what that meant. His truly were legion and of biblical proportions. I agreed to hold off for a month.

That month was up in ten minutes.

I knew why Sarge Winston, the Deputy Director of the Department of Mystic Affairs wanted to see me in his office. I had hurt yet another person, but this one wasn't my fault. Mostly.

I debated on waiting the ten minutes and taking care of matters, but Sarge had been good to me, making sure the seriál couldn't get into another host. He deserved me saying goodbye.

I knocked on his door.

"Come in," said a deep booming voice.

I pushed the door open. Sarge Winston was sitting behind his desk. He got his nickname back in World War I, when he was a sergeant in the Army.

His dress shirt sleeves were rolled up above the elbow, revealing forearms that looked like they were sculpted out of granite. His top shirt button was undone, revealing a ruby gem that was fused to his chest.

There is something dark and scary trapped inside that gem, a creature of primordial darkness that he'd stopped from getting loose back during the poorly named War to end all Wars. Sarge has been stuck with it ever since. He called it Sparky, no relation to the electric chair that I know of. Sarge claimed it hated when he buttoned his shirt because it blocked its view of the world it had wanted to destroy.

I guess Sarge is used to worse than me. His link to Sparky gives him power and made a guy who should be pushing up daisies spry enough to pass for about forty if it wasn't for the white hair and mustache.

"You wanted to see me," I said.

"Yes, Bart," Sarge said.

"Karver," I corrected.

He sighed. We'd been over this all the while he has been training me. Sarge thinks I should pick a different new last name. I don't. This way every time someone calls me by it, I'll be reminded of what I've done. Not that I'll ever be able to forget.

"Karver, please have a seat," Sarge said. "We have several things to discuss."

I sat, then folded my hands in my lap and stared down at my fingers. I didn't want him to see in my eyes what I was going to do. I didn't want to disappoint the old man.

He wasn't having any of it.

"First off, son, always make eye contact when you're talking with somebody. I know you've been through a lot, but you can't let it beat you. I know it's been a trifle unorthodox, not to mention difficult on you living here at the D.C. headquarters…" I'd been sleeping in an empty office. "…since your emancipation."

Despite myself, I laughed. "You make it sound like I was a

slave, instead of a serial killer on death row."

"I think that's a fairly apt description. The demon forced you to kill, gave you no choice. Yet you fought him, kept the body count low."

"I hardly consider more than five dozen dead a low body count," I said.

"But you know it was because of what was inside of you. And I thought you wanted to make up for what was done."

"I do, but I can't," I said.

"We've had this discussion. You've told me you wanted to try," Sarge said.

"I do," I whispered.

"I believe you, which is why I'm more than a bit upset about what I've been hearing. You are the last recruit I expected discipline problems from. Explain why I'm hearing that you hit the fleshsmith who was kind enough to give you a new face and new fingerprints?" Sarge said.

The fleshsmith was an ass, who did things to me I'd rather not relate. "Why? What did Adin say?"

"Adin didn't say a thing. Someone passing by saw you take the swing and reported it. I asked Adin if he wanted to press charges against you. He refused. Said you'd been through enough. You have anything you want to add?" Sarge said.

"No, sir."

Sarge gave me a long stare as if he knew more, but wasn't going to force me to say it. "Then let's move onto the matter of your latest shrink."

"I feel horrible about Dr. Berkle. I warned him, but he wanted to go ahead with it anyway."

Berkle was my eighth shrink in four weeks. Seems the DMA wanted to see if I was fit for duty after killing sixty-four people while possessed by a demon. The predominate school of thought held that the best way to go about this was to have me talk things through.

The first several shrinks didn't last a session. The next guy made it the better part of a week. Berkle made it a week and a half. Although he got me to talk to him about what happened, the good doctor didn't think I was progressing fast enough. Berkle was a telepath and could literally get inside my head. I guess that he figured he might be able to promote some healing in the process. Things didn't work out as he planned.

"Berkle vomited for three hours straight after he looked inside your noggin." Sarge said. "It seems to have subsided, but apparently he has developed a fear of knives and has to eat all his meals with a spoon. Not surprisingly, he's requested that you be reassigned to another counselor."

"I've told you I'm a mess."

"Well, your head should be. The seriál used you as his plaything, altered your body, twisted your mind. He did horrible, terrible things, all of which you felt and saw as if it was you doing them. That would mess up even the strongest person. You are the only known case of seriál demon possession where the body count didn't number over a thousand. And that demon was in you long enough to kill far more than that. *That's* why we rescued you. The fact that you were able to fight the demon, to keep him from killing more people shows amazing strength of will. Properly harnessed, that could make you a great agent, so we offered you the chance to help others as an agent of the Department of Mystic Affairs. You agreed, so I expect to you to toe the line."

"So are you going to assign me another shrink to ask how all this made me feel?" Honestly, five of the eight used that line.

"No. I'm working on having you paired with an agent named Mandi Cobb. I think she'll succeed where the others have failed. And the only question that matters is, are you willing to do what it takes to get past this?"

"Honestly, I don't know. I killed sixty-four people," I said.

"Son, you didn't do the killing. The seriál demon did. And you didn't kill sixty-four people, only sixty-three," Sarge said.

My heart felt like it had stopped beating.

"What! That can't be." I had kept count. "You mean someone survived?"

"Yes!"

"Who?"

"Lucy Innocent. You remember her?" Sarge said.

"I remember all of them." I know each one's name. Somebody has to. I jumped up and pointed at the floor. "You hear that you, bastard. I beat you!"

I stopped when I realized Sarge was watching and smiling.

"Yes, you did, every day when you held him back from killing more people. I'm happy to see you finally get excited over something," Sarge said.

"This is the first good news I've had since before the demon possessed me," I said.

"I would think having the seriál exorcised and getting your life back would qualify as good news," Sarge said.

I shook my head. "Not really. I have to live with the guilt of what I did, even if the demon was driving. It's overwhelming. On those rare occasions when I can sleep, I always wake up screaming."

"Nightmares?" Sarge said.

"Worse. Memories. My mind playing back what happened. The things it did, using me as bait. I can't bear to touch anyone because the contact triggers flashbacks of the things I did."

Sarge and I sat staring at each other in silence for a few moments. I broke first. "You should have let me die in the electric chair."

"I disagree, Bart." I didn't correct him this time. "Regardless, we can't have a DMA Agent functioning effectively in the field if he's racked by guilt."

Sarge opened up his drawer and put a knife the size of a machete on the desk. It had all sorts of mystic looking runes carved into it. Despite myself, I fell in love with the blade. It was a thing of sleek and deadly beauty. I knew what a blade could do -- what that blade could do in my hands. It both excited and horrified me that I couldn't wait to wrap my fingers around it.

Sarge seemed to read my thoughts. "Go ahead, pick it up. We had this and another made especially for you. It would be foolish to ignore the fact that you're stronger, faster and better with a blade than any mortal man. You can detect demons and Hell magic as an aftereffect of what happened to you. I don't want you crumbling in the field where other agents and innocents lives may depend on you."

I heard him, but all I could think was with one slash or stab and it would be all over. My dead would have their justice.

Again Sarge seemed to know what I was thinking. "Yes, your month was up about three minutes ago. If you really think you should have died, end it here."

I placed the perfect silver blade and held it against my throat. One flick of my wrist is all it would take to slice through both my jugulars. I'd bleed out in less than a minute.

I don't think Sarge was expecting me to actually put the knife against my skin. He looked sad and nervous.

"Before you take the coward's way out, I want you to think about those sixty-three dead. 'Your dead' as you are fond of saying. Do you think they would want the seriál demon to claim another life? Or would they want you to fight on against the evil of this world, to strive to protect others, to safeguard this country. And what about Lucy? What happens if someday she needs help? If she encounters something big and scary in the dark? Will you be around to save her again? If not you, then who?"

Sarge paused, letting his words sink in. He was right. My dead deserved more than me just offing myself. I could never make up for what I did, but at least I could try to balance the scales some. A second chance is better than just lying down to die.

"Fine. I've stared into the abyss. I'll fight the monsters," I said.

"Good, because I think you will make an exceptional agent and do your dead proud. We've been keeping you here just until the next class in the DMA Academy opened. It begins Monday. You'll be moving in tomorrow. George Knox and his team will train you in everything you need to know to become an agent."

I smiled for the first time in a long time. Maybe I could have a purpose in this world after all.

"Sometimes it's not worth questioning authority because it usually won't know the answer."
– Detective Bianca Jones, BPD

Few members of the Baltimore Police Department would dare to refuse a direct order from their commanding officer. Fewer still could get away with it. Bianca Jones was one of the few.

"No way. Absolutely no. I'm not going."

"I don't recall giving you a choice, Detective," Major Chester Williams said.

It wasn't the first time Bianca regretted her discovery that the supernatural was real, that there were things that lived in the shadows that saw humanity as playthings and cattle to hurt and kill. It was her own fault really. A case that had started out as a simple sexual assault led to her fighting a creature from another dimension. Then she remembered that in the BPD if you do a job once, it's yours forever. She'd stopped one monster. Now it was her job to hunt and stop the rest.

"I've done damn good on my own," Bianca said.

"Through a combination of courage, skill, and luck. But we both know that what you've faced so far is only a small part of what's out there and a 'learn as you go' attitude is going to get you killed."

Bianca opened her mouth to protest but Williams waved his hand to quiet her.

"And yes, I know about Morgan and the rest of your sources and associates, including that psychic from Brooklyn. That case was the one that got you noticed. You two took down a government operation."

"They were making monsters. They had to be stopped."

"You'll get no argument from me, but don't you think one federal agency talks to others. The Banner affair plus your past interest in The Carver case put you on their radar and got you this invitation to the DMA Academy. It's an honor in a way."

"One I can do without."

"Jones, the Department of Mystic Affairs has been dealing with supernatural threats for over two centuries. They're good. Hell, they've kept this country from literally going to Hell more times than anyone knows. But they can't be everywhere. That's why they started inviting officers from larger metropolitan areas to the DMA Academy for training. To fight the monsters, to keep us from going to Hell and to prevent Hell from coming for us."

"I know about Hell, I kicked its boss in the balls. Besides, the DMA, they're Feds, not real cops."

"Even if they are Feds, I'm not about to have you get killed in the line of duty because you are too stubborn to admit somebody knows something that you don't or that there is someone else better than you at something. You're going, Detective. You will learn every last thing they can teach you and then come back here better than any DMA jerk ever had a hope of being."

"Damn straight I will," Bianca said a second before realizing she just agreed to do something she didn't really want to do. "Still, I've been a cop and detective for years. I don't need to go back to school."

"Maybe not, but the city needs you to go in order to be able to protect it and its citizens," he said.

"That's hitting below the belt."

Williams smiled at her. Bianca rolled her eyes and sighed. "Fine, but I get a week's vacation when I get back."

"Fine, but only if you complete the entire training. Otherwise you're on hooker duty for that week, bait for the pervs that like young girls. Deal?"

Bianca nodded. "Those DMA guys won't know what hit them when I get there."

"Getting a good education hurts. Getting a bad one hurts even more."
– George Knox, folk hero, Commandant DMA Academy

George Knox never slept the night before the first day of a new class at the DMA Academy. True, the contemporary of Paul Bunyan had already gone over all the recruits as well as the guests from outside law enforcement. He knew them well on paper, but as head of the Academy, simply knowing wasn't enough. There was a largely unseen world alongside of the one most people knew. It wasn't that the supernatural hid. Some aspects of it did, but others simply stayed unknown because most people wanted rational explanations. They didn't believe in ghosts because ghosts didn't exist. They couldn't see pixies because they didn't believe in them. Vampires and werewolves might seem all nice and good in a romance novel, but people didn't want to think that they might be riding next to them on the late night subway.

DMA Agents and cops in local law enforcement who handle their jurisdictions' mystical crimes were going to be exposed to dangers that regular cops never even dreamed existed. It was ultimately Knox's responsibility to make sure that everyone who passed through his Academy left with enough knowledge to help them survive. Of course there was more to it than just knowledge. Like with any law enforcement agent, training was crucial, but when augmented by a quick thinking mind and good instincts, it was even better.

Knox picked up the stack of folders for guest students. The Department of Mystic Affairs had only a fraction of the agents that the FBI did. A fraction of their budget too. That meant quite simply that they couldn't be everywhere. It was the standing policy of Director Sam Wilson that the DMA assist local law enforcement whenever possible in learning more about mystical crimes and criminals. That included having local law enforcement go through the Academy alongside its agents. This had led to friction in the past. Feds and locals seemed to face off against each other in the field whenever jurisdiction overlapped or egos got out of control.

Some cops had been known to carry this attitude into the Academy. The raw recruits didn't have the same issue because most of them had not been in the field as agents. All of the guests, at least on paper, were good cops. Smart cops. Most of them had attitude, which served them well in departments that often mocked them for what they did.

Knox picked up one file on a cop who had more attitude than most – Bianca Jones. She seemed to have gotten by so far on a combination of hard headedness and quick wits. From all reports, her attitude spilled over even toward her own department and anyone she felt dismissed her because she was a woman and a small one at that. Knox's biggest challenge with her would be convincing her that there were things the DMA could teach her. Once he did that, she'd take care of the rest and probably end up being one of the best students in this class.

Some of the DMA recruits were coming to the Academy because they had survived something magical and deadly. Two cases in particular worried him. Both had been through Hell, one literally. Knox could relate. He'd barely gotten his own soul back from the Devil. The former Bartholomew Andrew Higgins seemed to be doing remarkably well after playing host to the seriál demon that controlled him as The Carver. There was a lot of self-recrimination and blame there. A suicide watch had already been done, but that didn't mean it should stop. Most minds would've crumbled under the strain of possession. Very often the possessed end up institutionalized, unable to cope with the things they had felt, done, and seen. Or worse, they got a twisted Stockholm Syndrome that had them justifying everything the demon did and worse, trying to emulate it. Higgins was one of the rare ones. No, not Higgins, Knox remembered, Not anymore. He had taken a new last name – Karver. He had been quite firm on it being the only way to address him and refused to answer to anything else. Believed it would help make sure he never forgot what he had done while possessed. Knox chuckled. That was not likely to happen. Karver kept a variation of his first name because no matter how hard you trained someone, an inner instinct could kick in at an unguarded moment to the sound of their own name being shouted. It could cause a reaction, often at the worst of times. Karver showed potential and because of that he was being given the Department of Mystic Affairs' version of witness protection, which included the new name and face.

As sad as Karver's case was, the case of Donna Winks was even worse. The poor girl had the misfortune of finding a jinn. Donna made her three wishes. The crucial one was done in a moment of teenage angst – she wished that nobody in the world knew she existed. An instant later, no one did. Her family, friends and classmates all forgot about her. Her public records still existed, as did photos and videos, but the wish made anyone forget them and Donna the moment they turned away.

Agent Rose Tower, a Department of Mystic Affairs Agent who was herself a jinn, put a charm on all DMA badges, including those given to Academy cadets. The charm allowed the agents to not only see Donna, but remember she existed. Despite just having turned eighteen, Winks was ready to fight the good fight.

George Knox put on another pot of coffee and again went over each of his files, making sure he would be ready for the first day of class.

"Be all that I can be? I did that already and it didn't work out so well."
– Karver, former demon possessed serial killer, DMA Cadet

Walking into the DMA Academy gave me visions of mashing up, going to college and joining the Army then putting them in a blender on puree. I wasn't exactly thrilled to be there, but for now it beat the alternative.

I felt out of place the moment I arrived. Most of the other cadets had friends and family seeing them off. I had no one. No one that I hadn't killed.

People tried to make eye contact and smile. I just gave a quick nod, and looked away. It was too uncomfortable. The demon had used friendliness to lure our victims. If I kept away from them, I wouldn't be able to hurt them.

There was a line to get our room assignments and class schedules. At first I thought they were letting tweens into the DMA because of one woman's height. She barely came up to my chest and seemed just as thrilled as I was to be here. Of course, I'd be unhappy to be anywhere, but her misery seemed specific to either the line or the Academy.

"Can you believe how unorganized they are?" the woman said, looking back at me and rolling her eyes.

"It's bureaucracy at work. Got to love it," I said.

"They knew we were coming. You'd think that they'd put more people working the line or e-mail us packets ahead of time," she said.

"What are you going to do?" I said, making with the small talk.

"Hurry up and wait. I guess," she said. "I'm Bianca Jones, Baltimore PD."

She held out her hand, but I pretended like I didn't see it. The idea of touching someone was still repugnant and made my stomach twist into knots. "I'm Karver, Department of Mystic

Affairs."

The woman gave me an odd look. "I assume that's your last name. What's your first?"

"I just go by Karver," I said.

"Kind of unfortunate name to have these days. Must get a lot of people pointing out it's the name of a killer," Jones said.

"You have no idea. Only mine is spelled with a K, not a C."

"At least they fried the bastard. I caught one of his early kills in Baltimore."

"The Innocent family," I said before I could catch myself.

The woman looked at me even more oddly. "That's right. How do you know that? The Carver had over sixty known kills. Across more than thirty states."

"It made the papers. I have pretty good recall," I said, but it sounded lame even to me.

Jones looked at my shoulder then back at my face. "Traveling light. No bags?"

I shrugged. "I don't need a lot. Besides, we have to wear an Academy uniform for the next three months."

Jones's ire rose again. "I can't believe I've got to be away from my job for three damn months for no good reason."

"I assume you're here to learn how to take down mystic bad guys," I said.

"I've already been doing that. I don't need Feds telling me that their way is right and mine is wrong."

"Maybe it's not a matter of whose way is right and whose is wrong, but to learn all the different ways, so you got more options when the time comes," I said.

"That's a good way of looking at it. Doesn't make me feel much better," Jones said. As we got to the front, somebody in red sweats, the uniform of an instructor, asked us our last names and pointed us toward the center of the waiting herd. Jones and I both ended up in the J to M line.

"Name?" said the woman behind the desk behind the table.

"Bianca Jones."

The woman flipped through a box full of envelopes and pulled one out. "You're in room 502."

She turned to me. "Name?"

"Karver."

The woman did the same trick and pulled another envelope. "Here you go. That's odd. You're in room 502 as well." The woman looked from one of us to the other. "Are you two married?"

"No," Jones said. "I know you Feds are all new agey and stuff, but I'm not rooming with a guy, at least not one I just met."

"I'm not looking to get any surgical adjustments just to be able to room with her," I said.

"I think we might be able to help out," said a clean-cut, well-built, good-looking man. In the right light he could pass anywhere from 15 to 25. "We seem to have the same transgender roommate issue. They put us in 501."

"I'm just happy to have a roommate," said a woman that I hadn't noticed was there until she spoke.

"Why don't we just switch?" I said. "You can go with Detective Jones and I'll go with…"

"James Pratt."

I turned my head to look at Jones, then turned back. "So who's going to room with Detective Jones?"

"Oh, I love this ever so much," said a young girl dryly, rolling her eyes. I hadn't noticed she was there until she spoke.

"Take your Academy badge out of your envelope and put it on your belt. That'll help you remember Donna," Pratt said.

I did as instructed and suddenly realize I had spoken to the woman twice, but had forgotten the first time entirely.

"So Karver gets a roommate, but what about me?" Jones said.

"Put on the Academy badge from your packet," I said, as Donna rolled her eyes.

Jones took out her badge, looked at it and stuck it in a front pocket.

"You're supposed to wear it," I told her.

"I was supposed to wear one at headquarters back home, but I kept losing it. After three replacements they started charging me. My pocket is fine." Jones looked around. "So where's my roommate?" she asked again.

"This is gonna be *so* much fun," Donna said, rolling her eyes.

"Come on, roomie," Pratt said, putting his hand good-naturedly on my shoulders. It took everything I had not to cringe away from the touch. "Let's checkout our new digs. You have any special abilities? I'm a bug."

"You seem to have the normal number of legs," I said.

"No, it's a classification of mage. I can pick up on conversations. I'm better with electronics than the spoken word, but I'm good with either," Pratt said.

"I guess I better watch what I say around you then," I said.

"Good one. Our room is this way I think. Pity we have to switch. That Donna is cute."

"Hello? What am I going to do about a roommate? Is anyone going to answer me?" Jones said. Donna took her hand and Jones reacted to her as if seeing her again for the first time, after which Donna led her off to their room.

"I want you…"
– "Uncle" Sam Wilson, living embodiment of the American spirit, Director of the DMA

Despite herself, Bianca Jones was impressed. With the exception of room assignments, the Department of Mystic Affairs Academy seemed to be well organized. Classes were broken down into a mixture of lecture and hands-on learning which covered everything from hand-to-hand combat with entities larger and stronger than the agents to making emergency wards with a piece of chalk, but it was the opening address that impressed her the most.

Bianca had expected to be bored by some politician's speech. Sam Wilson, the Director of the DMA, gave the address. After enough BPD functions with the Chief or Commissioner giving a speech, she made sure she loaded up on coffee before sitting down. The last thing she needed was to cause an interdepartmental incident by nodding off during the opening address.

Director Wilson entered from the back of the auditorium and marched up onto the stage with a technique that would have made a Marine Honor Guard jealous. Bianca could've sworn she heard a band playing *God Bless America* as the old man walked by, but there were no musicians or recordings playing.

Wilson looked old, but strong. His muscles were tight cords under his blue suit. His patriotic ensemble was made complete with a white shirt and red tie. His socks looked like two mini flags. The man had snow white hair and the lower half of a goatee, minus the mustache.

"On behalf of the Department of Mystic Affairs and the President, I welcome all of you to the latest class of the DMA Academy and to the service of your country. Each of you is here because you were chosen to be here. And what's more, you accepted the challenge to enter the fray. Each member of this class had been touched in some way by magic, be it for good or ill. You've seen the mystic world in action. Some of your experiences have been positive, others not so much."

Wilson seemed to look at Karver and some woman Bianca hadn't noticed before despite the fact that she was sitting next to her. "The DMA was created by the Executive Order of President Thomas Jefferson in order to combat mystic threats against this great nation of ours."

"Let us be frank here. And this will be hard for some of you to take. Many in our country and the law enforcement community do not take the Department of Mystic Affairs seriously. They have the mistaken belief that we deal with hoaxes and crackpots. These people think that they know beyond a shadow of a doubt that magic is not real. And they will wholeheartedly maintain that belief until magic rears its ugly head and bites them in the butt. And when that happens, when that which they doubt the very existence of rises up from the shadows to threaten those that they are sworn to protect, you will stop being a joke. They will then see you as their best friend because you will have the knowledge and the courage to stand up against the darkness of this world. For it has been said, and I believe it to be true, that when darkness falls, the DMA picks up the pieces."

"Of course there is danger in thinking that we know everything. That there is nothing new that can be thrown at us. That we have nothing else to learn." Director Wilson seemed to be looking directly at Bianca this time. "Down that path lies a greater danger than mere mystic threats because overconfidence will not only get you killed, but those you are trying to protect. I've been doing this for over two centuries and there are many, many things that I still don't know."

Bianca gave the old man a harder look. Wilson didn't look a day over 60 and that was only because of the white hair. Still from what she'd seen, Bianca supposed it was possible.

Wilson stepped out from behind the podium and strode to the front of the stage. Bianca was certain she heard *The Star-Spangled Banner* playing this time, but had no idea where it could be coming from. Wilson put his arm in front of him and pointed at the audience. The pose was very reminiscent of something, but she just couldn't put her finger on it.

"I want you to do your best to learn everything this Academy can teach you and then go out and protect this great land of ours and her citizens."

Suddenly, the Director transformed. His pants got red and white stripes. His necktie became an old-fashioned bowtie and a red, white, and blue top hat appeared on his head.

"Holy shit," Bianca whispered as she realized who Sam Wilson really was.

"Will you do this for your country? Will you take up the burden to protect America from the darkness and the enemies who wish to destroy her?"

The answer was a standing ovation with every person in the room yelling yes and clapping until their hand felt like they might fall off.

"I thank you and a grateful nation thanks you."

"Things are rarely as they seem. Especially when I'm around."
– Chester Coyle, Retired DMA Agent, member of The League of Shadows

The DMA Academy was fascinating, teaching us about everything from the known different breeds of vampires to the creatures of the outer darkness and everything in between.

Each day we had a guest lecturer in addition to class work and labs. Today, not so much. It seemed.

Cadets arrived before 8 o'clock. Knox didn't permit lateness. We all sat and waited for today's guest, but no one took to the podium. After about ten minutes, people started to grumble which seemed to be the cue for a deep dark laughter to start ringing out from everywhere. The lecture hall doors slammed shut. Then the doors disappeared as the walls melted around them like something out of a Salvador Dali nightmare. The room spun round and round. I don't mean I got dizzy – the lecture hall literally began to turn like some children's merry-go-round on steroids.

A flash of fire on the stage roasted the podium to ash and cinder. From the smoke stepped out a creature from the depths of Hell with skin the color of burnt flesh, teeth as big as my arm and horns that reached up to scrape the ceiling.

I didn't think this monster was the guest lecturer. There was no way I was letting another demon hurt anybody on my watch. I moved toward the stage and realized something. It didn't feel right. In the past, whenever a demon was nearby, I got a low-grade buzzing in my head. I didn't have it now.

"So you think you're all here to fight evil?" said the demon, laughing like it enjoyed the sound more than anything else in the universe. "What a joke all of you are."

"The only joke I see here is you," Bianca Jones shouted at the creature. "I sent your boss packing off to Hell and I'm going to do the same to you."

Jones reached for her gun but came up empty. We weren't allowed to carry weapons on campus. The knives Sarge had made for me were sitting in a weapons case back in DC.

Jones ran to the back. Behind me I heard the sound of something breaking, even as the demon laughed harder. "Pack me off to Hell? What a lovely idea. Let's all go together!"

Suddenly there were flames and smoke everywhere as an inferno erupted around us. In the distance we could hear the screams of the tortured and the damned. It chilled the soul and made me want to curl up into a ball, but I managed to refrain.

Some cadets panicked and ran around, looking around for a way out. They tripped and fell like bowling pins trying to stand against an avalanche. They had the right idea and I thought I'd join them when I realized I still felt my lecture chair. And I didn't feel any heat. Flames erupting thirty feet high should warm things up a bit, but there was a breeze still coming from air conditioning.

"You're no demon," I said. "None of this is even real."

The demon grew until it would have dwarfed King Kong. Its angular face turned towards me and grinned. "Really?"

Fire belched out of its maw straight toward me. I wasn't certain enough that it was fake to stay still and be barbecued, so I tucked and rolled.

The demon picked up a woman in its hand and she screamed better than any actress in any horror movie I'd ever seen. One problem. She wasn't a cadet. There were forty of us and we had been together day in and day out together for weeks. I didn't know everybody's name, but I knew everyone's face. The screamer wasn't one of us.

"Put the woman down," Jones ordered. She was holding a wooden club taken from whatever piece of furniture she had broken.

"Or what? You're in the Pit now, Detective Jones. My boss sends his love. He'll be by for you soon."

I was moving more by touch than sight. Groping with my hands and feet. What I felt didn't match the texture of what I saw.

We were still in the lecture hall. I found the outer wall and kept searching until I felt a fire extinguisher. It looked like a rock of similar size and shape.

Grabbing it, I rushed to the front of the Hell hall, tripping over what felt like a backpack that didn't seem to be there. Pushing off the ground, I headed straight for the demon. I got up in his face and sprayed it full force with the fire extinguisher. More insane laughter, but for the briefest instant, the spray went right through his face before the vision adjusted itself and the white cloud bounced back at me. There was no smell, no texture, no temperature to it. It had as much substance as a politician's promise.

The demon spun and slammed his giant hand down on me. I cringed, held the fire extinguisher over my head and closed my eyes. Nothing happened. When I opened my eyes, the demon's fist had closed around me. I closed my eyes again and walked forward, right through the giant charbroiled demonic flesh.

Just as suddenly as it appeared, the scene from the Pit was gone and there was a man standing off to the side, clapping. He was dressed in a suit and Fedora.

"Well done, Karver. You cannot always trust your senses. You can't always trust your gut either, but sometimes you have to go with it."

The man looked in his 60s and strolled over to me and shook my hand. I didn't want to offend a guest instructor, so I took the hand. He leaned and whispered in my ear, "Sarge said you're the one to watch. My old partner says you have the potential to be the best agent since, well, me." He laughed, but it was more genuine, less scary than the demons. "Very impressive how you held back that seriál demon long enough to get caught and sentenced to death row. Anyone with that strength of will and such a willingness to die to protect others is a man worth knowing."

I didn't agree with him, but said, "Thank you, sir."

"Take your seats and I'll begin my lecture. My name is Chester Coyle. I'm a Retired DMA Agent. I was on the job on and off for more than 40 years. I'm enjoying a well-earned pension. Like many of us, I'm a lot older than I look. Hang around magic long enough, manage to survive and you'll have the potential to live for a very long time. The average person touched by magic can live a hundred to a hundred and fifty years. It's why a friend of mine in Philadelphia set the age to qualify as an immortal at a hundred and fifty years old. What I'm here to teach you today is how to tell reality from illusion. My abilities allow me to create illusions of sight and sound. They are only as real as people believe them to be. Of course, in capable hands such as mine, illusions can surpass reality. As Karver here realized, there were certain things that didn't add up. Most likely the biggest was lack of heat from the fire. Also because it was such a big area, I had difficulty compensating for everything in the room. I memorized the layout of the chairs and stage, but if I couldn't see things like bags and coats, neither could you, which is why some of you tripped."

"In your careers you're going to run into a lot of people who will mask their power or trying to seem like they have more power than they do. Others will use illusions to bend others to their will or appear to be something they are not. And just because something is an illusion, doesn't mean it's not real. Had this not been a training exercise, I could have backed up the illusionary fire with a flame thrower or even a gun. It will be your job as DMA Agents and law enforcement to tell the difference between reality and illusion and figure a way to work around it. So let's begin with the basics…"

"Fool me once, shame on you. Fool me twice and it's your ass."
– Detective Bianca Jones, BPD

Once the lecture and lab on illusions finished, everybody rushed out towards the cafeteria for lunch.

Almost everybody.

"Hey, Karver," Bianca said, walking swiftly towards her classmate.

Karver seemed to pause as if debating about ignoring the detective, but finally he said, "What do you want, Jones?"

"How did you know demon wasn't real?" Bianca said, using the same tone she used on a perp during an interrogation. Bianca gave him the same look, although looking up from a shorter standing position was nowhere near as effective as standing up and looking down at a suspect in a chair.

"Deductive reasoning. I'm just a great detective," Karver said, then started to walk off.

Bianca grabbed his arm. "Bullshit. You weren't guessing. You knew. I want to know how."

Bianca had mixed reasons for that. On one level knowing how would help her do her job better, but her cop sense told her that there was something wrong with Karver. Maybe it was his name. It brought to mind her early obsession. Karver and Carver – they were too close. It occurred to her that maybe the serial killer and this soon to be DMA Agent were one and the same. It was a crazy idea she knew, but she was now in the crazy business. She couldn't think of how it could be possible, but could the serial killer have somehow survived the electric chair and infiltrated the DMA? Little did she know she was both right and wrong.

"Tell me your secret."

Karver met her gaze and to Bianca's surprise, he didn't look away. His eyes were filled with great sorrow and regret.

"I have the ability to sense demons and Hell magics at close distances.”

“So you cheated?” Bianca was smiling, as if she was joking, but her eyes were watching his reaction.

“Cheated?” Karver said, confused.

“Special Agent Coyle was testing us in there. No matter what I did, what any of us did to save the illusionary woman and stop the demon would have failed. You are the only one who passed, but it doesn’t count because you had special powers. Therefore, you cheated.”

Not yet comfortable around people, Karver couldn’t tell if the Baltimore cop was joking or not. Either way, he didn’t need special powers to sense the hostility coming from her.

“I didn’t cheat,” Karver said angrily. “Cheating would imply a purposeful run around the rules. No rules were set. We didn’t know it was a test. I made no conscious or unconscious effort to get around the nonexistent rules. Therefore I did not cheat. And for your information, if cheating is what it took to save a life, I’d cheat my ass off. But I didn’t cheat in there. You’re just pissed because someone showed you up and that someone happened to be me,” Karver said.

“Relax, I’m just yanking your chain,” Bianca said. “A cop does whatever he has to in order to get the job done. And you’re going to be some kind of cop, right?”

Despite her words, Karver’s comments had hit the detective a little too close to home. Because of her height, youthful appearance and gender, Bianca always felt driven to be three times as good as the next person. That had always been enough to make her the best at what she did. The fact that someone else was better than her was intolerable. Particularly if Karver was The Carver. She had to be better if she were going to take him down.

“Exactly how do you have this demon sensing power?”

“I’m not exactly comfortable talking about it,” Karver said. “Now if you don’t mind, I’d like to go get some lunch.”

“But we’re not done talking,” Bianca said.

“We are if you keep treating me like a suspect,” Karver said.

“That’s because you act like one, *Karver*,” Bianca said. “Just where are you every night? The other cadets all socialize with each other. You're nowhere to be found."

"I'm studying," Karver said.

"Nobody studies that much," Bianca said, then turned at approaching footsteps.

"How convenient to find you both together," George Knox said.

Both Karver and Bianca stood up straighter, almost at attention. The Commandant of the Academy had impressed both of them with his devotion to duty and his knowledge of the supernatural. Also, neither one wanted to run afoul of his strict discipline.

"I wanted to congratulate you both," Knox said.

"For what?" Bianca said.

"Your behavior in class today. The two of you were the only ones who took any positive action, even if one of you was a little hard on the furniture."

"Thank you, sir," came from both as Knox went on.

"Of course, I would expect nothing less from the two best cadets in the class."

Bianca should have left things there. But she had to ask, "Who's better?"

Knox hesitated, then said, "Karver did stop the demon, Jones."

Bianca heard a whispered "Maybe you should study more" from Karver before he said out loud, "Thank you, sir. I'll continue to do my best."

Knox put his hand on Karver's shoulder. "I know you will, son. And if you need anything, my door is always open."

"I appreciate that, sir. Now if you don't mind, I'd like to get some lunch," Karver said.

"Go right ahead," Knox said.

Bianca waited until after Karver left, then followed after Knox. "Commander, how carefully was Karver vetted before being allowed into the DMA?"

"Very carefully. Full standard government background check, plus a few mystic ones," Knox said.

"Is there any way someone could get around that?" Bianca

said.

"If you've learned anything in your weeks here, it's that anything is possible. However getting around our security measures is highly improbable. Why do you ask?"

"There's something off with Karver. He's not a typical cop," Bianca said.

"In case you haven't noticed, Jones, no one here is typical. It's practically a requirement." Knox said.

"You have a point, sir. But doesn't the fact that he has the same first name as The Carver and his last name is one letter different set off any warning bells with you?"

Knox tried to keep his face straight. He knew Karver's background, but didn't necessarily want anyone else to.

"There are coincidences, Jones. And I believe The Carver's first name was Bartholomew, not Barton although both are shortened to Bart. Perhaps you're so used to looking for criminals that you see them where they are not? And if I remember correctly, weren't you a detective on The Carver's Baltimore killings? Could there be some unresolved issues there? Perhaps an inner need to have been the one to catch and bring that killer to justice?"

"No. This is something more. I can feel it in my gut. And just like Agent Coyle said, 'Sometimes you have to go with your gut.' If I may be excused, Commander?"

Knox nodded, then headed back to his office to call Sam and Sarge Winston to let them know that Karver's cover might be in jeopardy.

"Be careful. Sometimes you don't carry a grudge. It carries you."
    – George Knox, DMA Academy Commandant

Ever since Knox told Jones that she was only the second smartest kid in class, she seemed to be gunning for me. Dirty looks were the least of it. She had taken to following me. I couldn't let that distract me. I had more important things than an obsessed cop with an attitude to worry about.

I may have been top in my class, but I felt like I didn't know anything. There was so much more I needed to learn to stop other monsters like me from hurting others.

It wasn't all mental. The workouts were grueling, pretty much like I imagine boot camp would've been if I'd joined the Marines. Jones had got me thinking. The demonic modifications had made me into the perfect killer, but now it did feel like I was cheating. It gave me an unfair advantage over the humans in the class. I was in top physical condition without even having to work out. I was stronger and faster than any man had a right to be. I breezed through most of the basic workouts, rarely breaking a sweat. Not that we ever stopped at basics.

There were plenty of supernaturals among the recruits who pulled ahead of us mere mortals, but I was able to stay only a few steps behind most of them. The funny part is George Knox was able to stay ahead of all of us, even a guy named Hunter who's supposedly some ancient Celtic God called Herne. Physically he was at the head of the class, but Knox was always two steps ahead of him. Rumor had him as a folk hero like Paul Bunyan and John Henry who sold his soul to the Devil for the ability to accomplish any task better than anyone. I can only assume that the power helped him turn the tables on the Devil and get his soul back. Seems a foolish gift to give on the Devil's part, but it seemed to be working out for Knox.

The part I hated most was sparring. Sure, it was smart to learn techniques to take on a werewolf or a vampire, but practicing had to be done on my fellow agents. I was always holding back for fear of hurting somebody else – except Hunter. He was strong enough that he could literally pick me up and throw me over a two-story building and fast enough to get on the other side to catch me. Damn impressive. But even with him I held back a little. I still wasn't comfortable with my powers and didn't want anyone knowing all that I could do.

Still, my abilities didn't go unnoticed. I went out of my way to avoid sparring with anyone smaller than me, which seemed to piss off Jones even more than she already was.

One day, I guess she'd had enough and swaggered over to me. "Come on, Karver, spar with me. Unless you're afraid?" Jones said with a smirk.

"It's not that I'm afraid of you, Jones," I said. "I'm afraid of what might happen."

"What do you mean?"

"You're a lot smaller than me. I don't want to hurt you."

That apparently was exactly the wrong thing to say. Her previous under the surface anger was nothing compared to this look of fury. It was like I insulted her mother or something.

"You. Me. On the mat. Now."

Jones stepped onto the mat, straightening her blue Academy sweats.

I guess I hurt her feelings. Holding back a sigh, I followed after her.

We were drilled in different martial arts techniques, but there was no bowing in a match. This was meant to imitate street fighting, not tournaments.

Assuming a relaxed defensive position, I watched Jones. She seemed to be a little bit of a hothead and I decided to use that against her. First, I smiled and watched as her jaw tightened. I stepped up my game and faked a yawn, lifting my arms over my head. Before my hands got back to my sides, Jones was coming at my knees with a kick.

Jones was fast, but I was faster. I stepped aside and sent an elbow towards her head. She got her arm up in time to block me. More than that, she got a hold of my hand and flipped me on my can.

Rolling with the attack, I got back on my feet an instant before Jones landed where I had been. When she got up, I swept her legs, knocking her back down. Jones leapt up, faking a kick to my groin. Male instinct made me overreact and she brought an elbow into my ear.

Adrenaline kicked in and I hit her in the stomach. Hard. Jones doubled over.

Crap. "Jones, are you okay?"

I moved in to check on her and she used the opportunity to punch me in the jaw with one hand and in the gut with the other.

It hurt. Now it was my turn to be pissed off.

Jones punched again, but I caught her hand and twisted it behind her back. Next I kicked her legs and brought her to her knees, then pushed her forward onto her stomach. Somehow, she got her free hand behind her, ignoring the pain I was causing her other shoulder and stuck two fingers inside my nostrils and pulled.

I let go and she pushed back, knocking me off of her.

Jones flipped over, but I was on top of her before she could get up, straddling her legs with mine and pinned her shoulders to the mat. I was stronger and I had the leverage. This time she wasn't going anywhere.

Apparently she didn't plan on it.

"Ready to tap out?" I said.

"When Hell freezes over." To accentuate her point, she brought her forehead up into my nose. I heard a crunch as cartilage and bone cracked and my vision was obscured by red. Worse, I was overcome by blind fury and my body had a flashback.

I drove my hand down into her throat intending to crush the trachea and realized what I was doing. It was too late to stop, but not too late to divert and instead I hit her shoulder. The fury wasn't satisfied and I chambered my fist, ready to hit her again and again.

"All right, this match is over. Jones, what the Hell was that?"

Knox shouted, his voice stopping me from doing serious damage. I got off Jones and walked to the far side of the mat, not trusting myself to not press the attack. I did some deep breathing to try to get my emotions under control.

"Making this as much like a street fight as possible. Does Karver think a perp won't use any weapon or body part at hand?" Jones said.

"You're also a trained police officer who is supposed to know the difference between practice and the real thing. You just broke another cadet's nose on purpose. There's no excuse for that kind of behavior in my Academy," Knox said.

"Sorry. I had a flashback to a time I was attacked, pinned and helpless," Jones said.

I could relate to the flashback part, but Knox knew she was lying.

"You have a flashback like that again and you're heading back to Baltimore on the first thing smoking, understood?" Knox said.

Jones got quiet and looked down at her sneakers. "Understood, sir."

"Karver, are you okay?" Knox said.

"I'm fine," I said.

"No, you're not. Your nose is broken and bleeding all over the place."

"I put blood, sweat and tears into my job. I expect nothing less from anyone else."
– Detective Bianca Jones, BPD

"He's bleeding all over the place," Jones thought, trying not to smile as she looked down at the assorted red stains all over her sweatshirt. Now she had a way to find out if Karver was the serial killer known as The Carver or if she was wrong.

Knox grabbed a hold of Karver's nose and moved it back into place. To his credit, Karver didn't even flinch.

Knox was muttering something about getting him to a fleshsmith, whatever the Hell that was. That seemed to bother Karver more than having his nose broke.

"Okay, Jones, Give me twenty laps on the track," Knox said.

"You're joking," Bianca said.

Knox frowned and gave her a hard stare.

"Do I look like a comedian? Make it thirty."

Bianca opened her mouth to argue.

"One more word and it'll be fifty."

"Sir, I lost control too. I should be running the same amount of laps," Karver said.

Knox and Karver exchanged a look that spoke volumes that Bianca didn't understand. Knox nodded. "Fine, but you're only doing twenty since you didn't mouth off. Now both of you move."

The pair double timed it out to the track.

"Taking the punishment is not going to endear you to me, Karver," Bianca said.

"I wasn't trying to. In fact, I think I just figured out why you're so pissed off at me all the time," Karver said.

"Oh yeah, why is that?"

"I think you have a thing for me. But you better forget about it. I'm in the wrong place to be in a relationship," Karver said.

Jones stopped short, her expression a blank stare. Sure, she noticed that Karver was more good looking than any man had a right to be and had the body of a male model. Plus, he had deep, dark eyes, but to be accused of pursuing a man she wasn't interested in infuriated her. "You've got to be kidding me."

"Don't insult either of us by denying it. And just so you know, I'm doing laps to teach me a lesson, not you," Karver said, then smiled. "Well maybe to teach you a little lesson."

"Oh yeah, what's that?" Bianca said.

"That I'm faster than you'll ever be. Not only am I going to beat you, I'm going to do it by a matter of laps," Karver said, taking off at a sprint. Jones didn't waste any time in speeding up and getting hot on his heels.

Bianca smiled. She'd taken a beating, one she had expected. But she also learned a few things about Karver, things that would come in handy if she had to take him down for real. As she ran, Karver lapped her for the first time. That didn't matter, he could have this victory. His blood on her sweats was her prize. She'd cut it out and send it to Joe Russo at the BPD Crime lab. Joe would run it against The Carver's DNA. If she was right, she'd end up winning the only race that counted.

"The Chase is the best part of the Hunt"
– Herne the Hunter, god and DMA Cadet

"You were right, Sarge," George Knox told the Deputy Director on video chat. "We just got word that one of cadets went off base. It's Jones."

"And she's carrying a package." This was less of a question than a statement.

"Just as you predicted."

"It's her sweatshirt, the one with Karver's blood on it. She's heading into town to that 24 hour UPS place. She'll send it to her crime lab by overnight express and in a week, two at the outside, they'll match his DNA to the Innocent case. Then the fun begins."

"We should stop her, I'll have …"

"With respect, Commander, we should not stop her. If we do, we just confirm what she believes and reveal that we're in on the cover-up."

"What can she do? She won't have proof."

"You've read her profile, George, that little lady doesn't need proof. Once she's convinced, she'll do her best to take Karver down."

Knox smiled and shrugged. "Let her try. Even without our support that's one thing she won't be able to do."

"By herself, an untrained Bianca Jones stopped a Mythos beast, destroyed a cult and stole a soul from the Dark One." Winston shook his head. "Now she's even more capable. If she thinks she's right, she'll do whatever it takes to bring Karver in, even if it means dragging the whole BPD Quick Response Team and an army of reporters along with her."

"So what do we do?"

"It's simple. We let her mail the package."

Fifteen minutes later, Cadet Hunter was standing before Knox.

"It's a training exercise," Knox explained. "Cadet Jones left here some twenty minutes ago, carrying a package. Your mission is to track her movements and retrieve the package without alerting her to your presence."

"If I may, sir. Will not Cadet Jones be aware that someone will be following her?"

"Jones has her mission, Cadet, and you have yours. Will you need something of hers with which to track her?"

Standing before a man who currently commanded his respect and obedience, Hunter did his best not to show offense at Knox's question. He almost succeeded. "Sir, I am not just a hunter, I am *The Hunter*. I am aware of Cadet Jones's scent. It is … pleasant, one that I would follow willingly. Her people come from my Isles, and she too is a hunter. The pursuit, the capture could be …"

"Cadet Hunter, must I remind you that this is training exercise."

"Sorry, sir, sometimes I just …"

"Yeah, sometimes we all just … Dismissed. Come back with the package and you'll move up in the class rankings."

"Where am I now, sir?"

"Higher than you'll be if you don't get moving and find the package."

Bianca was almost into town before Hunter caught up with her. *Odd*, he thought, *she has made no attempt at evasion or concealment*. He soon saw why – a brightly lit shop next to an equally bright convenience store. It was an all-night copying-fax-computer shop that offered shipping services. An efficient way to shed her burden and to keep it away from others, assuming those others did not have special training or powers.

Concealed in the darkness of the parking lot, Hunter watched Bianca make her transaction, hand over the package and leave the shop. Hunter left fifteen minutes after she did, the package under his arm, leaving behind a dazed, confused but otherwise unharmed store clerk.

An hour after she'd gone off base, Bianca was asleep with a self-satisfied smile on her face. As he stared at a bloodstained woman's petite-sized sweatshirt, George Knox had a similar smile on his.

"Sometimes no matter how hard you look, you just can't find what you're looking for."
– Karver, former demon possessed serial killer, DMA Cadet

I don't sleep well at night, or at any other time for that matter. Every time I close my eyes, I remember things that I'd give my life to forget. Ironically, thanks to the thing from the Pit that caused the nightmares, my body no longer needed much sleep. My roommate Pratt, on the other hand, seems to really enjoy snoozing. He snored from time to time, but it wasn't always the same sound. It was almost a symphony of snorts, pops and wheezes. And he tended to smile a lot. Good dreams, I guess. I envied him.

A few nights after my encounter with Bianca Jones during training, the snoring concert was cut short.

"All cadets to the main lecture hall," Knox's voice came over the speaker system. He repeated the message three times.

Pratt opened one eye, as if listening to see if it would happen again. Since the message didn't reoccur, he closed it back up.

I threw his blue Academy uniform at him.

"What's going on?" Pratt said, shocked by the impact of his clothes.

"The boss wants us in the main lecture hall," I said.

"For what? Some sort of test?" Pratt said.

I shrugged my shoulders. "Don't know. He's never done it before, so it's probably important."

Pratt looked over at me and gave me the once over. "You're already dressed? That's quick."

"Let's go," I said, not wanting to explain that I hadn't yet gone to sleep.

I was one of the first to get there. Pratt was one of the last. Probably wouldn't have made it at all if I hadn't woken him. He sat by me. Donna, the forgotten girl, sat on the other side of me. She seemed to like me for some reason. Not romantic. As far as I could tell, just as a friend. It was very… nice.

"What's going on?" Donna asked.

"I've no idea," I said

"Maybe some sort of test to see how we cope with lack of sleep," Pratt said.

Knox walked across the stage and stood at the podium. "Five hours ago, a seven-year-old girl named Amanda Decker was taken from her home. Local law enforcement needs all the help it can get for the search and has asked the Academy for assistance. You will divide into groups of five which will give us eight teams. Outside the hall, we have police radios waiting for all of you. You will each pick up one and report to Sheriff Shawkins. His department has the lead on this. You do whatever they need you to do. Knock on doors, search streets and God forbid search the woods. Any questions?"

Jones raised her hand. Knox nodded at her. "I assume an AMBER alert has already been issued. Do they have any suspects?"

"Not as of yet. However, in this county two girls have disappeared under similar circumstances in the past year. They've never been found. We want to make sure that we do everything possible to get Amanda back to her family. There may or may not be anything mystic involved. Remember, just because we've become involved, do not assume that magic is involved. Do not rule it out either. We have a few vans available to transport you to the Sheriff's Office, but we don't have enough seats for everyone. Those of you with personal vehicles, please take them."

The cadets filed out to get the radios.

"We can take my car," Pratt said. I tried not to roll my eyes as it was a convertible with a very tiny backseat. It could fit three people if they were all leprechauns or maybe the size of Jones.

"I guess we'll need two other people," Donna said.

I nodded. "We should get your roommate and Hunter."

Pratt tilted his head and gave me a quizzical look. "I thought you hated Jones."

"I hate her attitude and the almost creepy attention she's been paying me, but my personal feelings don't matter. We need to assemble a team that gives us the best chance of finding this girl and getting her back safely. Unlike the rest of us, Jones is a cop with the real world experience which none of us have. And Hunter claims to be the best tracker in two worlds. Time to put him to the test," I said.

I made a beeline towards the self-proclaimed Celtic god. Pratt and Donna trailed after me. "Hey big guy, why don't you come with us?"

Hunter was easily six seven, but then he took off the Academy baseball cap he normally wore and replaced it with a navy blue one with the initials DMA on the front. In the instant between headgear, he had antlers that easily gave him another three or four feet in height. Somehow, the hat hid the antlers from view.

"I assume you have a reason why?" he said.

"Yes. Because we're going to get that girl back to her family. To do that we need you. You're going to locate her."

"I can find her, with or without you. What do I need with the rest of you?" Hunter said with an impish grin.

"We need Pratt because of his car."

"Hey, I have powers too. I can listen in on any broadcast, be it radio or cell phone. I don't actually need a police radio to hear the chatter," Pratt said.

"Great, we need you for your car and to monitor broadcasts regarding the case. Can you try to pick up on cell phone conversations regarding Amanda, maybe pick up something from the kidnapper?" I said.

"I could, but there is so much traffic without narrowing down a frequency or a location, it'll be pure luck to pick one up out of the ether," Pratt said.

"Fine. Start trying," I said, turning back to Hunter. "We need Donna because she's our best shot at getting the kid out safely. You need me because none of the rest of you bothered to put the pieces together."

"Sounds reasonable. Who's our fifth?" Hunter said.

"Jones."

Hunter suddenly became more interested. Giving me the same tilt of the head and look Pratt did, he asked, "I thought you hated Jones."

"Why does everyone keep saying that? It's true I don't like her, much, but she seems to be a little too interested in me. Maybe the woman's got a crush on me. If so, I'm not interested. That's all there is to it. However, her law-enforcement experience will supplement what the rest of us can do and keep us from screwing up," I said.

"Does she know that?" Hunter said, looking over at Jones who had gotten to the front of the table. She had body armor on over her uniform shirt and had gotten her service weapon from the weapons locker. With that on one hip and a radio on another, she looked less like a little girl and more like a short, scary cop.

As I walked toward her, she turned to glare at me. "Jones, we need you as part of our quintet."

"Not going to happen. I work better alone." The look she gave me caused me to translate that "I work better without you."

"I doubt that. Baltimore PD has a whole team that you work with. You may be the best on the team, but that doesn't mean you'd get by without the other members. We are going to find the girl."

"We?" Hunter said, grinning.

"Fine. Hunter will find her," I said.

"Even assuming I am willing to work with you, who is your fifth?" Jones said.

"Your roommate Donna," I said.

"I'm standing right here," Donna said. Jones turned and looked at her.

"Who are you?" Jones said.

Donna rolled her eyes and screamed, pretending to smash her head into the wall.

"If you just wore your DMA badge, you'd know who she was," Pratt said.

"Know who who is? And I do have my badge," Jones said, as she turned away from Donna to look at my roommate.

Now I wanted to scream.

"Take it out of your pocket and put it on," Donna suggested, then wisely added, "Please."

Jones did. "Wait, I've seen you before. A lot."

"Duh, I'm your roommate," Donna said.

"You are, but why couldn't I remember you?" Jones said.

"She was cursed by a jinn. We don't have time for this. There is a little girl who needs to live. Time's a wasting. Are you in or out?" I said.

"I told you. I work better alone," Jones said.

"But with this team, we'll find the girl."

"The odds of finding this girl are lower than the odds of all of us winning the lottery this week. We don't know anything about her; she's been missing for hours. We know nothing about the family, acquaintances, suspects or the area. I'm going alone," Jones said.

"No, you're not. We need your expertise to make sure we don't make any rookie mistakes, so you're coming with us," I said.

"Exactly how are you going to convince me to do that?" Jones said.

"Remember when I said I'd cheat if it meant saving a life? I didn't want to do this, but you are forcing my hand. We both know you purposely broke my nose. I don't know why. Maybe you've got a crush on me. Maybe you just didn't want to lose the fight. Maybe you really are the nasty bitch some people think you are."

Jones looked ready to attack me again. I went on.

"Now we both know I could've filed charges against you, but I didn't. You don't help us, not only will I file charges against you, but I'll include harassment charges because you keep following me."

"Excuse me?" Jones said.

"You keep following me around, stalking me at every opportunity. It's a little bit creepy. Hell, you were even looking in our room one night," I said.

"Hey, how do you know she wasn't looking in the window at me," Pratt said.

We both ignored my roommate.

"I say that constitutes harassment. There are cameras everywhere. It wouldn't be hard to prove. I'm pretty sure those charges won't help your career any. I don't have any plans of pressing them, but we need you to make sure we don't screw up saving Amanda Decker. We don't like each other, but that shouldn't matter. So suck it up and do what's best for Amanda. Are you going to let your pride risk this little girl's life? Or are you with us?" I said.

Jones looked at me like she was seeing me for the first time or maybe like she had just looked at Donna moments before. "Fine, but you even try to imply that I sexually harassed you again and I will break both your kneecaps. Understood?"

"Understood. Now let's get out of here, and don't take off that badge."

"The best laid plans of mice and men can go astray, which is why it usually best to put a woman in charge." – Detective Bianca Jones, BPD

We were supposed to report with the search teams that were gathering at the Sheriff's Office. Instead we went to Amanda's house.

"You know those cops aren't going to let us anywhere near the family or the crime scene, right?" Jones said.

"I do. But we don't need them to let us in. We just need to distract them long enough for Donna to get in and search the crime scene."

"I still can't believe I had a roommate for months and didn't know it," Jones said.

"You get used to it," Donna said.

"Really?" Jones said.

"No," Donna said, her face a perfect model of sadness.

"Don't forget I need something that she's worn that hasn't been laundered and something with her genetics on it. A hairbrush is the best, but I might get away with a toothbrush," Hunter said.

"Got it," Donna said.

"I can do this part," Pratt said.

"Yes, you could, however you're the getaway driver. If things go south they may try to arrest us. You listen to the radio broadcasts on the police bands so you have an early warning if they're onto us. Your main job is to take Donna and Hunter so they find the kid. Besides Jones and I annoy each other so much that if we can share a fraction of that with the cop on the door, Donna will have no problem getting by."

"Ha," Jones said.

Jones and I strolled up to the cop on the door of the Decker home. I showed my DMA badge, Jones flashed hers from BPD.

"I'm Karver. This is Detective Jones. We're with the DMA Academy and we're here to provide any assistance that you might need," I said.

"This is a job for real cops. You baby voodoo cops can help comb the woods. We don't need you here," said the cop.

I tried not to get my dander up.

"Actually, maybe you missed it, but I'm Detective Bianca Jones of the Baltimore PD. I've worked quite a few missing persons cases successfully. I like to offer you my expertise if you'll have me," Jones said.

"I thought he said you were with the Academy?" the cop said.

"I'm there as part of my duties for the Baltimore PD," Jones said.

"Which marks you as a troublemaker or someone who pissed off her higher-ups. We do the same thing here. Those cops get the crap cases. Looks like you got thrown in with voodoo academy and that makes you a voodoo cop. You're welcome to each other," the cop said.

Jones and I exchanged a look. We both wanted to punch the guy. However, he had stepped forward far enough for Donna to get past him.

"We tried. They can't say we didn't offer," Jones said, looking at me.

"Absolutely," I said.

Making a point of looking at the cop's name tag, Jones said, "We'll be sure to tell Sheriff Shawkins about your cooperation, Officer Bell."

With that we turned and left, leaving the cop with the thought that maybe he should have let us in. We walked to the end of the street and stood there, pretending to talk on cell phones. The cop on door duty was watching us, but was still blocking the way. Donna simply tapped him on the shoulder and he turned around. She didn't make eye contact or speak to him, so as far as he was concerned she didn't exist. She could have done that on the way in, but he might not have moved and it might have drawn attention to her. Donna squeezed by and went around the corner to where Pratt was waiting with his convertible. We followed.

We all converged at the car.

"What'd you get?" Hunter said like a kid who was waiting to find out what presents his Grandma brought him back from her vacation.

"You seem a little cheerful and excited," Pratt said. Hunter looked at him. The horned god's entire face and continence changed to that of a predatory animal. Enough of the god he claimed was leaking through to make Pratt take a step back.

"I have a son about this girl's age. He's a little bit older and the reason I joined the DMA. In order to be a better father, I need to pay child support. To do that I need an identity and a job. The DMA is supplying me with both. So they have my loyalty as well. Whoever did this is not going to get away from me," Hunter said. "Just because I enjoy using my powers to save a little girl's life doesn't mean there's anything wrong with it. Capish?"

Pratt held his hands up in front of them and took another step back. "Capish, I definitely Capish. I didn't mean anything by it."

"Yeah, sure you didn't," Hunter said, turning back to Donna.

"I have clothes she wore to school from the hamper. I got a hairbrush, her toothbrush and a teddy bear," Donna said.

Hunter's eyes lit up and he sniffed the stuffed animal. "The teddy bear! That's perfect!"

The god pulled hairs from the brush and wrapped them around the teddy bear, closed his eyes and his hands began to glow. He bent forward, putting his entire face into the stuffed animal and breathing deeply. He took the hairs, put them in his mouth, chewed and swallowed, then spun around a few times, sniffing at the air with his hands up.

"He took her this way." According to the compass in the rearview mirror, Hunter was pointing north

"How do you know that?" Jones said.

"I just do," Hunter said.

We all got in the car and headed north.

Bianca Jones had never felt so ridiculous while acting in the line of duty. She constantly had to stop herself from complaining that this is not how a proper police investigation was done. Instead, she and the roommate she didn't know she had were trying to hold on to the legs of the self-proclaimed Celtic God as he stood on the back hood of Pratt's convertible. She would've put a stop to it if she hadn't seen the man's antlers and his hands glow. She had heard something of Herne the Hunter, not that she was entirely convinced that's who he was. The idea of a god needing to pay child support seemed a bit too outlandish even for her. If legends were to be believed, a lot of them should've had their divine wages garnished again and again.

"Turn right at the corner," Hunter said.

"Your wish is my command," Pratt said. He'd been taking the corners way too fast on purpose. He was having fun trying to knock the god from his perch, but so far Herne had maintained his footing with the help of the ladies.

Donna glared at Pratt. "I wish you would have phrased that a little differently."

Bianca and Donna held on, but the turn was too sharp and the Celtic god fell on his posterior. Thanks to their grip, he didn't fall off the car onto the asphalt.

"Pratt, stop this nonsense," Karver said.

Pratt laughed. "He said he's a god. A god should be able to car surf better than that."

From the backseat there was a primal growl and the man who claimed to be Herne moved into the tiny backseat. The big man reached forward and tore Pratt's seatbelt, then pulled the driver from his seat.

"Look man, I'm sorry. It was a joke," Pratt said, his voice trembling.

"You question my enjoying using my powers, yet you try to sabotage our mission? Give me one good reason why I shouldn't toss you out of this vehicle?" Hunter said.

Karver had reached over to take the wheel and was doing his best to drive. "I can give you one. We don't want to crash."

"I'll be fine," Hunter said.

"Then how about if anything happens to him, there will be a ton of paperwork you'll have to fill out," Bianca said. "Nobody likes paperwork, even someone claiming to be a god."

"True enough." Hunter pulled Pratt up right into his face. "You going to behave?"

Pratt nodded frantically. "Yes."

"Good, because the next time I fall, I rip a part of your car off."

Hunter plopped Pratt back in the driver's seat and got back on the trunk of the convertible.

"Prick," Pratt whispered.

"I have excellent hearing," Hunter said, already sniffing at the air.

"Sorry," Pratt said.

"Turn left here," Hunter said. The neighborhood had been going downscale. After a few more turns, Hunter said, "Stop. He's half a block ahead." He sniffed the air. "He's got her in an apartment building and she's still alive or at least she was when the wind started blowing this way."

"Which apartment?" Karver said.

"There, fourth floor, fifth and sixth windows in," Hunter said.

"Okay, Jones, this is why you're here. What do we do next?" Karver said.

"Donna, explain to me again how your powers work," Bianca said.

"Because of a bad wish no one remembers me or knows I exist. No one will even notice me unless I make an effort, with the exception of high-level magic users and jinn. I can hide others for a short time by wrapping my arms around them. I could basically walk in there, lift up the girl and walk out. As soon as I get her in a hug, the kidnapper won't even remember that he took her," Donna said.

"But then neither will she. That's got to stink, her not knowing you saved her," Pratt said.

Donna shrugged. "Credit is not what it's about. Just being able to help people and having anyone with a DMA badge remember me is pretty damn good."

"Hunter, how fast are you?" Bianca said.

"Faster than the fastest stag in the forest," the Celtic god said.

"What's that translate to – about 30 miles an hour?" Bianca said.

"Probably over 40. I can exceed 50 for short bursts," Hunter said.

"Still not faster than a bullet," Bianca said taking off her Kevlar vest. "All right, here's what we do. Hunter, you and I go up the fire escape; Donna goes in to get Amanda. If things go well, we just wait until Donna gets her, then you and I take down the kidnapper. If things go south, you go in through the window and cover the kid with my vest. I'll take the kidnapper out from the window." Her hand on her gun told us just how she planned to do that.

Isn't it great that it's already in a kid size," Pratt said.

"You're hilarious. Pratt and Karver will wait outside and take care of the girl. As soon as Donna lets go of her, she's going to forget how she got there. You'll need to calm her down, comfort her and get her away safely," Bianca said.

"Got it," Karver said. Bianca noticed he had no problem relinquishing control over the team where a lot of guys would have. "Donna, give us five minutes to get into position, then go get Amanda."

"Will do, roomie," Donna said.

"You don't think we should call in backup?" Karver said.

Bianca started to react like he was making a crack then realized he was serious. "It'll take too long and increase the risk of the kid getting hurt. The locals will go with tactical, which means snipers, which means they might take a shot. They might miss the kidnapper and hit the girl. I doubt a small town like this has much practice and they might screw up. Karver, the team you assembled is good. We go ahead with this and deal with the consequences later," Bianca said.

Karver nodded, almost in thanks.

Hunter and Bianca double timed it to the side of the building. Bianca tried to reach for the metal ladder on the fire escape, but it was out of her grasp, even when she jumped. Hunter reached up and pulled it down without even having to stand on his toes.

"Not one word," Bianca said.

"I wouldn't dream of it. In no way would I embarrass a lady such as yourself." Herne gave a slight bow. "Besides, I've lived among short people for many years. I know how sensitive they can be about it." Looming at the fire escape, Herne added, "Although even a pixie would've been able to manage that."

"Can't pixies fly?" Bianca said as she climbed up the ladder.

"They can, which I suppose would make it easier. Also rather foolish for them to use the ladder at all," Hunter said, leaping over her and up the sides of the fire escape, not even bothering with the steps. He was outside the window in seconds. It took Bianca a bit longer to join him. Amanda was inside, tied to a chair. There was one man who seemed to be ranting. The girl was terrified.

Bianca was amazed by how well things seemed to be going. They had found the girl easily and had a way to get her out that might work. Which is why she wasn't too surprised when the kidnapper walked over to the window that she and Hunter were hiding alongside and opened it. Nor was he terribly shocked when he stuck his head out, apparently to check the weather or get a breath of fresh air.

"It's a beautiful day to begin the rest of our lives together, my beautiful Amanda," the kidnapper said. "Although we may have to change your name and dye your hair, it'll save people asking too many questions that we won't want to answer. I've tried this twice before, but I know the third time is going to be the charm."

The kidnapper turned his head and saw Bianca's legs. "What?" He turned to the other side and saw Hunter. The kidnapper tried to pull himself back into the room, but the Celtic god grabbed hold of the hair atop his head and yanked the man out onto the fire escape.

"Donna, now!" Bianca shouted.

Donna was no stronger than an ordinary woman, but that didn't stop her from using a fire extinguisher from the hallway as a battering ram and breaking down the door.

Having lived for so long with no one being able to notice or remember her, Donna had learned to be self-sufficient and found one of her most important tools had always been a Swiss Army knife. She pulled it from her pocket and cut the ropes holding Amanda.

"Amanda, I'm here to get you out," Donna said, putting her hands on the girl shoulders. The poor girl had been so traumatized that it didn't take much effort on Donna's part to get Amanda to focus on her. The girl was already trying to find something to take her mind off the nightmare she was trapped in.

Donna grabbed hold of the girl and ran out the door and down the stairs.

"You've got information and a nice looking face. You're not leaving here with both."
– Detective Bianca Jones, Baltimore PD

As soon as Donna left with Amanda, Herne looked at Bianca then down at the kidnapper. "What do we do with him?"

"Throw him back in the room."

The Hunter did, none too gently.

Hitting the floor hard, the kidnapper was in no shape to try to escape through the door. Looking up from where he lay, he saw a short woman and a tall man staring down at him.

"What do you want?"

"What did you do with the other two girls?" Bianca asked.

"I don't have to tell you. I know my rights."

"Good," she replied, "then I don't have to read them to you. Are you willing to give me a statement now?" The kidnapper stayed silent.

"Okay, looks like it's time for good cop, bad cop."

Herne was confused. His Academy training had covered police procedure and interrogation methods and he was sure that you were not supposed to tell your suspect what technique you planned to use. Then he heard,

"Herne, take off your hat." He did. "Now think about Pratt." Herne caught on.

Looking up, the kidnapper saw the very tall man suddenly grow antlers. That didn't bother him as much as the bestial growl that came from the man's throat.

Bianca leaned in close to the kidnapper's face. "Now for the bad news. My partner is the good cop."

The kidnapper eagerly told them everything they wanted to know.

Herne hoisted the kidnapper over his shoulder and followed Bianca down the stairs.

"That went well," he said.

"Yes, it did," agreed Bianca, glad to be doing police work again, if only for the day.

"We worked well together," Herne said, adding "Maybe after graduation we can work together again."

Bianca considered the Hunter's proposition, for based on the way he had said it, that's what it was. "I don't think you have work in mind."

"I have several things in mind, Bianca."

"I'm sure." Remembering how strong Herne's thigh felt when she held it in the car, Bianca was beginning to think of a few herself.

"After graduation, if you find yourself in Baltimore, well, I don't suppose you'll have any trouble finding me."

"None at all."

"Good, maybe we can scare some more bad guys."

"Is that all?"

"It's a start."

"Sometimes being wrong is a good thing."
– Karver, former demon possessed serial killer, DMA Cadet

One of the most beautiful things I've ever seen in my life was Donna coming down the stairs with Amanda in her arms. The wave of emotion practically knocked me over and for once it was the good kind. I surfed it happily.

Donna put the girl down in front of me. "This is Karver, honey. He's the mastermind behind getting you out. He'll take good care of you."

Amanda rushed at me. I got down on one knee and she wrapped her arms around my neck. I stiffened for less than an instant, my body like a statue, but then I realized that's not what the girl needed. I forced myself to relax. More than that, I hugged her back. It felt good.

"Amanda, you're going to be all right. I promise," I said.

Pratt stood over me and looked down. "Karver, man, are you crying?"

Tears were indeed streaming down my face. Not that I cared one bit.

"Damn straight, I am," I said. I looked up to see Donna smiling at me. Jones and Hunter came out of the door behind her. They had our suspect in tow. The kidnapper looked frightened and kept staring at Herne's head. Hunter and Jones, on the other hand, kept staring at each other making me wonder just what had happened after Donna had gotten Amanda out.

Jones hung back with the perp so that Amanda didn't have to see him again. Hunter helped block the man from view.

I stood up with Amanda in my arms, turning her away from the man who took her.

"Good job, Karver," Hunter said, slapping me on the back.

"Thanks."

Even Jones nodded her approval.

The old man was right. I can do something good with my life. Thanks, God, I owe you for this one. We'll discuss the rest another time.

"No good deed ever goes unpunished or even appreciated"
– Every cop in the world

Bianca wanted to smile, but instead gritted her teeth. The rookies had all thought that finding the girl would make their flouting of the rules, their disobeying of orders, their insubordination go away, but she knew better. First and foremost, the job is about protecting the innocent, or it should be. Once they're safe, it's all about who gets the credit for the save. Having baby voodoo cops and an out-of-state detective be the ones to find and rescue the girl had the Sheriff's Department on edge.

Sheriff Shawkins had been yelling and chewing them out for being irresponsible, not calling in his people to do the actual rescue and a myriad of other assorted offenses. He had been yelling for fifteen minutes and showed no signs of stopping.

Bianca wasn't impressed. She had been yelled at by experts – BPD Academy instructors, Homicide sergeants, Jesuit priests and Franciscan nuns – all of whom could give this small town chief lessons in ass chewing.

Pratt, like Bianca was biting his tongue. Hunter was lounging against the wall, making as if he was bored. The sheriff started to yell at him, but the Celtic god stood up to his full height and gave him a look that no mortal man could manage. Hunter was left out of all the rest of the sheriff's tirade.

However, it was Karver's reaction that surprised her the most. He stood as if at parade rest, his hands behind his back, unable to wipe a goofy grin off his face despite the berating of the sheriff. The normally grim and somber man seemed almost giddy.

It had not escaped the sheriff's attention. "Do you think this is funny, cadet?"

"No, sir. We saved the little girl. That's all that matters. I don't give a damn about who gets the credit. You can take it all. We did good. And if you can't see that, that's your problem, not mine, Sheriff Shawkins, *sir*," Karver said, making the "sir" sound a little bit too insulting.

Donna walked up and hugged Karver and suddenly the sheriff forgot he existed, but he still remembered he had been yelling at someone, which only made him testier.

"That's enough, Cadet Winks. Release Cadet Karver and let him take his medicine," George Knox said. The commandant entered the locked roll call room much to Shawkins's surprise.

Donna let go and Shawkins sudden remembered Karver existed and spun back on him. "I'm going have you drilled out of your pretend cop academy and will make it my mission to make sure you never work in law enforcement again."

"Exactly how are you planning to manage that, Sheriff Shawkins, when the man is a hero?" Knox said, stepping between the angry lawman and his cadets like a lion protecting his cubs.

"Don't think you're getting off scott-free in this either, Knox. We asked for your help, not for you to throw a bunch of untrained amateurs in the middle of a sensitive investigation," the sheriff growled.

"Detective Jones has as much experience as any two men in your department. As for the rest, you know many of our agents and cadets have abilities that give them an advantage in the field over regular law enforcement. Apparently, they had the foresight to form a team that could safely rescue this girl. True, they should've coordinated this better with both myself and you. Rest assured, they will be reprimanded for that. However, none of us can argue with the results. Especially since the girl has already told the family that Karver and company did the rescuing and they have relayed that to the media," Knox said.

"Now just a minute…"

"Before you say another word, I want you to read these two press releases," Knox said, holding up the first paper. "This one gives the cadet team full credit and mentions how you criticized them after the fact, stresses that five cadets were able to outthink, out plan and outdo your entire department." Knox held up a second piece of paper. "This one relates how this team, under the direct supervision of yourself managed to assist the local sheriff's department in making the rescue. We have an entire PR department in DC waiting to go with either one, as soon as I make a call. They'll send one out to all the national media outlets. Which one is it going to be, Shawkins?"

The sheriff grabbed both and read them. "What do you mean five? There are only four of them."

"For once going unnoticed is not so bad," Donna said.

"Trust me, you're not unnoticed," Knox said.

"Who are you talking to?" Shawkins said, then crumpled and threw the first release at Knox. "Fine. Get them out of here. But you all better watch yourselves. And Knox, I don't want your cadets in my town from now on. I see a cadet spit on the sidewalk, they're going to jail."

"Thank you, Sheriff. All of you, march," Knox ordered. The five of them filed out.

"It's easier to get forgiveness than permission"
– Detective Bianca Jones, BPD

It went against every fiber of Bianca Jones' being to remain silent while she was being reamed out by someone who wasn't even a real cop, who wasn't even in her chain of command, but she held her tongue while George Knox read them the riot act in his office. It was worse than Shawkins.

"These four are rookies, but you're a seasoned detective, Jones. I expected better from you," Knox said.

"Sir, we got the girl back safely," Bianca said.

"Which is the only reason why the lot of you are still members of this Academy. Had Amanda Decker gotten so much as a paper cut, this would be a very different conversation, most likely ending with charges being brought against all of you in a court of law. I do not understand why you didn't come to me with this. I could have approached Shawkins and his department to have them assign an officer to your team. He probably would've been low man on the totem pole, but after this success, that officer would have been moving up the ranks. The department would have a friend in the sheriff's office instead of an enemy."

Knox took a deep breath, "What I want to know is whose idea was all this? Who am I to blame?"

Bianca knew how things were supposed to go. Everyone would keep their mouth shut and let the commanding officer blow off more steam. If it was her team and there was real risk of damage to their careers, Bianca would've taken the blame, but that wasn't the case here. Knox had already made it clear they were not going to be kicked out of the Academy. The worst that was going to happen to any of them was a letter of discipline in their file. However, not everyone realized that.

Karver raised his hand. "Any blame should be directed at me, sir."

"So this debacle was entirely your fault, then?" Knox said.

"Absolutely, sir," Karver said.

"What about the credit?"

"The credit for Amanda Decker's rescue should go entirely to Donna, Hunter, and Detective Jones," Karver said.

"Hey, I was there too," Pratt said. Knox turned a stare on him and Pratt withered. "Never mind."

Knox turned his attention back on Karver.

"And Agent Pratt was instrumental as well," Karver said.

"So you're entirely okay for them to get the credit and for you to get the blame. Which means you will be the one doing any punishment," Knox said.

"Yes, sir," Karver said.

"Very well," Knox said. "The rest of you can go."

"Sir, Karver should not be the only one getting punished," Donna said.

"Absolutely. We're all part of this. We all deserve equal blame," Hunter said.

Bianca rolled her eyes, but knew she had to speak up too. "They're right. At any point we could've left, but we followed Karver. We should all share the punishment."

The three cadets who had spoken up all turned to glare at Pratt, but he remained silent. It took Knox turning his stare on him for Pratt to finally speak.

"Hey, don't look at me. I just drove the car and listened in on the police bands," Pratt said.

"Very well. Pratt, you can leave. The rest of you have just become my special project."

Pratt practically ran out of the office and slammed the door behind him.

"I would like to say that while I am upset by the manner you went about what you did, that I am pleased with the results. In addition to a simple letter of reprimand that will be put in your permanent records…" Knox looked at Bianca. "Or sent to your home department, there will be a much more glowing letter of commendation. You did good work. Next time just do it within the bounds of accepted protocol. The lot of you be on the track tomorrow morning at 0500 and the fun will begin."

Karver and Donna left. Bianca and Herne stayed behind. The Hunter handed Knox a sheet of paper.

"What's this?"

"The locations of the bodies of the other two girls," Bianca replied. "We, er, persuaded the kidnapper to tell us where they are."

"Do I want to know how you persuaded him?"

The two cadets looked at each other then back at Knox. "No, sir," they said together.

The Commandant nodded. "I'll fax this to Shawkins. It might help smooth things over. What it will not do is lessen what is going to happen to the four of you."

"Sometimes life just feels like you are running in circles,"
– Karver, former demon possessed serial killer, DMA Cadet

Being Knox's personal project was worse than being back in the police academy. Bianca was sore in places she'd forgotten she had. Donna had it worse than she did. Her roommate had just been a typical teen, without even the benefit of being a jock. Karver and Hunter took turns helping her whenever they could, going so far as to sometimes even carry her on their backs. Of course Hunter always had someone on his back. Knox felt that being a god, Hunter had it a little too easy and made him carry the Commandant for his laps and calisthenics.

"I don't know how he's doing it, but somehow he's making everything extremely difficult. I can carry 50 times his weight and not be this tired," Hunter confided to the team doing a gasping for air break. Oddly enough, the one who seem to be doing the best with it was Karver. As far as Bianca knew he had no supernatural abilities beyond the ability to sense Hellish magic. Still, he was breathing the least heavily of the four of them.

Knox had just finished making them run a mile around the track backwards before they collapsed.

"All right, people, you've had five days of this. I trust that's enough to get my point across and none of you will be going outside of accepted protocol ever again, correct?" Knox said.

They all shouted in the affirmative.

"Fine, then your punishment is done. Go have breakfast and then get to class," Knox said.

"Sorry about this week, guys," Karver said.

"Don't be," Donna said. "I enjoyed being part of something with other people, even if it was a punishment. Plus, I'm a lot stronger than I was. It's a good thing. Or it will be when I can move without pain again."

"We saved a child. That's all that matters," Hunter said.

"We appreciate what you did, trying to take the blame,"

Bianca said as an instructor came into the gym.

"Jones, phone call from your office. Something about a case."

Bianca knew what the call had to be about. She looked over at Karver. From what she'd seen over the past several days, she was, for once, hoping that she had been wrong.

The caller was Joe Russo from the BPD Crime Lab.

"Hey Joe."

"Hi Bianca," Joe said. "You are amazing, you know that?"

"I do, but it's still nice to hear occasionally."

"I had Dolan run that DNA for you," Joe said.

"Yeah about that. I was overreacting…"

"Overreacting? I don't know how you did it, but you proved The Carver is still alive. The DNA is barely human, but it matches up. What is it? Some sort of government conspiracy?"

"I can't believe he fooled me. I can't believe I fell for it," Bianca said.

"Fell for what?" Joe said.

"It doesn't matter. I'm going to arrest a dead killer."

Bianca weighed her options. She could, right now, call Lieutenant Fredericks and get a warrant for Karver, rather, The Carver's arrest. That would take time. She could take him out herself. She had almost beaten him that time in the gym, but she sensed that he had been holding back and almost didn't count. She could go to Knox. Lay it all out for him and Winston. But they had dismissed her the first time and might even be part of a cover-up. No, there was only one way to handle this and that was with plenty of backup available.

Bianca stopped at her locker for her weapon and her cuffs, then ran across the campus, feeling like steam was coming out of her ears. She had started to actually like Karver. He seemed like a man of honor, someone who would make a good cop or agent. She had no idea what sick game he was playing, but she wasn't playing it anymore.

Karver had his food tray and was heading to a table. Bianca came up behind him and without warning slammed him face first on the table and had cuffs on him a second later. All the other cadets turned to watch as the drama unfolded.

"Jones, what are you doing?" Karver shouted.

"Bianca, let him go," Donna said.

"No," Bianca said. "Bartholomew Andrew Higgins, you are under arrest for the murder of the Innocent family."

"What are you talking about?" Hunter said.

"Karver is really the serial killer Carver," Bianca said. "I ran his DNA."

"Karver, is what she's saying true?" Donna said.

Karver's face was a portrait of pain before turning to stone. "Yes."

"But it is not the full story," Knox said, suddenly coming into the room. "Let go of him, Jones."

"No, there is still a warrant for him in Baltimore. Since he got the death penalty, Higgins was never tried for the murders of the Innocents. I'm within my rights," Bianca said.

Knox moved her aside and Bianca couldn't stop him. He flicked a finger, hit the steel restraints and the cuffs popped open.

"Attention, cadets. There is more to this story than meets the eye. Karver was possessed by a demon that used his body to kill. He fought the demon. We got rid of it and gave him a second chance. This information is covered by the national secrecy oath you all signed. If any of you speak of this matter, it will be a violation of that order and you will be kicked out of the DMA and prosecuted. Jones, follow me."

Bianca looked at Karver. "I'm not going anywhere, Jones."

"See that you don't, Higgins." Jones followed Knox to his office.

"Sit," Knox ordered.

"I…"

"Stuff it, Jones. You just spent a week being punished for going outside of channels and you pull this? You should have notified me first and I could have explained it to you."

"You could have explained it to me when I expressed my suspicions," Bianca said.

"What part of a national secrecy oath do you not understand?"

Knox said. "The man has been through hell. A seriál demon took control of him and killed 63 people. Karver saw and felt everything."

"Then he should have done something to stop it," Bianca said.

"He did. He fought it with every ounce of his being. It only claimed 63 lives."

"Seems like an awful lot to me," Jones said.

"We found a seriál operating in Rwanda during the massacres. We attributed tens of thousands of deaths to it. Karver is the only known case where the death toll was under four figures. The man saved hundreds by fighting it. He made sure it was caught. The only way he could be sure it would be stopped was for Karver himself to die, so he made sure he was sent to death row. He was willing to die to stop it from killing again. We exorcised the demon and gave him the chance to work for us. He took it. Our fleshsmith redid his face and fingerprints, but he couldn't change Karver's DNA. The man does not need this brought down his head. We've barely kept him alive this long," Knox said.

"He tried suicide?" Bianca said.

"What do you think his attempt to go to the electric chair was?"

Bianca looked down at the floor. "So he's just as much a victim as those the demons killed."

"Exactly. Only he's trying to have something good come out of it."

"And we just screwed it up," Bianca said.

"We?"

"You should have told me when I first expressed my suspicions. I would have … might have understood. And saved myself a beating."

"A well-deserved beating."

"Granted."

"One question, Jones. How did you get the DNA to your lab?"

"I mailed it, sir."

"We intercepted your package."

"I thought you would. While sending it, I also slipped the

clerk an envelope containing two swabs of blood I'd taken from my shirt. It was addressed directly to a friend in the crime lab."

"Very clever, Jones, only this time your cleverness may have ruined a man's chance at redemption."

"I realize that now, sir. I'm sorry," Knox said.

"I'm not the one you need to be apologizing to."

"Life sucks. This is news why?"
– Karver, former demon possessed serial killer, DMA cadet

I now knew what it felt like to be outed. Knox had tried to do damage control after asking me how I wanted to play things. The DMA is not big on fake cover stories, but it can do them very well when necessary. I opted for the truth. I thought I knew how much the truth hurts. I was wrong. It hurt a lot more than I expected.

Knox explained to the other cadets more details about my possession, stressing how I'd reined the seriál in. I don't think it made any difference once the Hellish cat was out of the bag. As far as most people were concerned, I was a brutal killer and the demon was only an excuse. Not that I blamed them. It's just I'd gotten used to being a part of something worthwhile. It had felt good.

Now things sucked worse than a vampire after a four day fast. Only Knox's threat with the national security oath kept people in line.

At no time was it more noticeable more than in the cafeteria. I felt like a loner in high school. No one would sit by me. If I sat at a table, those already there vacated. That wasn't exactly true. Hunter would still sit with me, but he didn't always eat in the cafeteria. He preferred to go out and hunt his own food. Donna would still dine with me as well, but she was working with the applied magic teachers on a way for her to be able to allow people to notice her, however briefly. The only time that they were available to work with her was during lunch and dinner, which left me taking those meals alone.

So imagine my surprise when a tray plopped down on the table across from me. I looked up and saw who it was.

"Hello, Jones. What do you want? To kick me while I'm down?"

Jones appeared sheepish and nervous as opposed to her usual

overconfident self, like she was gathering courage trying to say something. Finally, she took a deep breath and plunged ahead. "Karver, I'm sorry. I didn't know about the demon. You are as much a victim as the people the demon killed."

"Nowhere near as much a victim. I'm alive. My 63 dead are not."

"And thousands of others are alive, thanks to you. I acted harshly and rashly. After everything we'd just been through about staying inside channels, I should've gone to Knox first. I've been treating you badly because my gut was telling me there was something off with you and my subconscious was telling it was because you were The Carver."

"Your gut was right," I said.

"Maybe, but I should've had all the facts. I apologize and hope you'll forgive me," Jones said.

"Apology accepted. There's nothing to forgive. I've done a lot of evil things. It's not like I really deserved a totally fresh start anyway."

"Karver, it wasn't your fault," Jones said.

"My head knows that, but *my* gut knows different. I felt everything the demon did. It used me to entice those people to let down their guard so he could butcher, kill, and torture them. I remember everything. Every scream, every bit of begging for mercy. I felt the demon's joy in it all as if it was my own. The DMA shrinks have been working with me, trying to get me past it. What they don't understand is there is no getting past it. It's part of who I am and forever will be," I said.

"Then why are you here?" Bianca said.

"Sarge Winston told me that my dead deserved better. That I might do some good in this world. I didn't quite believe him, but I agreed with him that my dead deserve better. Ever since we saved Amanda Decker, I realized he was right. I can help save people from other monsters. Monsters like I was. It'll never make up for what I did, but the world would be better off with me trying than with me slitting my throat," I said.

"A dark, but reasonable viewpoint. Would you mind some

company?" Bianca said.

"Have a seat if you don't mind being seen with me," I said.

"Trust me, I've been seen with worse," Jones said.

The detective began to chow down, then noticed I wasn't eating.

"Not hungry? I've missed a few meals due to being Knox's new special project because of my actions, but you still have to eat."

"I do, but I'm not eating this. Some of the other cadets have added special ingredients." I pointed to the various foods on my tray. "The Sloppy Joe has Pratt's urine. The mashed potatoes have bleach and the milk has been opened and resealed with the addition of semen. My sniffer may not be as good as Hunter's, but it's enough to make sure I don't eat doctored food."

"And why come here and sit if you're not going to eat?"

"To show them that I'm going to keep going regardless of what they do. I'm not going to let some punks stop me from saving people from the bad guys," I said.

Jones smiled and started cutting her portions in half. She cleaned off her cake plate and put half of her food on it and slid it over to me. I nodded my thanks. She nodded back and we ate the rest of our meal in silence.

"People are supposed to live and learn but some just can't manage it."
– Karver, former demon possessed serial killer, DMA Cadet

The jury was in. I had an idiot for a roommate. Pratt had been trying to torment me from a distance and in secret, like his sabotaging my food and pouring Nair in my shampoo and the like. He was quick to talk trash from a distance, but never to my face unless he was in a group. All cowardly acts done from a distance. I had ignored it, but Pratt had just crossed the line.

I'm not sure what gave him and the other two cadets with him the push to move from sabotage to direct attack and I didn't care. I'd say courage, but it didn't take any sort of bravery to attack a man in his sleep.

From the smell they had filled pillowcases with flour. Easy to get rid of and we had community laundry, so it would be hard to match up the weapon to the user. Plus any bruises wouldn't be traceable to the weapon by mundane forensics.

My skin was sensitive enough to feel air currents change, so I could feel them come closer. They made little noise as they moved, but I heard their breathing and even faintly made out their heartbeats. When the air shifted because of something being lifted over my head, I decided it was time to let them know it would be best to stop.

"I wouldn't do that," I said.

Pratt took a step back as I opened my eyes and stared him down. "I wasn't going to do anything. I was just checking to see if you were still breathing."

"Why? So you could rectify the situation?" I said.

"Listen…"

"No, you listen. I've put up with your crap long enough. The next time you put urine or anything else in my food, I'm going to make you eat it," I said.

"I didn't…" Pratt said.

"Don't lie. I can smell that it was yours. You have a very distinctive odor. Stupid way to attack someone. Have you been paying any attention in class? A simple DNA test or mystic tracking spell and you'd get kicked out of the Academy. Not to mention I now know enough about voodoo and other sympathetic magic that I could use that urine to cast a spell on you. If you really thought I was still a serial killer, don't you think it was idiotic to give me the means to kill you from a distance?"

I almost smiled at the stupefied expression on Pratt's face. None of this had even crossed his mind or the minds of the two other cadets with him. "You helped me save Amanda, so everything before this moment is wiped away for you and your friends. Everything from here on will bring an equal or greater retaliation from me. Now get out. You need to find somewhere else to sleep from now on."

"You can't kick me out. This is my room too," Pratt said. "I'll tell Knox."

"I wasn't planning on turning you in, but if you're stupid enough to rat on me, I'm not about to lie to Knox to save you from your stupidity."

"You have no proof," Pratt said.

"You've watched as I took food out of the cafeteria with me. What do you think I did with it?"

Pratt fumed. "Fine, let me get my things…"

"Nope. I'll leave it in the hall in the morning. You can pick it up then," I said.

"There are three of us," said Tuckahoe, a cadet who was rumored to have some magical skill with locks.

"Exactly. Better go get reinforcements," I said. The third guy was Daniels, a minor psychic. "Right, Daniels?"

Tuckahoe and Pratt looked at the psychic who shook his head.

Pratt couldn't come up with anything else to say, so he and his cronies left the room and slammed the door behind them.

"No news may not be good news, but it sure beats bad news."
– Karver, former demon possessed serial killer, DMA Cadet

Knox called me to his office for an update on how my social situation was progressing. Knox didn't know whether or not to believe me, so he insisted that Jones sit in so he got an accurate picture. I would say things were fine, where Jones would be brutally honest.

"I don't like that it's still going on. DMA Agents are supposed be cut from better cloth than this," Knox said.

"It doesn't bother me. Really," I said.

"He's lying," Jones said.

"I am not," I lied. If I were being truthful I would have to admit that being ostracized did bother me, but I deserved far worse, so I wasn't going to let it affect me. "Besides, how would you know?"

Jones smirked. "I've done enough interrogations to know when someone's lying. Most people have a tell."

"I don't have a tell," I said.

"Yes, you do."

"What is it?" I said.

Jones smirked again. "If I tell you what is, you'll try to fix it. I'm not giving away the upper hand."

There was a soft knock at the door and in walked Sarge Winston. "George, sorry to barge in, but I need to speak to Karver."

"Sure, Sarge, no problem," Knox said.

Sarge motioned me out into the hallway and from the look on his face, I knew whatever he wanted to tell me wasn't good news.

"Karver, we've been monitoring Lucy Innocent as a courtesy to you. She posted some things on a social media site that sent up red flags."

Sarge handed me some print outs of her posts. Not a lot to go on there. "Lucy was worried someone was after her in Milton, Maine. Now, she's missing. We called the local police to check out her whereabouts, but they haven't been overly helpful."

"Let me go look for her," I said.

"Karver, you aren't an agent until you graduate the Academy."

"In three weeks, part of which is a four day weekend," I said. "I've got nothing to do next week when classes are closed. Everyone else has family or friends to spend it with. I don't have any family left. Let me do what I can to help her. I owe her at least that much."

"Normally I wouldn't dream of sending a cadet into an unknown situation, but three of our psychics had a vision of you heading to Milton. But you're still a rookie. You need someone with experience to go with you. Unfortunately I don't have anyone available," Sarge said.

Jones opened the office door. "I'll go with him."

"You will, Detective Jones?" The look in Sarge's eyes already told me he'd planned on that. Maybe even set up the whole thing by having Knox call us into his office at the same time. "But you aren't even a DMA Agent. You've made your opinions about Feds not being real cops very clear. Why would you volunteer?"

"I made Karver's life here more difficult than it had to be. This would help me make that up to him. And I was the one who realized Lucy was still alive. I helped save her. By some ways of thinking, that makes me responsible for her."

"I'm a little leery of sending not one, but two cadets into the field," Sarge said.

"I may be a cadet here, but in Baltimore I'm the best the city has to offer. I'll keep an eye on Karver and make sure he doesn't screw up," Bianca said. "No more than he absolutely has to anyway."

Sarge looked at Knox. "George, you have an opinion on this?"

"They started out at each other's throats, but that stopped. They are the two best cadets in this class. Honestly, even if they failed every test left, they'd still pass the Academy. So long as they are back by the time class starts on Wednesday, I'm okay with it."

"All right. I'm granting you both provisional agent status

for the next week." He handed us regular agent badges. "Go see what you can find out. Remember, our agency has restrictions we operate within. Based on her posts, Lucy was involved with some sort of cult. That gives us some possible jurisdiction if you turn up the slightest hint of magic. There's a department car outside. Be careful," Sarge said, tossing me the keys.

I nodded. Jones and I left.

"So you want to be partners with me, huh?" I said.

"Don't flatter yourself, Karver. I made a mistake. This is my way of making up for it, nothing more. I don't like you and I don't like playing errand girl for the Feds. I do this and we're even, agreed?"

"Sure."

We headed to our dorm rooms and each packed a bag. Bianca then raided the armory and met me at the car.

"We can never truly make up for past sins, but it is still better to try when the opportunity arises."
— Karver, former demon possessed serial killer, Provisional DMA Agent

Bianca and Karver made most of the trip from Virginia to Maine in silence. Karver wasn't one for small talk. In fact, he wasn't one for much of any kind of talk at all. Bianca suspected that if she didn't speak to him, he wouldn't utter a single word. He just drove, staring out at the road.

Bianca didn't even pretend to understand what he had been through. It was too terrible to even contemplate. The fact that Karver was functioning instead of in a padded room spoke volumes about his inner strength. As a cop, she had some idea what this girl meant to him. There had been people along the years that she had managed to save. And family members of some she had failed to save. She felt an obligation above and beyond that of a cop to protect them. She had helped save Lucy, so she had a personal interest, but she knew it meant more than that to Karver.

Karver drove nine miles above the posted speed limit with no variation without using the cruise control.

Both their cell phones went off at the same time. Bianca couldn't remember ever using a punk rock version of *Itsy-bitsy Spider* as a ringtone. She lifted up her phone and it turned itself on, the face of a purple cartoon Viking staring back at her.

It was the electronic avatar of the World Wide Spyder. He'd been one of the guest lecturers at the Academy. Spyder was a teenage hacker who was also into magic. An unfortunate mixture of the two caused him to be transformed into a digital entity that could live on the web or in any electronic device. He was the Department of Mystic Affairs' best cybercop.

"Sarge asked me to pass along that Milton PD found a Jane Doe murdered on the beach. They think she might be Lucy Innocent.

After Sarge's inquiries about her disappearance they called him. He informed them you were en route. They're expecting you at the crime scene. I've programed the GPS in your phones to take you there."

"Understood, Spyder. Please notify MPD that we will be arriving in twenty minutes," Karver said.

Bianca frowned. "GPS says fifty two minutes."

Karver put his foot down, pushing the gas pedal to the floor. The speedometer started rising. He reached over and put a siren on the roof of the unmarked car. "We'll be there in twenty."

They actually made it in nineteen.

Karver parked in front of a fire hydrant and the pair got out of the car and walked towards a beach blocked off by yellow crime scene tape. A couple of uniformed cops were standing behind it. Behind them detectives in suits and crime scene techs in jumpsuits were examining the area.

As they reached the tape, one of the uniforms stepped towards them.

"This is a crime scene. You need to leave the area."

Bianca pulled out her provisional DMA badge and flipped it open. "Federal Agents. We got an invitation to this party."

A plainclothes detective walked over. "It's okay. Let them through."

The pair ducked under the crime scene tape.

"I'm Detective Camp. You must be the DMA Agents."

"I'm Jones, this is Karver."

"We got your request regarding the missing girl. Unfortunately, I think we may have found her. It's not pretty," Camp said. He motioned for them to follow him and led them to a corpse with a white sheet over it. Karver bent down and lifted the sheet up, careful not to expose any flesh below the neck. It was obvious through the thin material that the girl beneath was naked and bloody.

"I thought she was dead once. She can't be dead again," Karver said.

"Dead again?" Camp said.

Jones put her hand on the detective's shoulder and whispered, "It's one of those cases."

Camp nodded knowingly. Cops saw lots of the bad that people can do. Sometimes it hits closer to home than others. Most cops had at least one of *those* cases.

"Who did this?" Karver said.

Camp smirked. "That's what we're trying to figure out, Agent Karver. You may have noticed we're doing a little bit of an investigation here."

Karver stood up faster than any man had a right to and turned towards Camp with a look on his face that made Camp start to reach for his sidearm. Jones stepped between them. "I think what my partner is trying to say is he knew this girl personally and he would appreciate the courtesy of helping Milton PD in any way possible in this investigation."

"You knew the girl?" Camp said, his manner softening.

Karver nodded. "This is Lucy Innocent."

"I'm sorry for your loss. Does she have any next of kin we can notify?"

Karver shook his head. "No. They were all murdered. She was the only survivor."

"I'm sorry, Agent Karver. Of course, I will keep you informed of our investigation, every step of the…"

"Who the hell are these people trampling around my crime scene!" shouted a man in a suit too expensive for any normal cop to afford.

"Lieutenant Fleming, these are the Federal Agents I told you about. Agent Karver was a personal friend of the deceased," Camp said.

"I don't give a damn if he's J. Edgar Hoover coming back from the dead. This is a Milton PD matter and none of your concern." Lieutenant Fleming paused his tirade and looked over at Bianca. "You Feds so hard up that you're hiring kids these days? Or maybe you're into the young stuff. Is that what you relationship with the deceased was? You her sugar daddy?"

Karver took a step forward, intending to clock the Lieutenant.

Bianca stepped in front of her partner again and put her hand on his chest.

Fleming laughed. "I told you to get off my crime scene. Get out of here now."

To emphasize his point, Fleming put his hand on Bianca's shoulder to shove her. It was a mistake. Bianca didn't like to be touched and had spent years learning how to take down people larger than she was. And she had spent the last few months drilling on how to fight creatures that were bigger and stronger than humans. Fleming hit the ground hard and fast.

Every cop on the beach froze. A couple of them had their hands hovering near their holsters. Karver leaned down and offered a hand. "Better be careful, Lieutenant. Sand can be awful slippery."

Fleming slapped the hand away. Before he could speak, Karver whispered, "Get up and make nice unless you want all these cops to know you just got taken down by someone who looks like a teenage girl."

Lieutenant Fleming stood and brushed the sand off his expensive suit. "Fine, but this is still a local police matter. Get the hell off the beach and stay away from this investigation."

"What if we don't?" Bianca said, her back up. She never liked anyone telling her what to do. It was only magnified when the order came from someone she didn't like.

"Then I guess I get to throw a couple of Feds in jail for obstruction."

"Do that, you'll have more Feds than people in this town," Bianca said. She'd enough experience with Feds in the past to know how they behaved and what buttons they pushed. She enjoyed being on the other side of things for once. "We'll shut this place down so tight you won't be able to write a parking ticket without asking, 'Mother may I'."

Bianca and Fleming locked eyes and looked ready to fight.

"Do things my way and we'll get along just fine."
– Detective Bianca Jones, Baltimore PD

"At least let me take a look at the body," I said.

"Thank you, Mr. Karver, but we're all qualified investigators here," Fleming said, making a big show out of not addressing him as "Agent."

"At least let me look for my own peace of mind. I need to know how she died. How would you feel if she was someone you cared about?"

I looked at the Lieutenant, trying for sincere. I was good at manipulating my expressions. The demon used my face often enough to get others to do what he wanted to help. Apparently I was just as good, because Fleming sighed and rolled his eyes.

"One look and you're gone. Do not disturb my crime scene," Fleming said.

"Thank you," I said in the interest of diplomacy.

"Detective Camp, you keep an eye on them," Fleming said. The detective nodded.

Jones and I went over to her body and pulled the sheet off. It was hard to look at. Lucy was naked and bloody, much like she had been the last time I saw her. Despite myself, I reached to check for a pulse, knowing full well there couldn't be one. Still, I had to be sure. After all, I had been wrong about her being dead before.

"She was killed from above with a knife," I said, unable to look away from the healed wounds I'd given her.

"I guess you would know," Jones said. The words sounded insulting, however the tone was not, so I let it go.

"No defensive wounds," I said.

"Ligature marks on the wrists and ankles," Jones said. "Whoever did this tied her down first."

Camp stood behind us, listening for our take.

"We found two more girls!" a cop down the beach started

shouting.

Camp looked at us then down the beach. It was obvious that this sleepy town hadn't had three murders in three years. The part of him that was the detective needed to see.

"Go on. We're almost done here," Jones said.

Camp nodded, but pointed to a uniform. "Chip, when they are done here escort them back to their car."

The detective ran off down the beach. Jones bent over and put her hands on the girl's shoulders.

"Help me roll her."

I put my hands on her shoulders and Jones got her hips and we moved her onto her stomach. Technically we were disturbing the crime scene, but from the impressions in the sand she'd already been rolled and probably photographed.

"Sand makes it hard to tell for sure how much blood is here, but it looks like enough for her to have been killed here. Some sort of tattoo, maybe a brand," Jones said.

I looked down and felt the blood drain from my face.

"Oh, shit."

The motel was of the cheap variety. Last time the place got new curtains and carpets was likely during the Clinton Administration. Bianca wasn't thrilled with the DMA policy about partners sharing hotel rooms when on assignment. The official line was it was so that partners can watch each other's backs. One was always supposed to be on watch. She chuckled as she wondered if the real reason was a government budget that was possibly too cheap to spring for separate rooms.

It took a few minutes to unpack her clothes and toiletries. Karver simply took his garment bag and hung it in a closet, then sat down on the chair in the corner.

Bianca turned and looked at the double beds, then at her partner. "Don't get any ideas, Karver."

His normally stony face crumbled for an instant. The man actually looked scared.

"I don't have those types of thoughts anymore. Not since… you know."

Bianca nodded, then tactfully changed the subject. "What do you know about this demon?"

"Most of it just from mind sharing during my possession. Before I bore you with too much detail, how much do you know about demons?"

"I've fought them. Not like you, not from within. I've never been possessed or made to do things I didn't want to, but let me tell you a secret. From the time she's old enough to understand, every woman wonders and worries *what if*. And before you ask, no, it never happened to me. That's because back in school there was this nun who, well, she had taken her vows a bit later in life than the other sisters. She knew what life was like on the street and made damned sure that her girls could defend themselves. Karver, I used to work in sex crimes and for three years, I met a lot of women and some men who had that question *what if* answered. Some I could help. Others I couldn't. Some broke.

Some got stronger."

Bianca took a deep breath. "You are one of the strong ones."

Karver nodded noncommittally.

"Now tell me about that scar."

"It's not a scar exactly. It's more of a brand."

"Like on cattle?" Bianca said.

Karver nodded. "Exactly. It's the mark of Leviathan. The guy's a major player in Hell. A lord. The one that possessed me wasn't scared of anything in this world, but he was scared of him. Leviathan is supposed to be able to take the form of a giant sea serpent. He guards one of the biggest gates of Hell, the Hellmouth."

"Like the vampire slayer show?"

"I don't watch much TV, but it's probably much worse. It's one of the gates that are supposed to be used during the Apocalypse. Opening it early might even cause a minor one. Lucy and those girls were likely either worshipers, sacrifices or both. Someone is trying to open the Hellmouth."

"Sometimes a scar is just a scar," Bianca said.

"And a kiss is just a kiss but this was a brand, Jones. I've seen it before."

"Memory road isn't worth the trip."
— Karver, former demon possessed serial killer, Provisional DMA Agent

Sometimes I think if I ever got a wish, I'd wish to forget. But that would be disrespectful to my dead. Would it be better if I didn't have almost photographic memory of my time being possessed? Probably, but if wishes could do any good without a jinn, there would be sixty-three more people alive. Sixty-six now counting Lucy and the other two girls.

It's a pity, but I can't remember anything from my life before my possession anywhere near as good.

I could call up the first woman I met with the brand as clear as watching a movie. She was a redhead, probably not long out of high school, but with the poise and confidence of a much older person. The seriál seem to hate that in a person, but then it viewed all of humanity with cold, hard hatred. Any sort of human happiness or the appearance of self-assurance was a trigger. It would target the happiest people. It hated how happy the Innocents were, so he butchered and killed them.

This girl was pushing all its buttons. Despite her poise, the girl didn't have much in the way of street smarts. She got cornered in a mall, in the back corridor that ran between the stores, far away from the eyes of noisy customers. We planned to kill her in a storage closet door after we dragged her inside.

The redhead yelled that she was protected. The seriál assumed she meant in an organized crime kind of way. That couldn't concern the seriál any less. It was too busy anticipating the redhead's struggles, hoping she would fight back because it'd make breaking her so much sweeter. We spun her around and ripped the shirt from her back.

She stopped yelling for us to stop and instead screamed the name Leviathan. That's when my eyes saw the brand of the serpent.

For the first time the demon froze, afraid and unsure of what to do. Slowly, he reached out with my hand and touched the serpent symbol. Contact triggered demon magic stronger than anything the seriál had. A message of warning exploded in our shared mind that brought us to my knees.

We saw Leviathan. It was bigger than huge and beyond human comprehension.

Some people feel small standing next to the ocean or looking up at the stars. This was like that tenfold only the stars and ocean wouldn't kill you without hesitation or regret in the most painful way possible. It was one of the few times I was happy some things were filtered through the seriál's consciousness. Otherwise just that glimpse would have driven me mad.

Leviathan was a giant and we were two bugs who had attracted its attention. Well, more a bug and a microbe. The seriál was enough for it to take notice of. I was not. It spoke in the original demon tongue, a bastardization of the language spoken in Heaven. It was the equivalent of someone shouting by way of using dynamite in a small tunnel.

"THIS ONE IS MINE."

It was then the seriál proved to me it was truly a coward. The warning made him want the redhead even more. It could have taken her and dealt with the consequences later. No human had ever posed it the least danger and it strutted around like it was cock of the walk.

Leviathan had no way of enforcing its threat unless the seriál went back to Hell. It hadn't been there in a long time and if it hadn't been for Father Sundry it probably still wouldn't be.

It was so scared of what Leviathan might do to it, it caved. I was glad for the girl and the seriál knew it and that pissed it off.

The seriál looked down at the weeping girl and wounded her the only way he could think of. "There will come a time when you shall wish I ended your life instead of leaving you to him."

We slowly walked out of the mall though the back corridors, the seriál furious over its impotence. A mall security guard had the misfortune to walk out into the corridor in our path. The seriál took one of our knives and beheaded the poor guy. It was the only time he didn't torture mentally and physically or stay to savor the killing. It was the equivalent of a child throwing a temper tantrum, only this one ended with some innocent man's death instead of a smashed toy.

The brand on Lucy was the same and she didn't have it the night her family died. I needed to convince my partner of that.

"Trust me, Jones. The thing that was once inside me was afraid of the demon whose brand this is. The gate opener…" Never a good idea to throw a demon's name around. It may make it want to listen in. "…protected the other one. It didn't protect Lucy which makes me think she was a sacrifice to him."

"How sure are you about this?" Jones said. She didn't want to believe me.

"Pretty damn sure."

"Then we need to assume you're right." Jones took a laptop from her bag and hooked up what looked like a cell phone.

"What's that?"

"Portable fingerprint scanner. I scanned her right index finger on the beach." She hit some keys, clicked some links and turned the computer screen toward me. Lucy Innocent's police record was staring back at me.

"How did you …"

"Court databases. In most states, this one included, they're public records. It looks like our Ms. Innocent wasn't so innocent. Lucy was arrested during a state police raid on a local house of prostitution. Charges were later dropped. Could be just some sicko. And maybe Lucy saw the tattoo elsewhere and just copied it."

"Maybe."

"You don't think so?"

I shook my head. "Only way to tell is to see if the other two girls had the brand. How do we manage that?"

"With Fleming heading up the case? Not through official channels, that's for sure," Jones said. "On her arrest record it gives her address as the brothel. We should probably check that out too. It's a sad but true fact that murders of working girls don't get the same scrutiny in some jurisdictions as they should."

"Think our badges will get us in the brothel?" I said.

Jones pointed to the screen. "Doubtful. Says here charges were dropped at the request of the Milton PD. Some BS about an ongoing MPD investigation. How much you want to bet Fleming is involved?"

"No bet. So you're thinking they're protected by the MPD?"

Jones shrugged. "Not out of the realm of possibility. If we ask, they probably won't let us see her belongings. They may even call Fleming."

"So what should we do?" I said.

"We split up. I'll take the morgue, you take the brothel."

"How do I get in?"

"The old-fashioned way. You're a guy. You have money. Those two things should get you inside. Once you're in, figure out the best way to search the place."

The idea of what I might have to do to prove my cover was making me sick to my stomach. "So we go first thing in the morning?"

Jones laughed at me. "The psychics got the call for help yesterday. Lucy was murdered today. Can we afford to waste the time, especially if you're right? Even if we're wrong, we still have to assume the next round of sacrifices will open the gate to Hell. Besides, how many brothels are open first thing in the morning?"

"Morning people have needs too," I answered weakly. My personal discomfort couldn't stop me from doing what had to be done.

Jones was pounding some more on the keyboard. "What are you doing?"

"Asking friends at the BPD to send requests up and down the East Coast to check if there have been any ritual killings and to cross reference multiple murders by stabbing with any information on tattoos or branding."

"Good idea, but why not ask Spyder? He'd probably do it in

a fraction of the time."

"Fleming may have friends in other departments. A federal inquiry might set off alarm bells," Jones said. "Besides we only have suspicions of magical involvement, so do we definitely have jurisdiction? Do you want to risk being told no?"

I sighed.

"You better get dolled up for the ladies at the Milton Gentleman's Club, Karver."

I fought to not sigh again.

"The dead do tell tales. You just have to know how to ask."
–Detective Bianca Jones, Baltimore PD

Milton City was too small a jurisdiction to have its own Medical Examiner, just a morgue with a few attendants and maybe an on-call doctor to do the unattended deaths and obvious murders. The difficult cases would be handled at the state level.

Bianca dropped Karver a couple of blocks from the brothel and headed for the Milton City Morgue. Like most morgues it was in the basement. She had never decided if that was because of a societal idea that the dead should be kept below ground or because basements had no windows and tended to leak so they were less desirable as office space. She tended to lean toward the latter.

There was just one attendant on duty. When you have no right to be somewhere, Bianca found it best to act like you owned the place. It didn't hurt that the attendant wasn't expecting company and had one of the sheets up and was looking at the unclothed dead girl beneath.

She flashed her badge. "Federal Agent. Are these the bodies of the murdered girls?"

"Does Lieutenant Fleming know you're here?" the attendant asked.

"Not my day to try to figure out what Fleming knows and doesn't know, Mister…" Bianca made a show of looking at his nametag. "Larry Mullins. However it could be my day to sic IRS Agents on someone who doesn't know how to do his job."

Bianca lifted up the sheet. It was Lucy. "I once saved this girl's life. If I find you did something to her, there is no corner of this world where you will be able to hide from me. And when I'm done with you, you'll be spending your prison sentence in the infirmary ward. We clear?"

Mullins swallowed hard, his face as white as the sheets over the bodies. "Yep. These are them."

"Now get out."

Mullins ran out. Bianca figured he was headed straight to a phone. Her window to examine the women was going to be a narrow one.

Milton didn't seem to have the budget for the traditional sliding body freezers, so all three victims were on examination tables, covered with white sheets with the air conditioning on full blast. She removed the sheet from one of the other girls and took pictures with her cell. The stab wounds were the same as Lucy's. Next she lifted her up, praying that Karver was wrong.

He wasn't. The girl had the serpent brand.

Replacing the sheet Bianca moved on to the other girl. Wounds matched, as did the brand.

She heard the stomping of feet and sent the picture to Karver. She was done, but remained standing over the dead girl.

Fleming stormed in, slamming the door against the wall. "I thought I told you two not to interfere with police business?"

Bianca resumed her already finished exam of the dead girl, deliberately dismissing the lieutenant.

Fleming moved closer. "Did you hear me?" The lieutenant reached to grab her, but Bianca turned suddenly and met his eyes. Fleming pulled his hand back like he had touched a hot stove.

"That was before you turned up two more bodies. I had to check to see if they are all killed by the same person." Bianca looked at the bodies. "They were. You got a serial killer on your hands."

"So what's that mean, you bringing in a bunch more Feds and taking over?"

"Hell no. Do you think I want to stay in this 'waiting for a Wal-Mart so it can have a life town' longer than I have to? I said *you* got a serial killer. Your town, your problem, unless you're asking for help? Are you, Lieutenant?"

The look Fleming gave said it all.

"Your morgue attendant is a perv. I suggest you have the M.E. check for postmortem sexual trauma."

"I wouldn't listen to your suggestion if I was on fire and you told me to go jump in the lake."

Bianca smiled. "Don't worry. I wouldn't."

"You leaving?"

"When I'm done. Unless you want to make a federal case of it?"

Fleming glared at her, but left. Bianca put the sheet back and decided to leave a note under the girls' bodies for the pathologist.

On her way out, she went out of her way to find Mullins. He was outside on a smoke break. Bianca stopped and gave him her best "I know what you've been doing" cop stare. In return, Mullins gave Bianca the finger.

Dumb shit, she thought and wondered if she had the time to teach him the proper respect for the law. Before she could decide, Mullins tossed his cigarette and ran back inside.

Bianca debated following him, but decided that Karver took precedence. She settled for picking up his discarded butt. Putting it in a small envelope, she would later have the DNA on it run against the sex offender database.

On her way back to the brothel to pick up Karver, Bianca never noticed the sedan that was following her at a very discrete distance.

"My biggest problem is that I'm often of two minds and one of them was never mine."
– Karver, former demon possessed serial killer, Provisional DMA Agent

The brothel was in a turn of the century building, only a few rooms shy of a mansion.

As is often the case, they had someone watching the door to keep out the riff-raff. I walked up to the outside door and he put his book down to stand up.

"Private club. No admittance," he said.

"Funny, Fleming said this was the place to get a little action," I said, playing Jones's hunch.

"Fleming sent you?"

"Well, considering his job, am I supposed to confirm that?" I said with a comradely smile. "Last thing I want to do is get him pissed off at me."

The bouncer laughed. "True. He explain to you the rules?"

"Just the basics. He said I'd catch on to the rest pretty quick."

"I'm sure you will. Arms up, please." He patted me down to make sure I wasn't packing, which I wasn't. I'd left my knives in something Bianca called her "Plan B" bag.

Stepping inside was like entering an erotic nightclub run by circus people. I wore a suit and I was overdressed. The club members who were dressed wore elaborate costumes. The rest were naked or at least made sure what little clothes they wore didn't cover any of the parts that are normally covered. It seemed to be game night, the most popular of which was tag where men chased girls. They didn't use their hands.

Despite everything I'd been through, I'm still a man and the sight so many beautiful naked women caused the usual male reaction. Unfortunately for me, the usual reaction triggered all the wrong memories. I pushed them down into a part of my mind from which they'd no doubt escape the next time I tried to sleep. *The mission, Karver,* I reminded myself.

The DMA manual states that agents should not drink while working unless undercover. I ordered straight whiskey from the topless bartender and downed it in one long sip. Then I had another one, the alcohol helping me to focus. I wasn't worried about getting drunk. Thanks to the seriál's modifications, the entire bottle would affect me about the same as a shot would a normal man. I ordered a third and turned to watch the festivities.

I tried to blend in as a dissenting customer, but apparently my undercover skills weren't fooling everyone.

A woman playing the role of hostess came over and placed her hand on my arm. She was dressed in an elegant evening gown and was not taking part in any carnal games. She had about twenty years on most of the working girls, but still was quite beautiful.

"Good evening, sir. Is there something the matter?" she asked with a disarming smile. I had to stop myself from pulling my arm away from her touch.

"Not at all. Why do you ask?"

"Because you have many beautiful women here at your disposal, yet you sit here all alone," she said. "We have a back room with many lovely men if that is your preference."

"Not at all. Just trying to get the lay of the land, so to speak."

The hostess gave a laugh at the lame joke, managing to pull it off as being genuine.

"Funny, but we can't let a big, strong man like you go to waste." The hostess lifted her hand to motion to a woman who would put most centerfolds to shame, even clad as she was in lingerie. The centerfold came over and wrapped herself around me like a shirt, running her hand along my chest and dry humping my hip. My demon rewired brain made me think that the proper reaction was not to return her touch in kind, but that slicing into her flesh was the right way to go. I stopped myself from reaching for a knife or running out of the room, but only just barely.

Her hand dropped down to rub my stomach and started moving further south. The thought of hurting her grew so strong that I reached down and grabbed her fingers before it could get to the place most men would want it to go to. From the looks the centerfold and hostess sent my way it was probably the wrong move to make. I brought the fingers up to my mouth and kissed them awkwardly. My brain thought the digits would make a tasty snack and urged me to bite one off and then suck out the marrow. I refrained and blocked out the urge.

An awkward silence floated in the air like the last balloon at a child's birthday party.

I tried to pop it. "Come here often?"

Fortunately the ladies here were paid to find men amusing and the lameness of the line didn't make a difference.

"Not as often as I'd like," Centerfold said. "Maybe you could help me with that."

"It's a wonderful offer, but sadly you're just not my type. I'm more into a girl who has body art – tattoos are nice, but I love branding." I turned to the hostess. "I heard this place might be able to hook me up. Is that true?"

"We have just about everything for the discerning customer," the hostess said, adding something that sounded like a cross between a cough, vomiting and someone being gutted.

I was impressed. It took a lot for an unaltered human throat to speak the most ancient of demon tongues.

What she said loosely translated as "Nothing else on the Earth is his equal."

This was too easy. It was obviously the password for the inner sanctum. Maybe even to finding out what they did to Lucy and the other girls.

I replied in the same language, "A creature without fear."

Her face turned to stone, her welcoming smile buried

beneath layers of beauty and makeup. I had gotten too cocky and screwed up. Verse 33 of Job 41 wasn't the right answer.

The hostess snapped her fingers and a large man who had been standing off to the side trying to do his best imitation of a statue broke character and moved towards me. Big guy, but I could take him. Unfortunately, he wasn't alone. He had six friends with as many guns. The doorman joined the party with his own automatic party favor and the big man pulled a piece of his own.

I was good, but taking on eight armed men while unarmed was suicide even for me. Choosing the better part of valor I fled up the stairs, past a rotund gentleman in a jockey outfit. He was swinging a riding crop repeatedly at the hindquarters of a nubile young woman who was nude save for a horse mask and a thong with a horse's tail. Horse lady didn't look sturdy enough to ride off into the sunset, so I kept running.

The gunmen didn't run after me. Bad sign. Meant they were professionals who knew it was better to take their time or that there was no way out. Probably both.

I needed backup and fast. The first door I came to was unlocked. I went in and locked it behind me, then hit Jones's number on my cell. She picked up on the second ring.

"I'm in big trouble. Time for Plan B, in a hurry. I'm trapped on the second floor with eight gunmen heading my way."

"On my way," she said. "Stay alive until I get there."

"I'll do my best," I said, piling furniture in front of the door. My cell phone had the same tactical advantage as a small rock. I needed a better weapon.

I ripped the chord out of the bedside lamp and stripped the torn edge insulation down to the wires with my teeth. The demon liked to do more than stab. Experience had shown me my chompers could bite through bone. It didn't take much to connect the bare wires to the metal doorknob and put the plug into a nearby socket.

Next I used the bedside table to smash the sheetrock wall. It crumbled nicely and I pulled out the pieces and went to work on the wall of the next room.

When the hole was big enough I pushed my way through. A man was chained to the wall with a leather-clad woman repeatedly ripping into his flesh with a bullwhip. His screams had masked my remodeling.

The dominatrix turned and was startled enough to stop her punishment.

I took the whip from her hands. "Official government business."

"Is this a raid?" she said.

"The raid's not until Tuesday. Today I'm just inspecting and doing the prep work. However I advise you to stay quiet and keep your head down. Things are about to get messy."

I crouched by the door and listened. A moment later I heard the sizzle of flesh and a man screaming, followed by a repeat performance by a second man. I guess he was foolish enough to try to pull his friend free and became a part of the circuit.

It was enough of a distraction that I dove through the dominatrix's door and nailed another gunman in the head with an end table. He went down.

The bullwhip snapped out and took out the big man's left eye. He screamed, brought one hand to his face and still managed to fire off a couple of shots at where I was standing. Fortunately I was already moving. He missed.

I didn't. A quick flip of the wrist put his gun in my hand and a twist had my arm around his throat in a headlock, his gun now resting against his temple.

"We can end this without further bloodshed. I'm a DMA Agent. Put down your weapons and surrender."

The gunmen hesitated, looking toward the hostess who had followed them up.

"Shoot him, you fools," ordered the hostess.

Tough boss. I fired first, putting bullets in three of them. They put a dozen shots into the big man. I backed into another room. The smell of sweat, urine, feces and fear hit me. Even before I turned I knew there were women captives there. The stench is different for men.

Unlike Lucy and the others, these women were still alive and I could sense the Hell magics of the serpent's brands even if I couldn't see them. Four women were stripped naked and tied to beds without mattresses. Flashbacks made me freeze for an instant, but it was long enough for the hostess to come up behind me and grab me by the hair and pull me out of the room. Apparently she didn't want the gunmen to shoot women branded for sacrifice.

Stupid more on her part because it gave me another human shield. I spun again and had the hostess in a headlock.

"Tell them to put their guns down," I said, making sure she was between me and the guns.

Instead she muttered a word that meant burn in ancient demon. A black candle that smelled of blood and heart burst into flame. I tried to go back into the room, but bounced off an invisible wall. I blew at the candle, but it was inside the ward the word had triggered.

"How do I get in there?" I said.

She smirked. "You can wait until the candle burns down. Or you can speak the counter incantation if you know it. I was never told."

The candle was huge and would take days to burn down, so I shot through a bunch of demonic words, covering everything from extinguish, off, dark, and open. Nothing worked.

Three bad guys left, three bullets. Not bad odds. Footsteps started coming up the stairs.

"What we have here is a standoff. I've already called for backup. This is your last chance to surrender," I said.

I really was hoping they'd stand down, but I really didn't expect them to. The hostess answered for them with a leg kicking back toward my groin. My gun hand smashed down reflexively. I felt her tibia crack under the barrel.

Despite the pain, the hostess was grinning. "There will be plenty of glorious bloodshed now. You put down your gun and I'll make your death quick. Two hours tops."

"Doesn't really work for me," I said, putting the gun back against her temple.

"Best offer you are going to get. You don't have any backup or they would have been here already."

An explosion rocked the front of the building. Everyone turned their head toward the sound.

"Want to bet?" I threw the hostess over my back in a fireman's carry which made her easier to lug and might make the muscle think twice about shooting at my back since the bullets would have to go through their boss first.

I ran to the window at the end of the hall and leapt through the glass and wood just as the bullets started flying.

"The cavalry usually arrives too late, so it's best to plan ahead."
– Detective Bianca Jones, BPD

Bianca smiled at the explosion. Part of her felt guilty enjoying being the cause of so much mayhem, but she reminded herself it was for a good cause and the guilt left to return another day.

The grenade was placed for maximum damage and minimal injury. The front doors absorbed the blast even as they were blown off their hinges.

The explosion likely made a few people hard of hearing for a while. Bianca was smart enough to have put earplugs in. There was no sign of Karver. She put her gun in one hand, another grenade in the other, a bag of weapons over her shoulder and got ready to go in after him.

Her phone vibrated, saving her the trouble. She put it to her ear, pausing a moment to take out the earplug.

"Good timing, Jones. Someone was questioning my integrity on whether or not I'd called for backup."

"You still inside?"

"Nope. Went out a second floor window and I'm running through the neighbor's yard to the block behind this one. Would it be too much trouble for you to come and pick me up?" Karver said.

"It is a little out of my way, but if you pay gas and tolls, I'll consider it," Bianca said, taking off in the car. She drove around the block and didn't have to wait long. Karver ran out from between two buildings with a woman over his shoulders.

"I didn't know they offered carry out," Bianca said.

"She wasn't exactly on the menu, but I think she knows what's going on." Karver threw the woman in the back seat and slid in next to her, pointing a revolver at the woman.

"This is kidnapping," the hostess said.

"Actually, you're under arrest. You have the right to remain silent or anything you do may cause me to shoot you," Bianca said.

"You can't do that. You're Feds," the hostess said.

Bianca shrugged. "You're trying to summon a demon to destroy the world. And I'm only a Fed temporarily. I think I can do anything I want."

Bianca put the pedal to the metal back toward their hotel. The car that had spent the evening following her gave up on staying hidden. Lieutenant Fleming pulled up alongside the car.

The hostess laughed. "Fleming is of Leviathan's Circle. You are both going to die."

Fleming shot out a tire. Bianca controlled the spin it sent them into.

Karver fired twice with his revolver, hitting a tire and shooting out the driver's side window.

Bianca reached into her bag and pulled out a pineapple style hand grenade, pulled the pin and threw it into Fleming's car through the shot out window.

Karver hustled the limping hostess out the opposite side of the car. Bianca was already running when their feet hit the ground. They were far enough away to not get caught in the blast and smart enough to hit the ground to avoid shrapnel. The hostess wasn't so lucky and stayed upright where a rearview mirror clipped her in the back of the head, knocking her unconscious.

Bianca noticed Karver checking to see if she was still breathing, but pretended like he hadn't.

The partners slowly got to their feet.

"You okay?" Karver said.

Bianca nodded. "You?"

"Dandy." Karver looked at the car. "Better change the tire and get out of here."

Sirens wailed through the night.

"Forget the car. We need to get out of here. If the cops here are honest, they aren't going to believe we killed their Lieutenant because he was trying to cause the end of the world. And it'll only be worse if they are in on it." Bianca said.

"We won't out run them on foot. We can steal…"

"Commandeer…"

"…a car, but they'll have roadblocks up," Karver said.

A man in black stepped out of the shadows between buildings.

"Quickly, follow me," he said, moving closer where they could see he was wearing a priest collar.

Bianca and Karver exchanged a look.

"In theory, the enemy of our enemy should be our friend," Bianca said.

"Best option we've got at the moment," Karver said.

Bianca looked down at the hostess. "Bring her for questioning."

Karver nodded. Bianca shouldered her Plan B bag and they ran off after the man of the cloth.

"God appreciates prayers, but he's even more fond of good actions in my opinion."
– Father Alexander DuPont, Universal Watch

Unsurprisingly, the priest led us back to a church, then around to the back and into the basement. I dumped the unconscious hostess on an easy chair that had seen better days.

"This is consecrated ground. They'll have to use mundane means to find us here," the priest said.

"Father, not that I'm not grateful for your assistance, but who are you?" Jones said.

"Father Alexander DuPont. I'm a member of the Universal Watch," he said.

We had an Academy class that outlined our counterparts around the world and whether we worked with them, against them, or some combination thereof. The Universal Watch was a special branch of the Vatican's Congregation of the Holy Office, a much reformed version of the Inquisition. Its agents were often referred to as the Church Police.

"I'm here in hopes of stopping the Hellmouth from being opened. I'm assuming DMA Agents would be here on the same mission?"

Jones eyed the man of the cloth warily. "How do you know we're DMA?"

DuPont grinned. "Police scanner. You were mentioned a couple of times, starting with the sacrificial murders at the beach and having blown up a brothel and kidnapped a woman. The rest was even less favorable, I might add," DuPont said.

Jones smiled at the last part. She seemed to enjoy causing chaos.

"Are you saying the Vatican only sent one agent to stop the end of the world?" I said.

DuPont's face took on a look of mock shock. "Heavens, no. They sent two of us. Same as the DMA."

"We were here on another matter and stumbled across this," Jones said. "Otherwise the DMA would have sent a larger team."

"Goodie for you."

"Father, where is your partner?" I said.

"Tina Parker is a member of the Watch's third order." Third orders as I understood it meant they were lay people who took lesser vows, but could still do things like get married and have families. "She went undercover as a runaway hoping to infiltrate the Circle and stop them. Unfortunately, it worked too well. She disappeared a few days ago and her trackers went dead. I'm praying she's not."

"Got a picture of her, Father?" I said.

The priest took out his cell phone, hit some buttons, then showed me the picture of a pretty young woman.

"I'm sorry Father, but they have her. She was tied up in a room on the second floor of that brothel along with three other women."

"The rest of the sacrifices they need to open the gate," DuPont said. "How could you leave them behind?"

"Outnumbered, outgunned and this one activated a ward trapping them inside." I told him the details. "I couldn't get through it. Do you think you might be able to?"

"Make no mistake, faith can move mountains and open doors that would otherwise be closed. I'm willing to try if that turns out to be our best option, but from what you described I don't think all the training in the world is going to get us in. What are the chances of us getting back into the brothel to take a look?" DuPont asked.

"Not too good, Father. There was a small well-armed force. We'd need a tactical squad," I said.

"Can't you get one?" DuPont said.

Jones and I exchanged a look. I pulled out my cell and dialed Sarge's number.

He picked up on the sixth ring. "Sarge, it's Karver. We have a situation here in Milton."

"What is it?" Sarge said, then the phone cut out.

"My phone's dead. No service," I said. Jones and DuPont tried theirs with the same results. "Father, is there a landline?"

"Yes," he said, pulling an old fashioned phone with a chord off the wall. "No dial tone."

"That's awful convenient for them," Jones said.

"No, it's a variation on a Babel spell, focusing on the means words travel by instead of the words themselves. Whatever they are planning is going on tonight," DuPont said. "Time for my secret weapon."

The priest pulled sheets off what looked like a moonshine still with about two dozen milk bottles full of clear liquid. "I have something that may help us."

"No offense, Father, but I think this is beyond holy water," Jones said.

DuPont smiled. "This isn't ordinary holy water. I use this contraption to distill holy water down to its blessed essence. It's been running for a few weeks. I was hoping for another few days, but this should be enough. Comparing this to holy water is like comparing dynamite to a nuclear blast. Similar, but on a whole different scale. Each one of those containers has enough blessed essence to destroy a lord of Hell on the mortal plane."

I reached out and touched a drop that was hanging from the spout.

"Ouch!" Smoke rose from my finger and it hurt like nothing I'd ever felt as a human and radiated throughout my entire body.

The priest took a step back and pulled out his crucifix. It had a disguised gun barrel in the top.

"I didn't think holy water could hurt you," Jones said.

"It can't," I said.

"If holy water does not hurt you, why would distilled holy water?" DuPont demanded.

"I was possessed by a demon. I got better and I'm trying to make up for things."

The priest put down his crucifix and nodded. "Who did the exorcism?"

"Father Sundry."

DuPont crossed himself. "The last living Disciple. You are both fortunate and blessed."

"Doesn't seem like it to me," I said, trying not to rub my finger.

"The demonic residue is reacting to the blessed essence. You'll have to handle it with care," Dupont said. "We need to find out where the summoning is and shove this down the Hellmouth's very throat."

I looked over at the still unconscious hostess. "I bet she knows the when and where of it."

We noticed blue and red flashing lights coming in the basement windows.

Jones pulled her gun.

"Put that away. They are probably searching the neighborhood. I'll talk to them and try and get rid of them. You sneak out the back." He tossed me keys. "I have a green sedan parked two blocks over."

"There's no alarm beeper. How will we know which one?" Jones said.

"It has a *Keep Christ in Christmas* magnet on the trunk. Take half the blessed essence in case you find the summoning and I don't. You interrogate her and I'll watch the brothel. May God be with you."

"Amen, Father," Jones said. I was already picking up a broomstick and some clothesline and jury rigging a way to carry a dozen gallon milk containers. I put the rope through the handles and tied them to the broomstick. I put the hostess back over my shoulder and the broomstick across both. DuPont went upstairs into the church proper and we crept out the back.

"No one likes asking the tough questions. And even fewer like hearing the answers."
– Detective Bianca Jones, BPD

"Where to?" Karver said.

Bianca looked at the unconscious woman in the backseat. "Somewhere where we can question her. They'll be watching our old hotel room, so it's a good thing we got a backup."

Karver had thought Bianca's idea to rent a second hotel room and pay only cash foolish, but he was beginning to see the wisdom of it.

The key was to get in without drawing any suspicions, which is rather difficult to do when dragging an unconscious woman. So instead they got the hostess between them with an arm around each of their shoulders so it looked like all three were drunkenly walking. The hotel was the type people used for romantic trysts, so the sight shouldn't have raised many eyebrows.

"So what are we playing – good cop, bad cop?" Karver asked.

Bianca reached into her duffel bag and pulled out a roll of duct tape. "Did that not too long ago. I was thinking more along the line of bad cop, demonic cop. Guess which one you get to be?" Bianca held up the roll of duct tape. "Care to do the honors?"

Karver held up his hand, but stopped half way. "Actually, if you wouldn't mind doing it, I'd appreciate it."

Bianca secured the woman's wrists to the chair and tossed the duct tape to Karver. "What happened to you sucks, but if you're going to work in this field, you have to get over it. You do the legs."

Without a word Karver duct taped the hostess's ankles to the legs of the chair.

"You think you can channel your inner serial killer, at least long enough to convince her?" Bianca said.

Karver nodded. "Convincing her won't be the problem. The hard part is the convincing everyone else that it's not there."

Bianca reached into the duffel bag and pulled out smelling salts, broke the tablet and wafted it under the hostess's nose.

"Is there anything you don't have in that bag?" Karver said.

"Just good planning. Get some of that blessed essence. If she's demonic or even possessed, that stuff will put a hole in her. I bet you could put a drop on her and she'll tell us anything you want to know to avoid getting the full shower treatment," Bianca said.

Karver nodded, adding, "But only start with a drop. It doesn't feel like she's possessed. And if she is, it may not be her fault."

"May?"

Karver ignored the question. The woman was rousing and started to scream. Bianca pulled a hunting knife out of the bag and handed it to Karver, who put the tip against the throat of the hostess.

"I do so love it when they scream, but it's too soon to kill you. I don't know what I want to know yet," Karver said.

Bianca put her finger into the milk jug and then let a drop fall onto the hostess's bare knee. It just rolled down as if it was water.

Bianca shrugged. So much for the easy road.

"You're Feds. Feds don't kill people," the hostess said.

"And of course everyone who claims to be a Fed really is," Karver said. "Tell me everything you know about the sacrifices planned for tonight and maybe you won't end up being one."

"Who are you?" the hostess said.

"He's The Carver. Surely you've heard of the seriál demon that got that nickname," Bianca said.

"But The Carver got the chair," the woman said.

Karver laughed and whispered in the demon language. "I got that and more."

"Why would you be working against opening a gateway to Hell?" the hostess said.

"Right now I have this whole place practically to myself. I don't need a crowd mucking things up. It'll take away from my fun," he said.

"So, what do you have to tell us?" Bianca said.

"You can't make me talk," the hostess said.

"Wow. You're really naïve enough to believe that. And here I thought you were a little savvier. Okay, it's your mutilation. I'm not staying around for it. The stuff that he's done so far still creeps me out. The stuff that he wants to do next is beyond reason even for a creature like him. You don't tell him something he wants to know, he's going to town on you. And I'm not staying to watch. I can't say it's been nice knowing you." Bianca moved towards the door.

"If I die, my lord will only reward me, so do your worst," she said.

This wasn't working. Time to go off script and improvise.

"I just want to be there when my brethren come through," I whispered in the demon tongue. "Can you imagine the destruction that will flow upon this world? It'll be glorious! I've been using her to get me closer, leading her on."

"I sense that you've been marked, so you might speak the truth. I may be able to get you near, but not her. She's not one of us," the hostess replied in the demonic tongue.

I laughed and roughly grabbed hold of Jones's arm and dragged her into the bathroom, shutting the door.

"What are you doing?" Bianca said.

"Improvising. You trust me?" Karver said.

"I do," Jones said.

"Then I need you to scream like someone's killing you." I grabbed a hold of her blouse. "And I'm sorry about this, but it's got to look good."

Jones nodded and helped me rip the blouse off of her, tearing it at the seams.

"Plan B is just the start. There are a lot more letters."
– Detective Bianca Jones, BPD

Karver walked out of the bathroom, wiping his blade on Bianca's shirt. It was a dark color and the knife shone as he tossed the seemingly bloody rag to the side. The hostess trembled as he came towards her. With four quick flicks of the wrist, the duct tape was sliced apart.

"You better not be screwing with me. I miss the party, you become the party. Understand?" Karver said.

The hostess swallowed hard and tried to speak, but no words came out, so she nodded.

"It's tonight?" Another nod. "So I'm guessing we're going to the beach?"

The woman nodded and followed Karver to the parking lot, where he pretended to decide which car to steal.

It didn't take Karver more than a couple of minutes to hotwire the green sedan Father DuPont had lent them by using his knife to pop the ignition. It would have been easier to use the keys, but Bianca had them. As Karver pulled away, sirens blared in the distance, heading in the direction of the motel.

"Guess some Good Samaritan called it in. Someone must've heard her scream."

Bianca waited a couple of minutes after she heard the motel door shut, just to be sure they didn't have any reason to come back in. She was wearing just a bra and her jeans. They had stashed some spare clothes in the room and Bianca grabbed a hold of a T-shirt she usually slept in.

Flashing lights filled the motel parking lot. Bianca looked out. Seeing the police cars, she knew they were there for her. Even if she were willing to hurt or even fight other cops, there were too many for her to take on by herself. Not wanting to be taken into custody, she sighed and said, "I hate doing this."

Bianca quickly washed off all her makeup, pulled her hair

into a ponytail and put on the T-shirt. Looking in the mirror even she had to admit that she looked like a teenager. Leaving her extra clothes, she took only her duffel bag. She was on the stairs when the police ran by her towards the room.

Bianca smiled to herself. Police can be so predictable. A cute girl gets ignored most of the time. In the parking lot, they had left several police cars, most with their doors unlocked, some with their engines still running. Cops did that in Baltimore too. They were so confident that no one would ever try to steal a police car that they didn't even bother to try and protect them. More than once she had seen a cop have to write up a stolen car report on his own cruiser.

A male officer was left watching the cars. Bianca ran up to him, trying for innocent and scared.

"Those cops up there," she cried, pointing to the motel, "something bad happened. They're all cut up and bleeding."

The cop ran off to help his fellow officers. Bianca hopped in a running patrol car and drove off.

"They never learn," she said, smiling to herself.

"The hardest debts to pay are the ones you owe the most on."
– Karver, former demon possessed serial killer, Provisional DMA Agent

Despite her early bravado, the closer we got to the beach, the more the hostess trembled. Even if I didn't already know what these cultists were trying to make happen, I would have been scared. As it was, I was already terrified. I thought of the damage one demon did using me and couldn't imagine that multiplied by thousands, maybe millions.

I knew beyond a doubt that there was a Hell, which meant there had to be a Heaven. Maybe this was what I was saved to do – stop Leviathan from opening the Hellmouth. I had no illusions about my own survival. Oddly, I was of two minds on that. My life in a trade to save millions was more than fair, but for the first time in a long time I found that I really didn't want to die.

I tried to call Sarge for backup again, but the Babel spell was still working, so no signal. Not that it would probably matter. Anyone not already here would arrive too late to help.

Options were running through my mind. I could try to sneak up on the sacrifices and take the cultists by surprise. Once I got there, that didn't seem the smartest route to go.

The members of Leviathan's Circle weren't bothering to hide what they were doing. Torches lit up the sand where there were four naked women tied down to makeshift altars. Even from this distance, I knew it was too late for two of them. I hoped one of the remaining two was Tina, Father DuPont's partner.

I hit the beach doing 60 and plowed into a couple of cops before they could even get their guns clear of their holsters. Unfortunately, sedans with rear-wheel-drive aren't meant for driving on sand and I quickly got stuck. I leapt out as another member of the MPD rushed at me. I sucker punched him and he went down. I hit him again to make sure he stayed there.

Two men in long dark robes got the drop on me. One of them

hit me in the back of the head with what felt like the hilt of a knife, while the other got me in a full nelson. I turned trying to get free. That's when Fleming put his gun up against my forehead.

"Hello, Agent Karver. Pity you weren't smart enough to follow my advice. A real pity."

Half his face was burned to the muscle. "And I can see you weren't smart enough to avoid Jones's grenade."

"I can see you've been touched by Hell and blessed by the Pit. What a shame. No, what a waste for you to have rejected that great gift. At least you are here for the last two sacrifices. In moments you will realize you backed the wrong side." Fleming was looking out on the water. I turned and realized I was too late. Out on the water the air was shimmering. The Hellmouth was forming.

"Have any last words, Agent Karver?" Fleming asked.

There were words to be had, but they weren't mine.

"Fire in the hole!"

"Bringing a knife to a gunfight. No problem for me."
– Karver, former demon possessed serial killer, Provisional DMA Agent

"Fire in the hole!" Bianca Jones yelled as she pulled the pin from a grenade and threw it into the middle of the Leviathan's Circle robed cultists.

Karver went limp and spun at the same time, putting the cultists who held his arms between him and the blast. There was much screaming and fleeing.

Bianca could hear Karver telling her not to spill blood near a ritual sacrifice. It tended to strengthen things. It didn't matter. Bianca could see they had already completed the ritual to bring Leviathan over. All she could do at this point was free the last two sacrifices meant to be a gift to him. A few more gallons of blood either way wasn't going make a hell of a lot of difference.

Bianca was no sharpshooter, but she was a very good shot. She started to pick off cultists with her pistol. A badly burned Lieutenant Fleming took cover behind one of the altars, using a still breathing girl as a human shield. Another robed cultist followed his lead, ducking behind the other living woman.

Karver rolled free of the men holding him. The blast had stunned them more than him, but they had knives out now. The one who had hit him from behind rushed at him blade first. In less than the blink of an eye, Karver had taken the knife away and plunged it in and out of the man's abdomen.

"You don't know how stupid pulling a knife on me is," Karver said as the man fell to his knees and crumbled into a ball. Unable to get beyond the pain and shock of being stabbed, the cultist didn't realize that Karver had managed to plunge the knife all the way in without hitting any major organs or blood vessels and that he'd done it on purpose.

Bianca stormed the beach, a pump action shotgun in her hand and her duffel bag over her shoulder. With one shot, she took out the two men still standing near Karver. The cultist hiding behind the human shield rose up above the woman, his knife poised to plunge down into her chest.

Bianca reached for her automatic, knowing full well the shotgun would do as much harm to the victim as the cultists. By the time she had her hand on the grip, it didn't matter anymore. Karver had thrown the knife in his hand. The point went through the cultist's throat and into his spine. The man lost all motor control and fell to the ground. The remaining robed cultists fled.

Bianca and Karver came around the other altar from opposite sides. "Hands up. No sudden moves," Bianca said, training her shotgun on Fleming.

Fleming complied, but he was laughing.

"You think this is funny?" Bianca said.

"I do," Fleming said. "It doesn't matter what you do at this point. Look!" The Lieutenant's face again turned towards the water. The Hellmouth had grown to the size of a small building and was positioned in front of a wooden pier.

"Leviathan is coming and is bringing with him the Legions of Hell and the end of days. The good guys lose. The bad guys win."

Bianca let the shotgun drop to her side. Something monstrous that might loosely be described as a serpent was sticking its maw through the burning gate. The opening wasn't big enough to let all of it through yet, but it was only a matter of time. Behind it could be heard the screams of damned souls. Their keepers were encouraging them to make ready to pour forth upon the Earth and ravage it, to make it ready for their Master. Bianca's blood ran cold and for the first time in her life she gave way to despair. "We've lost. There's no way we can stop that." Then she rallied and made ready to save as many people as she could

Karver had a different idea. Instead of getting despondent he looking around while trying to think of something. His eyes landed on the duffel bag on Bianca's shoulder and he smiled.

"Do you have anything else in your plan B bag? Preferably things that go boom?" Karver said.

"Grenades in the bag and more in the police cruiser over

there. Why?"

"I've got a plan and it's a doozy. You free the girls and leave the rest to me. Jones, it's been good knowing you." Karver ran towards the green sedan, opened the trunk and grabbed all the milk containers of blessed essence and ran to the police car.

Karver opened one of the bottles and poured it all over the outside of the car. He took another and dumped it on the bag of grenades. The rest he quickly attached, one each to a grenade.

Bianca felt hope until Karver got in the police car and sped away in the opposite direction of the Hellmouth.

Fleming laughed harder and Bianca knocked him out with the butt of her shotgun.

"Time for Plan Z."
– Karver, former demon possessed serial killer, Provisional DMA Agent

Yeah, I know driving away from Leviathan didn't seem like the bravest act in the world. And to be honest, a good part of me thought about driving away and getting as far from the Hellmouth as I could.

But I didn't. The thought of my dead would not have let me even if I had wanted to. My apparent flight was all part of the plan. I needed enough distance to try something incredibly stupid. I spun the car around and pushed the gas pedal all the way to the floor. Police cars tended to have good engines. This one was a V8.

I was doing 120 MPH before I hit the beach parking lot. If I pushed down any harder, my foot would have gone through the floorboards. I aimed for the pier, which fortunately rose up near the end. The car flew up into the air. The moment I was airborne, I grabbed my knives and pulled as many pins from the grenades as I could and leapt out of the car, throwing a bottle of the blessed essence down the throat of Leviathan with one hand, firing all the bullets in the gun I pulled out of the bag with my left.

The thing was monstrous, but that didn't do it justice. It had a maw that seemed made up of nothing but rows and rows of teeth. It could swallow two side-by-side semis and the highway they rode on so there was more than enough room to ram the police cruiser down its gullet. Leviathan opened wide and in went the car.

The first grenade blew just before I hit the water. Seconds later the others exploded in rapid secession, taking the gas tank with them. I gave the demon the sort of single finger salute it deserved.

The shock pushed me down into the cold waters of the Atlantic and everything went black.

"Sometimes a candle burning in the darkness is a more welcome sight than the most brilliant sunrise." – Detective Bianca Jones, BPD

Bianca took the knife the cultist was going to use on the woman and instead used it to cut through her bonds. The woman ran away screaming into the night.

Bianca turned to the second woman and had had her partly free when the woman yelled, "Behind you!"

Lieutenant Fleming had revived and found a sacrificial blade of his own that he was bringing down on Bianca's back. The woman's warning gave Bianca just enough time to spin and put her own blade into his dark heart. The look of disbelief on Fleming's face would have made Bianca pity him if he hadn't been such an evil bastard.

When she saw the police car take off in the opposite direction she thought the worst of Karver. Bianca turned and looked at the parts of the creature's head that were trying to poke through onto the mortal world and had to fight down a wave of nausea. She had faced pure evil before but nothing like Hellish slime pouring out of the gateway to the Pit.

She didn't blame Karver. Part of her wished he'd taken her with him. Not that it would have done much good. She didn't think anyone could run far enough to get away. The longer she looked at the creature, the more she felt humanity's chances slipping away.

She turned and finished freeing the woman. It had been hard to tell in the torchlight, but up close she recognized her.

"You're Tina Parker from the Universal Watch, right?" The woman nodded. Bianca helped her up and gave the naked women her jacket. "Any idea how we can stop this?"

"No, but we have to do it before the serpent comes all the way through. After that… the best we can do is form a beachhead here and try to stop as many of the escaping demons as we can."

Bianca nodded, checked her pistol and handed her shotgun to Tina. "Will bullets even do any good?"

Tina smiled. "Certainly won't hurt."

A shrill siren briefly drowned out the screams from beyond the gate of Hell. Karver's police car was coming back fast. It didn't stop at the cement or the wooden pier, just kept going straight into the literal mouth of Hell.

Bianca stopped transfixed at the car went right at the beast and Karver jumped out, throwing a milk container into the maw and shooting into it. When his ammo ran out he flipped off the demon and the car exploded.

Then Leviathan began to scream as its very flesh began to sizzle and boil.

"Did he have blessed essence?" Tina said.

"DuPont shared it with us, in case we found the demon lord first. Karver must've mixed that with the explosives," Bianca said.

"That was brilliant. It could have spit out the essence or shrugged off the explosion, but now it's in his bloodstream. Demons have to take on flesh to enter the mortal world. I think your partner just managed to destroy it."

"How do we close the gate?" Bianca said.

"We won't have to. If the serpent doesn't wedge itself through, it will shut itself." Leviathan writhed in agony, its screams drowning out those of the damned. "I can't see any demon risking destruction to get around that, can you? I am sorry about your friend."

"Don't be. Not yet."

Bianca Jones ran the length of the pier despite the urging of the fear center of her brain which could only hear the death throes of Leviathan's flesh. It was pleading with her to flee with all due haste.

Like any good cop, Bianca ignored it and ran toward danger. The Hellmouth was shrinking faster than it opened.

The ocean was littered with the debris of the exploded police cruiser. Bianca didn't care about the fender or the airbag. Gasoline floating and burning on the surface of the water gave her barely enough light to see.

She spotted a black shoe that bobbed to the surface, but there was no leg attached to it.

Bianca dove off the pier into the frigid waves, then tread water near the shoe, desperately searching for any sign of life. Seeing none, she dove beneath the water to continue her search, blindly grasping for a hand or foot in the black water, anything at all, coming up only when she needed air.

She dove again and again. Five times. Six. The seventh time was the one that proved lucky when she brushed against Karver's fingers. She grabbed his hand and dragged his limp body to the surface. Wrapping one arm around his chest, Bianca side-stroked her way toward shore and dragged him onto the sand. The man didn't move, wasn't breathing and she couldn't find a pulse.

Bianca put her hands in the CPR position over his sternum and did quick repetitions. Then she blew in his mouth and repeated the process.

It wasn't working. Bianca blew harder into his mouth, trying to force life into him by pure force of will. Karver's eyes opened and met hers. Something passed between them, a mix of the rivalry and the realization that they not only survived, but won.

Then something happened that neither of them would have expected in a million years.

"Sometimes people can surprise you."
– Karver, former demon possessed serial killer, Provisional DMA Agent

I figured I was dead. Instead I woke up kissing Bianca Jones. And that wasn't the strangest thing. Jones was kissing me back. It lasted only an instant before we regained our senses and pulled away.

I had told Bianca that I didn't get those kinds of ideas anymore. I still don't. But that day on the beach, with the adrenaline still flowing and the thrill of having saved the world and done something good for once, well, it was the closest I'd come since before my possession.

Then my body rebelled. I'd swallowed too much sea water and vomited onto the sand.

"I think I should be insulted," Jones said with a grin. I grinned back. In that look we came to an unspoken agreement. Neither of us mentioned what happened then or since.

"I take it we won," I said. The door to Hell was about the size of a quarter.

"Yep."

"Thanks for saving my hide."

"That's what partners do," Jones said.

"Any of the sacrificial girls make it?" I said.

"Both of them. One was Tina Parker."

"Good. Father DuPont will be happy," I said, then looked around at the corpses scattered around the beach. "Maybe this would be a good time to call for backup."

"Yep, cause I don't do cleanup," Jones said.

My phone was nowhere to be found. Neither was my right shoe. Jones handed me her cell. The spell that was blocking the phones before was gone because I got through to Sarge Winston on the first ring. I gave him the rundown.

"Good job, Karver. Tell Jones the same. Secure the crime

scene and I'll have the regional chief there ASAP," Sarge said. "Oh and I arranged for your new partner once you finish the Academy." He gave me the quick rundown on her and I hung up.

"Sarge says good job," I said.

"Did he expect any less?" Jones said.

"I don't think he did. And apparently he found me a partner named Mandi Cobb for when I'm finished with the Academy."

"Poor woman," Jones said, but she winked when she said it.

We locked down the beach and waited.

"Enough is enough."
– Detective Bianca Jones, BPD

Bianca Jones was getting tired of getting reamed out by people not in her chain of command.

Morning had come and with it the DMA Regional Director, a woman by the name of Jane Garrison. She instantly went onto the list of Bianca's least favorite people. She was more administrator than cop, more concerned about where blame was going to be placed, more than what had happened. She seemed bound and determined that it was all going to fall on Bianca and Karver.

"Of all the irresponsible, pigheaded, boneheaded moves. Taking on an incursion of Hell onto U.S. soil and not calling for backup is the stupidest thing I've seen in 25 years on the job," Garrison shouted. "I've had no less than four calls from the Ambassador from Hell complaining about what was done to one of the lords of the Pit."

"Hell has an ambassador to the U.S.?" Bianca said.

"You betcha and he's pissed and I'm the one having to deal with it," Garrison said.

"I've had enough of this shit. Karver and I just saved the world. Had that lord of Hell come through and opened up the Hellmouth, humanity would be on its way to extinction. And Karver tried to call for backup. Phones went down. Some Babel spell. Not unusual for someone with the power to destroy the world to be doing while they are trying to wreak havoc. So instead of yelling at us, yell at the ambassador and ask why his people were trying to destroy the U.S. and the rest of the world. Then thank Karver, Father DuPont and me for stopping them," Bianca said.

"Thank you? First up, DuPont and his partner were operating on U.S. soil without being sanctioned. Second, you're only acting DMA. And as such you will follow the rules. That means you answer to me. You do not tell me what I should do."

"Easy enough to fix." Bianca Jones turned to Karver. "Tell

Donna goodbye for me and that I'm sorry I won't remember her anymore."

"I will," Karver said.

Bianca took off her DMA badge and threw it at the Regional Director. "I quit. I have a job in a city where we fight evil instead of apologizing to it so you can take yours and shove it where the sun doesn't shine." Bianca turned to storm off, then stopped and looked back at Karver. "You coming?"

Bianca smiled at the look of confusion on the man's face.

"What? Where?" Karver said.

"It's time to blow this lemonade stand. You need to come to work for a real police department. I can make sure that you get assigned to my unit. As good as you are, you'll make detective in two years. Maybe less."

Karver actually grinned. "Wow, you do like me."

"Don't push your luck. You're good. You'd make a good cop. Any department would be lucky to have you. You interested?"

"Honestly, I am. But Sarge Winston and the DMA brought me to this party. It's only right that I leave with them," Karver said.

"I understand. The offer stands if you ever come to your senses," Bianca said.

"Appreciate it. Let me drive you to the airport," Karver said.

"Oh no, Karver. You are staying right here to clean up this mess," Garrison said.

Karver turned back to the Regional Director, his face stony. "Agent Garrison, have you read my file?"

"On my way here. Why?"

"You know what Hell did to me, correct?" Karver said.

"Yes. A real tragedy."

"Thank you. Tell me, did you ever think in your conversations with Hell's ambassador to file a complaint with him on my behalf over what his people did to me and my victims?"

Garrison seemed at a loss for words, but finally decided on "No."

"Well then, that gives you something to bring up if he calls again. In fact, I'd be happy to take his call myself if you like when I get back from driving my partner to the airport, at which time I will also assist in clean up." Karver turned and walked away, Bianca falling in at his side,

"You just pissed her off. You took her by surprise, but by the time you get back you will be in for it," Bianca said.

Karver shrugged. "Sure you won't come back to the Academy? I don't mind being number one in our class, but I prefer to earn it."

"And go back and deal with Garrison? No way. Besides Knox said I'd already passed."

"But didn't you say you owed your CO a week of pervert patrol if you left early?"

"I passed. That's all that matters. Mail me my diploma. Dummy one up if you have to."

"But from what he's told me, Herne is expecting to escort you to the graduation party."

"Too bad. He'll just have to go stag. Now get me to the airport. Take the scenic route."

"They say all's well that ends well. Occasionally it's been known to happen."
  – Agent Karver of the Department of Mystic Affairs

It would be a few years before I worked with Bianca Jones again. In the time between we would both visit our own respective Hells and fight our way out of them, always ready to face those things crawling in the darkness trying to find a way out, ready to fight to send them back where they came from. The case of Leviathan was our first true look into the mouth of the Abyss. Nietzsche said that when you do that, the Abyss looks back. That's fine with me. The Abyss needs to know who it's messing with.

THE DMA CASEFILES OF AGENT KARVER
Featuring stories with JOHN L. FRENCH & C.J. HENDERSON
DEAD
to
RITES
FROM THE PAGES OF MURPHY'S LORE
PATRICK THOMAS

DEAD to RITES

The DMA Casefiles of Agent Karver

Patrick Thomas

with crossovers featuring
C.J. Henderson & John L. French

PADWOLF
PUBLISHING

This one's for
Cory-
nephew and table monkey

THEN TERROR CAME

I'm not always crazy about my job, but it's better than the alternative. They pulled me almost literally out of Old Sparky's grasp. I was on death row because I had been possessed by a thing from the pit that used my body to commit the most heinous crimes. The DMA yanked me free because I managed to keep the body count to only double digits, which had apparently never been done before or since with a seriál demon. That made me mostly innocent, which gave the DMA the excuse to save me. The possession left me with certain aftereffects, which makes me useful in their mission to protect America from mystic threats. It also gave them the motive to mount the rescue mission. I guess I shouldn't complain. I got a new face, a new career, and a pension, assuming I live that long.

It's a big assumption.

Take today's case. Please. I sure as Hades don't want it. I'd say Hell, but it brings back too many bad memories. The victim waiting for the tape outline might already be there, cause he sure ain't here. However, he is over there. And there. And places I can't even see from where I'm standing. It was going to take a couple of rolls of tape to do the job.

It was taking everything I could muster to not vomit all over the closest cluster of remains. I hid it from the locals, but not my partner. She put a comforting hand on my shoulder.

"You okay?" she asked.

"You already know the answer," I said. Mandi knew how I was feeling, literally. "How about you?"

"Let's see. Over a dozen people in shouting distance, each somewhere between revulsion, disgust and sick interest. I'm just fine," said Mandi, each of the empath's words drooling with sarcasm.

"You need the meds?" I asked. Of all the people I've got to deal with in my new life, Mandi's the one I like the most. What's even odder is that she claims she likes me. There's no accounting for taste.

"Nah. This is nowhere near as bad as last minute shopping in the mall on Christmas Eve. The local sheriff thinks somebody threw Mr.

Harrison into a wood chipper, then tried to fertilize," said Mandi.

"I can see why he'd think that," I said.

"You don't agree?" she asked with a knowing grin.

"No. We wouldn't be here if that were the case. A human can inflict that much damage, but it'd be a lot of work," I said. Mandi knew how I knew and I was grateful she didn't break eye contact. Most of the agents who know my history would have.

"Demon?" said Mandi, not bothering to beat around a bush that had withered and died a long time ago.

"Don't think so. I'm thinking animal or beast of the large, supernatural variety," I said.

"Yep, that's my gut too. I'm just troubled by the lack of foot or paw prints; might mean we got something that can fly or be partially immaterial."

"You been at this longer. You got any inkling what it might be?" I asked.

"Nope," said Mandi.

"Great. I love a mystery," I lied.

I'm told the procedure is the same for a mystical crime as for a mundane one. Inspect the scene, take forensic evidence, interview witnesses and make your best guess.

We took care of number one; the crime scene lab boys and gals did number two, which meant it was time for number three.

I figured it'd be quick as there were no witnesses or if there were, they were probably mixed in with the human meat strewn about the place. Thankfully, it was the medical examiner's job to sort out the pieces.

We headed straight for Sheriff Weeks to see who had been first on the scene.

He was still shaking his head and talking non-stop. It was one way to cope and I couldn't criticize. I tended to shut down.

"I ain't never seen nothing like this in eighteen years," he said. The years seemed about right. You don't see many law enforcement types with more than twenty on the job. They see too much bad. So when the half pay pension comes at twenty years in, most take it and get out. I'll probably start counting when the number is further away from twenty.

"Let's hope you don't see it again," I said.

"You think whoever did this will strike again?" asked Weeks.

"Unless he turned him, her, or itself in while we were inspecting the crime scene," I answered. "Harrison have any enemies?"

"Not that we've been able to find. He was the quiet type, dealt in artifacts for the Boston museums and some collectors; been some talk that some of his merchandise is stolen, but as most of it happened overseas, it's a bit out of our jurisdiction. And Boston PD didn't want to be bothered with questions from a small town sheriff in a neighboring state," said the sheriff. I just nodded.

"He been selling anything recently?" asked Mandi.

"We're not sure. We are looking for his business associate now, but other than that he had no family or close friends to tell us if it looks like anything was taken," said the Sheriff. The fact that most of the outside of the house was covered in blood and gore would have discouraged even the most helpful of friends anyway. "What do you think did this?"

"Not happy with your wood chipper theory?" I said.

The Sheriff shook his head. "No tire treads inside the house or out and a chipper would leave some trace. Still, people are asking questions and I have to tell them something. We haven't even been able to find a single footprint." He looked at us. "We're not going to, are we?"

"It's possible," I admitted. As hard as it was to fathom, it was conceivable that something this brutal might not leave behind any secondary physical traces.

"Some of the men are saying animal, but I'm a hunter. I've seen what a bear or a wolf can do to its prey. This ain't it. I have to admit, I've always thought the Department of Mystic Affairs was a waste of my taxes, mainly because I assumed you always dealt with crackpots and hoaxes, but now..."

"The DMA gets its share of that, but the criminals we deal with are real. They just have different MO's than most police departments are used to handling," explained Mandi. We get that reaction a lot. Unlike fictional agencies, the DMA does not keep its existence a secret nor do we operate clandestinely in the shadows. The criminals do that. We work in the open. Our unofficial motto is *When darkness falls we pick up the pieces*. The problem is nobody tends to believe us. It makes what we have to do even harder, because everyone out there, from police to the public, is looking to explain away the darker parts of reality. It's easier than accepting it. I envy them.

"So what are we dealing with here?" Sheriff Weeks asked.

There is a tradition of friction between federal departments and local law enforcement. The DMA has enough trouble being taken seriously, at least until the monster droppings hit the fan, to play things that way. Orders straight from the top are to share all information and theories with the locals, unless they are suspected of complacency. Uncle Sam, the real Uncle Sam, is our bureau's Director and is unbending when it comes to that.

"Supernatural creature," I said.

"Like a werewolf?" asked the Sheriff.

"Not a lunamorph," said Mandi.

"A what?" asked the Sheriff.

"Classification for werecreatures. Wolves are the most common, but there are over three dozen separate classifications. It's not one of them," said Mandi.

"How can you be sure?" said the Sheriff.

"Used to work with one; tracked a few more; a lunamorph kill doesn't look like it's been shredded," said Mandi. "We're not sure what kind of creature this is."

"Great. What should I tell my people and the reporters? You have a cover story?" asked Sheriff Weeks.

"Truth works as far as I'm concerned," I said.

"Agent Karver, you can't be serious. We do that and we'll have a panic on our hands," said Weeks.

I shrugged. It wasn't worth arguing with this guy. "It's your call."

We got the details Weeks had on the case so far. The only thing resembling a witness was a guy walking his dog. The dog found part of Mr. Harrison early this morning. The crime scene techs think it was his pancreas. The dog walker called 9-1-1 on his cell phone. The dog had a nibble or three. The locals canvassed the neighborhood and so far had come up with jack and squat.

"We're going to give the inside the once over," said Mandi.

"Okay, Agent Cobb."

"Call me Mandi."

The Sheriff smiled. Mandi was giving him an emotional tune up. He'd end up stronger and able to deal with this mess easier. And he'll find himself very fond and extremely trusting of my partner. It was against regs for her to be doing it and Sam would have a fit, but I wasn't going to tell.

"Call me John," he said. "What's your first name, Agent Karver?"

"Just Karver," I said.

The Sheriff looked perplexed. "Must be rough getting by these days with that name, what with the serial killer that the media nicknamed Carver."

"Bart Andrew Higgins is dead," I said. "And comparisons don't bother me." The DMA let me choose a new name, as long as it wasn't one of my original names. My choice makes sure I will never forget what something did using me as its vessel.

The house was relatively untouched, other than one door smashed in and another smashed out. And an overturned couch. There was no blood or remains inside, which was a blessing. We worked our way through the residence. The guy seemed to decorate in modern clutter. Papers, books and other assorted junk were everywhere, but were organized into neat piles.

"This will take weeks," complained Mandi.

"Not necessarily. Let's start with a couple of assumptions. Ernie Harrison made a living selling presumably stolen artifacts. He may have gotten ahold of something mystic in nature, possibly cursed. And it was probably a new acquisition or he'd have been dead sooner. He'd have kept it somewhere..." Walking into a closet, I lifted up a small throw rug, and found a trap door revealing a dial and handle. "...safe."

We had the crime scene techs dust for prints and test for blood. There were some minute traces of blood on the throw rug.

"I doubt whatever killed Harrison then went into safe cracking," I said.

Mandi nodded. "It could have ripped it open instead."

We were both thinking someone could have sicced this thing on Harrison.

There was an envelope of pictures on his dresser, recently developed. Most were of artifacts, one in particular – a couple were of Harrison and another man. I recognized Harrison from a printout the Sheriff had of his driver's license photo. Of course, we were all aware that the remains might not be Harrison's, but his wallet was found in one pile of shredded corpse. The lab would test the DNA against samples found in the house so we could be more certain of whose murder we were investigating. My next question was who else was in the picture.

Before I could voice it, a female deputy came into the room. "The Sheriff wants you to see something outside."

We followed. The medical examiner's techs had bagged some of Harrison's remains, revealing the ground beneath. The Sheriff and several of the rest of the locals had lit up cigars – old cop trick to help block out the stenches associated with a crime scene. He offered us stogies, which we turned down. I was sucking on one of the nastiest mentholated cough drops you can buy. It only helped a little.

"This help?" He pointed to a trio of prints. They looked vaguely canine, if there was a pooch the size of a rhino.

"Maybe," said Mandi. In addition to what the crime scene techs did, we took pictures with our phones and sent them back to DC for analysis. Our equipment was easily the match of any local department in the country and usually better.

While the crime scene techs made plaster molds of the prints, I held the picture of the two men up to the Sheriff. "Any idea who the other man in the picture is?"

"Yes, that's Harrison's alleged partner, Don Baker. He's the one I sent a unit to question a while ago. I haven't heard back from them yet."

"You see the necklace in this picture?" I asked.

"It looks like it's made out of jade," said Weeks.

"It could be. You find it anywhere outside or in the house?"

"No. Is it important?" he asked.

"It may be. If you or your people come across it, treat it with extreme caution. Instruct everyone not to touch it until you call us. It may be nothing or it could very well have something to do with this killing."

I handed him two of the photos. One showed the front of what looked like a jade amulet. There were some symbols I didn't recognize, but then again it wasn't my specialty. The symbols were around the image of a creature that looked like a cross between a winged dog and the sphinx. It wasn't pretty. The second showed its backside, which had a skull.

"Will do. What's your next move?" asked Sheriff Weeks.

"We go to talk to Baker."

But Don Baker wasn't at home. We called the office psychics. Luckily, they were having a good day and directed us to a nearby gym. We had to get by a trainer at the door, who demanded to see our membership cards. The ones for the DMA we showed him weren't what he was expecting, but they worked just as well.

A few well-placed questions later, we found Baker toweling himself dry in the locker room. He was relatively well muscled, at least in comparison to his dead friend.

"Miss, I don't think you're allowed in here," said Baker, using his towel to cover his manhood.

Mandi flashed her badge. "Federal agents, Mr. Baker. We'd like to ask you a few questions."

"Normally, I'd be happy to, but I'm kinda naked. Can't this wait a couple of minutes until I get dressed?" he asked.

"I'm afraid it can't. Tell me, when is the last time you saw Ernie Harrison?" I said.

"Last night. Why? Did something happen to Ernie?" Baker asked. It was obvious he was trying to appear concerned. I'd say he got more like suspiciously interested.

"I'm afraid Mr. Harrison is dead," said Mandi.

He fell backwards onto the wooden bench, even dropping his towel in the process. He was good, but one look at Mandi's face told me he was faking.

"How did it happen?" Baker asked, absently picking up his towel.

"We were hoping you'd be able to help us come up with an answer for that. Where have you been for the last twenty four hours?"

"At home alone, except for my visit to Ernie's last night and my trip to the gym today, but I can tell you Ernie was alive when I left him."

I held the picture of the amulet out in front of me. "Have you seen this?"

"Of course. The Jade Hound," said Baker, reaching into his gym bag. "It's right here..."

Mandi and I drew our guns so fast I wasn't sure who cleared their holster first.

"Sir, do not move or speak or we will have to shoot you," I said, unsure if the amulet could be activated by incantation. "Drop whatever is in your hand and step away from the bag."

Baker listened. I kept my weapon trained on him while Mandi secured the bag.

"It's here," she said.

I nodded and cuffed him. "Let's go."

"Why? For what?" he asked.

"I think you already know," I said and read him his rights.

"Can't I even get dressed? At least wrap a towel around me," whined Baker.

Mandi held up a washcloth. "You shouldn't need more than this. Waste not, want not."

I actually helped him into a pair of sweat pants and sneakers and we took him to the local police station. As we left I could hear a distant howling. Baker seemed to hear it too and he looked around nervously.

It didn't go well. He asked for his lawyer right off the bat. The only thing we got out of him was his claim that Harrison had given him the Jade Hound as a gift. Baker was smart. By washing up in a public shower, any blood or genetic evidence we found could never be tied to him beyond a reasonable doubt.

Next we had the usual issue of convincing the local DA that magic means could be used to murder. Unfortunately, the DA was a fundamentalist Christian and was offended by the very thought of magic. Don't get me wrong, I'm not anti-religion. I still go to church on occasion, although I prefer to stay in the back. I figure I need it more than most. The problem is so many people are so blinded by their own beliefs, it shuts them off from seeing reality. He figured we were trying a frame job and wouldn't even agree to hold him for twenty-four hours. I tried to get him to go out to the crime scene with no luck. Even Mandi's propathic persuasions did nothing to change his mind.

In less time than it took us to track him down, Don Baker was back on the street with the Jade Hound amulet in hand. There was definitely something magic about it, like it was charmed to make people want to have it – never a good sign.

Mandi and I stood on the steps of the jailhouse as he left. He shot us a jaunty salute, which pissed me off. I marched over and blocked his path.

"Is there a problem, Agent Karver?" asked Baker.

"Yes. You had something to do with your partner's butchering. This ain't over," I said.

"I'm innocent. Even the DA agreed with that," said Baker, with a smirk that made me want to mop up the pavement with him.

"Well then, you have a nice day then," I said, matching his grin with one of my own.

Baker tilted his head and looked at me, obviously doubting the sincerity of my words.

"Why, thank you," he said, pushing past me.

I politely touched his shoulder. "We've sent pictures of your lovely green accessory to our office in DC. In a day, maybe two, we'll know everything there is to know about it. If it had anything to do with Harrison's death, we'll be back for you, so enjoy what time you have left on the outside."

"The DA will just let me go again," he said smugly.

Mandi, who was watching from the sidelines, chimed in. "We learned from this mistake. You won't be going to the DA. We'll be taking you straight to a Federal prosecutor, one who specializes in magic based crimes."

"I didn't cross state lines," said Baker.

"To do what?" I tried. He didn't take the bait.

"Absolutely nothing," he replied.

"Using magic in the commission of a felony automatically makes it a federal offense," said Mandi.

"Don't leave town or try to get rid of the amulet," I said. "Not that it'll matter. This arrest already established you had it in your possession. Destroying evidence will only add to the charges against you," I said. "So, like I said, have a nice day. It may be your last."

Clutching the amulet to his chest, Baker turned and stormed off. We watched him go and again there was howling in the distance. Baker walked faster.

"Better ask the Sheriff to put a tail on him," said Mandi. I nodded. She flipped open her department issued cell. "Let's see if Spyder found out anything."

We spent the next two days doing more grunt work, tracking down anyone Harrison had recently had contact with. Several museums and private collectors of questionable repute were moderately forthcoming in answering our questions. Many of them had bid on artifacts recently, but none had even heard of the Jade Hound, let alone been offered the opportunity to buy it. Mandi felt that all of them were being truthful on that point, although from past experience we'd learned that a sociopath can have such tight controls over their emotions that Mandi's empathic abilities were useless. Unfortunately, it was hard to tell if any of those we questioned fell into that category.

According to the deputies assigned to Baker, he hadn't left the house except to get groceries or work out.

We were back in town on our way to question one of Harrison's neighbors who had allegedly been out of town for a week, when our cell phones rang. The ringtone was a punk version of "My Country, 'Tis of Thee", which was the default for a call from Spyder. He's a good kid, even if he's a little on the wild side. When I say "kid", I mean it. Spyder was a master class hacker who messed with magic and ended up being transformed into an electronic life form. He generally lives on the Net and calls himself the World Wide Spyder. When that happened, he was all of eleven.

I flipped open the phone. The view screen showed his current avatar face, a blue faced alien Elvis, complete with antennae. "Hey Spyder, you got anything on the Jade Hound?"

"That's why I was calling. Jana in records found a series of murders tied to it over the last several decades, most scattered around Europe. Harrison was the first on US soil. And guess who just got back from London?"

"Harrison and Baker," I said.

The screen exploded in electronic fireworks and the words *We Have a Winner* flashed across it.

"How does it work?" I asked.

"Apparently, Baker may not be the perp. As near as Jana can figure, the Jade Hound was dug up back in the 1920's in the Netherlands from the grave of a man who, ironically, himself was a grave robber. The first deaths happened in England soon after. There have been more killings sporadically over the years. There seems to be a connection to having the amulet stolen and it has been stolen a lot. When it ends up in a private collection via a will, nothing happens. When it's stolen, all hell breaks loose. No offense," said Spyder.

"None taken. So we can safely assume Harrison stole it and Baker took it from him," I said. "Probably came by, saw what had happened and used the situation to his advantage."

"That'd be my guess," said Spyder.

"Any specs on the hound?" Mandi said, looking over my shoulder.

"Neither Jana nor I could find much, outside of a couple of old stories. Nobody's been able to take the thing down or as near as we can tell, even tried. It likes to stalk its victims. It can stay unseen and has some association with bats. It plays mind games, letting its prey know it's there. Want to guess how?"

Mandi and I exchanged a look. "It howls."

"Got it in one," said Spyder.

Mandi's cell rang and she stepped away to answer it.

"What's Jana's best guess on how to kill it?" I asked.

"Major body damage, but how to do that is anybody's guess," said Spyder. "You'd better take Baker into protective custody."

I frowned. Okay, maybe he wasn't guilty of murder, but that didn't mean I liked the guy. I mean, who climbs over the still warm remains of a buddy to rip him off? Still, protecting people was part of the job, regardless of what I felt their scumbag status was. "Will do. First we'll have to find him."

Mandi shut the lid of her flip phone. "Already done. That was Sheriff Weeks. Baker ran into the police station, trembling and sweating, demanding protection. The howling followed him and is getting louder. John didn't know what to do, so he called us."

"We need to get him and his men to evacuate the area," I said.

"Already taken care of. Spyder, we'll need armored airborne transport ASAP and a warded safe house," said Mandi.

"Nearest safe house is in Maine, about five hours by car from your current location," said Spyder.

"Which is why we asked for airborne," said Mandi.

"There's a little bug in the K-Y," said Spyder. "We only have two classified to be able to withstand an attack by something as powerful as the Jade Hound. One's in the shop following an attack last week."

"Last week? What's the problem?" I said.

"Plating got torn apart. That stuff is custom made to resist missiles to monsters to mystic attack and it's on back order," said Spyder.

"And the other one?" asked Mandi.

"Sarge and Mox are using it to transport a prisoner to Eastern State Penitentiary," he said.

The Quakers built that prison almost two hundred years ago and they knew a thing or two about holding inmates, arcane and otherwise. In 1971 it was converted fully to a maximum security facility for mystically inclined criminals. The place looks like a castle.

"ESP is in Philadelphia. They could be here in less than an hour," I said. Plus the pair of them had enough firepower between them to fry almost anything.

"They could if they hadn't started out in New Mexico," said Spyder.

"Great," I griped.

"I'll have our esteemed Deputy Director and resident fire demi-goddess en route to you ASAP," said Spyder.

With my luck, it wouldn't be soon enough.

We made haste to the police station and had to flash our badges to get past a police manned barricade.

"You think a block away is enough?" I said to Mandi.

"I suggested three, but John's manpower is limited."

I nodded. The fact that he took Mandi at her word put us a step above the usual situation.

A sharpshooter with a high powered rifle was positioned on the station roof, but it made me feel only marginally better.

Weeks met us at the door. "Glad you're here. Ever since Baker showed up, the damned baying hasn't stopped. What the hell is going on?"

We gave him the short version.

"Our best bet is to get him out of town to protect any innocent bystanders. John, could you get a hold of an armored car?" asked Mandi.

"Yeah, I should be able to. Give me half an hour," said John, moving toward the phone on his desk and pointing us toward Baker.

"I guess you didn't listen to me," I said.

"What?" asked Baker.

"I told you to have a *nice* day. But I guess anyone stupid enough to steal an amulet with a death curse ain't exactly bright enough to take good advice," I said.

"We should get him into a cell," said Mandi.

"I didn't do nothing," Baker said.

I grabbed him by the shoulder and yanked him to his feet. "Shut up and move. We're here to try and prevent that monster hound from pureeing you like it did your buddy. A cell will make that a little bit harder for this thing."

Just then there was another howl and it sounded close. Shots rang out from the roof.

"I guess it figured that subtle wasn't going to work if we got him to a safe house," said Mandi.

The upper half of the front wall of the station was all windows and they shattered inward, glass rocketing everywhere. A piece caught me above the eye and pretty soon I was seeing red.

The hound had a face even a mother would abandon in a well and bury under a ton of cement. The thing was hovering in the air. Fortunately, the ceiling wasn't very high, which forced it to land. I'll take a grounded monster over a flying one any day of the week.

Mandi held out her hand to Baker. "Give me the Jade Hound."

"Gladly," said Baker before I could tell my partner no.

"Everyone get into the cells and lock the doors," ordered Mandi. Baker sprinted, but the cops stood firm, their revolvers drawn – an incredibly brave and stupid thing to do. If we survived this, I was buying every one of them a drink.

Mandi was trying to get the hound to chase her, but it was ignoring her in favor of the retreating Baker.

"This isn't working," she said and put the amulet in a wastepaper basket. Mandi pulled her automatic out and fired a shot at the Jade Hound. The amulet was unharmed, but it did get the monster's attention. It stopped and turned its head to glare at Mandi, but continued to move toward the cells.

Mandi picked it out of the garbage. "This isn't working."

No it wasn't and I figured out why. I ran over to my partner and snatched the Jade Hound out of her hand.

"Karver, what are you doing?" she said, but there wasn't time to answer. My partner would figure it out momentarily.

The hound stopped and turned around to see who the latest idiot was to have stolen its jewelry and saw me. The key word being stole. Baker *gave* it to Mandi. I waved, aimed my gun at its left eye and fired. The bullet made it go splat, but we have very special ammo at the DMA. That particular load had everything from iron to silver to holy water and the kitchen sink mixed in – never know what you'll be facing down.

The blood poured out and congealed into something that resembled a bat, if Salvador Dali got to design it while on crack. I fired a second shot and the bat returned to blood and had the secondary effect of hitting the beast in its shoulder. I had the hound's attention, but it looked like the eye was already starting to heal. I had to get it away from the cops. I leapt out the gaping hole in the front wall and the monster followed.

I'm not a powerhouse like some in the DMA. I can't cast spells or bench press a semi or shoot energy blasts out of my chest. The demon that possessed me did some tuning up of my body. I was stronger and faster than a normal person and had some enhanced senses and perceptions. I can sense most demons at over a half-mile and have an unexplainable love for polka music and yodeling, as if the memories of what it made me do weren't bad enough.

I knew the hound wasn't from Hell, but I wouldn't mind figuring out a way to send it there. At the moment, I was just trying to get away. There was a motorcycle out front, which I set out to hot wire before the beastie got outside. The cops and Mandi were helping me by distracting it with gunfire. The locals' bullets were only annoying it. Mandi's ammo was taking chunks out, but even that was only slowing it down and making more bats. Fortunately, the regular ammo seemed to work fine on the winged rodents.

The hog roared to life as the hound's head cleared the jagged glass of the remaining window shards. I raced away seconds ahead of winged death, infinitely grateful for the remnant skills of a misspent youth.

Without looking behind me, I turned the accelerator to the max. I felt rather than saw the hound dive-bombing me and made a sudden turn around a corner, leaning into it. I got low enough for the hound to pass over me, but I ended up spilling the bike in the process. Ignoring the case of road rash, I got to my feet and spun around, searching the town skies for a flying killer.

I saw a dot outlined against the sun, which probably would have gone unnoticed by someone with normal eyesight. I limped over to the bike, my gun in hand. I stood over the cycle, waiting. Once it was at about three stories, I leapt backwards and started running in reverse in the opposite direction of its dive. I managed to leap onto the hood of a parked car.

I shot as the hound pulled out of its dive and was almost on top of the bike. My shot hit its target and the gas tank exploded, engulfing the winged monster in a fireball. I had thrown myself behind the car and slowly lifted my head to look.

Flames were licking the sky and devouring blood bats. Smoke obscured my view, but I could make out a smoldering carcass mixed in among the remains of the motorcycle.

I wasn't dumb enough to approach the hound, but I did stand up to get a better look.

"That wasn't so bad," I said, but instantly regretted it. That horror of a face lifted up and looked at me. It wasn't made any prettier for having been charbroiled. It started baying and the sound made my blood run cold. I did the thing that you're never supposed to do when facing a predator. I ran away down the street, my gun pointing and firing behind me.

The hound got up slowly. I had hurt it, but not enough to keep it down, but maybe enough to keep it grounded. The skin on both of its wings was bubbling and blistering. One appeared torn part way through. The hound started running after me instead of taking to the air, which, if I overlooked the fact that I was being hunted at all, would be considered a good thing.

I headed back toward the police station in hopes that Mandi had come up with something. My partner didn't disappoint. As I rounded the corner, an armored car smashed into the hound, crushing it between the grill and a brick wall. Again it was stunned. Mandi was at the wheel and threw the vehicle into reverse. Spinning it around, she pulled alongside me and waved, then sped ahead. I could hear the hound shedding bricks as it got back to its feet.

The rear door of the armored car opened and I jumped in. In the front of the rear compartment there was a bulletproof glass window that allowed the driver to see the guard in the back. Mandi had it open.

"Go, go, go!" I shouted when I looked behind us and saw the hound gaining.

"Not part of the plan," she said.

"We have a plan? I must have missed the memo," I said.

"Paperwork's not your strong suit. Wait for the hound to get inside with you," Mandi said.

"Have I been that bad a partner?" I screamed. The monster was getting closer.

"No. As soon as it's in, crawl through to the cab. I'll hit this switch and the back doors will shut..."

"Trapping the hound," I said, finishing her sentence.

"See, I knew you'd catch on," she said as the front paws of the hound scratched and scurried their way inside the armored car.

By the time the third leg was in, I was halfway through the window. It was a tight squeeze. "I guess it's a good thing I skipped dessert at lunch."

Mandi grabbed me by the back of my suit and pulled. I saw her eyes go wide as she looked behind me and then slammed the brakes. The sudden stop threw me into the cab and onto the dashboard, a split second ahead of the hound's jaws clamping down on the air occupying the empty space where my legs had just been. The momentum also shut the doors part way, so by the time Mandi hit the button, there wasn't far for them to go to lock shut. The hound spun and realized it was trapped.

I started to slam the window shut, but Mandi motioned for me to hold and tossed a tear gas grenade she got from the locals in and shut it herself.

Mandi smiled and shrugged her shoulders. "It couldn't hurt."

I nodded and collapsed on the seat.

"You okay?" she asked.

"I will be," I answered as the entire armored car started to shake as the hound tried to claw its way out. It was a high tech armored car with extra thick metal and so far it was holding. Sheriff Weeks popped up at the driver's side window.

"Everything okay in there?" he asked.

"John, you should know better," I said, wagging a finger at him. The man was one of those who didn't run when the hound came in. That earned my respect, so I honored his request to use his first name.

"What are you talking about, Karver?"

"You shouldn't come a knocking if the car is a rocking," I said.

"In your dreams," said Mandi. Turning to John she said, "He's fine, but we better get this vehicle to a deserted location just in case."

"You don't think it'll hold the thing?" John asked, his face losing all color.

"Not sure, but I don't want to take the chance," said Mandi. "According to Spyder, our backups' ETA is in forty minutes."

Spyder told Sarge what had happened and he and Mox made it in twenty-nine minutes.

We were in a ball field on the edge of town when the armored Crete-class helicopter touched down.

Sarge disembarked while the helicopter was still fifty feet off the ground. He landed as easily as I would have jumped down four stairs. Not bad for a guy who was drafted back in WWI. As a soldier, Sarge Winston's unit came across a summoning of something old and threw himself on the jewel that was the catalyst for the spell. The thing bonded to his chest with the summonee trapped inside. They have a curious relationship, but it makes Sarge hard to hurt.

"Heard you had some fun, Karver," said Sarge, shaking my hand, then Mandi's

"Yeah, you missed the party," I said. I pointed my thumb over my shoulder at the still rattling armored car. "Mandi saved you a party favor."

The helicopter had touched down at this point and Mox nodded at us. Her hair was blond this week, which went surprisingly well with her Polynesian features. Spyder had brought her up to speed.

Mox went halfway into the cab and opened the window. The hound tried to come at her and got a face full of fire for his trouble. She had her shoes off and one bare foot on the ground. A moment later the lawn seemed to disappear and red-hot lava poured out of her hands to fill the back of the armored car. Her mama was Pele, the Hawaiian lava goddess. Inside the baying of the hound got louder and sounded like a cry of pain, but it was a natural born killer so I didn't have any pity for it. Once the magma was up to the ceiling, Mox reached inside and touched the sizzling lava to draw out the heat. It slowly cooled to hardened ash. Her magic kept most of the heat in the lava so the steel armor plating warped a little, but mostly stayed intact except for some minor melting on the interior.

When she stepped out, the armored car was in a crater over ten feet deep. The raw material to create all that magma had to come from somewhere.

Sarge opened the back door and a red beam shot out from the crimson stone in his chest, carving a box shaped stone of the ashy mess. The Assistant Director reached in and dragged it over to the copter and loaded it in the back all by his lonesome.

We made sure the hound was put in a secure containment area, but where is one of the few things we do keep secret.

I got a halfhearted lecture from Sarge the next day about taking unnecessary risks.

"You don't have to always put your life on the chopping block," he said.

"If it could save someone else, yes I do," I said. I had a lot to make up for.

Sarge's lecture was based on department policy, but the smile I got showed his true feelings on the matter.

We even managed to have Don Baker charged with taking evidence from a crime scene and not reporting a murder. The penalty was only three years and he could have gotten less if he plea bargained, but he didn't. Of course, the fact that we didn't tell him the hound had been captured until after the fact may have had something to do with it. Plus since he was involved in multiple and organized crimes including theft, smuggling, and bringing a dangerous magic artifact into the country that was used in the commission of multiple killing, injuries and property damage we managed to take his house and property away to pay for the cleanup of the town using a little known provision of the RICO Act.

That just about wrapped things up, except for the fact that the Jade Hound disappeared from the evidence lockup a few months later and is presumed stolen.

THE BEAST WITH TWO BACKS

They called my partner and me in to investigate the beast with two backs. No, we didn't go undercover as peeping Toms; it was more complicated than that. This beast did indeed have two backs, as well as two fronts that were pressed close together. When I say it was hard to tell where one began and the other ended, I'm not waxing poetic. This writhing mass of flesh had at one point been two people, and my best guess was they were engaged in making the figurative beast with two backs before their sexual union turned very literal.

There was a male and female head which seemed to share only one mouth where two sets of lips had fused together. Arms wrapped around torsos, but the hands disappeared, each set of fingers melting into the flesh of the other. At the points where their groins met there was no trace left of sexual organs, just one smooth lump of flesh, as if someone had taken Ken and Barbie and held them together over an open flame.

The pair that were now reluctant Siamese lovers hadn't stopped moving the entire time I stood trying to get a grasp of the situation. Neither paused as each of them thrashed around in pain, desperately trying to pull away from the other. It was a goal they were never going to be able to make happen on their own.

"Isn't this the damnedest thing?" asked Detective Turner. He was one of San Francisco's finest, and had pulled the short straw when it came to this case. "Have you ever seen anything like it?"

"No," I answered honestly.

"How can something like this happen? Radiation?" asked Turner.

"Magic," I answered. The locals never like that answer.

"I don't believe in magic, no offense to the DMA. My superiors called you in," said Turner. The Department of Mystic Affairs is never treated with respect by the locals until some bad mojo moves in and does something they can't explain. We make no effort to hide the fact that magic is real and monsters exist. It's not our fault that most people choose not to believe us until it's too late.

"By the time we're done, you're going to probably want to rethink that," I said.

There was a sound of dry heaving coming from the bathroom. It was an improvement over the sound of the wet ones that had preceded it for the last several minutes.

"Your partner going to be alright in there?" asked Turner.

"Yes," I said.

"Weak stomach or flu?" asked Turner, being polite enough to give her an out for rookie behavior.

"Neither. She's been doing this longer than I have, and I've seen her look at remains where you couldn't tell how many people or what parts of them were left, all without batting an eye. My partner has certain abilities which make her sensitive to emotions, and these two must be pouring out a great deal of terror," I said. Mandi's an empath with propathic tendencies, which means she can send out as well as receive emotions. Usually she can stomach what other people are feeling. This must have been especially bad.

"It's not just the emotional terror these two are churning up. I'm blaming part of this on breakfast at that greasy spoon this morning," said Mandi. She had pulled her long blonde hair back into a ponytail. I guess that helped keep the puke out of it.

"Then I guess you don't want to stop at the all-you-can-eat pea soup, chili, and gefilte fish buffet for lunch? I hear they have a chocolate sauce raw oyster platter that has to be tasted to believe," I said with a smile.

My partner shot me a look. "Keep it up, Karver. I throw up again; I ain't going to the bathroom. I'm aiming for your shoes."

I pulled out a roll of chewable antacids and handed them to her.

"Where'd you get these?" she asked, taking the roll and popping three of the tablets.

"Motel lobby had a machine." Mandi had been in there a long time. I noticed it on the way in, so I ran down at the first sounds from the bathroom. "They also had an assortment of condoms, if you want to stock up."

"I don't know how you can think of sex after seeing something like this," said Turner. "I was hoping you'd know what happened."

"We know," I said.

Turner gave me a cop look. If I had been a suspect under

interrogation, it would have meant I was in trouble for an inconsistency.

"I haven't seen something like this, but I know something—or rather, someone—that can do it. It's called a fleshsmith," I said.

"Which is what?" asked Turner.

"It's a mage that can manipulate and mold any type of human or animal flesh," said Mandi. "There's very little we can do for the victims at this point, except calm them." Since Mandi had come out of the bathroom, the painful movements had slowed. Mandi had been sending calming emotions their way in an attempt to relax the couple and block their pain. It seemed to be working.

"What can you do?" said Turner.

"I already called for assistance from the home office," said Mandi. "The Department of Mystic Affairs has its own fleshsmith and he's on his way."

I cursed. "You called Adin?" My feelings toward him fell on the far side of loathing. Adin had been the one to give me my new face when the DMA rescued me from death row. The fleshsmith thought he had a sense of humor, which is the last thing someone who just had a demon use his body to murder more than five dozen people needs.

"How else do you suppose we could separate them? The flesh has changed to the point where, even if a surgeon could separate them, the body parts that should be there, aren't. The doctor wouldn't even know where to begin cutting."

"Fine, you're right, but I don't have to like it," I conceded. "What do you have so far on the victims?"

Turner pulled out his notebook. "To be honest, we're not entirely sure which is which. Neither have any special identifying characteristics. Each of them seems to have a single male and a single female breast. According to the IDs we found, the victims are Barney Diamond and Bambi Boosh. What we've been able to find out, Bambi is an exotic dancer." Turner pointed to a pair of silicon sacks that lay on the floor. "We're running down the serial numbers just to verify. Barney was a partner in one of those dot com IPOs that raised hundreds of millions in capital. He was smart enough to cash out enough of his stock before the bubble burst. He's worth about eighteen million."

"Either of them married or seriously involved?" asked Mandi.

"Diamond is married. His wife's name is Susan. We're trying to find her now," said Turner.

Cheating husband certainly is a motive. "What does Susan Diamond do for a living?"

Turner flipped open Diamond's wallet. There was an entire gallery of pictures of a gorgeous blonde, her features and figure perfect in every way. "Near as we can tell, she had no outside income." Turner looked at Mandi. "No sexism intended, ma'am, it looks like she was a trophy wife."

"None taken. I'm looking for a trophy husband, myself," said Mandi.

"Yeah, but she has trouble getting them to stay up on the mantle," I said.

Turner smiled. "We've been afraid to move them. We don't want to hurt them, and we don't know what would."

"Good call. Our man will be able to give us a better idea of what has to be done," said Mandi. "Karver, why don't you and Turner go see what you can find out about the missing missus."

"You sure?" I asked. I knew Mandi was using her propathic powers to keep the victims calm, but I also didn't want her in a position that would put her back to praying to the porcelain god.

"I'll be fine. Go."

So Turner and I went, starting with the house, the neighbors, the country club, and a few other places. No one had seen Susan Diamond. Apparently, she was a sight to be seen, from what we heard from the men and even the women. If she had been around, somebody would have remembered and told us, if only to brag.

My phone rang. It was Mandi. After I heard what she had to say, I whispered, "Damn."

Turner looked at me, worry in his eyes. "The victims die?"

I shook my head. "No, our fleshsmith is at the motel. Feel free to take the long way back."

Turner ignored my suggestion and instead turned on the sirens. We were there in record time.

Adin saw me and gave me a perfect smile. Fleshsmiths are notorious for being uber-beautiful people. When you can adjust your looks on a whim, it's not that hard to do. I doubt anyone but me would have seen the sadistic glee in that grin.

"Karver, good to see you," said Adin, rushing up with his hand outstretched to touch mine. That wasn't going to happen. Touch is how their powers work.

I pulled my piece and pointed it between his eyes. "Don't even think about touching me."

"Karver!" scolded Mandi. I could feel the calming waves pulsing off her towards me. They didn't do a thing.

"Pulling your weapon on a fellow agent. That's a suspendable offense there, Karver. I could have you up on charges," said Adin. His perfect smile just kept getting bigger.

"Yeah, maybe I'll get suspended or maybe I'll shoot you. I know where to shoot you that it won't kill you, just hurt like hell until you mold the flesh back into place. However, if I tell about what happened when you worked on a certain new recruit—" namely, me "—I think you'd end up without a job. Maybe even some jail time. You want to continue this pissing contest, or do you want to back down?"

Adin put his hands up in mock surrender. "Fine. I was just saying 'hi'."

"We both know that ain't true." Adin was still too close for my comfort, so I didn't holster the weapon until he took two steps back. Then I put my gun away.

I looked at Diamond and Boosh. "Why are they still connected?" I asked.

Adin's perfect smile faded into a look of embarrassment. "We've run into a few problems."

I was surprised. I didn't like the guy, but he was master level at what he did. "What kind of problems?"

"For starters, we have two entirely separate people that were merged," said Adin.

"We already knew that. It's why we called you in," I said.

"No, that's not what I mean." Adin motioned Turner and me away from the fused lovers. The rest of the conversation, on his part, was a whisper. "When you merge two separate beings, it's common to leave a differentiation point, a clear line where one begins and the other ends. The person who did this just merged flesh without regard for bone, muscle, fat, or whom it came from. I can't tell who belongs to what."

"Can you just guess, separate them, and reform what's missing?" I asked.

"I could, but it could have disastrous results. The two of them have different blood types and different tissue types. If I leave any tissue from the other person still inside, the body will start attacking it. Their own immune systems will kill them. In fact, at this point, I don't think I'd even be able to get all their blood separated because it has mixed so much. And that's going to be a problem, because he's B and she's A. The two don't mix well. Worse, one's positive and the other is negative. If I separate them, we may still have to take all the blood out of both of them and do a full transfusion."

"Can't you just morph the blood into the right type once they're separated?" I asked.

"Too much and too delicate. I can manage a few pints if it's in a jar, but in and among all the capillaries mixed through all the flesh, there's no way; same goes for the foreign tissue. When I worked on you, I changed fat to bone and muscle. But the genetic code in all of them would still be yours. I can't change that."

That's something I hadn't thought about. My DNA was still in criminal databases.

"I'm waiting on two medical teams to arrive. I'm going to separate the pair and have them start the transfusions on the way to the hospital. The problem is that I'm going to have to treat this as an amputation and take the overlapping pieces of flesh away. Unfortunately, they're both in good shape."

"What difference does that make?" asked Turner.

"I can change one type of flesh to another. To do most of my work, I usually use stored fat. Both of them are in good shape and are thin. We may be able to use some of the muscle mass, but it's not going to be enough to grow entire hands and pelvises. We'll just have to see if they survive, then fatten them up and see what I can do later on."

Turner cursed. I concurred. The medical teams Adin was waiting for arrived.

"Anything I can do?" I said.

"Yeah. Catch the sick bastard that did this," said Adin.

"I will," I said. "Can I take my partner with me?"

"Yeah, now that the medical team is here, we're going to sedate both of them. Their eyes are open, and they don't need to see this. I actually had to adjust their eyelids. They were locked in the up and open position. They couldn't have shut their eyes no matter how hard they tried."

I had to agree with Adin's assessment of sick bastard; problem was, the sicko was also pretty creative. That pointed toward intelligence, and a smart monster is harder to catch than a dumb one, human or otherwise.

"Remember, a fleshsmith's power only works through the hands, so don't let this one touch you," said Adin. "Either of you."

"We won't," Mandi said.

The conjoined pair were both being injected in the gluteus muscles, as they were large fleshy areas that neither one seemed to share with the other. In less than a minute, they were both unconscious, their heads lolling to opposite sides, their lips looked as if they were going to be torn apart from the strain. Adin started with the faces, putting one of his hands on each. There was a soft glow, and the space where their lips should have been was removed, leaving a pair of skull-like grins.

I had seen worse. Hell, I had done worse when the demon controlled my hands, but I had no desire to see more. Although I was impressed by the fact that he sealed the flesh that was left behind without a drop of blood being spilled. God forbid a seriál demon possessed Adin. There's no telling what kind of destruction it would be able to do. I looked at my partner's face. Mandi had seen what I had seen, but she was turning a little green. Part of it was probably what she ate for breakfast, but part of it was the nausea of everyone in the room who was watching. I went over, put my arm around her shoulders, and led her out of the room, picking up a wastepaper basket on the sly as we left. I closed the door behind us and got her around the corner from where the uniforms were standing guard. We went to the top of the stairwell and I handed her the basket. Mandi started to say thanks, but the end of the word was drowned out by a heave.

Finding one person in a city the size of San Francisco was not an easy thing. Fugitives were able to stay at large for a long time if they were smart. Fortunately, most weren't. Amazing how many are caught getting some nookie at their significant other's abode. Sometimes the only way to catch the smart ones was to put their picture on TV and hope for the best. That wouldn't happen until we had proof that the wife was indeed the fleshsmith – not that it would be effective in this case, with a perp who can change their appearance. It could just as easily be that one of Bambi the dancer's regulars got a little too obsessive and possessive. We decided to check out her club next and ask some questions. The name of the place was the Pole Barn. The door was decorated with cartoons of overly endowed women wearing pasties with hats, chaps, and spurs. We were in time for the lunch rush. When the guy at the door asked us for the cover, we could have pulled our badges. We didn't. Instead we forked over the money. Sometimes it's better if people don't know who you are. The hope was that people might open up more to a fellow purveyor of the fleshy arts. If that didn't work, we'd pull out the badges, go backstage, and talk to the dancers.

We made like a couple out for a little bit of excitement. We weren't the only ones there. Somewhere along the line, strip clubs had gone from a dirty little pleasure to a place to take a date – progress takes all forms.

I sat down on a chair near the stage. Mandi went over to the bar to work her wiles. She came back over with a pair of rum and Cokes.

"What's this? We're on the job," I said.

"Two drink minimum," she said. "I said we were fans of Bambi. Bartender said she hadn't shown up for her shift, and no one seemed to know why. He says the next dancer up is good friends with her. She might be where we start."

There was something a little off in my partner's tone when she mentioned the dancer. Not that something specifically was wrong, but something was up. "What's the dancer's name?"

My partner sighed. "Mandi."

I guess I didn't have to laugh so loud or so hard, but it's so rare that I find something funny enough to laugh at these days that I couldn't help myself. My partner's eyes narrowed, and she frowned. It was her face of intimidation. It only made me laugh harder.

The DJ announced Mandi, and the speakers belted out "Cotton-Eyed Joe." Cowgirl Mandi was energetically swaying some parts, shaking others while making the faces that mimicked ecstasy, but you could tell by her eyes that this was just a job. When her number was done, she came down onto the floor to wander among the crowd to try to separate the patrons from their cash.

Mandi waved a couple of bills to get her attention. "That was great. I was wondering if I could get my man here a lap dance."

Now it was my turn for the face of intimidation. I guess my laughing must have really pissed off my partner, because she knows I'm not good with the touching. It brings back all the butchery, which to the seriál that rode my soul was like foreplay, sex, and orgasm all rolled into one.

Mandi had the right to get even with me, but that didn't mean I was going to let her get away with it. When cowgirl Mandi came over, I said, "I appreciate it, but I can't accept." The stripper gave me an odd look. "She's my mistress. I'm cheating on my wife with her. To let you do the lap dance would seem like I was cheating on my wife with two women, and that would just be wrong."

"I understand," said the stripper. Apparently, this wasn't the first time she heard that line.

"However, you were paid for a lap dance." I handed her another twenty. "I think she could use one more than me."

Mandi's jaw dropped.

"The customer is always right," said the dancer.

"Except when it's him. He's never right," said my partner.

"She's just feeling a little bit awkward because we're in here trying to gear her up for a threesome," I said.

Mandi the stripper was rubbing her bare back and thonged behind against my partner Mandi's front. "I thought you said another woman would be too much cheating on your wife?"

I shot her a smile. "Who do you think the third person's going to be?"

Mandi the stripper swung around, straddling my partner and rubbing her arms up and down Mandi's side. My partner rolled her eyes and stood up, dropping the stripper on her thonged behind.

"Sorry, this isn't working for me," said my partner.

The stripper shrugged. "Hey, I get paid either way. So why are you wearing a gun? You a cop?"

"She's good. Maybe you could frisk our perps that way. We'd probably have a lot less resisting arrest," I said.

"I'd never get the outfit past the director. We do have a dress code," said Mandi. She flipped open her badge and showed the stripper. "We're federal agents. We're looking into the assault of Bambi Boosh." The stripper stopped her playful act. Her expression became one of genuine concern. "Oh my God! Is she okay?"

"No, but if we find who assaulted her, there might be a way to undo what damage was done," I said. "Have any of her customers been acting odd of late? Either regulars or new ones?"

The dancer thought about it. "Nobody I can think of. She was seeing this one married guy, Barney Diamond."

"He was hurt in the same attack," said Mandi. "Is there someone else that you can think of? Anybody or anything out of the ordinary at all?"

"No, I'm sorry. I'd tell you if there was. I could tell you about most of her regulars if that'd help," she said.

I pulled out a pad and pen. "It might." I wrote the names down.

The dancer's face got pale as she looked at something over our shoulders. "Didn't you say Bambi was attacked and hurt?"

"Yes," I said.

The dancer pointed to the stage. "She doesn't look hurt. Hell, she looks great. Looks like she got some liposuction and bigger boobs."

Mandi and I jumped up and had our guns drawn.

"Freeze! Federal agents. Don't move."

Either this really was Bambi and she had a lot of explaining to do, or the criminal fleshsmith had altered herself (or possibly himself) to look like her. Either way, she was going into custody.

We had found her easily enough, but she wasn't going to come along quietly. There was another dancer on the stage, who she quickly got behind and lifted off her feet with a single arm around her waist—seemed impressive for such a petite woman, until I realized that she had probably altered the density of her own muscles to make her stronger and faster than any normal person should be. Her other hand touched the terrified woman's face.

"Come anywhere near me, and I'll fuse her nostrils and her lips shut," said the fleshsmith. "I'm not joking."

With her powers, that was a real threat. "I know you're no joke." I took an intuitive leap. "I saw what you did to your husband and his mistress."

I had definitely hit some buttons. "That cheatin' bastard and his whore got what they deserved."

On some level, I suppose that was true… at least from her point of view. Their bodies were her pain made manifest. Problem was, that pain was going to kill them if Adin wasn't able to save them. There's nothing in the regulations that says you have to be 100% honest with a perp in a standoff situation. "It was impressive. It took the Department of Mystic Affairs fleshsmith more than four hours to get them apart."

The fleshsmith swung the dancer around, squeezing her small waist even tighter. The woman was having trouble breathing. "That's impossible! I mixed their bodies so far together that even I wouldn't be able to undo it."

I shrugged. "Well, no offense, but you may not have the same level of skills as the man the government employs. He's been to medical school. Have you?"

"You mean after all that, they're both fine?" she said between gritted teeth.

Mandi had gotten to the side in an attempt to get a clear shot. Our conversation was keeping the fleshsmith distracted enough that she hadn't noticed yet. "Well, as I understand it, he used some sort of radioactive marker that bonded to the specific blood and tissue types to separate the flesh correctly. There were parts he couldn't get," I lied. "So basically, he had to replace the distal parts. Just means neither one of them has much fat to spare at this point, and I think your husband's private parts may be a little smaller than when he started."

"He's just smaller? Oh, that is so wrong!" said the fleshsmith.

"Be that as it may, if you'll just let the woman go, we need to take you in for some questioning," I said.

The fleshsmith laughed. "You think I'm stupid? You think I'm just gonna let you arrest me? Not a chance. I walk outta here, and this floozy gets to keep her face."

"Taking a hostage out of this building will qualify as kidnapping. The death penalty is still on the books for that," I said. I forgot to mention that using magic to kill also carried the death penalty, but that was a law most people weren't familiar with.

"I have a suggestion. Let the woman go, and take me as a hostage instead," I said.

The fleshsmith laughed. "Why would I want to trade a helpless woman for a trained DMA agent?"

"Well, you know how we law enforcement types are with acceptable casualties." That was a lie. I knew of no decent cop anywhere who thinks any loss of any civilian is anything less than a tragedy. However, public perception can be different. "We're a lot more hesitant to risk one of our own." The fleshsmith turned so the woman was between her and Mandi. Apparently, she had been watching out of the corner of her eye. "That makes sense, but not you. Your partner."

Mandi had her gun out in front of her pointed at the fleshsmith. "No problem. Let the woman go and I'm all yours."

"First lose the gun," said the fleshsmith.

Mandi looked at me, put the safety on and tossed me her gun. Putting it on the floor would only invite the hostage taker to pick it up and we have some pretty impressive ammo, which would only strengthen the fleshsmith's position.

"So how are we going to do this?" said Mandi. I could feel the waves of calm she was sending with her propathic powers.

"You put yourself in the same position she's in, in my other arm, and I let her go," said the fleshsmith who looked like the stripper Bambi.

"How do I know you'll let her go once you have me?" asked Mandi.

"I guess you'll just have to trust me." The smile on the fleshsmith's face was less than encouraging, but Mandi did as she asked. As soon as her arm was around my partner's waist, she lifted her off the ground and threw the stripper ten feet. The fleshsmith's free hand pulled up Mandi's blouse from her pants so that the hand that restrained her was able to touch the bare skin on my partner's abdomen. I guess her powers wouldn't be able to work through the clothes. Her free hand then came to rest on Mandi's face.

"Now we're just going to walk out of here, and as soon as I'm safe, I'll let her go," said the fleshsmith.

"There's not a chance in hell that's how this is going down," said Mandi, using her emotional powers to try to scare the fleshsmith. It was having a limited effect. "Let go of me, lay down on the floor with your hands behind your head, and you get out of this without being hurt."

The fleshsmith's power pulsed and sealed both of Mandi's nostrils. "I don't think you're in any position to be giving orders Agent."

"You're not leaving. That's non-negotiable," said Mandi with a nasally tone. "Karver, you let her get away and I will never forgive you."

My partner wasn't bluffing, to either of us. Since I wasn't about to alienate the only person I could let down my guard around, I started narrowing my options down to what I would actually do.

"When my partner has made up her mind, that's all there is to it. I'm afraid I'm not going to be able to let you go," I said, lifting up my gun.

The fleshsmith shook her head and let out a raspy laugh. The power surged again, and Mandi's mouth sealed seamless. My partner was moments away from suffocation. At least I saw her take a deep breath when she felt the power surging. That gave her a couple extra seconds.

The fleshsmith rushed towards the stripper she had thrown a minute ago, who hadn't had the sense to get up and run. I shot the perp in the shoulder. It barely slowed her down. She put one hand on the wound. The bullet was pushed out, and it started mending instantly.

I leapt on the stage, running to intercept her. She may have altered her flesh to make her faster than normal, but unluckily for me, the demon that had possessed me had done similar things to my body. Even so, she was going to get to the girl an instant before I was, and I could already feel the power surging in her hands. I couldn't let her harm an innocent. With my free hand, I reached back underneath my suit jacket and pulled out one of a pair of very special knives, about the size of a short sword or machete. I jumped, swinging my blade. I sliced off her right hand above the wrist. It was a clean cut, and bled terribly. She grabbed it with her left hand and started healing the flesh. I could see the palm starting to grow back already.

"Stop," I ordered. Her hands were the same as deadly weapons. As long as she had one, she could hurt somebody else, and if she managed to grow back the other, we'd be back at square one. "Lie down and put your hand behind your head, or I'll slice it off."

"You're a Fed. That would be police brutality," said the fleshsmith, her thumb and the stubs of her other fingers were already back.

"Last chance."

She raised the middle finger of her injured hand, which was already half-way restored, and pointed it at me. I cut it off again, and the other one for good measure. Then I cuffed her wrists to one of the poles on the stage. Normal handcuffs would slide right off. But with the runes that were on the DMA cuffs, they wouldn't go anywhere, and they'd act as a tourniquet for her wounds.

I rushed back to Mandi. She was already a deep red. There was no sign of lips, although the nostrils were still recognizable. I took my other blade out from behind my jacket and held the point up to her face.

"Don't move," I said. With the surgical precision that only an ex-demon-possessed serial killer could have, I sliced two nostril holes where the other ones had been. These bled profusely, but that was dealt with easily enough. I took Mandi's cuffs off her waist and looped them around her nose. The bleeding stopped. It would stay that way as long as the cuffs were on.

I needed help to make sure she stayed okay. Time to call in backup. I took out my cell phone and hit speed dial one. A small purple dinosaur head appeared on my phone's screen.

It was the agent known as the World Wide Spyder. "Karver, what's up?"

"Mandi's been hurt by a fleshsmith, Her face is sealed up. I've got her enough air to breathe, but I need Adin here now to fix her." The purple dinosaur head morphed into the Spyder's real face, something he rarely did, as he was always too busy playing games on the web. As an electronic entity, it wasn't that hard. "He'll be there as soon as he can. Tell Mandi to hold on." I turned the phone screen toward Mandi; she nodded and gave Spyder a thumbs up. It's easy enough to forget that the kid was really just a teenager. Even though we dealt with death and darkness all the time, it's different when it's one of your own.

I may not have liked the guy, but Adin was there in less than fifteen minutes. The DMA takes care of our own. Adin rushed in and ran to where we were on the stage. This caused the fleshsmith who I had cuffed to a pole on the opposite side of the stage to scream about the injustice of having her hands cut off while Mandi only had a couple of holes closed.

"If you like, I can close your holes and see how much you enjoy it," said Adin. The perp fleshsmith shut up.

Adin put his hands on her face and did a quick assessment. "Karver, you did a nice job. The cuts are clean and in the right places. I'll be able to fix the nose easy." He slid the handcuffs off, and the nostrils weaved themselves back together. Not a single drop of red stuff fell. Next, a hole where her mouth should have been opened. Mandi sucked in large amounts of air.

"Mandi, give me your badge," said Adin. He must have seen the odd look I was giving him. "This way I can get her lips to look the same way they did before. Memory's only so good. Unless you'd want some cosmetic changes made?"

"No, the way they were is fine," slurred Mandi. A moment later, you wouldn't have been able to tell that her face had ever been anything other than normal.

"Thank you," said Mandi.

"It was my pleasure," said Adin.

"How are Diamond and Boosh doing?" asked Mandi.

Adin's face dropped. "I was able to get them separated, but it wasn't good. Bambi died. She had asthma, and her system couldn't handle it. Diamond is stable, but he's missing a lot of his pelvis and everything below his elbows. It'll be a matter of time before we find out whether or not he'll survive. He's getting a full transfusion as we speak."

The fleshsmith chained to the pole laughed. "I knew it. The bastard deserves everything he gets for cheating on me."

"What about the woman? She never did anything to you," said Adin.

"She's no innocent. She's the slut who slept with my husband. She deserved what she got."

"So you have no regrets about what you did to both of them?" said Adin.

"None."

Adin smiled and revealed a tape recorder. "That's too bad, but you're going down for what you did." Adin looked at me. "I hope you read her her rights."

I nodded. I did it while we were waiting for him.

I motioned Adin aside. "That was nice work you did there."

Adin gave half a shrug. "It's bad enough what she did to those people, but don't mess with one of the DMA and expect to get away with it."

"Agreed, but that wasn't the only part I was referring to. Thank you for fixing Mandi," I said.

"Karver, you're the one who saved her. All I did was fix the damage the perp did." Adin got a glint in his eye, and grinned every bit of his thousand-watt smile. "Does this mean you'll shake my hand now?"

Adin extended his hand to me.

"Sure." I took it, but I slipped one of my cleaned blades out of the sheath and let it dangle obviously by my side. "Good advice from you about how to take care of a fleshsmith. Cutting off her hands worked great. Now I can take care of any fleshsmith who tries to attack me."

To his credit, Adin chuckled and let go of my hand. "Good. I'll take her in for you guys if you like."

"You sure?" I asked. Paperwork is major on something like this. I'd still have a ton to explain why I decided to perform amputations on a perp.

"Yeah. Give Mandi a little time to collect herself," said Adin. He took her away.

"You okay, partner?" I asked.

Mandi nodded. "I will be. I appreciate the surgery, Karver."

"No problem. To be honest, I think I'm going to miss having you like that. I don't think I've ever seen you be quiet that long," I said, smiling.

"Well, it's not like you can hold up your end of an intelligent conversation," she countered.

"So, you still want that lap dance?" I asked.

"Only if you're the one giving it," Mandi countered. "And I can find a video camera to immortalize you in a g-string."

"Give me the forty bucks," I said.

"For you? I was thinking of digging around for some spare change, and even then, I'm probably overpaying."

"Forget it, then. I have some pride," I said.

"Since when?" asked Mandi.

"Since I got you as a partner," I said.

"No fair. You cheated by being nice," said Mandi.

"Then you can make it up to me by giving me a lap dance. I know you have some experience, but do you think you'll be able to do it without an entire group to perform for?" I teased.

"I guess that's something you'll never know," said Mandi.

"I'll add it to the list."

HECATOMB

I hate serial killer cases. They hit a little too close to home, considering my past. That's why the old man has a tendency to assign me to them. Sarge says I have a unique perspective, having spent time in the mind of one. Technically, the seriál was in mine, but it wasn't worth arguing about. Not with the body count we were dealing with. The latest pushed it to double digits, which was enough for the locals to actually put a call into the Department of Mystic Affairs.

There was nothing overtly mystical about the deaths, but that's often the case. Otherwise we'd be involved before the dying.

"Agent Cobb," said Police Chief Buster of Greenville PD shaking my partner Mandi's hand before turning to me. "Agent Karver, thank you for coming."

"We're here to lend whatever assistance we can," said Mandi. My partner is the diplomat. I'm more likely to point out that if they had called us sooner, a lot of innocent people would still be alive. "What makes you think the killing might be magic related?"

The chief coughed and his belly, which was barely contained by his suit jacket, jiggled up and down like a watermelon tumbling down stairs. "Actually, I don't. Don't believe in it."

"Then why'd you call us in?" I asked, not bothering to hide my annoyance. Mandi gave me a look and sent relaxing emotions my way for a brief moment. It was her way of asking my permission to calm me down. I've let her do it under certain circumstances. Today wasn't going to be one of them. I hated my time being wasted, especially when more people might end up dying because of it. Mandi sensed my increased annoyance and turned off the psychic valium.

"FBI agent name of Pine suggested I do it. He is the profiler the feds brought in and he felt there was enough here to warrant calling you in. I don't see it, personally. Whole DMA is a waste of perfectly good tax dollars, if you ask me," said Chief Buster.

"I didn't. How about I refrain from mentioning the amount of tax revenue being squandered to get enough doughnuts in your mouth to swell your belly to that size and you keep your trap shut about my agency?" I said. I stopped short of asking if his first name was Belly.

Mandi glared at me and rolled her eyes back in her head. She has had talks with me on more than one occasion to not antagonize the locals. I said I'd try if they didn't start anything. Chief Belly Buster started this.

Mandi was working her particular brand of psychic magic to calm Buster down. On him it worked. "Chief, we've worked with Agent Pine before. He had a reason for what he suggested. Why don't you explain everything you have to us?"

"Fine." Buster led us to a conference room, boards plastered with crime scene photos.

"Sue James was the tenth victim to be killed near the Tar River over the last seven months. Each victim had their eyes, teeth, and all their finger and toenails removed. Each one was found exactly three days later at or near the spot where they disappeared. The medical examiner found ligature marks around the neck of each victim, but says that's not how they were killed. It was as if they were put in a vacuum and the air was sucked out of their lungs. The alveoli in the lungs in some cases were actually turned inside out.

"Pine examined the body and the reports on the others. Neither he nor any of our ME's were able to find a single tool mark to show how the missing parts were removed. We did find hair, but our labs haven't been able to identify it, other than they are sure it's not human. Pine has much more experience in this sort of investigation than we do and he said he's never seen anything like it. He thought you might. He asked for you specifically, Agent Karver."

In a way, I was flattered. Pine was the man who caught me when I was possessed by the seriál demon – got me sent to death row. I was grateful at the time, before I was shanghaied by the DMA, exorcized, and given a new face and life.

"Pine's the best," I said. Pine had no idea who I once was, but I respected the hell out of him. And I owed him. If he hadn't caught me when he did, a family of five would have been slaughtered.

"Yeah, he caught The Carver. No offense to you, Agent Karver," said the Chief.

"None taken," I said. It made sure I never forgot what the seriál had used me to do.

"Look, sorry I insulted you earlier. Sue James was a close friend of my daughter's. I may not believe in magic, but if there is something you and your partner can do to stop this psycho from killing again, you will have my eternal gratitude."

What could I say to that? "We'll do everything we can."

Of course, that involved a lot of leg work. First, we sent samples of the hair to the DMA lab in DC. Our DNA lab has a tad more samples to compare it to. We spent the rest of the day reading the case files. At one point I was starving. Chief Buster brought in doughnuts, but after what I said to him, there was no way I was having one. Mandi had no such problem and had three jelly, my favorite, making sure to tell me how tasty each was. I responded by ordering a pizza with extra mushrooms. Mandi hates mushrooms.

The next two days we spent re-interviewing witnesses. Although calling them witnesses was stretching it. No one had seen a thing, but in three of the cases there was someone who was walking with the victim before their disappearance. Each of them reported hearing a baby crying and splitting up to find it. The other person never came back, but showed up dead three days later in the same area. Each of them also reported seeing some sort of vermin. One described it as a badger, another a fox. The other wasn't sure what it was, except it had a long tail.

At the start of the fourth day, we got a call from the World Wide Spyder. He thinks it's a cool name. I like him so I reserve judgment.

Our cell phones have a few attachments you can't get at the local dealer yet. One was a working, real time video phone. Spyder's chosen avatar of the day was a blue barbarian.

"Playing games on the job?" kidded Mandi.

"I get down time, same as you. Anyway, the lab managed to identify the hair," said Spyder.

"What is it?" I asked.

"Sarge…" The old man, one of the Deputy Directors of the DMA. "… wants you to meet with one of our consultants who's an expert. All I can tell you is that it's Native American in origin."

"Who's the consultant?" I asked. He told me. "Great. I hate meeting with gods, especially tricksters."

"How come we never get to meet with hunky, love gods?" asked Mandi.

"Probably too intimidated by me," I said.

Mandi laughed. "I said hunky love gods, not brooding, dark agents with delusions of grandeur."

"Meet him at the diner outside of town," said Spyder.

It could have been worse. It could have been Coyote. That trickster's got an active grudge against the federal government. I heard a couple years back, Congress was trying to back out of an old treaty because oil was found on a reservation. He gave them all dysentery until the bill was shot down.

Not that this trickster was much better. We were sitting at a table, sipping coffee and waiting. A couple opened the door and a black bird flew in, then circled the room once before landing on our table.

"Raven," I acknowledged. Mandi did the same.

"Agent Cobb, Agent Karver. I've been waiting out there for ten minutes. You think they'd keep a window open," said the bird.

"Probably don't get a lot of feathered customers," I said.

"With these prices, who can blame us?"

The owner came out from behind the grill and over to our table with our waitress. "You have to get that thing out of here. No pets."

"But he's housebroken," said Raven, referring to me.

The waitress giggled. "You're a ventriloquist."

"No, he's a government consultant we're having a meeting with," I said. I always go with the truth by way of explanation. It's not my fault nobody ever believes it.

"Whatever funnyman. The bird goes or I'm gonna throw y'all out of here," said the owner, who came over to back up his waitress.

"That'd be a real bad idea, tough guy," I said.

"Why's that?" he asked.

"For one thing, the bird is a god. Never a good idea to tick one of them off." I flipped out my badge. "For another, the lady and I are federal agents. I've seen a dozen health code violations since I sat down. You don't leave us alone; I make a call and do a ride along with the health inspector so no bribe will get you out of being closed down. The last thing is if you lay a hand on me, I'll break it and run you in for assaulting a federal agent."

Out of the corner of my eye, I saw Mandi cover a smile with her hand.

"Oh, c'mon, let him try to throw me out. I'll ravage this place to the ground," Raven said, bobbing side to side in what I guessed was his imitation of a human boxer.

The owner looked from me to the bird, trying to figure out if I was serious. With a sigh, he decided that I was.

"Fine, but if the bird makes a mess, you're cleaning it," he said and stormed back to the grill. "And I saw your lips move."

Raven cocked his head. "I don't even have lips. What do you think they put in the coffee here?"

"Cream and sugar," I said. "Don't make a mess. Please." Politeness helps when dealing with gods and the bird was on our side.

"I'll think about it," said Raven. He looked at the waitress. "You ready to take our order, sweetbuns?"

The waitress was very amused. She looked at me. "What do you want?"

"Hey, missy, don't be looking at him. I'm the one talking to you," said Raven.

"Okay, what would you like?" she asked like she was playing along with the gag, her pen poised over her pad.

"Omelet, with sausage and Swiss. That sign outside right?" asked Raven.

"Which one?" she asked.

"The one that says you sell live bait," he said.

"Yes," she said.

"Throw in a cup of night crawlers," he said.

"I don't think we can do that," she said.

"Whatever happened to the customer is always right?" said Raven.

"Clyde…" she said, pointing her thumb over her shoulder at the owner. "… says he's always right."

"Mammals have an over inflated sense of importance," said Raven.

"That's an unusual order," said Mandi.

"What, you're shocked I eat worms?" said Raven. "Early bird and all that, although, I try to sleep in till at least nine, which is why I have to eat in places like this."

"Not the worms – the eggs – seems a little cannibalistic," said Mandi.

"They're chicken eggs. Do I look like a chicken to you?" asked Raven. Mandi shook her head. Raven turned to the waitress. "They are chicken eggs, right?"

"Yes."

"Good. I'm done. You may serve the humans next," said Raven.

The waitress chuckled and bowed. "That's mighty kind of you," she said and turned to me. "What can I get for you?"

Normally, I let Mandi order next, ladies first and all that, but if I get asked first she gets offended if I defer to her. "I'll have two eggs over easy, a side of home fries, and corn beef hash."

"And for the lady?"

"A yogurt and a blueberry muffin," said Mandi.

"Nothing hot?" I said.

"After the way you just ticked off the cook? I'm not ordering anything off the grill. I don't want my food spit on or worse," said Mandi.

I hadn't thought of that. "Cancel my order. Make it a yogurt, bagel with cream cheese and a jelly doughnut." I heard Mandi snicker. I ignored her. "Make it two doughnuts."

The waitress left to get our food.

"What do you have on our killer?" I said.

"It's vermin," said Raven, picking up a sugar packet with his beak and swallowing it in two gulps, paper and all.

"Most killers are," I said.

"I mean literally. The Zuni and Hopi used to call it Ahuizotle, the life sucker. They say the first one was created when fox mated with the shadow of rattlesnake and gave birth to the creature. Not that I put much stock in legends," said Raven.

"Most people would consider you a legend," I said.

"Exactly my point. I've killed a few of these things in my time. I thought the last of them was slaughtered years ago. They use the baby noise same way a human would use a duck call, to attract their quarry. They like to live around rivers and are amphibious, but tend not to attack in the water – makes the prey too slippery to hold. Ahuizotle are about the size of a fox with a long tail that opens like a hand or the jaw of a snake. They use it to grab their prey around the face. If the victim is larger, they wrap the tail around the neck and drag it away. An Ahuizotle then literally sucks the life out of whatever it has caught," said Raven.

"Does it eat the eyes, teeth or nails it takes?" asked Mandi.

"No, takes them as trophies, but ones with practical use. Ahuizotle use sympathetic necromancy to employ the eyes to see. They arrange them around their lair, making it nearly impossible to take them by surprise. The nails and teeth they attach to living trees or bushes, making weapons and defenders out of the branches."

"So we search the river for branches with human teeth and fingernails and capture the thing," I said.

"It won't be that easy. They camouflaged well three hundred years ago. Any that have survived to this day probably mask their presence to damn near invisible. And, no offense, they are too fast for a human to catch. Why don't you call in Agent Buck? A werewolf would be a far better match for an Ahuizotle," said Raven.

"Buck's no longer with the DMA," said Mandi. Which was an understatement. Buck went bad, kidnapped a family, tried to rape the mother. He's doing hard time. "We can handle it."

"If you say so," said Raven. "I better check to make sure that human can handle my omelet." He flew over to a cup of bait, tasted one of the night crawlers. Apparently it met with his approval because he flew into the kitchen with it. Using stealth, he knocked the owner's spatula on the floor. When he bent to pick it up, Raven dumped the worms on his open omelet and managed to drop a piece of cheese over them before the owner was able to stand back up.

Raven returned to our table. A couple of minutes later the waitress brought our food. Mandi and I thanked her. Raven just said "Yum" and used his beak to devour his sausage, worm, and cheese omelet. We were polite enough to wait until he was done to continue with the questions.

"So how do we kill it?" I asked.

"Do enough body damage, but it'll be stronger the more it's fed on life forces. Takes about three days to suck it all out properly. But the question is, how long can you hold your breath?" said Raven.

"Why?" asked Mandi.

"Because if it can get to your mouth and nose, it will literally suck the life out of you," said Raven.

"How does it remove the trophies?" I asked.

"The tail creates a suction and it just yanks them right out," said Raven.

"Lovely," said Mandi.

A customer across the way was screaming that there was a worm in his eggs. Raven flew over and landed on the guy's table. "Sorry, that's one of mine." Raven pecked into the guy's eggs and pulled it out. The guy, a trucker from the looks of him, took the cap off his head and swatted at the black bird who was a second faster. Raven landed on the guy's head. The trucker bellowed and tried to knock him off with the hat. Raven managed to yank the cap free with his beak, then flew to the other side of the dining area and proceeded to taunt the trucker.

"This might be a good time to go," said Mandi.

"Yep," I agreed, waving over the waitress for our check. I handed her cash, including a nice tip and told her that the trucker's meal was on us. I kept the receipt so I'd get reimbursed later. When we got to the door, I yelled, "Raven, we're leaving."

By which point, the trucker and a small group of friends were chasing the bird, trying to use table cloths as nets. They were having no luck catching him.

When we exited, Raven noticed and flew toward the already closed door. He flew to the waitress. "Hey, toots, could you get the door for me?"

The waitress obliged and Raven plopped the red cap on her head as he flew out.

Catching up to us, he landed on Mandi's shoulder.

"All you need now is the eye-patch and the peg leg," I said.

"You make a crack about my pirate booty and I'll slug you," she said.

"Wouldn't dream of it, except maybe over a bottle of rum. Raven, will you help us search for this Ahuizotle?" I said.

"I'll do what I can," he said and flew off. As gods go, Raven was all right, but by his nature got easily distracted, sometimes by shiny objects. We couldn't count on him to find this killer. We'd have to do it before it claimed another victim.

Turns out, we were too late. A high school senior, Ken Jerry, disappeared while looking for a place to make out with his girlfriend by the Tar River. The circumstances were the same as the other ten.

We mobilized the locals, used bloodhounds and helicopters, searched the shoreline and surrounding area. Even with Raven helping out we came up empty.

The hardest thing to do is accept when you've lost. At the end of day two, we knew we had lost Ken Jerry. All we could do was avenge him.

Mandi and I had a plan. Starting at the midnight that began the third day, we staked out the area of the river where Ken Jerry disappeared and waited for the Ahuizotle to bring the body back. We took up positions away from each other to have a larger area covered. We hid. A standard issue amulet is built into the DMA badge that helps keep us off the mystic radar, so all we had to do was stay quiet and hope it couldn't smell us. Raven was watching the skies.

Nothing happened for hours. I don't sleep well, but that is a plus on a stakeout. However, quiet time is not my friend. My mind tends to wander and where it goes is not pretty country. I remember everything that the seriál used my body to do – vividly, down to the feel, the taste and the smell. I see my dead and I get angry that I couldn't save them – and that I was used to kill them. The fury makes the adrenaline pump and that keeps me alert.

About twenty minutes after sunrise, I saw Raven circle overhead counterclockwise and then fly off toward the river. That was the signal. The Ahuizotle was coming from the direction Raven flew off in. I slid the safety off my gun and did a silent check of my equipment. I was as ready as I was going to get.

The Ahuizotle came out of some brush. It did look like a swollen fox with a massive tail, which was easily twice the length of his body. His tail was wrapped around Ken Jerry's neck, dragging his lifeless body. I waited until he was in the clearing before I stepped out.

I may never be in the movies, but I can act when I need to. I let out a startled scream and started backing away as if I was afraid. Like any criminal, it had to somehow deal with witnesses. I was betting it leaned toward eliminating them.

The murderous thing had a voice. "Going somewhere, human?"

I was still in character, so I cringed and trembled. "What are you?"

"Your death."

I fell backwards and the creature crept forward, leaving the corpse behind. When it got close enough, I threw a pocket ward circle into the air. It unraveled and fell, adhering itself to the ground when it touched. I was at the exact center. The life sucking thing didn't know what was happening.

"*Lockdown*," I intoned, activating the spell circle. The circle flared to life.

Too late, the life sucker tried to flee. It crashed into invisible containment walls.

"Mage!" It said the word as if it was a curse. I wasn't, but saw no reason to point it out. The pocket circle was standard issue. It was only moderately strong, meaning it would only hold a demon for a few minutes, but this thing wasn't in that class. Normally, it is supposed to hold a perp until transport or backup arrives, but considering all you have to do to avoid it is dive or jump out of the way, it's pretty limited with a conscious perp. And it's against regulations to use one to trap a perp and an agent inside. Usually pretty stupid too.

The thing wasn't sapient and it worked alone. We have orders not to kill anything vaguely human or associated with a major power to avoid political repercussions unless there is no other solution. Even the monsters have rights. We have a little more leeway with the beasties. This thing had a body count of at least eleven, so there was no way it was making it to trial. I'd catch hell for it, but this thing could escape or make parole and that would put any future victims on my conscience. I already had enough guilt so there was no way I was letting that happen.

I opened fire before it had finished speaking. Raven was right. The thing was fast. I only hit it with two of my first five shots and I qualify as an expert marksman. I used the distraction to put on my defensive gear.

The fox thing attacked, leaping on my chest as its tail went for my mouth and nose. It hissed when it realized I had strapped on a mini-air bottle of the sort used by scuba divers that covered both my airways. Its claws couldn't slice through my body armor vest. I managed to get a shot off that caught the tail. It didn't cut it off like I hoped, but it did take a good chunk out.

The next few minutes were target practice. I wounded it several times with DMA special issue ammo—each bullet was part silver, iron, blessed, among other things. There was enough in there to hurt most anything that could be shot, but the Ahuizotle had just finished feeding. It was at its strongest. Bullets weren't going to be enough and the life sucker knew it. It was playing with me the way a cat does a mouse until I ran out of ammo. Our ammo is expensive and we don't get issued much at a time. It laughed when my last clip clicked empty.

"That all you have, human?"

I holstered the gun. The Ahuizotle couldn't see me smile under my breathing apparatus as I pulled out two blades that resembled machetes. Each was forged in a very special way, and was lined with runes and other symbols of power. I often brag about certain skills I have from a misspent youth—I can hotwire a car, know how to pick locks and get past some alarms. The skills I have with a blade were even more finely honed into my motor memory and mind, but I have never bragged about them. Normally, I feel nothing but shame, especially about how I got them.

This was one time I was almost happy about it. The life sucker tried to run as it began to realize that I wasn't locked inside with it. It was trapped with me.

I attacked the thing that had slaughtered eleven people, most of them practically children. I saw the children among my dead and for the first time since my body was given back to me, I let my inner rage loose. I held nothing back. It was a relief and a release. A surgeon or Jack the Ripper couldn't have done better. Even the goddamned seriál would have been hard pressed to match me as I butchered the life sucker. Everything that had been inside me, eating my soul alive with guilt came out through those blades. There was nothing I could do to bring back even one of my dead. I'd trade my own life to make that happen, but that's never been an option. Death would end my pain, but that's the coward's way out. I owed my dead much more than that.

So I spent as much time as it took to make sure that this thing would never hurt anyone else ever again. When I stopped, there wasn't a piece left bigger than a coaster and its heart was a pile of bloody pulp.

It took effort to rein back in what I had let loose. When I finally came back to myself, Mandi and Raven were staring at me. I was covered in blood and gore, none of it my own.

"*Open sesame*," I intoned and the spell circle shut off.

"Holy worm guts," said Raven. "I never want to get you mad at me."

I didn't care what the bird thought. There were only two people whose opinion meant anything to me and of the two, Mandi's was the one I cared about more. How much had my partner seen? I must look every bit as horrible as the monster we've gone after.

"Mandi, I…"

"Did your job," she said.

"I look…"

"Fine, at least inside," she said.

"So empathically, I'm okay?"

"No, you're a mess, but somehow you're less of a mess than before," Mandi said.

"Are we okay?" I said.

"Yep, but if you think you're getting in the car like that you're nuts," she said.

"It's an agency car. What's the big deal?" I said.

"I signed it out. I'm not explaining to Sarge why it's a mess," Mandi said.

"What do you expect me to do? Walk?"

"Take off your clothes," she said.

"You just want to see me naked," I said.

"In your dreams," Mandi said. I wish my dreams were that simple and nice, instead of the sideshow of horrors that they are. Mandi sensed the change in my mood and shot me a sad smile, but no emotional mojo. I guess she figured I was okay.

I gathered the pieces of the life sucker thing into a body bag. I did a striptease that confused the bird and made my partner giggle, but it wasn't because of how I looked. The demon had enhanced all of me. We won't even talk about my episode with the fleshsmith.

After cleaning the blades on my shirt, I bagged the clothes in an evidence bag. I strapped back on my three holsters—two for the knives and one for the gun—and got in the car. I held my badge in my hand.

Leaving Raven to guard Ken Jerry's body, we went to take care of business. Back at our motel, I walked out of the car and into my room au natural without batting an eyelash, even when I passed a geriatric couple. I gave a simple nod and hoped for cataracts. No such luck. The wife took one look at me and gave a wolf whistle that cracked my partner up. I took a scalding shower, put on a clean suit and we went to see Chief Buster.

"We took care of the killer," I said, showing him the life sucker's corpse pieces. Then I told him where to find the poor kid's body. I don't know if we made a believer out of him, but he thanked us and shook our hands. Sometimes that's all you can hope for.

We stayed the night in Greenville and for the first time I can remember I slept through until the morning without waking up screaming even once.

CARDIAC ARREST

In my line of work, shootouts are terrible. Don't get me wrong. I'm sure shootouts are bad for anybody, but they tend to be worse for DMA agents. When the Department of Mystic Affairs gets involved, there are times when bullets won't do the job.

Mervin Ketzel was the perfect example. He had robbed fifteen banks in the last eight months. Ketzel didn't wear body armor and he had been shot at in six of the robberies, including two headshots, yet he walked away.

The FBI got called in and when they saw the video passed the case onto us. The sad part is we knew what was happening within seconds.

"He did what?" asked Agent Pine of the FBI. The profiler and I had a long history, although he didn't know it. I was once possessed by a demon. I did a lot of bad things. Pine brought me in. Although, it took everything I had to control the demon long enough to allow him to do it. We've worked together before and he doesn't recognize me. For one thing, I'm supposed to be dead. For another, a lot about me has changed, not the least of which is my face.

"Took his heart out and hid it," said Mandi Cobb, my partner. There's nobody else I'd trust as much to watch my back. To be honest, there's almost no one else I trust period.

"Then why isn't he dead?" asked Pine.

"Old time mage trick. Mystically remove the heart and as long as it remains hidden, you can't be killed," I said.

"Karver, tell me you're joking," he said.

I shook my head. "Wish I was."

"How does he survive without something to pump his blood?"

"Magic," said Mandi.

"If it's such an old trick, how did this guy learn it? Everything we've found out about him points to the fact that he's a geek with no real skills."

"Internet," I said.

"The internet?" he said.

"Yep. Some idiots posted several old grimoires online. With all the translation sites available, it doesn't take a genius to make the text readable. We've had a rash of these lately," said Mandi.

"So to stop this guy, we have to find his heart?" he said. I nodded. "How the hell do we do that?"

"And there's the rub," I answered. "The only thing in our favor is these people weren't bright enough to learn this on their own, so they don't think through the hiding of the heart part. We found one in a shoebox under the guy's bed."

"So does this heart thing mean you couldn't catch this guy if we knew where he was?" he asked.

"We didn't say that," said Mandi.

Pine wasn't one to ask questions out of idle curiosity. "Where is he?" I said.

"Bar outside of town. We have him under surveillance, but after seeing the type of punishment he can take, we didn't want to engage him near civilians," he said.

"Smart move," I said.

"Can we gas him or poison him?"

"Nope. Got to catch him like a rat in a trap," I said. "And since it's a guy, guess who gets to be bait?"

Mandi rolled her eyes. Pine chuckled a little too loudly for my tastes.

"Actually the gentleman lives an alternate lifestyle so he wouldn't be interested in the lovely Agent Cobb," he said. "He might, however, find the dark and brooding Agent Karver strangely titillating."

"You're kidding," I said.

"Nope," said Pine.

"Oh joy."

"I'm sure we can dig up a nice leather outfit for you," he said.

"Only if you want him to make me as a cop," I said.

Pine looked at me sideways. "I expected you to put up more of a fight."

I wanted to, believe me. There was a time where the thought of trying to entice a man by pretending to come onto him would have me heading for the hills. It was a lifetime ago, before I had been an unwilling party to perversions of a much higher caliber.

I shrugged. "I'm secure enough in my manhood, but I'm decking him if he even tries to get to first base." That's not so much homophobia as touch-phobia. Simple human contact was how the demon helped lull and lure our victims.

I discarded my suit in favor of blue jeans and a red t-shirt. That made up the extent of my undercover gear, along with my watch, which had a transmitter in it, and a small speaker deep in my ear canel where Mandi could feed me any information I needed. Usually she just used it to make wisecracks. My ankle sported a holster, but it wasn't like a gun of any size would do anything to Ketzel except tick him off. For the same reason, I left a pair of blades I normally carried under my suit jacket. The simple act of touching my back could alert him that I wasn't actually looking for love.

I was expecting the place to be a dive, but it was nice, in a middle-class suburb kind of way. I paused for a deep breath before going in. The seriál demon that took control of me had had its way with me in more ways than one. It modified my body in order to better do its dark deeds, including giving me an ability to attract people sexually and it wasn't limited to the opposite sex. I kept it reigned in most of the time. I let it loose before I walked in the door.

I played it cool, but all the covert stares made me uncomfortable. One of the not-so-covert stares was from Ketzel. I parked myself at the stool next to his.

The lady bartender was in front of me before I sat down. "What can I get for you?"

"Beer," I said. She poured and put it in front of me.

I pulled out a five, but Ketzel beat me to it. He had a hundred in his hand.

"Let me get that for you," he said, leering at me.

"That's my partner, the love machine," broadcast Mandi in my ear.

For obvious reasons I ignored her and feigned interest in Ketzel. "That's neighborly of you."

"I'm Merv," he said, putting his hand out.

I shook. "I'm Jim," I lied, but it sounded nice and normal, something I'd never be again.

"Well, Jim, tell me, did you hurt yourself when you fell from heaven?"

"Ask him if he's from Iowa. With a line that corny, he'd have to

be," said Mandi.

"Just a sprained ankle, but I stayed off it for a couple of weeks and I was fine. Got a nice settlement from the lawsuit too," I said. Ketzel laughed. "You going to ask me my sign next?"

Ketzel's cheeks turned red. "I've never been good at this kind of thing. I came into some money lately and I'm just looking to celebrate."

"Tacky lines and bragging about money you may or may not have isn't going to do it for me," I said.

"It's a lot of money," he said, raising his eyebrows suggestively.

"How much?" I said.

"According to the file, $1,875, 312," said Mandi.

"Enough to cover your naked body," Ketzel said. "Including some big bills for those special places."

"Ick."

"That's a lot," I said, leaning closer in feigned interest. "Look, I've got to be honest with you. I haven't done this kind of thing a lot. It would kind of be bad for me and my reputation in my community. I drove two hours to get here so nobody would recognize me. I have a fiancé, so I'm not looking for anything long term."

"Me neither," Ketzel said. "Honest."

"You can be discrete?" I asked.

"It's my middle name."

"According to the FBI file it's actually Lloyd," said Mandi.

"There is a motel not far from here."

I made a worried face. "They have security cameras and clerks." I took a deep breath. "I borrowed my future brother-in-law's van. He has it all set up to score with the ladies, so I figured..." I paused. "It has a bed."

Ketzel laughed. "Sure. It sounds fine."

"The van is ready and waiting," said Mandi. *"You're doing good, partner."*

We stood and he tried to hold my hand. I pulled away. "Not yet," I whispered.

"Tease," Ketzel whispered back.

"Don't forget to put a wiggle in your walk," teased Mandi as we went into the parking lot.

The van was a classic from the eighties. I walked to the back door and opened it. When a method worked, we stuck with it. The van wasn't as reinforced as an armored car, but Ketzel was not in the class of the Jade Hound. To make sure he didn't get suspicious, I went in first. He followed, a little too hot on my tail.

There was a mini-door connecting the front seat to the back. I opened it. "I got some protection up front."

He grabbed my wrist. "I don't need any protection," which was true enough.

"I do," I said. He pulled. The hidden heart made him strong, but I was no weakling. I yanked at the weak point between thumb and index finger.

Ketzel looked at my free hand. "You're pretty strong."

I didn't answer. I moved backwards through the mini-door. Ketzel lunged at me, but he was a second too late. I was through and had the door shut and locked.

"What the hell is this?" he screamed.

"Department of Mystic Affairs. Mervin Ketzel, you are under arrest," I said and read him his rights.

He started wailing and smashing into the walls and the partition, but the van was reinforced for FBI stakeouts and was bulletproof. Even the windows were built to withstand much more than he could dish out.

After a few minutes, he was tired and breathing heavy. He began to get the idea that he wasn't going to be able to bust out. "This is entrapment!"

"Nope, just plain, ordinary trapment," I said. "Now I think it's time for a heart to heart talk. It would help if you could tell us where yours is."

The interrogation didn't go great, but I really didn't expect it to. Ketzel knew he couldn't be seriously hurt or killed, just bored. He didn't even lawyer up.

We couldn't force him to take a lie detector test, not to mention polygraphs are unreliable. The only thing they're good for is intimidation, maybe fooling someone into thinking they'd get caught in a lie so they tell the truth. If someone can keep a cool head, they can beat a polygraph as often as not, despite what the experts will tell you. Back in my bad days, I beat one – twice.

We could, however, use Mandi's empathic powers to gauge his

reaction to questions. When we asked him where his heart was, he said, "I left it in San Francisco. You might as well give up. You'll never find it."

"I bet it's in Mobile," I said, which is where most of his heists were. Mandi's hand signal told me no.

"No, it's in Clearwater, the town where he grew up," Mandi said. Ketzel's pupils got wide, but otherwise showed no reaction, but Mandi's smile told me we hit the jackpot.

However, some jackpots are harder to collect on than others. Clearwater was a small town compared to New York or Boston, only forty thousand residents, give or take, but that left a lot of hidey-holes. We had a warrant for his parents' and sister's house, but found nothing.

We touched base with the local police department to alert them to what we were looking for. As it turns out, the Clearwater PD had already found the heart.

"Jon Gunther's dog dug it up in Van Dover Park about three months ago," the sergeant on desk duty informed us. "Our ME verified it as human. We've had no luck in finding the body it was taken out of."

"We actually have it," said Mandi.

The sergeant got that look cops get on their faces when they hear about a death. Somewhere between *that's too bad* and *not another one*. "Was it a local?"

"Used to be. It's now in custody awaiting trial in Philly at ESP Federal prison," I said. Eastern State Penitentiary is the Alcatraz for mystically inclined convicts.

The sergeant's eyes went wide. Our story was outlandish enough that he actually called the home office in DC to verify who we were. It's supposed to be standard protocol, but rarely gets done. Badges impress people; federal badges impress even other people with badges.

The long and the short of it was, at the end of the call, he knew we were the real deal and was trying to get his mind around it. "How is that possible?"

"Dark magic," I said. "Didn't you guys ever notice the heart was beating?"

He shrugged. "It only did it every couple of hours. At least I thought it did, but I knew it wasn't possible, so I didn't say anything."

And that was the advantage those who used the darker side of magic depended on. It doesn't exist, so don't speak up or you'll be judged mad. That's why the DMA has a policy of openness in regards to our cases. It's not our fault most people choose not to believe us.

"Where is the heart now?" Mandi asked.

The sergeant looked sheepish. "We don't know."

"Why's that?" I asked, not liking where this is going.

The sergeant seemed to shrink down on himself. "It kind of got lost."

"From out of your evidence room? How's something like that happen?" I asked, unable to hide the disapproving tone from my voice.

"Technically, it was out of our morgue. Doc Johnson, our ME, thought it was best if we kept it refrigerated. We only noticed it missing about a month ago."

"What did your internal investigation reveal?" I asked. I had been a Fed long enough to know it would have been checked out and the results kept in house, especially if the issue wasn't solved.

"Nothing. We don't have video surveillance. Never needed it before. The last person to have signed it out was Johnson, but he only works an eight-hour shift, Monday to Friday. Anyone could have gone in after hours."

"Great," I muttered. Without that heart, there was no way to control Ketzel shy of reinforced walls. One screw up at ESP and he'd get free. I doubt even my demon-carved good looks would get him in a trap van again.

"Why would someone take a human heart?" Mandi asked.

"Snack for some sicko?" joked the sergeant. "They say it tastes like chicken."

"More like dried pigs feet," I answered before I could catch myself. The sergeant looked at me oddly. "That's what I hear, anyway." It was a poor cover, not that it mattered. "It wasn't eaten or our prisoner would have died, ditto for being destroyed."

"I wonder if the heart itself has any innate magic?" asked Mandi. "The traditional spell doesn't give it any, but these mage wannabes tend to change things around. Think something could have empowered the heart?"

I shrugged. "No idea." I pulled out my cell phone and hit "1" on my speed dial. It wasn't technically a call, instead connecting me with a web address for the World Wide Spyder.

A man's face in a finned sci-fi helmet appeared on my screen. Spyder changed his appearance frequently. Being made of sentient electrons, it wasn't difficult. "Karver, what's up?"

I brought Spyder up to speed. "We need to find the site Ketzel used for his spell, see if there are any major differences between it and the traditional one. Assuming he was able to follow directions and any changes weren't made in his execution of the spell."

"I'm on it. I'll have the spell lab see what they can figure out."

"Thanks, Spyder." I hung up.

"Any unusual activity in Clearwater recently?" Mandi asked.

"Lots. About five people have dropped dead in the last month. Last one was yesterday. The lot of them from no apparent cause "

"Says who?" I asked.

"Johnson, the ME. At least on the first four. He's autopsying the fifth today," answered the sergeant.

Mandi and I exchanged a look. "The dead have anything in common or unusual about them?"

"Not that we've been able to find. Although, …" The sergeant hesitated.

"What?" asked Mandi. She had been exuding trusting emotions since we started the conversation. Now she turned them on high.

"I really shouldn't say anything, but the first victim was Rudy Daniels. Word was he was doing Doc Johnson's wife. Don't think he knew and since there was no evidence of foul play…"

"You let a man who was a suspect do the autopsy on what was possibly his own victim?" I said.

The sergeant shrugged. "He don't have an assistant. Nobody else was qualified."

The guy who's sneaking around with the wife of a man with access to a magically removed heart conveniently drops dead. I believe in things that go bump in the night, but I don't believe in coincidence. "I think we need to talk to your ME."

"He's in the morgue," said the sergeant. "I'll take you down."

For whatever reason, morgues are usually in the basement. Maybe it's because they're underground which is where we as a society put dead people. Or it could be because basements flood easy and nobody else wants their office there.

The Clearwater City morgue was pretty typical. A bunch of metal exam tables and about a dozen coffin-sized coolers built into the wall. It was also dark. No one seems to want to give these guys good lighting.

The man we had come to question was elbow deep in a body.

"Doc, got a couple of Feds here who wanna talk to you about the missing heart."

Johnson froze. It was half an instant, but I caught it. So did Mandi, who used a hand signal to let me know the subject made him very nervous.

Mandi turned to the sergeant and shook his hand. "Thanks for your help. We can take it from here." The cop stood, debating whether or not to stay. It would be easier if he didn't, so my partner sent out feelings of unease and revulsion, normal enough around the dead. It was enough to convince him to make his exit a hasty one.

We introduced ourselves. "Dr. Johnson, I was hoping you could tell us everything you know about the missing heart," said Mandi, again making with the trust mojo.

The ME paused and removed his gloved hands from the victim's chest cavity. "Not really much to tell."

I moved alongside him and peered inside. He had most of the organs from the abdomen out and weighed, everything, except the heart.

"Really, doctor? I think we all know that isn't true," I said.

"I really have no idea what you're getting at," said Johnson.

"Right," I said. "We can play it your way for now," which is when my phone rang. The ring tone let me know it was Spyder. "Excuse me."

"Doctor, when is the last time you saw the heart?" asked Mandi.

"When I put it in the freezer – Number 11. When I checked a month ago, it was gone."

"Don't you lock the morgue?" she asked.

"Sure, but there's a key upstairs on the pegboard. Anyone could grab it and put it back when they were done," suggested Johnson.

"Did they dust the key for fingerprints?" asked Mandi.

"I have no idea. Would that help catch whoever did this?" he asked.

"Probably not," I said, hanging up the phone. "Agent Cobb was asking to see your reaction." I put on a pair of gloves that went up to my elbows and moved over to the body. With the information Spyder had dug up I now had a working theory. It was time to test it. I reached inside the corpse.

Johnson freaked. "You can't interfere with my autopsy. You may destroy evidence."

"Don't worry. I know my way around a body." Better than I'd like to. "I can't seem to reach what I need. May I borrow this?" I said, taking the Stryker Saw next to him. I turned it on and he started screaming reasons at me as to why I had to stop. By revving up the saw, I drowned out his commentary. It was a good saw, cut through the ribs easily. I reached back inside and found what I was looking for. When I pulled my hand out, a shriveled human heart was in it. Johnson seemed shocked. I put it on the scale. "Interesting. I'm no doctor, but I think the average adult human heart weighs in the neighborhood of 300 grams. This poor guy was well over two hundred pounds, but his heart only weighs 87 grams. Agent Cobb, do you think this could possibly have kept this man alive? Ignoring of course the obvious state of necrosis it's in."

"No, Agent Karver, I don't think it could," said Mandi.

"That means that whatever killed him was able to kill his heart from the inside. Any idea what could cause that?" I said.

"I'm going to take a wild guess and say the very heart we came down here searching for," said Mandi.

"You are good. That call was from one of our fellow agents. Turns out our lab was able to test the spell Ketzel used. Due to a scanning error update on the part of the owner of the website, it combined the invulnerable spell with a decay spell. The missing heart can feed on the living variety. Unfortunately, that tends to kill their owners," I said.

"I don't have any idea what you're rambling about. You're talking crazy," said Johnson.

I didn't need Mandi's hand signals to tell me he was lying. "Johnson, it's over. The agent I was speaking to is already getting a warrant to search your home and car. We're going to find the heart."

Johnson smiled. He probably sucks at poker. "You won't find it."

"That's what the last guy said. Who knows? You may be right, but we will also be checking DNA. You yourself took the samples," said Mandi.

His smile got bigger.

"We will of course be double checking your samples against the prisoner's," bluffed Mandi. There was no way we could get a tissue sample from Ketzel without risking someone's life.

Johnson's smile lessened.

"And we will get a court order to have an outside examiner check the bodies of the four other deaths you've ruled natural. My guess is they will find hearts just like this one in each of them. Then we'll find proof that your wife was sleeping with Rudy Daniels. How hard will it be to convince a jury that you knew about it?"

"Like a jury would believe a magic heart could kill somebody," he smirked.

I walked over and wiped my gloves on his lab coat, then took each one off, making sure I snapped them, before putting them in his pocket. "Our jury pool pulls from those who not only believe in magic, but have it as part of their lifestyles." Not only humans are eligible for US citizenship. And all citizens can pull jury duty. "Plus we have nice footage of Ketzel being shot during the bank heists and not being hurt. Not to mention video of him walking around with a gaping hole where his heart should be. It won't take much for them to convict. And using magic in the commission of a crime makes it a federal offense. Using it to kill gets you the death penalty."

Johnson's smile was as dead as the people he worked on. He was looking for a way out. We gave it to him. "The Attorney General looks favorably when someone works with us to prevent further crimes. The incidence where the death penalty is asked for is greatly reduced," offered Mandi. It was the truth. The death penalty was saved for the more extreme cases, like demon-possessed serial killers.

Johnson didn't take our way and opted for the highway. "I want a lawyer."

"Fine. You're under arrest," I said.

There was another interrogation. This one was less successful than Ketzel's. Lawyers tend to have that effect, especially when they are pointing out little things like lack of a murder weapon, even if it was a heart. The search warrants hadn't turned up the heart, but we had gotten some trace evidence. It would be some time before we got lab results. We had put the locals on sifting through video surveillance. We had video from a bank camera that put Johnson near the second body twenty minutes before it was found. With luck, there'd be more. According to Spyder, the heart had to be close to each victim, touching them in order to kill them.

Mandi pulled me outside. "I think he's good for the first four victims, but not the fifth."

"Why?" I asked. "Guy lives right behind him. Maybe he played his music too loud and that upset the good doctor."

"No. I felt total shock when you pulled that shrunken heart out," she said.

"It was an unusual thing for a Fed to do," I suggested.

"That wasn't what the shock was at. When we asked him about Rudy Daniels he felt smug and vindicated. The next three he felt significant guilt, but no personal attachment. The last, Randy Leon, there was much confusion. The other guilt seems to be eating him up. When we asked him where the heart was, there was more confusion. My hunch is he ditched the heart and someone else found it."

"And that someone used it to kill Leon," I said. "Think he'd be stupid enough to stash it in his backyard?"

"The dogs smelt human remains in the backyard and there was freshly turned dirt there, but nothing we were able to unearth," said Mandi.

We ran a check on priors on Leon. He had no convictions, but he had been charged with molesting his ten-year old son. The kid was removed briefly from the house, but when the investigation turned up nothing concrete and the kid recanted, they sent Randy, Jr. back. Kids tend to be curious. If he saw Johnson bury something, he might have dug it up. And Leon was found dead in the boy's room.

School was still in session and Randy, Jr.'s mother had sent him in rather than have him underfoot while she was planning her husband's funeral – her words. Not a pleasant woman. I didn't have trouble believing she'd let Leon hurt her son. I'd like to bring her in, but there was nothing to charge her with. Nothing we could prove anyway. I felt for the kid. We offered to let her come with us when we questioned her son. She declined, signing a consent form rather than make the ten minute trip to her son's place of learning.

When we got to the school the metal detector went off, but our badges got us in to see the principal. We told her we were investigating the death of Andrew Leon, Sr. and showed her the consent form. She called the mother to double check, then, led us out to the playground. Randy, Jr. was a small kid and three larger ones were pushing him around like a pinball.

When they saw the principal, the trio of bullies stopped. She seemed happy to leave it at that, letting them move a short distance away.

"You aren't going to reprimand or suspend the bullies?" I asked.

The principal smiled the type of grin that I remembered adults in authority using when I was a kid to try to beguile someone. "It's just boys being boys."

"Odd attitude for a principal to have, especially toward a kid who just lost his father," I said. "Which tells me one or more of the boys has a parent you're afraid of professionally."

Mandi brushed an imaginary something from her eye, our signal for bullseye.

"I'll thank you to leave the running of my school to me, Agent Karver," she said with all the indignity that she could muster. It was considerable. "Room 101 is empty if you'd like to talk to him there." Then she left in one of the finest huffs I'd ever witnessed.

Mandi walked over to the kid. "Hi, I'm Agent Cobb, this is Agent Karver. We'd like to ask you a few questions."

"What'd you do now, Andrew?" asked one of the bullies mockingly. I hate bullies.

"It's none of your damn business. Now drop and give me twenty," I said in my best disciplinarian voice.

"You ain't a teacher. I don't gotta listen to you," he said.

"Really? I just saw you assault Andrew. How about I arrest you for it? Andrew wouldn't even have to testify since you were dumb enough to do it in front of two federal agents," I countered. I knew it'd never hold up, but I wasn't about to take crap from a 'tween. He did the push ups.

The classroom was a kindergarten room. The class that usually occupied it was on a field trip.

"We'd like to ask you some questions about your father's death," said Mandi.

"Okay," he said meekly.

"How did he die?" asked Mandi.

Randy shrugged his shoulders. "I don't know."

I sat down across from him. "Randy, was he trying to do something he shouldn't?" Mandi was broadcasting trust at full blast.

His nod was barely a movement, but the tears spoke volumes.

"You dug the heart out of Doctor Johnson's lawn and had it in your room, didn't you?"

Another nod, this one less meek.

"When he tried to hurt you, you used the heart, didn't you?"

A third nod. "It told me to. Not in words, but with pictures inside my head. My father told me he'd kill me if I told, but I finally did. Then he told me he'd kill my Mom if I didn't say I made the whole thing up. I said I did, but I didn't. I had to lie."

"I know," I said and I did. Mandi didn't bother with signals. Tears were falling down her cheeks from the kid's inner turmoil. He did this for a woman who couldn't be bothered to take an hour out of her day to be there for her son.

"Am I going to have to go to jail?" he asked.

"Even though you killed him, it is pretty clear it was self-defense. You saw Doctor Johnson bury the heart?" I asked.

"Yeah," he said.

"Would you be willing to say that in court?" I said.

"I guess."

"I think I can get the Attorney General's Office to make you a deal if you are willing to testify. You won't have to go to jail. And you'll have to give us the heart. Is it a deal?"

"Yeah, sure."

I made a quick call and got lucky. They wanted Ketzel more manageable ASAP so in less than five minutes we had the deal.

I told Randy and he led us to his locker. The heart was in an insulated lunch bag, wrapped in aluminum foil. I put it in a warded evidence bag being careful not to touch it.

"So that's it?" he said.

"Yes," said Mandi.

"I have to go back outside?" he asked, obviously reluctant to go.

"You worried about the bullies?" I said.

"Yeah."

"You were planning to use the heart on them, weren't you?" I said.

"I thought about it. It wanted me to. I brought it to school, but I didn't bring it out on the playground, even though I could tell it wanted to go."

"You did the right thing. Let us help you out with your problem. The only way to stop a bully is to stand up to him and beat him down," I said.

"I can't fight," Randy said.

"Anyone can fight, it's just a matter of doing it well," I said and proceeded to give him a very abridged self-defense course.

"Now you are going to go out and take care of them," I said.

Mandi gave me a questioning look. I whispered in her ear. "Give him confidence." With her powers, it would be easy. "Give the bullies so much fear that they won't be able to fight back. Make it enough so they won't forget it."

"You sure about this?" she asked. "They're just kids."

It was my turn to nod. "Randy had enough inner strength to save their lives by not feeding them to the heart. He stood up to something dark and far more powerful than he was and he beat it down. Randy saved those bullies' lives. Least he deserves is to not spend his days in fear because of it."

"I guess someone who did that would deserve a break," Mandi said. From the look she gave, she wasn't just talking about the kid.

We went back out. "Go over there and demand an apology."

Randy did. They laughed and pushed him. Mandi upped his confidence and poured on their fear. The fight was lopsided, lots of hitting and pushing, but when it was done the three bullies ended up running away in front of all their other classmates. One wet his pants.

Randy ended up being brought into the principal's office. Mandi and I went in with him.

"Agent Cobb and Agent Karver, this is a school matter and doesn't concern you," she said.

"Wrong. We're witnesses. You allowed the first attack to go unpunished, so Randy had to defend himself the second time," I said.

"I have three boys blithering and crying in the nurse's office. He had to have done much more than defended himself," said the principal.

"Actually, he didn't. We saw the whole thing and it was self-defense. If we have to file a report, that's how we would write it up," said Mandi.

"And the fact that had the principal dealt with the earlier fight instead of ignoring it, this wouldn't have happened because those boys would have been suspended," I added.

"Being law enforcement agents, we'd be obligated to send copies to the local police and the school board of course," said Mandi.

"Maybe even the State Board. And any attorneys Randy's mother wanted brought into the matter," I added.

We got glared at, but the principal caved. Mention lawyers to an administrator and they quake worse than if they were facing a hungry vampyre. Needless to say, things went relatively well for Randy. He was suspended for the next three days—it was mandatory in the school's zero tolerance policy—but he would have had one of those days off for the funeral anyway. We also managed to get him some counseling with the school shrink. He was hurting and needed it.

His mother was called. She asked if we could bring him home. We stopped for ice cream on the way.

When we got to his home, I handed him my card. "If you need anything, just call. I don't want to hear you turned into a bully like those other kids."

"I won't," he said and went inside walking a little taller than he had earlier that day.

"Think he'll be okay?" I asked my partner.

I wanted to hear "yes." What Mandi said was, "Maybe." She's honest to a fault sometimes.

Once we showed Johnson the heart and told him we had an eyewitness linking him to burying it, he started to sweat. He broke in less than an hour, even with the lawyer. The heart offered him the chance to kill his rival, but he didn't have to take it. It seems the heart suggested the other three victims and Johnson had gotten a guilty rush from the murders. They were people who had done Ketzel wrong and Johnson figured they'd never be traced back to him.

Ketzel was more manageable after that. We tried to get a court mandated mystic surgeon or fleshsmith to put the heart back in, but he got a lawyer who contended that it was a violation of his civil rights to have surgery forced on him. The matter is pending an appeal. Until then, they had the heart in a separate section of ESP with electroshock pads on it. Ketzel gets out of line, his heart gets a jolt. The invulnerability doesn't pass to the heart and anything done to it causes him some serious discomfort. If he gets the death penalty, they'll probably have to administer the injection directly into his heart. That or hit it with a sledgehammer. Considering all the loved ones his victims left behind, there won't be any shortage of people volunteering to do it.

There certainly wasn't for my execution.

SNIPS AND SNAILS

This definitely qualified as the oddest undercover assignment I'd ever had. Usually tucking babies in isn't something an agent of the Department of Mystic Affairs has to do unless the child is his. Or hers. The odds of me ever having kids are somewhere below slim and barely above none. The seriál demon that had once possessed me had done a lot to change my body. Who knows what that would do to a child, let alone having me as a father.

I held the baby awkwardly. Every time I hold an infant I remember the one whose brains were bashed out with my hands. The demon may have been the one killing, but I could still feel and see everything. The scent of talcum powder still makes me want to retch.

The baby was puckering his lips. I turned to my partner Mandi Cobb. For the sake of this assignment, we were husband and wife.

"I think he's hungry and we're out of formula," I teased. "I think we'll have to go back to basics."

"Karver, that's not happening. Best I can do is nuke some frozen pizza or a burrito," said Mandi.

"That's not exactly baby food."

"I'll run it through the blender," she said.

"I think little Gus isn't ready for that. It would probably be best to put him to bed. Want to kiss him goodnight?"

Mandi looked at him and made a face. "He's an ugly baby."

"You are supposed to be his loving mommy," I said. "And who knows what is watching us?"

"Fine." Mandi planted one on Gus' forehead.

"C'mon little guy." We were in the master bedroom of a three bedroom in the sleepy town of St. Albans, Vermont, which stank of lavender candles. The room not the town. There had been a rash of baby kidnappings, the children taken right out of people's homes. The first had been a toddler over eight months ago. Then over the last six weeks, six more children were kidnapped, all of them under a year old. The patterns of the taken were too similar for it not to be the same perp and it stank of magic. Sad that it took this long for the locals to call the DMA in, but that's about par for most places. Nobody believes in magic until it's staring them in the face while standing atop a pile of corpses.

I put the baby in the crib at the foot of the queen-size bed, putting the soft blue blanket over his shoulders. "Goodnight, little Gus. Do you need your diaper changed?"

Gus gave me the finger. I laughed, which was rare enough. The DMA was not going to risk a baby's life, so Gus got the job. Normally he looked like a man, although the type of man varied. Easy enough to do for a changeling. A baby was a bit more of a challenge as it required more control to maintain a smaller form, but he was up to the task.

"Sleep tight. Don't let the bed bugs bite." One of Gus' fingers briefly transformed into some sort of insect which he put on his throat and moved like it was attacking his jugular. I put a pacifier in his mouth. Gus made a face but began to suck on it. It wasn't just to help his disguise. It had a charm that would make him appear human to any high level mystic and shot up to three very small, but potent, bullets if he bit down on it.

I turned and Mandi was already in bed, dressed in a flannel nightgown. In theory I should get in the bed next to her, but I don't do well with intimate physical activity, even the casual kind. The seriál always used it to lull victims into a false sense of security and allowing myself that comfort when my dead were denied it always makes it feel like my insides are ripping apart.

Mandi sensed what I was feeling, child's play for an empath.

"Coming to bed, snookums?" teased Mandi.

It shouldn't have bothered me. We had actually spent the night in a bed before in a purely platonic sense. When I was first recruited from death row, my nightmares wouldn't let me sleep for more than an hour at a clip. Once we were partnered, she'd stay with me, using her propathic abilities to let me feel more than guilt and revulsion at what I had been forced to do. "I have some reservations."

"You could have mentioned it earlier. I hope it's Italian. Now I have to change my outfit."

"I'm actually quite shocked by the outfit," I said.

"Really?" she replied.

"Oh yes. I figured with your reputation, it would be something a little more scandalous." Mandi is only a little less promiscuous than I am, and I haven't been intimate since the demon was exorcised. For her it has something to do with being able to sense everything a partner is feeling. Putting on a game face doesn't cut it with Mandi. "Where's the leather? And the spikes?"

"All my good stuff is at the cleaners," Mandi said.

"Do you have to pay extra to get all the stains out?" I asked.

"Naw. My cleaner has a fetish. He does it for half price."

"Truth be told, I'm a little hesitant to get into a bed next to you. Instinct might kick in and you'd attack me. I might not be able to walk for a couple of days."

"You have nothing to worry about. I prefer good looking men." She patted the empty side of the mattress.

I went into the bathroom and came back out with a can of Lysol.

"What's that for?" Mandi asked.

"I figure it'd be safest to spray the sheets down. With all the action you go in for, you've got to have just about every STD going, maybe even a few new ones caused by the others breeding together."

"I think you're thinking about toilet seats not bed sheets," Mandi said.

"Nope, but I have that covered too. Since we have to share a bathroom, I got the industrial strength disinfectant, the kind they use in leper colonies. And a blowtorch."

There was snickering from the crib. Mandi threw a baby bottle at Gus. "Anything more from the peanut gallery and when I get you, I'll make it look like SIDS." The baby bottle flew back out and hit Mandi in the shoulder, a tiny bit of formula squirting out on her sleeve.

"Honey, is that anyway to talk about our son?" I teased.

"What do you mean ours? You actually think you're the father?"

"I had hoped. Whose is it then?" I said.

"Not really sure. Either one of the State U football team or a sailor."

"Just one?" I said.

"Probably, although which one would be hard to narrow down. It was around the time of Fleet Week."

"At least you were doing your best to give the troops something to fight for. And test to see if they learned anything from watching those VD films."

The bantering had the desired effect. My mind was dragged out of my cesspool of a past and I was able to climb into my side of the bed.

Mandi used the remote to turn on the TV. We had rigged all our security systems into the cable system. Any alarms would override the programming and flash on the screen. Plus we had another agent outside, blending into the woods on the neighbor's property, not so close to scare off the kidnapper. We were on communications silence for obvious reasons. We needed to capture or follow the perp in order to find the missing children, hopefully before it was too late. It's the kind of thing that is always in the back of your mind, but you try hard not to think about because it erodes focus and hope.

We had put all the other families in town with children three and under in a large safe house outside of town. Luckily, it was a small town and it was only forty-seven families. In a larger city, I'm not sure what we'd do. There were enough wards on that place to make sure nobody got in, so if the perp was looking for another baby, we were literally the only game in town.

I put my hand out. "Using the remote is a man's job, you know."

"I do. If you see one let me know." Mandi opened a hardcover book, pretending like she was reading it. In reality she was checking the gun that was hidden inside.

The show that was on was one of the true crime variety. I don't much care for them. Too much like work. This particular one made me break out in a cold sweat.

"Although eventually given the electric chair, the serial killer known as The Carver left a trail of bodies across the country, leaving law enforcement baffled."

The last thing I needed to do was watch a documentary on my victims. I remember each of my sixty-three dead without any outside help.

Mandi felt my emotions go south and handed me the remote without a word. The next channel was a cooking show, which didn't help. The demon employed many different methods to dispose of bodies. With enough spices, any meat can be made to taste good. I gagged as my pallet remembered tastes best left forgotten.

I put on some mindless sitcom and no one spoke for the next hour.

Stakeouts are generally a whole lot of boring. At least on this one we had the TV.

We hadn't discerned enough of a pattern to figure out when and if the kidnapper would strike. The best the locals were able to piece together was sometime between eleven and three.

In the cases when parents were awake, something had put them to sleep. There are dozens of common and hundreds of not so common ways to knock someone out. We had made preparations for several.

Sadly, we hadn't made the right ones. Neither Mandi nor I remembered falling asleep, but we woke with her curled in the crook of my arm. I don't know about my partner, but I lay there for a couple of minutes in that state between waking and sleep before I realized what had happened. It was very peaceful. That ended once I realized that there was light coming in the window and the TV was off. We had tied the TV and the security systems into our own generator, so even if the line was cut the TV should have stayed on. That meant magic was employed to kill the power.

My jumping out of bed caused Mandi to roll out and pull her gun out of her book holster.

"Gus is gone and the power's down," I said.

Mandi tried her cell and got nothing. DMA issue phones have a power source that can last half a year on standby. It also meant we couldn't use the phones to track the pacifier. It wasn't a good sign.

Mandi stripped off the night gown, fully dressed underneath, and we ran outside, but there were no telltale signs of an intruder. Our next stop was the woods where we found Hunter snoring in a tree.

Shouting didn't wake him, so Mandi threw a pinecone, which smacked him right in the head. That did the trick a little too well as Hunter dropped out of the tree in a shower of leaves ready to attack. Mandi sensed the change in his mood in time to move; only Hunter was faster. Luckily, so was I, thanks to the demon's reengineering of my body. Even with my enhanced strength and speed, I was no match for the Celtic god of the forest. Fortunately, I didn't have to be. I made like a linebacker. It felt like I had tackled a tree. Hunter didn't move, but he stopped his attack on Mandi.

I landed on my butt, leaves crunching beneath me. "Not a morning person, are you?"

"Sorry. I'm not used to someone being able to sneak up on me in a forest, even one as pathetic as this one. How did you find me?" he asked, offering me a hand up. I took it.

"We just followed the sound of cutting wood," I said.

Hunter looked around, his eyes narrowed and sniffing at the air. Smelled like a forest to me. "No one is harming any of the trees in this vicinity."

Not all gods keep updated on the affairs of man, let alone slang. Rumor has it that Hunter showed up for his interview with Uncle Sam in clothes that hadn't been in fashion since the Renaissance. Still, being a god looks good on the resume and he had a reference from Paddy Moran, the owner of Bulfinche's Pub. Even Sam treads carefully around him. Hunter had become the best manhunter in the agency.

"He meant you were snoring," Mandi said.

"I don't snore." Hunter seemed generally offended. "Wait, I was on watch. I shouldn't have fallen asleep. Why, once I went a year and a day without so much as blinking when I was hunting…"

Mandi cut him off. "Herne, did you see who took Gus? The cells are down, so we can't use the tracker."

His eyes went wide, answering the question even before he spoke. "No, but I will find him."

Dropping to all fours, Hunter sniffed the ground and ran over to the house faster than a deer, using a gait that should have been awkward, but instead was oddly graceful.

"I smell magic. The kidnapper went this way." Hunter rose to his feet and sprinted off into the woods that became Vermont state land. We followed as fast as we could, but trailed far behind.

Hunter had stopped at a small cave, practically covered by shrubberies and other growth. I wouldn't have found it easily had Hunter not been standing in front of it.

"Are the children in there?" asked Mandi.

"They were taken in there and have not come out."

"So why are we not going in after them?" I asked, but as I stood there I answered my own question. My demon altered senses picked up a low hum, like a mosquito-sized bee buzzing at the base of my skull. "There a nexus in there?" Hunter nodded. "Any idea where to?"

"Faerie." That helped explain the tech outage. Faerie is not very kind to anything more modern than transistors. Without the right shielding, even automatic guns might not work for long. And there are a lot of things there that love to steal human children. It's a dark tradition. "I am persona non grata in Titania's kingdom and that particular Faerie Queen is not known for her mercy." Hunter stood silent for a moment. "Did you know that I returned to Earth at her request? I was sent to kidnap my own son, a boy I didn't even know I had. I betrayed Titania for my child and she has not forgotten. Corny..." Short for Cornelius. "...is the reason I became a DMA agent."

"To help protect his country?" I asked.

"Nothing so noble. I had to pay child support. I have grown to love Corny and if someone dared take him, I would move heaven and Earth to get him back. I will do no less for the parents of these missing children. Nothing is worse than losing a child."

Just then, Mandi's cell beeped. The face of the World Wide Spider appeared on the tiny screen. We must have moved outside the range of the spell. "Are you all okay? We've been trying to reach you for hours."

"The perp got Gus. Hunter tracked them to a nexus," said Mandi.

"Any idea where it leads?" asked the electric agent.

"Faerie."

"Which kingdom?" asked Spyder.

"Unknown," said Mandi.

"Hold on," said Spyder.

Spyder was undoubtedly already talking to Deputy Director Sarge Winston or Uncle Sam himself to get further instructions.

He came back on less than three minutes later. "Since we do not know which kingdom, Sam says you have to stop. DMA incursion into certain territories of Faerie would violate US-Faerie treaties."

I grabbed the phone before Mandi could respond. "Hasn't Spyder gotten back to you yet?"

Mandi caught on pretty quick. "Not yet."

"Maybe the Faerie magic has affected the technology again," added Hunter. "Every minute we waste waiting possibly puts the children and Gus into greater danger."

"Then we better go now," I said.

Mandi put her phone down on a rock. "I'll leave this here in case they can track it and send backup." Hunter and Gus were normally partnered with Mox and Trevor, a lava demi-goddess and vampyre, respectively. At the very least they'd come looking for us if things didn't go well.

"Guys, I'm right here. I can hear you. You should be able to hear me," said Spyder. "Sam ordered you guys to stand down."

"You two better turn off your phones to protect them," I said. When you turn them back on it should give our backup at least a couple of minutes to track us before Faerie magic stops them from working too."

"Are you sure you want to come with me?" said Hunter, ignoring Spyder's yells at us to listen to him. "Depending on where the nexus opens up, it could go badly for both of you."

"We aren't letting a fellow agent go against an unknown enemy without backup. We aren't going to abandon Gus and if we don't join you, those six babies may be forever lost. Let's go," I said.

The cave was tiny, damp and at least fifteen degrees cooler than the air outside. We crawled in the dimness on our elbows over dirt and stones until we reached the end of the cave. The nexus took on the appearance of what was nearby, in this case, the cave wall. When Hunter got close, it glowed ever so slightly, turning the cave an odd combination of orange and blue. The buzzing increased, making it feel like the tiny bees had relocated their hive to the back of my head. Hunter crawled through the muck to the nexus first, Mandi went next and I took up the rear.

Going through a nexus is a lot like going on a roller coaster that races through a Jello lake that has a live electrical wire hanging in it. Despite the hard ride, we emerged unscathed on the other side. We appeared to be in a second cave, not much bigger than the first. This one smelled of mold and something sickly sweet. I could see no light at the end. Hunter crawled ahead of us, pausing briefly at each fork in the cave to sniff long enough to make a decision. We followed him as quietly as we could crawl.

"I should have brought knee pads," mumbled Mandi.

"Don't you have a spare set in your purse?" I teased. We were both shushed by Herne.

Twenty minutes later we emerged into moonlight, but Hunter had us hide in the mouth of the cave, before he disappeared into the woods. In the distance, birds did some nocturnal cawing. I didn't hear or see Herne return until he was fifteen feet away from us.

"You can come out now," he said, taking off his DMA issue cap and folding it in his belt. Antlers, far too long for the hat to conceal naturally, appeared.

"We in enemy territory?" I asked.

"Yes, but not the one I was worried about. The kidnapper stopped hiding his scent once he came through the nexus," he said.

"He? You know who did this?" asked Mandi.

"No, but I know what he is – a bodach."

"What do you know about them?" Mandi said.

"They appear generally as winged old men and steal children," he said.

"What do they do with them?" I asked.

"Rumors vary – slaves, servants, meals and mates are popular ones. We may be too late for some or all of them."

"Why too late?" I asked.

"I felt it when we came through the nexus. Time flow here is faster than on Earth. Our friend Murphy calls it quantum geography. How much faster, I can't say. It may only be a few hours or it may be centuries. If he let the children live, they may be dust by now," said Hunter.

"And Gus?" asked Mandi.

"He's gentry. For Faerie, this area is rather magic poor, but he's a native. He'll be older, but still alive if the bodach didn't kill him because of the deception. They went this way."

We trailed far behind the forest god who swung and leapt from the trees like he was in a jungle movie.

"I feel like I should be wearing a loincloth," I said.

"Please spare us," Mandi said. "You'll frighten the natives. Besides you haven't even loosened your tie."

"Clip on." But she knew that. With what we do it doesn't make sense to wear a potential noose around your neck.

When the brush got too thick, I resorted to pulling out one of the two blades I keep holstered on my back. They were both slightly bigger than a machete and specially made to be effective against some of the things we have to deal with and arrest. It seemed almost disrespectful to use them to slice through the undergrowth, but there was no other way to keep up. And since our automatics were as likely to fail as shoot, I figured I was better off armed than not.

At one point, we lost sight of Hunter before we realized that he had clawed markers in the trees for us to follow. It didn't take long for me to wish I had traded in my dress shoes for a pair of hiking boots. I had mud stains up past my ankles on both legs and feet.

When we finally caught up, we saw that Hunter had found the kidnapper, so we stayed back in the shadows to help if he needed us. He was confronting one of a pair of identical old men, each of whom had what looked like wasp wings. They were surrounded by six boys who looked to be stair step kids, probably about two years apart. The youngest looked two and the oldest twelve. The boys were confused, probably because there were two identical bodachs giving them conflicting orders. One was obviously Gus. The other was furious and had an arm around the neck of a boy who looked about eight and held a knife to his throat.

Hunter was trying to diffuse the situation without the boy being harmed. The bodach's eyes were glazed over with fury. Blood was already trickling down the hostage's neck from where the blade tip was being pressed against it.

"You can't have them. They're mine!" he screamed.

"You know the boys all have families who miss them and want them back," reasoned Hunter.

"Their families don't care, don't care at all. The only one who cares is Brody Bodach." Got to love it when a perp talks about himself in third person. "Their families don't care if they are gone."

"That's not true. Parents miss their children terribly," said Hunter.

"All parents miss their children?" asked Brody Bodach.

"Yes. They would do anything to get their kids back."

"LIAR! I will kill my brothers before I let them go to be with those who don't love them." The blade pressed in deeper and the eight-year-old boy whimpered.

"Nobody has to get hurt here." Hunter had his hands out at his sides, attempting to look harmless.

"Too late. Brody Bodach was hurt and nobody cared."

"If you really care, you won't hurt these boys," reasoned Hunter.

"Killing them will stop them from getting hurt. Death is better than pain."

There were days I agreed with Brody Bodach, but that was a personal preference. As near as my math and age estimation skills could make out, the kidnapped kids had already lived through about two years here for every week they were gone from back home. They'd been through enough without this psycho slicing them.

Gus had positioned his disguised self between Brody Bodach and the other five kids. We signaled him to distract the perp, which he did by moving away. Mandi started broadcasting trust to the kids and we motioned them to be quiet then got them away.

"You okay getting back to the nexus?" I asked.

Mandi nodded. "You cut a big enough path." I didn't have to tell her I was going back to help. I handed her my second blade. She raised an eyebrow. I didn't easily give up my knives. In addition to having traces of iron, silver and other substances mixed in with the metal to make sure it hurt most things magic, there were runes carved in them. In the right hands they could do more damage to a monster than an Uzi or a hand grenade. In the wrong hands… well let's just say I have too much personal experience regarding what happens when a knife is in the wrong hands.

"Just in case." We didn't know if the charms on our guns would be enough to let them work and who knew what else was out there. "Be careful."

"You too, partner."

By the time I got back to the standoff, Gus was in his natural gray form and Brody Bodach was yelling at Hunter and the changeling that they had scared his brothers off. His arm was still around the one boy's neck and his knife still at his throat.

I had learned from body sharing with the demon how to move quietly and I could be damn near silent when I needed to be. Gentry can be deceptively strong. I'm stronger than the average man, but trying to overpower this guy in Faerie would be a losing battle, so disarming was most likely a losing proposition.

I just had to convince him that giving up was the best option, which meant I had to make not letting the kid go seem more frightening.

He didn't realize I was behind him until I grabbed hold of both his wings with one hand and put my blade up against the base where they attached to his back.

"You hurt the kid and I'll slice off your wings and burn them." Magic is funny. If the wings weren't destroyed, he might be able to reattach them.

"Those wings are mine. Billy Bodach gave them to me when he

died. Without them, I not Brody Bodach, just plain Brody. You let them go!"

"I will if you let Jordan go." I took a risk and a guess based on when the kids were taken that this one was Jordan Allen. "Please, before he gets hurt." I didn't need to see the front of the boy's neck to know he was bleeding more. The alkaline smell was enough.

The thought of losing his wings seemed to have calmed his anger. "You promise not to hurt brother Jordan? Or Brody Bodach?"

"You have my word."

The perp let out a huge sigh. "Fine." The kidnapper dropped his knife and let go of Jordan. "Brody Bodach too tired to fight any more."

I cuffed him with DMA issue restraints. The charms built into the handcuffs would hold this guy easily enough. I put away my blade and the three of us took Jordan and the perp back to the nexus. Actually, Gus turned into a horse and the kid and I rode him while Hunter took Brody Bodach.

We got there as Mandi was prepping the kids to go through.

I got off Gus the horse and moved toward my partner. She handed me my blade and I sheathed it. No need to upset the children any further. "How are they doing?"

"Not good," said Mandi. "Very few of them even remember their homes in St. Albans or their families. It's almost like we're the ones kidnapping them."

"Great. How are their families going to deal with this?" I said.

Mandi shrugged. "The best they can I hope. We are going to have to call in counselors to be on hand for the reunions."

"Let's worry about that after we get them home," I said. The longer we spend here, the more time passes for the families back home. Every minute would make returning harder on the kids.

Hunter made a rope from some vines and linked us all together, to make sure we all emerged one after the other instead of hours or more apart. He went through the cave first, carrying the baby boy who was stolen last week who was now a toddler. Mandi followed next and helped the four year old who had been kidnapped two weeks ago. The six and eight year olds were next, with me behind them taking Brody Bodach. The ten and twelve year olds were in back of me. Gus took up the rear.

We had been gone less than a day, so mere minutes had passed in

St. Albans when we emerged.

Spyder had been waiting and watching on the phone. "You're back."

"We have the children," said Hunter.

"But those aren't babies," Spyder said.

"Quantum geography," Hunter replied.

Spyder cursed. "I'll have a counselor team en route for the families within the hour."

"We are going to take all of you back to your parents and families. We're also going to help you get adjusted to life here in St. Albans. It will be difficult at first, but you will all get through it," Mandi said, broadcasting a mixture of courage and optimism.

Brody Bodach was weeping. "What about me? Will I see my parents?"

"What are you talking about?" I said.

"Billy Bodach took me like I took my brothers. When he died, he gave me his wings and told me my parents had long since forgotten me and had a new baby to replace me. He told me my parents didn't care enough about me to come for me, so I came here to save my brother from our uncaring parents. But I had forgotten where they lived, so I couldn't be sure where my brother was, so I took all the babies to save them. But their parents cared enough to have you come for them. Why didn't you come for me?"

"Dear God," Mandi gasped. I looked at my partner. The first kidnap victim had been a three-year-old boy named Brody Dannan. Eight months gone in Faerie at two years a week would make Brody a sixty plus year old man.

"Is he for real?" I whispered.

"Emotionally, yes. We very possibly are looking at Brody Dannan," whispered Mandi, her face ashen.

"Damn." This old man was really a poor kid brought up by some psycho fey. There's no telling what horror the bodach did to him before he died and passed on his power, transforming the poor kid into something other than human. I felt sick to my stomach. This guy was as much a victim as the kids. It didn't excuse the kidnappings, but it did make my heart bleed for him.

By noon we gathered the parents in the local high school auditorium. Mandi stood up and explained what had happened to their children. My partner used no emotional propathic sugar coating, so her explanations were greeted with anger and accusations of government manipulation. Like I've said, most folks didn't believe in magic, even when it was staring them in the face. It took Gus going through a host of transformations and Hunter levitating all the parents before they even considered believing.

The kids had a long road ahead of them. The DMA was providing adjusted identification paperwork to account for the boys' rapid aging. The two- and the four-year-old, even the six-year-old would be better off in the long run. The others couldn't read or write, or even converse on any normal topics for kids their age. All the parents had a tough road ahead of them. The DMA ran DNA testing to make certain, but even that wasn't enough for one single mother. She was sixteen and now her infant son was ten. She ended up signing over her parental rights to the Allens who took in the boy along with Jordan.

When most of the parents and kids left with their individual counselors, we still had Mary and Joe Dannan left. They were confused.

"Where's our Brody?" Mary asked.

We explained that he had been gone so long that he had aged much more than the others. We explained what little information Mandi had learned in the past few hours regarding what Billy Bodach had done to Brody. It hadn't been pretty and his intellect hadn't developed much beyond that of a pre-teen. And she told them it probably never would.

Finally, we brought Brody out to meet them. We dispensed with the handcuffs, but made clear what we would do to him if he tried to do anything to harm his parents.

Mary Dannan saw him and began to sob on her husband's shoulder. Joe Dannan's jaw dropped and showed no sign of rising again any time soon.

"Mom? Dad?" said Brody, wrinkled and tiny, easily twice the age of his own parents, neither of which was able to look at him for long.

"This can't be our boy," said Joe.

"I remember we had a cat named Tickles. Mom, you made me a chocolate cake for my birthday. Dad, you had a red car and used to carry me around on your shoulders."

That only made Mary Dannan sob louder, but she was looking at her son. "He looks like my father."

"Grampa Dave?" said Brody.

"Oh God," she sobbed and ran out of the room.

"We'll need to see the results of the genetic testing. We have to know for sure before we go any further with this. I'm sorry, Brody," said Joe Dannan, barely able to speak between his own weeping. He ran out to follow his wife.

Brody watched as his parents left him alone. His tears didn't start until his father's last footstep faded away. "I thought you said all parents love their children."

"They do love you. It's why they're crying," said Mandi.

"And sometimes love ain't enough," I said. Mandi glared at me, but that didn't make what I said wrong. And sugarcoating things would only make it worse for Brody.

The fact that society failed Brody didn't excuse his crimes, but it did allow him to plea bargain to be put in a psychiatric center for the mystically damaged. It was referred to as Ringvue, mainly because people had trouble speaking its real name.

The testing came back positive on everyone. All the families tried to make a go of it, except for one. The love the Dannans had for their radically aged son wasn't enough for them to reconnect. Sometimes I hate being right.

To their credit, the Dannans visited Brody once a month and called every week, at least until his mother actually became pregnant again. When she started to show, Brody had a bit of an emotional breakdown and his parents stopped coming.

They still call occasionally, but it's just not enough for Brody. His shrinks are trying to work through his many issues, but it's an uphill battle. I don't know if he'll ever be released back into society and that's probably safest for everyone that way.

Mandi and I visit him whenever we can. Apparently, we're the only ones. Poor guy's so desperate for human contact outside the asylum that he actually asked if he could call us Mom and Dad. Mandi explained how it wouldn't be appropriate. I just reiterated that he had enough issues without having me as his father figure, although this was probably the one case where it wouldn't mess up the kid any worse than he already was.

GET A ROOM

I knew things were going to be bad when Sarge's briefing started out with the fact that two past presidents had wanted to nuke the place. Zachs had been the one recommending it, but luckily cooler heads prevailed and Tennessee was prevented from becoming a nuclear wasteland. Like Sarge Winston, Zachs was a Deputy Director of the DMA, but he was in charge of Black Ops. Not a nice guy or one I trusted. Zachs had planned to play the mystic terrorist card with the last administration, but Sam found out and expressly forbade it. He was too worried they might actually consider a nuclear option.

The place was a nexus. It wasn't just a door between worlds like the one we followed Gus and Brody Bodach through. The one at the Scarlet Star Motel actually attracted evil. People disappeared, dead bodies were a mainstay, and the place had more demonic possessions than Congress. The last was a personal sore point with me – the possessions, not Congress.

"Sarge, there has got to be some other way to destroy the place short of a suitcase nuke," I said.

"Karver, if there was we'd have done it already. The place basically behaves like an evil magnet. Unfortunately, it's not the only one. The only upshot is these types of places tend to attract a lot of the really bad mystic stuff within a couple hundred mile radius, limiting it to a single location. We've tried to monitor the place, but the owner has filed complaints. Since the courts, even with the Patriot Act, don't usually accept evil magnet as an excuse for surveillance warrants, our hands are tied."

"So why are we going in now?" asked Mandi. My partner was trying to get a read on Sarge, but the elder thing in the ruby fused to his chest always made it hard for her to gauge his emotions. It annoyed Mandi because it made her feel the equivalent of being blind or deaf.

"Because someone else is going to try to do what Zachs has been wanting to do for decades," said Sarge. Both of them were Deputy Directors of the Department of Mystic Affairs and were as different as night and day, Sarge being the day.

"Someone is going to nuke the place?" I said.

"Worse. They're going to try to undue the binding that holds the nexus together and let loose all the evil that has been collecting there for millennia. The initial release will result in an explosion that will devastate Tennessee every bit as thoroughly as a small nuke. What will happen after is unclear, but it won't be pretty."

"So how are they going to do it?" asked Mandi.

Sarge frowned. "That's the problem. We don't know. The two department psychics that got the information are in comas from the overload, but were able to communicate what they found to a third."

"Will they be okay?" asked Mandi.

Sarge shrugged and dropped his tough veneer, letting his concern shine through. "Hopefully. This kind of fallout happens a couple times a year. The fleshsmith is making sure their bodies are fine and the psychic shrink is working with them. According to what little intel we've got, the forces in the nexus surge and wane. Tonight it's going to surge to its highest point in a long time, which will make the unbinding easier. It also means the pull of the metaphorical magnet will be at its strongest."

"So we're going down in force?" I said.

Sarge shook his head and sighed. "There's been a threat against the President and various members of Congress. An attack of a mystic nature is supposed to happen at the State of the Union Address tonight. Every free field agent has been pulled to cover security."

"Except the two of us," I said.

"Can't Sam do anything?" said Mandi.

"He did. You're it. The mobilization at the Capitol is on direct orders from the President in conjunction with the Secret Service. He doesn't feel the impressions of two unconscious psychics are worth a hill of beans and Sam had to yell and scream for ten minutes to free up the two of you."

It's a sad state of the country when the President ignores the advice of Uncle Sam himself. "I guess the lives of the people in an entire state don't measure up."

Sarge sighed. "Karver, it's politics."

"Sad. You'd think he'd show more concern for a state that he won in the last election," said Mandi.

"Why didn't Sam pull two of the heavy hitters?" I asked. In

terms of firepower, my partner and I are pretty much lightweights. Other agents can change shape, shoot fire, bend steel, and the like. Compared to that, being able to sense and affect emotions and being a little stronger and faster than the average guy and sensing magic in play is not a lot of use in a spell fight. We pretty much depend on hardware for our muscle.

"One of the psychics mentioned the two of you by name," said Sarge.

"Maybe he dated Mandi and was having a flashback," I said and got slapped for my trouble.

"You only have a few hours. I suggest you get moving," said Sarge. "Here's the file on the Scarlet Star Motel. Read it on the way."

The file was the size of a phone book for a major city.

"I can't believe this much goes on in the middle of nowhere," I said.

"Easy to get away with it. Local law enforcement probably keeps hitting their collective heads trying to figure out why so many victims are being killed," said Mandi, who was driving as I went through the file.

"Surprised they're still in business," I said.

"There are people who are looking for a place like this to do business. Others are probably just tired or unwary travelers. There isn't much else around the area," she said, fixing her hair in the rearview.

"You look fine." Better than fine actually. Mandi was wearing a red dress that reminded me in no uncertain terms that my partner was a gorgeous blonde woman. Believe it or not, I don't think of her that way most of the time. Things would get too complicated. I don't have many friends since I stopped being the possessed serial killer The Carver and became Agent Karver. The details are still classified, but a handful of agents know. Most avoid me like the plague. Mandi doesn't. I'm not going to risk losing that. "Why did you get all dolled up?"

"We need to be undercover, so why not as a honeymooning couple?"

"But why the dress? Honeymooners can wear jeans and t-shirts," I said.

Mandi wiggled her eyebrows and smiled. "I was slotted to guard some senators' wives after the State of the Union at some gala. The department picked up the tab for the dress since it was for an assignment. It cost over a grand and looks great on me. This way, I technically still needed it for an assignment and even Zachs won't be able to give me grief."

"Well, if the bad guys are male, you should be able to provide a distraction just by taking in a deep breath," I said.

"Which will make you window dressing, as usual," she said.

"Looks like room nine is over the center of the nexus. Intel says they don't typically rent that room, meaning they have some idea of what is going on. My guess is that is where it will go down." But it was only a guess.

"Any hints in there about what we should expect?" Mandi asked.

"According to these files, practically anything," I said.

"So in other words, the usual," she said.

"Pretty much," I answered as we pulled up to the place. The sun was setting in the distance and it bathed the Scarlet Star in red light, making the motel look like it was covered in blood. Not a good sign and in this business you learn to pay attention to signs or you end up hurt – or worse. If it wasn't for the mood lighting, the place would have looked like any other run-down motel.

We pulled the car in by the registration office and stepped out. Mandi put her arm around me and I managed not to cringe. Mandi read my emotions and pulled back a bit. I still had problems with casual physical contact. One of the other reasons I tried not to think of my partner as a gorgeous woman. Carnal thoughts tended to bring back bad memories. A lot of people died at my hands. Plenty of them were lured to their lives' end with some use of sex. Sometimes it was even part of their end.

I can still see the faces of all of my dead. My head knows the seriál demon was doing the driving, but my gut still feels responsible. Sarge assures me I have the lowest body count of any seriál possessed on record. My dead are only double digits. It wasn't uncommon for a body count to reach the thousands. Sarge credits my willpower with minimizing the death toll and managing to get caught. I helped make sure I got convicted, rejected any appeals I could and got sent to the electric chair. Now I have a job hunting down monsters like I used to be.

Mandi knows me better than anyone, sometimes maybe even me. She even knew how to deal with my emotional cringing. Her hand slid down until it was holding my hand.

I didn't have to tell her it was better – benefits of working with an empath. The office door was locked. I shook it a couple of times to make sure. My finger pressed on the call bell, but no one answered. I peeked through the half open blind slats and saw a head peeking up from behind the counter. I banged on the door.

"Go away! We don't have any more open rooms," said the man.

"He's lying. And he's scared," Mandi said.

I reached for my badge with my free hand, but Mandi stopped me.

"Let me try something," said Mandi, pulling the hem of her shirt up so she could fix her stocking. The head of the man behind the counter raised up high enough so I could make out shoulders. His eyes were locked on my partner's leg.

Mandi leaned forward and I started to feel certain stirrings in my loins. It wasn't that the view was turning me on. Mandi was—quite literally. In addition to her empathic skills, she was a propath. All that means was that she could project as well as sense emotions. Right now she was projecting what would be best described as horny. The red dress was cut low enough that my partner's leaning over was the equivalent of waving a jug of cold water in front of a thirsty man in the desert.

The clerk came out from behind his hidey-hole and made his way cautiously to the door. Mandi's from the South, but only tended to have a strong accent when she was trying to get something from someone. Mandi thinks it helps distract people so they don't realize what she's doing. Tonight her dress could do that by itself.

"Excuse me, sugar, but I need a room for the night," Mandi drawled.

"Trust me, you don't want to be here tonight," he said.

"Why not, sweetie? This place looks just darling," she said.

"Looks can be deceiving. Working here long enough, you pick up on things and the signs are bad tonight. You'd be better off staying at my place," he offered with a leer through the parted blinds.

"That's such a sweet offer. What's your name?"

"Jim," he said.

"Jim, why don't you open up the door so we can discuss matters?" suggested Mandi.

Jim hesitated and looked out the door. Only Mandi and I were in sight, so he opened first the lock, then the door.

He seemed embarrassed by his fear. "Normally, I don't lock up for any reason. It's just every few years…"

"You don't have to explain yourself to me, sweetie," said Mandi, wiggling her way through the narrow opening. When I went to follow, Jim tried to shut the door in my face.

"Sorry, sir, but the office is closed," he said.

My foot prevented the door from reaching the jamb. I let down my nice face and looked at him with the one I try to hide. Even Adin the fleshsmith couldn't get rid of that one, no matter its shape. Jimbo flinched. He's not the first one to look away from my eyes. I'm told the windows to my soul are more than a little grimy. "I'm with her."

I shoved, the door moved, and in I went. Jim muttered quietly under his breath, but locked up quickly.

The pegboard behind the counter was almost empty, but only almost. "Looks like you still have three rooms available."

"Actually, room eleven is a crime scene. The sheriff hasn't released the room back to us."

"What happened?" I asked.

"The owner doesn't like us to discuss... active investigations."

"How about room nine?" I said.

Jim literally jumped and put his hand over the peg. "No, it's reserved. This is the spare. They're already in the room. This is for the rest of their party."

"Fine, then give us room seven," I said.

"The same people who rented nine asked us to not rent that room out. They wanted privacy."

"No problem there. We just got married over in Pigeon Forge and we'll be making enough noise of our own that we won't notice anyone else. Isn't that right sweet pea?" I said.

Mandi leaned over the counter, giving Jim another view of spectacular peaks every bit the equal of the nearby Smokey Mountains. "He just got out of prison and he's raring to go."

"Then I guess my place is out," said Jim, not bothering to hide his disappointment.

Mandi nodded. Jim got a little pissed that he wasn't going to be getting any tonight and his protective intentions toward Mandi faded away. "Fine, take room seven."

We paid him cash and got the key.

As we exited, I noticed a woman dancing in the moonlight out by the pool. She wasn't wearing a leotard, a tutu, or even a top hat and tails. It was something much more unusual.

"What does she have tied to her body?" Mandi asked.

My sight and sense of smell were better than my partner's. "Raw meat, mostly pork chops."

"Why the hell would someone..."

The answer was hiding in a nearby hedge with a video camera. He wasn't watching the meat dance, but only had eyes for the filthy water in the pool, which was filled and cluttered with junk that ranged from a cracked big screen TV to a baby carriage. There was a dark stain that looked red on it.

"According to the file something big, bad, and carnivorous lives in the pool. It seems to be able to vanish when search teams have gone in after it," I said.

"It's got to be tough or desperate to live in that. Maybe bush boy's trying to sacrifice her to it."

"And maybe a ritual sacrifice is how the binding will be undone. Let's go ask him," I said.

We drew our weapons and split up so we approached the hedge from opposite angles of the parking lot. We were both pretty good at stealth movements, but we could have been doing the tango for all this guy cared. His gaze never left the murky water.

We got within five feet before I piped up. "Federal agents, sir, please put down the camcorder. Miss, please step away from the pool."

The woman listened, but the man got agitated and leapt up. "You don't know what you are doing. This is in the name of science."

I aimed my gun at him.

"I'm sure it is, sir. Are you familiar with the science behind the firing of a bullet? I can assure you it will work just as well if you're not. Please put the video camera down," said Mandi, who also had him in her sights.

With a nod, she indicated she had him under control. I moved toward the woman. "Take off all that meat and please explain why you are acting like bait."

"I told you, this is in the name of science. I'm a professor at a major university," boasted the man.

"Steve, you're a teaching assistant at a community college," said the young woman.

"Brenda, shut up!" Steve ordered.

"Steve promised me an A if I did this," said Brenda. "I offered to sleep with him, but he turned me down. I think he's gay."

"I am not gay. I have a girlfriend," said Steve.

"Who nobody has ever seen," replied Brenda.

"Why did you have this woman act as bait?" I asked.

"I have an eyewitness account of a dinosaur that lives in that pool. I drove three hundred miles to get here. Video of it would make my career," Steve said. A look at Mandi told me he thought it was real.

"What career?" countered Brenda.

"What eyewitness?" I asked.

"An Elvis impersonator. I bought him a couple of rounds in Vegas and he told me how it ate his wife," said Steve.

"Ate his wife? You never told me this thing ate people, you son of a bitch!"

I hesitated to point out that she was wearing raw meat. I decided not to ask why she thought she was out there.

Brenda started tearing meat off where it had been duct taped to her and threw it at Steve. One steak clipped him pretty good on the side of the head. Steve managed to catch or scoop up most of the projectiles and ran toward the pool, tossing bits of meat in as he ran.

"None of you are going to take away the greatest discovery of modern times away from me!"

"Stop!" Mandi said.

"Freeze!" I tried.

Steve didn't listen. He seemed like more of a crackpot than a real danger, so neither of us really wanted to shoot him. Of course, he had been willing to risk a woman's life for a video clip, so he wasn't exactly a nice guy.

We moved after him slowly, so not to spook him. The shallow end of the pool was dry. Steve jumped in, still throwing meat. The would-be cryptozoologist slipped on the slick surface and landed on a pile of spheres.

"Who the Hell left all these beach balls here?" he screamed.

Crap. They didn't look like beach balls. "Steve, move away from those. They aren't beach balls—they're eggs."

Steve's eyes went wide. He picked up one of the eggs and started doing a geeky happy dance. "This is even better than video. With this, I'm set for life. I'll be hired with tenure!"

There was a small ripple in the deep end and a reptilian creature burst out of the water. Alligators can move at speeds of 30 miles per hour for short bursts. This thing would have left them in the dust. The pool surface was basically a ramp and there was nothing between man and beast.

Mandi and I started firing an instant after the creature made it out of the murkiness, but it was too late for Steve. It was too big for normal ammunition to do much more than annoy it. The reptile had ripped Steve's legs in a single bite and had quickly started to swallow the rest of him.

My partner and I switched clips to explosive rounds we brought with us from the DMA armory. We took out the creature's legs and torso with some well-aimed explosive blasts. Brenda screamed behind us.

It wasn't long before the creature was lizard-burger. Mandi moved to check Steve for signs of life and I covered her. Large bodily harm does not always equal dead in this business. Mandi looked up and shook her head. The only fame Steve was going to find would have to be posthumously.

Mandi and I looked at each other.

In the field there were always gray areas where agents had authority to take out a clear and present danger, even if that danger is not an immediate one. The two of us had a simple policy on the matter. We forgo questions and investigation. Too many people have died in the pursuit of answers when the monsters under the microscope get free.

We made a decision without having to speak. We turned our guns on the future threat. A few well-placed rounds obliterated the eggs. Oddly, the pool was undamaged.

"Is he?" asked Brenda as we walked toward her.

"You won't be getting your A," I said.

Mandi moved to the student's side, attempting to comfort her. "Brenda, do you have a car?"

"We came in Steve's. I don't have the keys," Brenda said.

I went over to the lower half of the corpse and checked his pockets. I took out a key ring, wiped the blood on Steve's pants and tossed them to Mandi.

"Brenda, I need you to get in that car and keep driving until you get home, understand?" Mandi said, handing Brenda the keys.

Brenda nodded. "What about Steve?"

"The local authorities will take care of his body and contact his family," Mandi said. I was already on the phone making arrangements. The dispatcher didn't seem surprised when I told him where we were.

"Is there going to be a cover story?" she asked.

"No. Tell everyone the truth," Mandi said. We both added in our own minds *for all the good it will do*. The DMA doesn't cover up the truth. It's against Sam's policy. People just choose not to believe this kind of thing unless they see it for themselves.

Brenda drove off. We debated on waiting for the locals to secure the crime scene until screams roared out from inside the motel. I felt the surge of magic. Inaction was not an option. We sprinted across the lot. I made it inside ahead of my partner. The yelling was coming from two sources – rooms five and eight. There was so much dark magic lingering I couldn't pinpoint anything. The noises from five were louder and more frantic, so I kicked in that door first, my gun drawn.

Inside was a sight that made my eyes sore. It was like a bondage convention for people who couldn't afford entire suits of armor, so they bought just the underwear instead. A dozen men and women had wrapped themselves in chains, spikes and other metal implements of destruction, including shackles and handcuffs.

My actions barely slowed down the orgy. I had to give them credit for focus. A few heads turned my way and a woman who could have been mistaken for a dominatrix Tin Woodswoman came up to me. "This is an Iron Ring soiree. Invitation only"

"Federal agent. We have reports of illegal activity. I heard screaming," I said. I scanned the room. Everything appeared to be consensual. "Sorry for the interruption."

"If you have time later, please stop back. Consider this your invitation. We always have room for one more. The more the merrier and I like a man who's forceful and knows what he wants," she said.

"I'd probably need a can opener and it's in my other suit," I said.

"Cute, forceful, and funny. A triple threat. I'd love to wrap you in a chain mail loincloth and some gladiator gear."

"I appreciate the offer, but I'm on duty."

"Pity," she purred. "I could teach you an entirely new use for your gun."

"I'm sure that would be against regulations," I said. Not to mention if they ever have to run tests on my weapon, I couldn't imagine how I'd explain how her DNA got there.

I exited quickly, closing up behind me. Mandi had already kicked in the door on number eight where there was undeniable illegal activity that ran the gamut. Forget the drugs and the underage drinking. There was human sacrifice by naked men in ceremonial robes that we were too late to stop. A young man lay splayed naked and filleted in a spell circle. A small wormhole was open and green tentacles were already slithering out, followed by a body larger than a king-sized bed. It looked like the illegitimate offspring of a slug and an octopus.

"Freeze, DMA agents," ordered Mandi, her gun drawn. She aimed between the eyes of the man holding a large bound book. Experience teaches that during a summoning the person with the book is almost always the leader.

A couple of the other men tried for the window. I cocked my gun. It's amazing how well such a small sound carries because all of them stopped in their tracks. "When she said freeze, she meant everyone. Over in the corner. Any of you move, you die. Comprende?"

To the last, they nodded and obeyed rather meekly. Of course the appearance of an otherworldly monster can have that effect on people who really didn't think the summoning would work and just realized that they might be there as an appetizer for the new guest.

Mandi's gun hadn't wavered from the leader. "Return the extra-dimensional now."

"The book doesn't say how," said the leader. He was far more whiny than I was used to.

I grabbed the tome from him and a piece of paper fell out. It was a phonetically written out version of a spell from the book. The original was written in Greek. "You obviously didn't translate this. Who did?"

The leader pointed at the butchered kid. "He was a language major."

I looked at the cover. It had three Greek omega symbols. These bozos weren't masterminds. They were idiot frat boys. The monster was standing still as if waiting for instructions. That happens with some of the less intelligent summonees—they can't do anything but destruction without marching orders, which would have to come from the Tri-Omegas. It would be best for us to keep them off balance so they didn't realize that. Fortunately, they didn't strike me as the types who were at college on academic scholarships.

"Why'd you kill him?" I said.

"We didn't plan on it. The book kind of took over."

Sentient tomes are to be avoided at all costs. It's in the DMA agent handbook, which hasn't achieved self-awareness, at least as far as I knew.

"Anyone else know Greek?" Lots of shaking of heads, none of it in the yes direction.

I looked at my partner and she joined the head shaking parade. "Not enough to risk a spell."

"We'll have to drive it back into the wormhole," I said and fired an explosive round that splattered a tentacle. The creature took a step back, but I felt the book hum. The hole between worlds collapsed on itself. The omega slug shrieked. I would have said it was loud enough to wake the dead, but the butchered kid would have proved me wrong. If I had picked room eight first maybe he'd still be alive. Judging by the look of the wounds, probably not, but I might have been able to abort the summoning.

"Any other bright ideas?" asked Mandi.

"I have one or two," said a voice inside my head that seemed to originate from my gripped palm. *"Why don't we try them?"*

Great. The damn book was trying to take possession of me. Better me than my partner. I've had some experience in this department and a lot of time training to make sure it never happened again. "Ain't going to work. You're an amateur and you're badly written."

Mandi looked at me with a pretty good idea of what was happening. "You got it under control?"

I nodded. Despite my bravado, it was an effort to fight the book off, but it wasn't as strong as a demon. And I wasn't exactly weak-willed. Then again, neither was the book.

"Attack them," ordered the book and the omega slug obeyed. A green, suckered tentacle snaked out, wrapping itself around Mandi's waist. A moment later, the agent in the red dress was lifted off the ground and dangled above its maw.

My partner was too close to the thing for me to use explosive rounds—the risk of shrapnel hitting her was too great. Time to go old school. I reached for one of my blades, grateful and ashamed of how comfortable I was getting in using them. I aimed and tossed, nailing the thing in the right eye.

Mandi fired off two explosive rounds at the slug. One hit its hide with minimal damage. The second hit its wounded eye and blew off part of its head. Slug slime splattered everywhere. The frat boys weren't going to be getting their room deposit back.

Mandi signaled me to toss her my second knife. I did. Of late, throwing our weapons back and forth was a skill we'd perfected on dull stakeouts where we had hours upon hours of time to kill.

Mandi didn't have my finesse with a blade, but she could handle one with a decent amount of skill. The knife sliced through the appendage she dangled from and she dropped to the floor, managing to land in a crouch. She backed away firing. Angry and hurt, the slug's thrashing tentacles lashed out and smashed the windows and part of the ceiling. More damage was done to the room than the slug.

"We need to hurt it more," Mandi screamed.

The frat boys had the room set up like a party, including the typical range of refreshments. Otherworldly creatures often tend to have similar physiology to their Earth counterparts, which gave me an idea. I lifted a keg and threw it at its face. All living things, even monsters, have protective instincts. The omega slug caught it with an unwounded tentacle.

"Down!" I yelled, grabbing the end of the mattress and flipping it up while pumping an explosive round into the keg. Mandi and I took cover behind it. The Tri-Omegas were on their own.

Beer and keg shrapnel rained everywhere. Where the omega slug was hit by the beer it was melting, just like the garden variety.

Mandi took another keg, pumped it to the max and cut off the nozzle. She had her thumb on the hose and was spraying the omega slug's wounds. The creature was slowly dissolving. I picked up a case of beer and started shaking, then opening each in rapid fire succession and lobbing them at the creature. I got a few right down its gullet and it started melting from the inside out. The explosive rounds did a lot more damage now – made more of a mess too.

A few minutes later the slug was omega goo.

"Shall we try again with something a bit more durable?" said the book. It had remained quiet through the attack, all the while trying to use the distraction to worm its way past my defenses. *"Open me and I will guide you to the right pages. I'll even help you sound out the hard words."*

"I don't think so. Besides, it's all Greek to me," I replied. I took a warded evidence bag out of my pocket and dropped the tome in. I heard its psychic screams as I closed the seal. "It was overdue."

Mandi shook her head. "Best leave the wisecracking to me. You can help me with the rest of the perps."

Thus far, the Tri-omegas had remained relatively docile while we took out the monster– easier to see who won before choosing sides. Neither of us forgot that this bunch were guilty of murder, illegal summoning, and conspiracy. The fact that the book may have influenced them would probably get them a relatively light sentence, but the truth of the matter is even possessed you can fight. That leaves the possessed with some level of guilt to live with every day – at least those of us with a conscience.

I admit that based on how easily they were cowed I expected them to go quietly. I was wrong. Children of privilege believe the rules don't apply to them, especially the ones they break. Once the obvious danger was gone, they felt brave enough to fight back against two mere mortals.

Three of them pulled guns. One dimwit even pulled a fraternity paddle.

That left us with few options, but none of them good. We still had explosive rounds loaded. The round gave a concentrated blast, which cut down on injuries to bystanders, innocent or otherwise. Problem was if a human was hit in the torso, it didn't leave much by way of a corpse. Besides, I have enough deaths on my conscience and I could somewhat relate to what the Tri-omegas had been through. Of course, in their case everything was of their own volition, which knocked my pity level down to zero.

"Karver, get out of the room," Mandi ordered, putting her weapon by her side.

I raised an eyebrow. The frat boys raised their guns.

"Neither of you is going anywhere," said the leader. That's when Mandi hit them with an emotional whammy that was the equivalent of a love potion. The Tri-omegas had eyes only for her. Hell, I had trouble to not swoon when I looked at her. Mandi pointed with her eyes toward the door. I raised both eyebrows, asking if she was sure. She repeated the gesture.

I trusted my partner, so I left quietly. As soon as the door shut behind me I heard the Tri-omegas screaming, but they didn't sound very upset about it. In fact, they were all very happy noises.

I opened the door once I heard Mandi reading them their rights. All the Tri-Omegas were on the floor glassy-eyed and smiling stupidly. My partner had the comforter held up in front of her as a shield. All the men had gotten off a shot of a very different kind, even the ones without guns— easy to tell since all their robes were hanging open.

"I didn't know that orgasm was considered an emotion," I said.

"There are plenty that lead up to one," she said, putting a pillowcase on each hand to handcuff the nearest Tri-omega.

"I didn't know you could do that," I said, cuffing anther one to an old style cast iron radiator. "Must make one hell of a party game."

"I don't do it often. You won't believe the amount of paperwork involved in explaining why a suspect has ejaculated during an arrest. Sarge gives me grief, but we already had a confession and an attack on federal agents," she said. "We still aren't done here. This was just a summoning, not the unbinding we were sent to stop." Mandi immobilized another set of wrists. "And I'm out of cuffs."

I had just used my last pair as well, which left us with six more unbound perps. "How long will they be like this?"

"A few minutes at most," she answered.

I grinned. "I know where I can get more cuffs. I'll be right back."

I rushed across the hall to room five, knocking this time. The Tin Woodswoman answered. "Change your mind? I have the loincloth all ready."

"Actually, I was wondering if I could borrow a cup of handcuffs." I said, explaining the situation. The Iron Ring members were thrilled to help, so long as I guaranteed the return of their shackles and promised a letter verifying that they had been used by the DMA to restrain actual suspects. The idea was a turn-on for the lot of them and I soon had more restraints than I really needed. I returned all the fur-lined ones.

As I began my way back to room eight, I observed a man in a two thousand dollar suit leading a woman who looked like she shopped out of *The Little House on the Prairie* clothing catalog. They were moving toward room nine. I ducked back to listen and caught the tail end of their conversation.

"So you'll let Frank go once I go inside?" she asked.

"Your boyfriend will be free to leave, the money he owes us will be forgiven," said the guy in the suit. "We won't hurt him anymore. It is very generous of you to offer yourself in his place."

"I love him. I'd die for him," she said and they went inside.

A hunch that my gut knew was right knocked me upside my head. Everything fell together for me. I knew how they were planning to undue the binding on the malevolence in this place. Evil deeds couldn't do it or it would have been undone long ago by the horrors done here. They needed a pure act, maybe an act of love. Probably made up some cock and bull story about gambling debts or the like, weaved a yarn about this Frank guy being about to die for it. They would have gone to the woman asking for the money, an amount that she didn't have and couldn't get. Then the messenger told her the next time she saw her honey would be in a body bag. The girl probably offered her life for his on the spot and the scumbag agreed and brought her here.

I'd bet my spare clips that the boyfriend is in on it. The girl seemed like the quiet and dowdy type. She probably hasn't had a lot of dates or social outings, which made her naïve and the perfect mark. This Frank is probably so good looking it hurt for this girl to look at him. It wouldn't take much for her to fall in love with him. The scum undoubtedly showed her the time of her life, all the while setting her up to surrender hers. I'd seen it before, up close and personal. I wasn't going to let it happen this time.

I ran across the hall and tossed cuffs to Mandi and explained my theory as we secured the rest of the Tri-omegas.

"So we need to stop her selfless act," said Mandi as she secured the last frat boy. She returned my knife. I cleaned them both off on a clean towel and tucked them back under my jacket in their sheathes.

"If we go in there with our guns blazing, she'll probably dive to protect him. We'll finish their work for them," I said. "We need to make her take back her offer. How do we make that happen? You got another trick up your sleeve?"

"Emotional manipulation probably wouldn't help. This girl offered herself willingly. She would have to rescind the selfless act the same way," said Mandi, her brow creased in thought. A moment later, she smiled and I almost saw a light bulb go on over her head. "I've got a plan. Follow my lead."

We ran across the hall. Mandi put away her gun and motioned for me to do the same. I switched to a more traditional clip first. My partner waved at the door and I kicked it in. It was re-enforced and took three kicks before it gave. I stepped aside to allow Mandi to rush in. A man I took for the boyfriend was tied to a chair. He looked like he had been roughed up, but it was all a show. The pooling of blood in the bruises was superficial, only one blow each. When you work someone over for real, you hit the same spots over and over. A group of men in suits stood around with clubs and large blades. Not to brag, but mine were bigger.

They didn't know how to react. If they confronted us physically, there would be a fight, maybe blood spilled. That would ruin the noble sacrifice motif they were going for and maybe prevent the binding from being undone.

Mandi ran over to the tied man and started kissing his face. "Oh Frank, what have they done to you? Are you okay? I came as soon as I heard."

The girl's face dropped. "Frank, who is this woman?"

Mandi turned and looked at her like she was nasty something on her shoe. "I'm Frank's girlfriend. Who the hell are you?"

"I'm his fiancée."

"Frank, you told me you broke up with her!" said Mandi. "You might as well go home, little girl. I mean, what do you think he really wants? You? Or this?" My partner twirled in her red dress motioning toward all the good parts with her hands.

"Sue, I don't know this woman," said Frank, pleading with his face for her to believe him. And Sue actually seemed to be buying it.

"Don't know me? Then how were you able to scream my name so loud, so many times, sugar?" Mandi rubbed her palms all over

Frank's body and with each pass Sue's face became more crimson.

"Frank…" said Sue, her tone practically a growl. The mouse was ready to roar.

Frank turned to look at Sue to work some more of his magic with his puppy dog eyes and movie star good looks, but Mandi pulled his face back toward her. "You promised that you'd kick Sue to the curb if I had that ménage à trois with you and my friend Bambi. You said that being with her was like having sex with an inflatable doll, only not as satisfying." Mandi took a deep breath and straddled Frank. "Is this because I asked Bambi instead of Suzy? Okay, we can have just one more threesome if it will get her gone."

"Bitch!" said Sue, throwing Mandi on the floor by her blond hair. She spun on Frank, fire and fury in her eyes. "You said you loved me!"

"That's what he told me. And Bambi," said Mandi. "Over and over until he collapsed."

"Sue, honey, this woman is lying," said Frank. The desperate pleading in his eyes for her to believe him was genuine. Not the truth, but genuine.

"Then why would this man come to me to see if I would get rid of your debt to them? He said they didn't think your fiancée had the guts to do it. You want proof? You want me to tell you about what he looks like naked? About where his mole is?" bluffed Mandi, but her gamble paid off. Sue believed her.

"You bastard!" shrieked Sue as she raked her fingernails across his face. "I hope they kill you!"

A single drop of blood flew through the air and landed on the green carpet and changed the entire feel of the place. The evil became almost palpable and the room actually shuttered. I could feel the evil beneath hungering for more.

The gentlemen in suits lifted their knives and eyed my partner and I like we were a pair of Thanksgiving turkeys.

"I can see that you gentlemen are unhappy that we ruined your plans for the evening," I said, pulling out my gun. "We are DMA agents and you are all under arrest. I would however like to point out that whoever sent you on this mission did not plan for any of you to return. The magics you were attempting to release would have killed all of you in a display of dark fireworks that you would not have been able to appreciate. Kindly put down your weapons, get on your knees, and put your hands behind your heads."

"We outnumber you, so how about we just carve you up instead?" said one of the seven men in the room.

I ignored him, instead lifting up my collar and speaking into it. "This is Agent Karver. They are in room nine and not giving up. Send backup."

A couple put down their knives and assumed the position. The wave of submissiveness Mandi was sending their way didn't hurt.

One brave soul against the wall actually threw his blade at me. Good shot too – right at my throat. If it weren't for the enhanced reflexes the seriál demon left me with, I would have been skewered. As it was, I barely caught the blade in time, but they didn't know that. I was scared and I was pissed. I probably shouldn't have done what I did next, but it felt so good.

I tossed the knife back, but my aim was a little lower. The knife stuck in what remained of the wall, close enough that it cut through the crotch of his suit. The look of terror on his face was priceless. This was immediately followed by the sounds of the rest of the knives and clubs falling to the floor, followed by the rest of the men dropping to their knees, even the supposedly tied up Frank.

"Anyone tries anything and I won't be so nice next time," I said. Mandi looked at me. We were again out of cuffs. "Go to room five. I've got this covered," I said, picking up a knife off the floor. Mandi led Sue out. "Anyone moves, I'm thinking left."

"Left what?" stammered Frank.

I just looked at him, then lowered my eyes and smiled.

They barely breathed until Mandi got back. This time we had no choice but to use the fur-lined variety of restraints.

The locals helped us transport the lot to the local jail. We did some questioning and found out that the men in suits had been recruited online for the job and promised great wealth and power. As they'd be dead, there was no reason the folks who hired them would have to pay off. The World Wide Spyder was already tracking down the people behind the plot. The suits were charged as domestic terrorists. Most accepted a plea to avoid the death penalty. Frank decided to fight it out and lost. It'll be years before he exhausts all his appeals. Sad part is, once Sue found out Mandi made the whole thing up, she decided to stand by her man. I hear they got married, but Frank isn't allowed conjugal visits yet. Sue plans to wait it out. I guess she'll still be young when she becomes a widow.

The frat boys clammed up and demanded lawyers. Using magic to summon an extra-dimensional monster more than crossed state lines, it made it a federal crime. Turns out, it didn't take much to get them all to accept plea bargains. One of the geniuses had recorded the entire thing on his phone, including the murder.

A DMA cleanup team got the lizard carcass, its eggs, and the omega slug remains and disposed of them safely. Nothing's more dangerous than a mystic biohazard. Problem was, we didn't get all the eggs. It seems Brenda got some ideas in her head on her way home, deciding that Steve was right about the value of an egg to an academic career. She must have turned Steve's car around and found one we missed and loaded it into the trunk. Once Brenda got home, she contacted the biology department at her community college and told them she had a fresh dinosaur egg. They didn't believe her, but humored her with a meeting. When she didn't show, they sent someone to her dorm room. Brenda was dead. Her corpse had large chunks of flesh missing which were never recovered. Pieces of a large eggshell were found at the scene.

The local papers were given the full story, but they still changed the details so the public would believe them. They alleged we took out an alligator in the pool that killed one of the guests. Hazing at a frat party got out of control, leaving one young man dead. There was nothing at all about the happenings in room nine.

One interesting consequence is for the first time I find myself almost agreeing with Zachs. I still stop short of recommending the place be nuked, but I can see his point. The Scarlet Star is still open for business despite it all. I have a lot of unused vacation time. I'm thinking about taking some and staying there, seeing what I can do to discourage things when the nexus surges again.

I mentioned it to the owner and for some reason he told me he wouldn't ever rent me a room again.

Guy's obviously never heard of a fleshsmith.

THE TIES THAT BIND

by

Patrick Thomas and C.J. Henderson

Hell is said to have no fury like a woman scorned. I'm considered by some to be an expert on the former, but I'm anything but an authority on women. Any male who claims to be is either a liar, a miserably deluded fool, or someone I haven't met yet.

However, I am something of an expert on Mandi. Not to imply that she wasn't a woman, because she definitely was, right down to her stereotypical all-American gal next door, blond hair and blue eyes. Looks can be deceiving, though. She may look the part, but she doesn't exactly fit it, unless of course most folks' neighbors fight monsters for a living at the bequest of the federal government.

Mandi's been an agent longer than I have and she's good at it. A lot of folks figure she must have ticked off one of the higher-ups at the DMA to have been partnered with me. The real reason was mainly so Mandi could monitor my mental and emotional health at the start of my law enforcement career. It's a task that an empath is uniquely suited for. The pairing has been a blessing for me, something far and few between in my life.

Case in point—I was first recruited by the Department of Mystic Affairs from death row. My mind and soul were more than slightly ripped apart by my time as a serial killer. Now, I was possessed by a demon during that period, but that only does so much to keep the guilt in check. It's just enough to keep me from the coward's way out. With my skills with a blade, slitting my throat would only take half an instant. It would be too easy and I don't deserve easy.

Mandi does, but she'd never gotten any of it, either. Early on, my partner learned either to shield herself from the emotions of other people or go mad. Despite her best efforts, Mandi hasn't always been able to avoid the latter.

Her stays in a rubber room may have been worse on those around her. My partner is also a propath—meaning she's able to make others feel her projected emotions. When her control is shattered, anyone in her range experiences whatever it is she's experiencing. Suffice it to say at those times there can be a run on rubber rooms.

During saner times, Mandi works hard at ironclad control. My partner always comes across as in charge of any room she walks into, but I've seen the kinks in her armor. Underneath she's just like the rest of us, her skeletons shoved to the back of her closet under the old clothes and shoes. At least she didn't strip the meat from their bones and sauté it in butter. My skeleton closet was converted into a bunker long ago to be able to hold all my dead.

In short, it was a rarity to see her lose it.

But, the day in question was indeed going to be that rare kind of day. Things had started out typically enough with a stakeout in Alabama. Any mystic threat against the United States or its citizens falls both in the DMA's lap and jurisdiction. Most people, law enforcement types included, assume we deal with crackpots and hoaxes. They usually can't accept the fact that they're wrong until after the darkness creeps out and beats them over the head or leaves behind some dead--in an unexplainable manner, at least by traditional means.

It's a sore point with me. How many agents in Homeland Security have gone head to head with a terrorist? Yet they mock what I do when I've faced down things that would make them and the terrorist curl into a ball together while hugging each other and screaming for their mommies to come and make it better.

We were parked across the street from a Wiccan supply store. Now most Wicca are relatively harmless, having no real powers of their own. The few that actually have some magical ability generally use it to help, not hurt people. The owner of the shop was a woman who called herself Hilda. We had gotten tips that she was selling love potions. Now there are a lot of mages out there who made the occasional love potion, but it's very hard to track down and prosecute. Hilda had made a business of it and her potions worked, at least for a time. It was the mystic equivalent of a date rape drug. Worse even. Not only could the user take advantage of the victim physically, but also emotionally and financially. And the victim does it willingly until it wears off. Then they are never quite right again. They only get worse with repeated use.

No one deserves to be forced to act against their will, to do things they wouldn't normally dream of. Trust me on this. I know.

Our warrant had allowed us to place listening devices in and around the shop. So far we'd been drinking coffee and eating sandwiches for two days with nothing to show for it besides stiff backs and the slight beginnings of caffeine headaches. We used a modified glamour charm to change the van's appearance each day to alleviate suspicion.

A sting operation is usually quicker than a stakeout, but DMA policy dictated the way we did things. Our director, the actual Uncle Sam, was a stickler for the rules and the letter of the law. We tried to catch criminals in the act if at all possible before setting up a sting operation. The plan was for us to be here four days and we had two to go.

Mandi's cell phone rang with a non-DMA number. It's unusual for her to get a personal call on a stakeout. It would have been even odder for it to happen to me. I haven't been very good at the friend thing since the beast from the pit used my body to slaughter 63 people. Most of the people I know these days are work-related acquaintances.

"Millar, what's up?" Millar was Mandi's brother, the only member of her family she cared to have anything to do with. He was a good guy. Mandi spent as much time with him, his wife and kids as she was able. She's even dragged me along on Thanksgiving and Christmas, not wanting me to be alone. I did a lot of dark things on the holidays. Just the sight of a Christmas tree is enough for my guts to go nuclear.

"I'm kinda in the middle of something for work here." Whatever her brother said next made her face drop.

"Oh my God! Charlie's missing? I'll be there as fast as I can."

This was when Mandi started to lose control. I could feel my blood pressure rising, a pounding in my ears. My fingers were drumming themselves, scratching the seat, my legs; I wanted to smash something to pieces. A woman passing by the van kicked the dog she was walking, then started apologizing to the canine by picking it up and kissing it profusely.

"Karver, somebody kidnapped Charlie. We need to get to New Jersey. Drive." With what she was throwing off, neither of us was in much condition to be behind the wheel.

"Mandi, driving is not the fastest way. You're not thinking straight or you'd realize that. First, you need to rein things in or we're going to have a riot on our hands." Outside passersby were shouting at each other and were seconds away from punches being thrown. "And we'll have to explain how and why we blew cover."

Mandi inhaled and exhaled in a carefully prescribed, ritual pattern. This caused her parasympathetic nervous system to kick in and calm her down. I knew her mental shields had finally gone up, because I wasn't furious anymore. Next, I felt a combination of calm and regret wash over me. The confused people outside on the sidewalk felt it as well. They stopped yelling and awkwardly apologized to each other before moving on. Mandi speed dialed Sarge Winston, the assistant director of the DMA and our direct supervisor.

"Sarge ..." Winston had been a sergeant in the First World War and the nickname had never left him. People in our line of work tend to age well. "My nephew Charlie is missing and my brother thinks he's been kidnapped ... no, he's not the type of kid to run away. He's only seven years old. I have to head up there. What can you arrange?" Mandi's face got very dark.

"You've got to be kidding me," she snapped. "Can you at least get us air transport to get there ASAP?" At Sarge's answer Mandi's hand hit the van wall and her eyes rolled back in her head. Someone outside responded with a sympathetic primal scream.

"A commercial flight is not going to cut it. You know as well as I do every minute after a kidnapping matters ... fine, but I need you to do me a favor. The locals are giving my brother a problem. They're treating it more like a missing child than a kidnapping. They haven't even notified the FBI. I need you to get an Amber Alert issued ... yes, I realize the trouble a false alert would cause, but I don't care. He's family and, and I doubt it's false ... Thanks, Sarge."

Mandi was gritting her teeth.

"I can't believe this. We can't get transport because it's personal and not department business. Apparently Congress has been slashing budgets and Sarge will catch hell for authorizing mundane or mystic transport. Worse, he told me I have to stay here until relief arrives – said I need to calm down. He's calling the Mobile office and having them send two agents to relieve us. Sarge said he'd have two tickets at the airport ready for us on the first thing smoking, military or private." I started contemplating faster ways to travel 1,200 miles.

"How long is that going to take?" I asked.

"Sarge promised no more than two hours – probably less. I'm not willing to wait that long."

Disobey orders or not help the only friend I had left in the world take care of her family. I put the key in the ignition and turned it. It wasn't a tough choice.

"Then we go."

Mandi was glaring at the witch in the window. "No Karver, I have a better idea." With that, my normally rational partner opened the car door, got out, ran across the street to the Wicca shop.

"Oh crap," I said. This was not going to end well.

Mandi threw open the shop door and let the tears of worry she had for Charlie stream down her cheeks. With a nervous, but directed energy, she began furiously searching through the shop's shelves. It wasn't long before she attracted the owner's attention.

"Can I help you with something?" said the owner, wearing a puffy white shirt and a peasant skirt. She held a broom like it was a scepter. Mandi sniffed and wiped her face on her sleeve, answering;

"I'm sorry. I'm not usually like this. I just got dumped. I'm hurt and pissed off. I know this stuff's not for real, but do you have anything that I could give him that would make his hair fall out or his penis shrivel up?"

On the plus side, all the bugs were working well. Time would tell if the recordings would be used as evidence against this wicked witch of the south or at a disciplinary hearing against Mandi. Since she hadn't asked specifically for a love potion, we had sidestepped entrapment, but barely.

"I think we can do a little bit better than that." The shopkeeper smiled, asking, "Do you still love him?" Mandi nodded her head.

"I do, but he dumped me for this other woman. She's prettier, younger, and rich. I can't compete with that." Hilda raised an eyebrow.

"What if I could give you something that would not only level the playing field," she asked, "but wipe out the competition?" Mandi let herself look aghast.

"I don't want to kill anybody."

"No, no." Hilda chuckled. "It's nothing like that. I sell love potions here." She reached over and picked up an old-fashioned perfume atomizer, the kind with the rubber ball you squeeze to spray. "All you'd need to do is get close enough to spray this in his face and a moment after he breathes it in he'll be madly in love with the first person he sees. He won't care about anyone but you."

"I don't know ..."

The shopkeeper laid a sisterly hand on Mandi's shoulder. "It's your decision, but this way the both of you get what you deserve."

"How much?" asked Mandi.

"Two thousand dollars for this bottle." Mandi whistled.

"That's a whole lot of money."

"Yes it is, but despite what the song says, you can buy love, but it don't come cheap. The spray in the bottle will last about six months. You'll have to spritz him every three or four weeks. I really feel for your situation, so I'm going to help you out." Hilda pulled out a smaller bottle.

"This has got enough for one dose. I'll give it to you at cost." She looked Mandi over, paying attention to the quality of her clothes, mentally making calculations.

"Two hundred dollars. It's practically free." Pushers are smart that way. The first one's free or cheap, then once they have you hooked, the price gets jacked up. Her materials cost is negligible. A barrel probably cost her about fifty bucks. The only real cost is the power it takes.

"It really works?" asked Mandi.

"If it doesn't, I'll give you your money back."

Mandi pulled her credit card out of her wallet, asking if Hilda took plastic. The shopkeeper smiled and took the DMA issued credit card out of her fingers.

"Absolutely." Hilda ran the card and gave Mandi the receipt to sign. "Here you go."

"Great," said Mandi, flipping over her wallet so the shopkeeper could see her badge. "Department of Mystic Affairs. You're under arrest." By this point, I was already in the shop to act as backup, but Mandi didn't need it. She had the woman frisked and in handcuffs before I got close. The woman tried to cast a hex on us, but nothing happened.

"That adds attempted assault on federal officers to the charges," said Mandi.

"But the spell didn't work," protested Hilda.

"Pulling and firing a gun will get you the same charge, even if it misfires or jams. If it wasn't for the runes of power on those handcuffs, it would have worked," said Mandi.

Mandi read Hilda her rights and loaded her into the back of the van. We headed to the DMA office in Mobile. Mandi drove as I made some calls. When I hung up, Mandi asked;

"You get us a faster ride?"

"Close enough," I said. "It'll be waiting for us in Mobile."

It took us fifteen minutes with the sirens on to get to the DMA office and another ten to get the shopkeeper processed. I filled out the paperwork by hand as quickly as I could instead of typing it so we could get going sooner. Then we handed off everything we could about the case to the regional director, Agent Mountak. We explained to him what was happening and why we had to leave.

"Can I offer you a ride to the airport?" he asked.

"Don't need it." We were walking down the hallway to a pair of elevator doors. Mandi hit the button.

"That's not our elevator," said Mountak perplexed.

"Nope, it's ours," said Mandi. The doors opened, and inside were two women. One was the elevator operator, a woman of slight build with hair so white it would make driven snow look dingy. She went by Gani and was the twin sister of Merlin. Unlike her brother, she was still free to roam the Earth and tap into his powers. The second one was a woman with shoulders so broad she'd make a linebacker envious, and an hourglass figure of gargantuan proportions.

"Thanks Terrorbelle," I said. The two of them work for Nemesis & Co., an independent agency out of New York. Their boss is the enforcer for the Council of Thrones, a mystic court of last resort and final appeal. DMA agents have standing orders to not antagonize her or her trio of agents and render aid so long as it falls within our jurisdiction. I called in a marker.

"No problem, Karver. You helped me out with that werewolf serial killer," said Terrorbelle. "Mandi, I'm so sorry to hear about your nephew—anything we can do, you just ask."

Mandi nodded and we got in. "Thank you. I need to get to Edison, New Jersey."

"I can get you as far as Newark," said Gani, hitting the close door button. "My elevator spell is limited to places I've visited. Luckily, I've been to Mobile before."

When the doors opened again we were in New Jersey. Now there was the little matter of how to get the rest of the way from here to there, but it looked like Terrorbelle had it covered. She handed Mandi a set of keys and behind her in the elevator was a mint condition black Harley.

"Get it back to me when you can," said Terrorbelle. "And take good care of it. The last person I loaned a bike to wrecked it."

"And they're still standing?" kidded Mandi.

Terrorbelle looked sheepish and shrugged. "It was Murphy." I held back a smile. Terrorbelle had a major crush on the man. She was tough as nails, but had a very soft spot for the Bulfinche's Pub bartender. "And, well ... he sorta saved my life doing it."

"I'll do my best to return it intact. Thank you both," said Mandi, rolling the bike out of the elevator in what appeared to be an office building. The elevator doors closed behind us and promptly disappeared. Mandi walked the bike down the hallways and out the front door, then off the curb and into the street. She swung her leg over and started it up. Then she put a helmet on and tossed me another.

"What are you waiting for, Karver? Get on," said Mandi.

"You mean you want me to ride in back?"

"Why you got a problem with that?" asked Mandi.

"Not terribly masculine. I'd be more than happy to drive," I said.

"I'm sure you would, but it's not happening. Now get on or do you want to argue with me some more?" asked Mandi. Normally I would have loved to, but there's a time and a place for everything. I swung my leg over the back, put the helmet on, then wrapped my hands around my partner's waist.

"And don't think you can use this as an excuse to try and cop a feel," teased Mandi. I was the last person in the world that anyone had to worry about the odd inappropriate touching; it still brought back a flood of memories—all of them bad. Too many of my dead started their final trip with my hands doing things that are better left unsaid. Instead, glad to see she was coming out of her mood, I teased her back, asking

"Why? You worried I'll smudge all the fingerprints that are already there? Cause without those prints how else are you going to keep track of whose hand went where?" I said.

"Well the Twister t-shirt I wear helps. I usually try and keep to the same pattern. My spinner's rigged." And with that she revved the motorcycle and we were off.

When we got to Millar's house, the FBI had already arrived. Agents were cordoning off the perimeter. As soon as Mandi set foot on the cement path, an agent placed himself in front of her, holding his hand in the air like he was an overdressed crossing guard.

"This is a crime scene. You can't come in here," said the agent.

"I'm Charlie's aunt," said Mandi. "And you are Agent...?"

"Glenn. Who's Charlie?" asked the agent, fumbling through a pad.

"The kidnapping victim," said Mandi, not bothering to hide her irritation. It leaked out onto the agent, which didn't help matters.

"Oh you mean Charles Cobb."

"No, I mean Charlie. Now get out of my way."

The agent was already irritated and now he had his backup. If she were thinking straight she would have been oozing helpfulness and he would have personally escorted us in and offered us refreshments.

"Sorry, but as I said it's a crime scene. Only law enforcement allowed in."

"You want to play it that way? Fine." Mandi flipped open her badge. "DMA Agent."

Glenn made an effort to show that he was chuckling. "You're a voodoo cop? So what? You might as well have told me you work for the Department of Wildlife and Game. You ain't getting in here."

Things went downhill from there. The normally cool and collected Mandi Cobb began to rave and shout like a lunatic. Since that was usually my job, I decided it was up to me to fill in for my partner's usual place in the scheme of things. I pulled out my cell phone and dialed.

"Sandra, this is Karver. I need to talk to Sam." The living symbol of America could be notoriously hard to get a hold of, but if anyone could do it, it was his elfin secretary. Not that I normally had his ear, but I had also never called directly from the field before either.

"No, it's not exactly an emergency," I explained, "but it's urgent. Mandi's having a meltdown and it's going interagency."

My partner had been with the DMA since she was barely legal. Since she's a little sensitive about her age, I won't say exactly how long, but she's more than halfway to her pension. Sandra told me to hold. A moment later Uncle Sam picked up the phone. I explained the situation. Sam might get tied down in bureaucracy, making sure all of us follow the letter of the law, but loyalty was one of his strongest qualities. He wasn't about to let someone mess with one of his own.

"Karver, stand by. It'll be taken care of momentarily."

When the director told me what he was going to do, I couldn't help but smile. All told, it took less than three minutes until the agent's phone rang. He looked at the number and his face blanched. "Holy shi—"

"I called my boss. He called your boss. That ringing sound ... that would be the director of your FBI. Me—I wouldn't keep him waiting," I said. If it was just me the guy had been arguing with, I would have handled it myself. But Agent Tude was messing with my partner as well as the safety of one of the few kids that I've actually had the pleasure of playing with since my new life began. Mandi's the closest thing to family I have these days, which by default makes her family mine. I wasn't about to let a pissing contest get in the way of pulling together every resource available to find Charlie.

Agent Glenn was doing a lot of "yes, siring." When he ended the call, his face was beat red and veins on his forehead and neck were pulsing. I didn't need Mandi's abilities to know that he was pissed at me for what I did. He didn't need them either to know how much I didn't care. With a great deal of effort to control what came out of his mouth, Agent Tude said;

"Please come inside." We followed discreetly behind him as he walked up the path.

"Since when are you the hothead? I thought it was my job to create friction with anybody else working the same case as us. I don't have a lot of skills, you know. You start stealing my bits and I'm going to feel pretty useless." Mandi took a deep breath and smiled at me. It was genuine, but it still took a great deal of effort on her part. She didn't let sentiment cloud the air for too long, however.

"It's about time you pulled a bit of your own weight," she added, doing her best not to grin. "For the most part you are pretty useless on a case."

I considered bantering a good sign. Wanting to encourage it, I asked, "Then why do you keep me around?"

"Pretty much just in case there's any heavy lifting or someone needs to be chased through a sewer tunnel. Those are two of your skills I won't try to replace," said Mandi.

"Thank you," I said warmly. "I need some sense of job security in these troubled times."

Inside the house, agents were questioning the rest of the family. Agent Tude got a glare from the agent in charge of the crime scene, so he decided to introduce us.

"These are Agents Cobb and Karver of the DMA." Mandi ignored all of them and went straight for her brother, embracing him in a bear hug. The agent in charge gave her a funny look and turned back to Agent Tude, who explained that she was the victim's aunt and what the FBI director had told him. The agent in charge nodded. By this time Mandi was hugging both of her nieces. That lasted a minute before she turned her intentions on her sister-in-law. The agent in charge waited patiently until she was done.

"Agent Cobb, I'm Special Agent Woods. I want to assure you that we're doing everything that we can to find your nephew." Mandi shook the outstretched hand. The embraces had done her as much good as they had her family. With her walls firmly back up in place, she said in a professional tone;

"Thank you. Please bring us up to speed."

Woods did. It wasn't a lot. A window was open and there were a couple of adult male sized footprints in the dirt outside Charlie's window. There were a couple of peanut butter candy wrappers inside his room, which couldn't have been Charlie's because he was allergic to peanuts. Otherwise, there was nothing – no witnesses, no security footage. The FBI was already canvassing registered sex offenders in the neighborhood, but so far had come up empty.

"What can I do to help?" asked Mandi.

Woods seemed a genuinely good guy. He couldn't think of any way to use us at the moment, but he programmed Mandi's cell number into his speed dial and gave her his. Promising to keep us in the loop, that we would be involved in any tactical moves, he simply suggested Mandi take care of her family and that I watch out for her. Mandi thanked him before walking off to call Sarge. I played with the girls to give Millar and his wife a chance to discuss more with Woods. When my partner came back, she was somewhere between unhappy and irritated.

She had tried to get Sarge to have us take over the investigation. Of course, he had said no. There was no evidence of anything other than the mundane. Without magic, we had no jurisdiction. Sarge had even gone the extra mile to put all the agency's psychics on it, but they came up dry. Which is the problem with most psychics—they can't always turn it on and off at will. Mandi wasn't about to give up, however. To sit around and wait for the FBI would drive her crazy.

"So what are you going do?" I asked.

"I don't care if we don't have jurisdiction. I'm going to do something," said Mandi.

"That much is a given. I meant since we can't use DMA resources what are we going to do?"

"The last thing that I want to."

We took the motorcycle and ended up in Manhattan. Mandi hadn't spoken much on the way. Truth be told, at one point I thought we were going to end up at Bulfinche's Pub. One of their patrons is probably the greatest psychic in the world when he's not drunk. Problem is, he's always drunk. Mandi took her helmet off and stared at one brownstone in particular. With a sigh she said;

"Better get this over with." As we started up the walk, I asked;

"Who are we here to see?"

"Lai Wan. She's a psychometrist."

"A what?"

"She can read the history of an object, including anyone who it's come in contact with. And any person." Things were falling into place.

"That explains why you swiped a candy wrapper."

"Because of his allergy, we know the wrapper wasn't Charlie's and it was already dusted for prints. I figured it would do us more good here, assuming she'll agree to help us."

"There's a child kidnapped. Why wouldn't she help?"

"The woman has her own agenda," snapped Mandi. "Lai Wan's worked as a consultant for the DMA before, but her price is usually high and it's not always money. Emotionally she's a mess. She's in a constant state of anger mixed with a superiority complex and a great deal of arrogance mixed in. I can only imagine what it's going to cost me to get her help, but it doesn't matter. She's Charlie's best hope and I'll do whatever it takes."

As the pieces started coming together for me, I began to wonder how exact her description was, and how much of it was compensation on Mandi's part. Testing my theory, I asked;

"I take it the two of you have a history?"

"We've worked together before and let's just say we didn't hit it off. Lai Wan hated the fact that I knew what she was feeling. She thought I was jealous that she was able to not only gauge people's emotions, but by touching an object she could see what actually happened. Which is a lot more detailed than what I can do," said Mandi.

"Was she right?" I asked. It took a suspiciously large amount of seconds for her to answer.

"Maybe."

My partner knocked on the door heavily; her way of changing the subject. We heard footsteps approaching. The door opened revealing a slender oriental woman; every patch of skin other than her face was covered by clothing. I met her eyes. They were the type that had seen things that shouldn't be seen and could never really be spoken of. There was something oddly familiar about them. Then I realized I saw eyes with that look every morning in the mirror. Our shared glance lasted only a moment until she turned her attention toward Mandi.

"Agent Cobb," said Lai Wan. "Does the Department of Mystic Affairs have another case they are unable to solve?"

"Actually it's not DMA business. It's a personal matter," said Mandi.

The woman's face expressed no glee, but there was a glint in her eyes as she said, "Not interested." As she moved to close the door my hand shot out, stopping the motion. In the process, my bare finger accidentally brushed up against the smallest sliver of exposed skin between her glove and sleeve. Lai Wan stiffened as if having a seizure. She stumbled but did not fall, her hand not letting go of the door as if it had a will of its own. It was a moment a normal person might not even have noticed, but it spoke volumes to Mandi and me. With her free hand, the woman wiped away the slightest trickle of drool that had forced its way from her mouth as we'd made contact. Her faraway, mystical eyes were suddenly filled with pity, and it took me back a step that in that moment they looked more like mine than ever. Her voice sounding suddenly hollow, she said;

"I never thought I would meet someone worse off than myself, Agent Karver. Self-pity can restrict the boundaries of one's world.

Still, I am not interested. And if I were, my fee for you, Agent Cobb, would be far in excess of what you could afford."

"I'll pay whatever you need," Mandi blurted, "only please help me. My nephew Charlie's been kidnapped. The FBI has got nothing but dead ends and the DMA can't get involved because no magic was used. I can't let anything happen to him. Please, Lai Wan, *please*—help me find him."

The woman hadn't actually moved, but there was a subtle difference in how she was standing. There was the slightest tilting of her head, and then she motioned us to enter. I started for the door, but Mandi held back, asking, "About your fee ..." The psychometrist lifted her gloved hand and waved off the comment.

"We will worry about such things afterward. Would either of you care for some tea?" Mandi started to open her mouth, but knowing it was going to emit something combative rather than gracious, I touched her wrist while saying;

"Thank you. We would."

Over tea we explained everything we knew about Charlie's disappearance. Mandi handed Lai Wan the wrapper. The psychometrist looked at the orange square for a long moment, carefully removing her glove at the same time. Finally, after she'd learned whatever it was she needed to by sight, she closed her eyes, reached out and touched the paper.

"This wrapper has seen much. For instance, in the factory where it was made, the woman who boxed it is dying of breast cancer, but is unaware of it."

"What's the woman's name and where is she from," I asked.

"It is not relevant to finding Agent Cobb's nephew. Why would you wish to know?" she asked.

"I'll locate her and make sure she gets treatment," I said. Lai Wan tilted her head and stared at me. The look seemed to say that she already knew my answer. Well, I figured, if that was the case, there was no harm in letting her know.

"I have a lot to make up for," I told her.

"Indeed, Agent Karver." Lai Wan gave me the woman's name and address. I can't explain it, but in a way I felt like I'd just passed a test. The feeling was enhanced when, with the faintest of grins, she asked, "The man who stocked the candy on the convenience store shelf is cheating on his wife. Would you like to know who he is so you can inform the woman?"

"No, I think I can pass on that one," I told her. She smiled. I must admit, it looked good on her.

Turning to Mandi, she said, "The name of the man who kidnapped your nephew is Jeremy Joseph Johnson." She gave us his address.

Something in the building's construction, or perhaps even Lai Wan herself, was interfering with my cell reception, which was unusual. DMA phones worked most places.

"May I borrow your phone?" I asked.

"I would prefer not," she said. "Perhaps if you stepped outside you might find better reception."

"I'll pay for the call," I offered.

"It is not a matter of payment. As I am certain you can understand, I would prefer for someone with your unique history to not come into contact with any more of my things than necessary. Although I make a point of not sitting in the guest chairs in this room, or indeed, actually entering it without the necessity of entertaining guests, your aura is so ... shall we say, remarkable in its endurance. I'm afraid it might upset others. I'm actually considering burning your chair when you have left, Agent Karver. No offense."

"None taken. If burning a chair would get rid of the memories of what I've done, I'd do it in a second." I meant what I said, too. Having said it, though, it prompted a question within my head I found I just had to ask. Knowing it would bug me, I let it rip.

"I apologize for our accidental brushing up outside, but couldn't you kind of tell something about me just from us being close?"

"Of course," she acknowledged. "I knew it was Agent Cobb at my doorstep before she began pounding on my door. I sensed all that had been done through you before I opened the door."

"Then, if you don't mind my asking, why did you flinch?"

"I had no idea you were so innocent in all that happened to you." She paused for a moment, then added, "I know something about how that feels."

"I'll go outside to make the call."

I told Woods what we had learned and, bless him, he didn't go into the how we had learned it. Instead he dispatched FBI agents and a tactical team to Triple J's home. I returned inside and informed the ladies.

"I do not believe he is at his home. Perhaps if I was allowed access to the crime scene, I could discern something more."

"We'll make it happen," said Mandi. "One problem – I don't think we're going to be able to manage three on a hog. Do you have a car?"

"No, but there are ways." Lai Wan picked up the phone, and after a moment said, "Zachery, how would you like to meet some DMA agents? I thought you might. We need a ride. If you could meet us in front of my building in, say ... fifteen minutes? Yes, that would be fine."

As Lai Wan put the phone back in its cradle, Mandi asked, "Who is this?"

"Zachery Goward, professor of theology, doctorate in philosophy. His studies center greatly in areas you walk on a daily basis. He will be happy to transport us for the chance to ask you scores of annoying and personal questions."

I had no idea if this was some way for Lai Wan to stick pins in Mandi for whatever it was from their past, but if my partner wasn't going to say anything, neither was I. We drank tea and she even brought out some cookies I can't remember the name of, but that weren't like anything I'd ever had before. Goward was right on time, and we met him in the front.

I opened the front passenger door for Lai Wan, who slid in and greeted her friend. Then, I opened the rear door for myself, only to have Mandi scowl at me over the roof of the car.

"You never open the door for me," she teased.

"You never wait long enough," I answered. "I'd open the back door for you, but you'd probably be confused as to proper behavior, having never been in a backseat without a date – or fully dressed."

"You're just jealous because the last woman low enough to get in a backseat with you made you wear a paper bag over your head," Mandi growled, finally opening her own door and sliding inside.

"Hey, she had a grocery fetish," I answered, joining her in the backseat.

"Our tax dollars at work," Lai Wan said to Goward.

"You should see your tax dollars on vacation," Mandi quipped.

"Oh, the things they do. Of course, if you did see that, then we'd have to either shoot you or recruit you."

"Please," the psychometrist answered coldly, "If I accidentally see anything you deem I shouldn't, I'd prefer the bullet." I couldn't see her eyes that time, but something told me a part of her would prefer the bullet regardless.

I thought we'd die a thousand times as Goward drove along, peppering us with questions. He loved to make eye contact, but that's a bad thing when you're driving and the eyes you want to contact are behind you. Finally, Mandi hit him with a bit of calm, and although he didn't stop asking questions about every kind of thing we ever faced, found or fancied, he did keep his hands at ten and two, and his eyes forward which, believe me, after our first few blocks, was good enough for me.

In Jersey, Goward stayed with the car under orders from the FBI while the rest of us went inside. Lai Wan went over the crime scene and found nothing new. Agent Tude was left in charge and I could tell he'd like nothing better than to stop us, but he didn't want any additional surprise phone calls more.

Approaching the techs who were still there, Lai Wan asked the one holding the evidence bags, "May I?"

After Tude gave the go ahead, the psychometrist went through everything perfunctorily until she came to the bags holding dirt samples from the footprints found outside. Carefully, Lai Wan opened the zip seal of one, removed her right glove, then placed her index finger in the dirt, specifically touching a fleck of paint she had sensed.

"Johnson is not at the house. He has set up a work area in an abandoned building ... it possessed a sign before he took it over ... 'Curly's Electronics.' I believe he is there now."

"I know where that is," said Millar. "That's not ten minutes away. I'm coming with you."

"No, little brother, you're not. You'd only get in the way and endanger Charlie. I'll bring him home, I promise."

"You don't know the address ..." He said weakly. It was a feeble gambit to be allowed to come along, but before he and Mandi could get into it, Lai Wan said;

"And what you know, I know, sir. Please contain yourself. It is best for your son."

Mandi did a bit of a double take, but then simply turned to Agent

Glenn, whose 'tude had, if anything, grown worse, even without any prodding from my partner. "Call Woods. Tell him to have the tactical team meet us there."

"Right," said Glenn, then under his breath muttered, "Damn voodoo cops."

We ran to the car; Lai Wan followed.

"You're a civilian," said Mandi.

"With more than enough experience with this type of situation," she answered. Then, to seal the deal, as she slid back into the front seat, she added, "Besides, I am the only one who knows the address."

I have to admit, I liked her. Lai Wan told Goward what was happening and where to go. We had no sirens, but he drove like we did. Funny, it never bothers me when I do it, but this old professor's glee behind the wheel unnerved me to no end.

We were there in seven minutes. Lai Wan had Goward pull over a block away from the building. While he stayed with the car again, this time on DMA orders, the rest of us moved on the building. We snuck around to the back where there were no windows. As Lai Wan touched the building, she told us, "They are both in there alone. Your nephew's hands and feet are bound, but he is physically unharmed."

I didn't like the way the word "physically" was put in as a disclaimer, but Mandi was too emotionally involved to notice.

"Where the Hell is our backup?" she said and whipped out her cell phone. "Woods, this is Cobb. What's your ETA to Curly's?" Mandi's shields dropped for the briefest second, but it was long enough for her anger to burn me.

"Glenn didn't call you? That son of a bitch. I want him up on charges. I told him that the bastard that took Charlie is in there and ..." Mandi went silent, her face paling as she suddenly felt, "... and he's terrified."

Lai Wan, her hand still on the building, interrupted, telling us, "We can wait no longer."

"Woods, we have to go in," Mandi said and hung up. "What's happening?"

"Johnson is a monster, human but a monster just the same," said Lai Wan. "He has a knife, much smaller than the ones Agent Karver has under his jacket. He also has a gun. Both are on his person."

Mandi was trying to get a reading on the kidnapper's emotional state. "A standoff with this guy is going to end badly. He's too unstable to deal with rationally."

"I concur. What we need is a distraction. I offer myself," said Lai Wan.

"You're still a civilian," said Mandi.

"And your director allows the use of qualified civilians when necessary. The former owners of Curly's were Chinese like myself. There is a picture still hanging there of the family. He's seen it. I can convince him I'm one of them long enough for you to subdue him from behind."

"Do you look enough like the family?" asked Mandi.

"And here I thought all Orientals looked alike to you Caucasians."

"You are putting yourself in the line of fire," said Mandi.

"To rescue your nephew."

"Lai Wan, I know we don't get along but I want to thank ..."

"Mandi, let us save Charlie."

Lai Wan simply walked in through the front door and started going through the storefront, making certain to be loud enough to attract the attention of the perp in the back.

"What are you doing here?" demanded Johnson, his gun by his side. Lai Wan yelled at him in what I can only assume was Chinese. Johnson pointed his gun between her eyes. "Speak English!"
Lai Wan suddenly could only speak in broken English, pointing at the picture on the wall. "This my family store. What you do here? Why you in my store? What for you come my store—you come rob my store? Joke on you, nothing to rob here. Robber too late."

"I'm not a robber ..."

His words were cut short by the click of Mandi's automatic at the back of his head. "No, you're a sicko pedophile kidnapper. I'm a Federal agent. If you want your brain to stay inside of your skull, you do exactly what I say. Finger off the trigger and slowly put the gun on the floor."

"You shoot me, I shoot the chink bit—" Johnson's words trailed off in confusion as his head snapped this way and that, trying to find Lai Wan. I don't know how she worked it, but he was blind to the sight of her, not even noticing when she neatly took the gun from his hand and the knife from his waistband.

"He have any other weapons?" asked Mandi, figuring the

psychometrist's powers were better than any frisk.

The first pass had cleaned him out. I was glad Lai Wan had moved in and helped Mandi because my partner had insisted I get Charlie out instead of backing her up. He collapsed crying onto my shoulder. I don't do so well with physical contact, but I fought off my inclination to push him away. Instead, I held him until the sobbing stopped, telling him he was going to be "okay." It was a lie, or at least, it would be at first. Charlie had a good family and I figured with time they would eventually get him through. Still, there was nobody else there yet to hand him off to and Charlie was better off with someone he knew. That also meant I couldn't go back in to help Mandi without bringing Charlie with me and DMA policy and common sense dictate that you don't bring a freed hostage back into a possible fire zone.

"You are now and forever on my list of favorite people," said Mandi to Lai while she cuffed Johnson.

"But you still don't like me."

"I don't have to."

"You bitches got lucky. I'll never see the inside of a jail. That kid's going to be too damn afraid to testify against me for the rest of his goddamned life," sneered Johnson.

"Then I'll have to make sure you are never able to hurt anyone ever again," Mandi said, raising her gun up slightly. Johnson's eyes opened wide and he started to shake.

"Wait a second. You're a Fed. You can't hurt me."

"Now what kind of world would we live in if I couldn't hurt you for what you did to my nephew?" asked Mandi.

"Your nephew? I didn't know. I'm sorry," Johnson's voice cracked badly, his body trembling.

"Too little, too late," Mandi said, stepping closer. Lai Wan spoke up, her voice barely a whisper.

"Are you certain you wish to do this?"

"Oh yeah, I'm sure," said Mandi, holstering her weapon.

Johnson looked confused but relieved until Mandi took his face in her hands. Her eyes met the pedophile killer's and my partner would not let him look away. A few seconds later, his screaming began.

When Woods and the tact team arrived, Johnson was curled up in a ball, whimpering softly to himself. The slightest movement of anyone near caused him to recoil. Johnson was going to be living with fear for a very long time.

The next day we were back in DC, called on the carpet in the deputy director's office. Sarge was not at all happy. He did start by asking if Charlie was okay. But, as soon as Mandi told him he was as fine as could be expected under the circumstances, he shifted gears, saying, "I'm glad to hear that. What I am not glad to hear are the details of this case."

Even though the DMA isn't a military organization, Sarge had learned his management style in the army. Mandi and I were standing pretty close to attention in front of his desk. Neither one of us said a word. "I told you the DMA did not have jurisdiction and that the case belonged to the FBI. You seemed to have entirely disregarded my directives."

"Not in the least, Sarge. Working as a civilian on behalf of my brother, I hired Ms. Wan. Hiring a private investigator is entirely legal for any citizen." Technically, Lai Wan doesn't actually hold a private investigator's license, but she's been called in as a professional assistant by so many government agencies, including ours, that the boss seemed willing to let that one slide.

"I handed over all leads she gave me to the FBI," said Mandi, "including who and where Johnson was. It's hardly my fault Agent Glenn didn't take Ms. Wan's abilities seriously enough to do as I instructed him and contact his superior."

"Glenn has been suspended pending a full investigation. My understanding is his defense is that there was no reason to believe a couple of 'voodoo cops.' I assure you that will not hold up, even if I have to attend his disciplinary hearing personally. But, that was his screw up. You used powers on a non-powered citizen and seem to have crippled his psyche. This is unacceptable," said Sarge.

"Sarge, I can explain ..."

"I'm sure you can, but if your explanation even hints of personal revenge, not only are you suspended, but I'll have your badge and gun," said Sarge.

"Deputy Director Winston, if I may interject at this point?" asked Lai Wan, who had been sitting serenely in a chair off to the side of the room. Sarge sighed.

"Please, Ms. Wan."

"This man has molested and murdered at least seven other

children." She handed a piece of paper to Sarge. "This is a list of his other victims. Five of them have never been found. I have detailed where he buried their bodies. I trust you will find these remains. The families need closure."

"It will be taken care of. Thank you," said Sarge. Lai Wan nodded, continuing.

"Knowing Charlie Cobb was in danger from this monster, I offered myself as a distraction. While I held Johnson's attention, Agent Karver got the boy out. Agent Cobb then got the drop on the perpetrator, but he also got the drop on me. Johnson ordered your agent to put down her gun or he would shoot me. She obeyed and had no choice but to use the means at her disposal to assure he did not harm or shoot either one of us. Yes, the amount of power used was excessive, but this man had just done terrible things to a member of Agent Cobb's family. Yes, her control was slightly affected by her fury. But really, you and I both know that had she meant him harm, she could have frightened him to death."

I wasn't aware Mandi could do that, but neither she nor Sarge argued the point, so I guess it was true. Or maybe Lai Wan just distracted the boss as she kept going, telling him, "She did not use any such force, however. What she did could only be considered the equivalent of shooting to wound as opposed to a killing shot. Agent Cobb saved my life and her nephew's. Is she to be punished for these acts of heroism and bravery?"

I give the woman credit; she could be very convincing while lying through her teeth.

Not caring to argue with the psychometrist, Sarge turned to my partner and demanded, "Mandi, is what she said true?"

"I wouldn't dispute a word of it, Sarge," Mandi answered.

"Karver, do you have anything to add?" Mandi had told me what had actually happened, but there wasn't a chance of me ratting her out.

"Sarge, I was outside with the hostage, but up until the point I left the building, my recollection is the same as Lai Wan's."

Sarge looked at each one of us. None of us flinched. The crimson gem embedded in his chest started to glow bright enough to shine through his shirt. He was using his powers to verify our story, although I don't know if the thing trapped in there has any way of detecting lies.

"All right. I can *accept* this story." He seemed relieved. "Cobb, you're on one week administrative leave, starting immediately."

"Sarge?" asked Mandi, wondering if she had just been suspended anyway.

"Go be with your family. That's all. Get out."

"Thanks Sarge," she said. The deputy director nodded and we exited. Once the three of us reached the parking lot, Mandi and Lai Wan stood facing each other awkwardly.

"Lai, I can't tell you how much what you did means to me. Charlie would probably be dead if you hadn't helped. And what you did in there ..." The psychometrist waved Mandi into silence.

"There are many ways to the truth. I simply gave the one closest to the facts that gave history the outcome it deserved."

"But why did you come all the way down here and defend me? We've never gotten along," said Mandi.

"I had a niece who was killed. I was not able to save her. I carry the pain of her loss with me every day. Helping to save your nephew has taken some of the evil that was done to her and transformed it into something good. I don't know if I would have let Johnson live were I in your shoes. There will be days you will punish yourself for your generosity. No one deserves to be punished further for choosing the lesser of evils."

"Thank you." Lai Wan nodded again.

"You are welcome."

"What do I owe you for your fee?" Mandi said.

"As you said earlier, you do not like me. That is fair, as I will probably never come to like you. So, since I believe holding an enormous debt over your head will make you most uncomfortable, let us say you owe me a large favor and that one day I will come to collect. How is that?"

Mandi fidgeted for a moment, then answered, "It's not so much that I don't want to owe you a favor ... I don't like owing anyone—anything. Couldn't you think of something I could give you, or do, or ..."

Lai Wan raised her hand to her head as if thinking, her look saying she was doing so merely for comic timing. After a moment of mock concentration, she announced, "Yes, there is, you will be sweet and wonderful to Agent Karver. Forever."

I know it's a cliché, but trust me, Mandi actually did turn green. As I held my breath, trying not to howl, the psychometrist added, "Yes, that would please me well. You shall greet him with respect —"

"Respect?"

"Walk his dog, if he has one, dust his home once a week, give him daily back rubs—"

"Excuse me?!"

"Keep his car clean, and his gun, and shoes ... oh, and bake him cookies. What kind do you prefer, Agent Karver?"

"Ah, macadamia white chocolate chip crunch ... with coconut."

"They sound wonderful. Enjoy them. Shall we say five dozen, the first Tuesday of every month?"

"A large favor," Mandi muttered in defeat. "A very large favor, to be collected at any time you ask."

Blinking, as if caught off guard, Lai Wan pretended to be something like flustered, then finally said, "Of course, Mandi, as you prefer."

For me, it was Christmas in July. I wanted to comment, but Lai Wan moved her head slightly, her attention distracted for a moment, which lead me to believe her ride was approaching.

As if to confirm that our time together was coming to a close, she suddenly got very serious, telling Mandi and me, "You two are very good for each other. You are both seeped in darkness, but you each try to carry one another into the light. It is a generosity few know, and fewer appreciate."

Neither one of us knowing how to act more mature than one of the Three Stooges, though, Mandi just lowered her eyes and said, "He's seeped in something."

"It's the aftershave you got me for Christmas. Don't think I don't know it came from a dollar store," I countered. "As for what Mandi's seeped in, I'd rather not say, but if you shone one of the tech UV lights on her she'd look like a ghost." As we saw Goward's car coming into view, I added, "And hey, I'd like to say 'thanks' for everything as well."

Still serious, she answered, "Agent Karver, I must tell you that despite your horrific past, the way you have fought your demon and struggle to make right acts that were not entirely your fault is commendable – even noble. Your spirit impresses me far more that your past horrifies me. For your own sake, as you relive the things you have done, try to revisit some of the good things as well."

Goward pulled up to the curb and Lai Wan climbed inside. Whether or not she bothered to wave, the car's tinted windows hid her from view as they drove off. As Mandi and I stood there watching them fade from sight, I said, "Well, she didn't seem so bad."

"This time she wasn't," answered Mandi. "Let's see if you think so next time when she calls in that favor."

"She won't be calling me, partner."

I won't tell you what Mandi did to me then, but it hurt for about forty-five minutes.

ASK NOT

I felt like I was back in high school, being called into the principal's office, only my principal hadn't yanked me out of the electric chair. Sarge Winston had. Actually, my principal had always said that I would end up in prison, although his gloom and doom forecast for my life stopped short of including death row as my final destination. Not even he had predicted I'd be possessed by a seriál demon to get there.

Getting called in on the carpet by the Deputy Director of the Department of Mystic Affairs was nothing new for me. Every other time it'd happened, I knew why. This time I didn't and that worried me. Sarge Winston was a good guy, especially for a high-up Fed, but he was still my boss. It was his job to make sure I toed the line and that wasn't exactly easy. I'm not a suit and tie kind of guy, despite the DMA dress code.

Still, Sarge saved my life, had Father Sundry exorcise the demon, and put me to work as an agent for the DMA. I owed him, but that didn't mean I made his life easy. Although I'd never admit it, disappointing Sarge felt like someone was ripping a hole in my chest.

Problem was, I hadn't done anything trouble worthy for weeks. Certainly nothing to warrant Sarge leaving me cooling my heels for ten minutes before he showed.

"Sorry to keep you waiting, Karver," said Sarge.

He had never apologized before either. Something was definitely up. "No problem. What'd I do this time?" I figured it was better to have it out in the open.

Sarge laughed. "Nothing I know about yet. Why? You have a guilty conscience?"

After a demon used my body to slaughter 63 innocent people, I have a permanent guilty conscience. "Not about anything recent."

"I want you to accompany me on an assignment," he said.

"Why me?" The DMA had plenty of powerhouses. I wasn't one of them. Compared to a jinn or the Celtic god of the hunt, I was strictly bench warmer material. I'm one of the few agents who actually wears

Kevlar. One of the few mystic abilities I have was being able to sense hell magic in play. "Demon problem?"

"Not that," he said. "But I have my reasons. Besides, you haven't done much with your partner on leave this week."

With Mandi trying to help Charlie and the rest of his family through his trauma, I'd been riding a desk.

"Any reason for the mystery act?" I asked.

"Lots. Grab your overnight bag from your locker and meet me in the lobby in fifteen," he said.

"Can you at least tell me where we're going?" I asked.

"Dallas."

We flew from Dulles to Dallas/Fort Worth International.

When Adin redid my face he made me good looking and Mandi tells me I got the dark and brooding act down, which apparently adds up to irresistible to some women. That and the demon made some other adjustments to me that made the ladies notice me. It helped him lure some of our victims. It was likely the reason that our flight attendant was very interested in me. I got extra pretzels, free headphones, two dinners, and my pillow fluffed half a dozen times – not to mention a whispered offer that would have made my month a few years ago. Even the idea of sex sets off flashbacks to my monster days. I took a phone number I never planned to use just to get some peace.

Sarge looked on and smiled. He had a white crew cut and a thick white moustache and, despite his advanced years, had the build of a bear. The flight attendant, apparently looking to hedge her bets, whispered in his ear too. Sarge gave her a look of apology and pointed to his wedding ring. She seemed both surprised and disappointed.

We didn't talk the rest of the flight. Sarge isn't a motormouth, but silence was unusual even for him. Whatever our assignment was, it was troubling the old man.

Getting off the plane, I had to duck into a duty free shop to lose the persistent flight attendant.

"Good to see all that academy training we gave you is going to good use," he said.

"Ha, ha," I said. "I consistently scored high on every test I was given."

"Then we better make those tests harder," Sarge said, laughing and pointing across the corridor to where the flight attendant was standing. She had enough buttons undone for me to know she was wearing a pink push up bra. She had her finger in her mouth, trying for seductive. It just reminded me of a six year old that the demon had…

I almost threw up all my extra pretzels right then and there.

Sarge didn't have the empathic abilities that my partner did, but he had some idea of what was happening inside my head. He put his arm around my shoulder, making sure the woman could see, before he pointed to his ring finger and then to me.

The woman's jaw dropped, she pouted, but turned and left.

"You don't take that arm off me, I'm going to tell Emmy," I said.

"She'd get a chuckle and a half out of that. I was very homophobic back in the day," he said. "Different time."

I'm not a big one for thank yous, but his save was appreciated – helped get my mind off darker times. "Sarge…"

"Don't mention it," he said cutting me off. Sarge veered off toward car rental row. That was a surprise. I was a lowly field agent, so I was expected to take care of things like that. Sarge was the number two man in the DMA, or number three if you listened to Zachs, the other deputy director. I didn't – safer that way. Guy can use his voice to put a whammy on you and make you do anything he told you. In short, even in the DMA there's enough brownnosing to make sure someone should have been there with a car.

"The Dallas office isn't sending someone to pick us up?"

"Not on this one. They have a standing order to pass the situation on to me," he said.

"Which is?" I asked.

"Revenant," he said. That's government speak for a ghost or spirit that's tied to one spot.

"Where?"

"Dealey Plaza," he said, looking for a reaction. I tend not to react overtly, so I wondered what about this place was different enough for him to expect me to. The location didn't ring a bell. "People in the area for a two-block radius have been complaining of things being knocked out of their hands on the street, cars not starting, even being thrown around. One elderly woman broke a hip on the sidewalk."

"You sure she didn't just trip?" I asked.

"Yes."

"Isn't it unusual for a revenant to have that much area to roam and enough power to affect the physical world to that extent?" I asked.

"It is, but this one is fed by belief," he said.

I was confused. "Belief is how gods get power, not ghosts. Are we dealing with a dead god?"

"Not exactly. If you knew your history better, you'd already know what we were dealing with."

I racked my brain for famous Texans. "Jim Bowie? John Wayne?" I wasn't sure if he was really from Texas, but enough of his movie characters were.

Sarge just sighed and we went to get the car.

When we got to Dealey Plaza, we scouted the area on foot. I had never been there, but I had to admit it looked familiar. Three streets— Main, Elm, and Commerce—all met under a railroad bridge. Three sides were surrounded by buildings over ten stories. And on one side there was a grassy knoll.

I stopped short in the middle of the street. I realized where I was and I think my jaw even dropped. Sarge turned to look at my face and smiled sadly. "You figured it out, did you?"

"You've got to be kidding me. We're here to deal with the ghost of a dead president?" I said.

Sarge nodded. "One of the good ones too."

"You knew him?" I said.

"Not well, but I did."

My mind started working out the details. "Most revenants are tied to the physical world by something that is unfinished. An important task that remains unfinished or an unpunished killer are the most common. I'm assuming passing some old piece of legislation isn't going to fix the problem."

"Not hardly. The former president is fixated on his assassination and the lack of resolution," Sarge said.

Before I could ask more questions, screams came from Commerce Street. Sarge ran fast, especially for an old guy and I had to hustle to catch up. As we got closer, we saw a misty presence in which hovered several shopping bags, a pocketbook, a cowboy hat, and a black high heeled shoe. They were swirling in a variety of directions.

An American flag had come lose from a nearby flagpole and floated behind the spectral presence. The wind seemed to be making the notes that comprised *Hail to the Chief.*

People were running any way they could to get away. It was a stampede. A well-dressed woman in business attire with a single black shoe had fallen on the sidewalk. Her arms were covering her head to protect herself from the fleeing feet of her fellow Texans.

I rushed through the crowd, blocking them with my own body. One middle-aged man with a potbelly and a bolo tie who outweighed me by fifty pounds was shocked when he bounced off my back and into the building.

I was on duty, so I turned with a smile. "Watch where you're going, sir." He didn't say a word. His eyes were fixated behind me and I guess the ghost was coming closer by the speed with which he ran away. I turned and ducked. A flying pocketbook barely missed conking me in the head. A black shoe came at me next and I managed to catch it and pull it free. Reaching down, I pulled the other one off the woman's foot and handed the reunited pair to her before pulling her up. Hopefully, this way she wouldn't fall again.

"What is that?" she screamed.

"Apparently, the ghost of JFK," I said. DMA policy is to tell the truth. Unfortunately because of what we deal with, nobody ever believes us.

"I think it's a dust devil." It was easier to make up an explanation than consider the truth. "Thanks for the help," she said, then ran off.

The street around the revenant was deserted, but crowds were gathering out of harm's way to watch. I saw a few camcorders. Although we don't cover up, we do have orders from the current president to not show off either.

Sarge got right in front of the presence, blocking its path. The crimson crystal that was fused to his chest glowed through his shirt faintly. "Mr. President, you have to stop this before someone gets hurt."

"Too late. In case you haven't noticed, someone's already been hurt," the ghost intoned and vanished. Everything that had been aloft plopped to the sidewalk, except the flag which floated over to Sarge and landed in his hands.

I walked over to him, trying to figure out our next move. Sarge, once a sergeant in the army, handed me one end of the flag and motioned to me to help him fold it. He tucked the finished triangle under his arm and started walked toward Main.

I trotted to keep up. "Why not Elm Street?" I knew he had a reason; I just had no idea what it was.

"They've redone Elm. It doesn't look the same as it did in '63. He won't manifest there as he'll have less power. Sadly, the city planning board got the money and is going to restore it."

"I'm assuming that Oswald didn't do it," I said.

"He was part, but only part. Kennedy won't be able to rest until the entire truth comes out," said Sarge.

"None of the conspiracy nuts got it right yet?"

Sarge shook his head. "Some have got parts of it, but no one has released the full story."

"And until that happens, the former leader of the free world won't retire to the afterlife," I said. "Why don't we just release the whole story?"

"It's not that easy. I was one of the ones investigating the assassination for the DMA and the whole story is more complicated than you can imagine. For one thing, the entire Warren Commission report was ordered sealed by the order of President Johnson until 2039," said Sarge.

"Which makes his involvement suspect of course." Sarge put on his poker face. "Not to mention, sixty five years later, anyone involved would be dead. Except you, of course," I said. Sarge has already celebrated his hundredth birthday. He won't be around forever, but he'll still be around long after I'm pushing up daisies.

"I wasn't involved. I only investigated," said Sarge.

"Obviously, you've had to deal with the presidential ghost before. If you couldn't send him to the beyond, what did you do?" I asked.

Sarge stopped and stared me in the eyes. "Only what I had to."

"Did you ever read the report?" I asked.

"Yes, after the second time. Right over there is the Texas School Book Depository. That's where the Warren Commission issued its public explanation. A single copy of the full report was hidden and locked away by one of the members there. It has several items left out of the one secured in Washington. I broke in, intending to hand it over to the media so he could finally rest in peace," he said.

"But you didn't. Why?" I asked.

"I read it first. Even so many years later, what was in there had the potential to actually destroy this country. I had thought the commission members moral cowards, but after I read it, I understood why they did what they did. I couldn't go through with releasing it. I wasn't going to be the man who destroyed America. I put it back and did my job," Sarge said.

"But it's not something you're happy with," I said.

"Son, I've been defending this country in one way or another since before your father was born." True enough. Sarge fought in Europe in WWI, which is where he was bonded with that thing on his chest. It's the reason he's still alive and when it's in the mood, makes him as powerful as a tank. "I've done a lot of things in the trenches that I'm not proud of, but most of them were necessary. In a perfect world, I never would have had to do 'em, but this ain't that kind of world. We do what we can to make sure the bad guys don't win and try not to become the bad guys in the process."

Sarge spied a black limo and moved toward it. "That's just what we need." A driver was seated behind the wheel. Sarge flashed his badge. "Federal agent, sir. I'm afraid we have to commandeer your vehicle."

"Like Hell," said the driver.

I opened the door. "Sir, we are going to get the vehicle. You can do it the easy way or the hard way."

"What's the hard way?" he asked.

"We arrest you for obstruction. True, you'll make bail in a day, but then we'll make a phone call to the IRS. I'm guessing you deal with a lot of cash only business and I suspect not all of that gets reported. It'd be a shame if they found you had been underpaying your taxes, what with all the penalties and interest," I said.

"And the easy way?"

"You give us the car, we give you a receipt. Anything happens, the government has to fix or replace it," I said.

"You'll take good care of her?" he asked.

"We will, sir," said Sarge.

The man willingly got out of the car; Sarge gave him a receipt and took down his personal information. Then the old man got in the back.

I gathered I was driving and got into the driver's seat. The partition window was down.

"Drive up and down Main and Commerce slowly until we see something, then pull up alongside the commotion. I'll take care of the rest," said Sarge.

I drove for the better part of an hour, until I noticed a post office without a flag.

"I think he's nearby," I said, pointing to the bare flagpole. Sure enough, a flag was floating behind the ghost of JFK. Again there was the flotsam of personal possessions flying through the air, only this time there was a baby in the midst. Before I could stop, Sarge was out of the car and had managed to grab the baby and return her to her father. Sarge ordered the people to evacuate the immediate area and they obeyed. He had that kind of voice and that kind of presence. Sarge waved me to bring the car closer.

"Mr. President, your car is waiting," said Sarge to the ghost, opening the back curbside door.

"*Thank you,*" the spirit ex-president said and floated into the backseat. Everything but the flag dropped to the pavement. The stars and stripes followed JFK, with Sarge behind it.

I looked over my shoulder looking for instructions. If we strayed too far, the ghost would fade. Sarge motioned back toward an alley.

The revenant looked at Sarge. "*I know you, don't I? Agent Winston, DMA. Helped us out when the Russians tried to attack the White House with that invasion of igosha sprites. My wife hated having to put out all those spoons and loaves of bread at the table and the staff thought I was crazy when I ordered everyone to knit them hats and mittens, but it worked. You even managed to somehow ship them all back to the Kremlin. Oh, to have had a working spy camera to have seen their faces. You still a field agent?*"

"No, Mr. President. I'm deputy director now."

"*Uncle Sam still in charge?*" he asked.

"Yes, sir, he is," answered Sarge.

"*I liked him. Always felt inspired after I met with Sam.*"

"He has that effect on me as well," said Sarge.

"*Who is driving?*"

"That's Agent Karver behind the wheel."

"Mr. President," I said, turning my head.

JFK nodded at me, then turned to Sarge. *"He looks normal enough."* Not all DMA agents do.

"We have a situation here, Mr. President," said Sarge.

I'm not sure the dead president heard or comprehended. *"My back doesn't hurt at all. It did when I was alive. I'm dead again, aren't I?"*

"Still, I'm afraid."

"It's so hard to think. My head hurts so much."

"That's where you were shot, sir."

"And nothing's been done about it."

"That's not exactly true, Mr. President. Our hands are tied," said Sarge.

"I order you to untie them. I deserve at least that much."

"I'm afraid you are no longer president, sir. I can only imagine what you've gone through, but you are beginning to get out of control. You fractured a woman's hip and almost hurt a baby."

"I would never..." The spectral presence paused. *"But I did, didn't I? I didn't mean for anyone to get hurt. It's just I hurt so much, I'm so confused and nobody is telling the truth about what they did to me."*

"The truth is many years away," said Sarge.

"How long has it been?"

"More than three decades," said Sarge.

"Damn."

"Sir, do you think you can control yourself and stay apart from the public?"

"I have to let the truth be known."

"I can't allow that at this time. You know what would happen. You would destroy the land that you love. And I can't risk you hurting or killing someone else in the process."

"I'm the goddamned President of the US of A. What makes you think anything you do is going to make me do anything?"

"Because a great man once said 'Ask not what your country can do for you, ask what you can do for your country'."

The ghost of JFK was silent again. *"We've been through this before, haven't we?"*

Sarge nodded. "Many times."

"I remember now. That thing on your chest is going to blast me.

Everything that I am is going to be spread out so far that it'll take years for me to get myself back together again, to be able to think a coherent thought again, won't it?"

"Yes, sir."

"Couldn't it just destroy me?"

"Not on my watch, sir," said Sarge.

"I always thought when I died I'd see Patrick again."

Sarge noticed my look of confusion. "His son – died in infancy."

"And I'd finally get to meet poor Arabella."

"Their stillborn daughter," whispered Sarge.

"Let's get this over with before I change my mind. Will you tell my wife, my daughter and my son I love them?"

"I have told them each time before when you asked me, sir. I'm sorry to report that your wife and son have since passed on."

The ghost wept.

After the spirit of the former president composed himself, Sarge opened the door. The spirit exited in what I can only describe as a presidential manner. Sarge followed. I got out the driver's side, but just to watch.

Sarge stood at attention and saluted. The ghostly president returned the salute and they both held that position for several moments.

"Do it," said JFK.

Sarge unbuttoned his shirt so the crimson jewel was exposed. A ruby beam shone out, enveloping Kennedy's spirit. It dissipated and dissolved until there was nothing there.

Sarge's eyes were misty, so I felt obliged to ask a stupid question. "You okay?"

"No, I'm not," said Sarge. "You understand why I brought you along?"

I shook my head. Other than drive the car, I hadn't done anything useful.

"This will happen again. I may not be here to handle it." Sometime before I was recruited, Sarge had been imprisoned off American soil for five years. "I wanted someone I could trust to know how to handle the situation."

"I don't have the power to get rid of a revenant," I said.

"When we get back, I'll help the lab boys and girls whip you up something that'll take care of that."

"Why me?"

"I need someone who would be able to do this if the time came. Sam would have problems disobeying a past president; Zachs would turn the situation to his own advantage. Others would have trouble seeing the forest for the tree. After what you've been through, your only agenda is to make right. I will warn you, he doesn't always go quietly. Will you do it?"

"I'll have to think about it," I said.

Sarge walked around to the driver's door and got in. "Our flight leaves at 2042." Took a second of math to translate the military time to 8:42 PM. Then he told me where the uncensored report was.

"What makes you think I'm planning on…?"

"Because it's what I would do." Sarge drove the limo away. "What I did do."

The report was relatively easy to get to. The building had only average security. The man who hid it had no mystic powers, set no mundane traps. Just a hidden door in a monument that would never be gotten rid of.

It would have taken me days to finish it. The thing was as thick as the DC, New York, and Boston phone books piled on top of each other. I didn't have to go through all of it. The censored findings were all in one section, barely ten yellowed pages long. There were footnotes, but I didn't check most of them. I didn't have to.

Even the wildest conspiracy theorist would have been shocked at what was there. It would have destroyed the federal government, not to mention that of Texas. Our government is very far from perfect, but it's far better than what would follow in the wake of this getting out.

I put it back where I found it and headed for the airport.

I'd tell Sarge I'd do it. I wouldn't like it, but I'd do my job – same as him.

ZOMBIE AND SPICE

It's rare that the Department of Mystic Affairs gets called in on a stalker case. I hate to call enduring the attentions of someone who's off in the head mundane, but it usually is. Folks with mystic power tend to skip obsessive fantasies in favor of making their sick dreams a reality. The perp in this one just hadn't managed to make that jump yet. Hopefully, we'd catch him before he could.

What makes this case a little odder is not only did I ask for it, I threatened to quit if I didn't get it. The woman at the center of the depraved attention had never met me, but I owed her. I took away something from her life that could never be replaced.

When my partner and I arrived at Lucy Paxton's home, she invited Mandi and me in for coffee. If the DMA hadn't given me a new face when they recruited me, she would have never let us in the front door.

"I have to say I'm surprised that Federal Agents were sent to help me. Before this, I could barely get the cops to take me seriously," said Lucy.

"This was a little bit out of their realm of expertise, but it falls squarely in ours," I said.

Every night for the past week, someone had sent Lucy a gift. The last three were zombies. The first was a rat, the second a squirrel, and the last a raccoon. It took two animal control officers and four cops to take down the raccoon. When we stopped by the morgue on our way here, its dismembered body was still moving. At least the locals were smart enough to separate the body parts into stainless steel containers. Three of the men were bitten by the living dead rodent, and were terrified they were going to become zombies. When I explained to them it didn't work like that, one of them offered to name his first-born child after me. I declined. Karver was a bad enough name for me to bear, let alone an innocent kid.

"I have to admit, I'd never even heard of the Department of Mystic Affairs before," Lucy said.

"Most people don't hear about us until they need us," said Mandi. It wasn't like we were a secret agency, but most of the cases we dealt with seemed to only be reported in the tabloids.

"Do you have any idea who has been stalking you?" I asked.

"I've been over this with the police. I have no idea of his name, but I have seen him a few times. He's got a medium build with dark short hair."

"That's not much to go on," Mandi said.

"I know," she said. "How did he send those animals after me?"

"There are different ways of raising the dead," I said. Not all of them were limited to zombies, but Lucy didn't need to hear that. If this guy was a necromancer, the danger for this poor woman was enormous. "We're going to stake out your house and see if we can catch him or his next present. We'll get a better idea of what he can do then."

"Wouldn't it be better to find that out before then?" she asked.

"Of course, but life's rarely that easy," answered my partner. Lucy wrapped her arms around both her shoulders and shuddered. Mandi's an empath, and it was obvious she was confused by the emotions coming off our victim. "Are you okay?"

"No," Lucy admitted honestly. "I want to kill this guy."

"Normal enough feelings," said Mandi.

"No, not for doing this to me. Not entirely anyway – for using a raccoon. Raccoons were Winnie's favorite. She had more than a dozen stuffed ones."

"Winnie?" asked Mandi.

"She was my daughter."

Mandi glared at me as the name Winnie Paxton clicked in her head.

"She was killed by the serial killer Carver," said Lucy. The lady was tough. Her eyes got runny, but she didn't let a single tear escape. "It must be rough for you, Agent Karver, to have to go through life with the same name."

I didn't point out the difference in spelling. It was the only way they'd let me use the name.

"It's a burden." But one I choose to bear so I never forget what that demon forced me to do.

"When they gave him the death penalty, I thought it would help. I even went and witnessed the execution." I stopped myself from saying "I know." I wasn't there, but I saw the video of my supposed death, and all the faces of those who came to watch. Gus did a great acting job pretending to be me dying. "But killing him didn't bring back my little girl. And now this stalker is messing with the only thing I have left of my little girl—my memories."

"I won't let him hurt you. I promise," I said.

"Ms. Paxton, will you excuse us? We need to examine the perimeter of your house to determine the best way to secure the area," said Mandi.

"Of course," she said.

I followed Mandi outside. I didn't need to be an empath to know she was pissed.

"You volunteered us for a case involving the mother of one of your victims? And didn't mention it to me?"

"I took away her daughter. She's in danger. I owe her that much," I said.

"The seriál demon killed her…"

"Using my body," I said.

"It wasn't your fault," said Mandi. I remained silent. I had been told that, time and time again, after the DMA had pulled me off death row and exorcised the demon. Logically, what they said made sense. Logic only goes so far. There was no way for me to fully explain that to anyone, even Mandi. My only answer was silence. "How'd you get Sarge to agree?"

"I can be very persuasive," I said. Mandi tilted her head. "I used guilt and when that didn't work, I begged."

"You?" Mandi said. "I've never seen you beg for anything."

"Been saving it," I said. "Too bad the same can't be said for you."

Mandi raised an eyebrow and glared at me. "Begging?"

"No, saving yourself. I mean, you're the only woman I know who sailors follow from port to port instead of the other way around," I teased.

"Anything to support our troops. Now that you've started begging, don't stop. It might actually help you get a date that you don't have to inflate."

"Say what you will about Belinda Blowup, but she has the most amazing pair of balloons. And when I fill her with helium and take some out of the nozzle, I can make noises for the both of us," I said. Mandi and I had an odd dynamic, but it worked for us.

We did a perimeter check. Typical suburban house, a small lawn in front, a little yard in back. We set up motion alarms along her fence line so we'd know if anything came through the back. We gave Lucy a radio that tied directly into the ear sets we both wore, and parked our car a couple of houses away. Her home was at a T-intersection, so we had three blocks to watch.

We had thermoses filled with coffee, soup, and the traditional box of doughnuts. Nothing happened for the first several hours, except that our food supply got low. Around nine o'clock in the evening, Mandi pointed to a little girl in a dress coming down the bottom of the T. "Something's wrong."

"Not all kids have a curfew," I said.

"That's not it. I'm getting no emotions off of her," said Mandi.

Then I felt the slightest tingle on the back of my neck. My time as a possessed left me with the ability to sense different types of magic. Those involving Hell or demons I'm most sensitive to. If the girl was a demon or possessed herself, I would have known she was coming long before we could see her.

"I think it's a dead girl walking," I said.

The demon also enhanced my eyesight. As soon as the girl in the pink dress passed beneath a streetlight, my heart skipped a beat.

"It's Winnie. The bastard raised her daughter," I said, getting out of the car. A rage that wasn't entirely this sicko's fault took me over.

"Karver, get back in here. The raiser could be anywhere. We don't want to give away our position," said Mandi.

I was beyond listening. One of my dead was walking, and I had to stop Winnie before her mother saw her, or the emotional damage to Lucy would be something I couldn't imagine.

When I got close enough to the zombie child, I realized I didn't have a plan. Protocol dictates the best way to stop a zombie is to dismember it and separate the pieces. I had already sliced up this little girl once. I carried two blades under the back of my coat, but I couldn't bring myself to use them on her – not again.

I needed another option. There was a sedan between me and the girl. I used my gun to smash open the driver's window and pull the trunk release. It popped and I opened it all the way. Zombies are not terribly creative. If Winnie's raiser had just told her to go to her mother's house, she'd only attack me if I tried to stop her. The magic used to raise and hold zombies together makes them very strong. There was a very good chance Winnie was stronger than me, so I had to be careful. I waited until she was near the trunk, grabbed her around the waist, spun her, and threw her into the trunk, slamming the lid down hard.

The metal wouldn't hold her long. I could already hear her pounding against it.

Which is when the sensor alarm went off.

"Karver, he's heading in the back. I'm going after him," said Mandi into her radio.

I ran back toward the house, pulling out my gun with one hand and one of my knives with the other. I could hear Mandi shooting at something in the backyard. I assumed it was similar to what greeted me in the front.

A zombie pit bull ran to intercept me. I swung my blade at the canine's neck and sliced the undead head clean off. Each of my blades was covered with some pretty powerful runes, which made slicing and dicing much easier. I picked the head up and threw it up into a tree. I got lucky—it stuck on the first throw, but wouldn't stay up there long. The jaws were moving – trying to knock itself free. The body tried to run away from me, so I shot out two legs. That slowed it down enough for me to slice off the other two. I threw the pieces onto nearby roofs, where three of them landed in rain gutters. I picked the body up and impaled it high up on Lucy's fence post. I hoped that would make it harder for the parts to reunite.

I charged the front door, smashing it in. The enhanced strength and durability the demon had given my body for its dark deeds did come in handy.

The stalker had already reached Lucy, who had curled up in the fetal position on her own kitchen floor. The man who thought zombies were a sign of love was cradling her head on his lap and petting her head as if she was a dog. He had a long, slim knife with a black hilt and carvings of its own pressed against her throat. Her eyeglasses lay thrown to the side of the floor.

Mandi had already gotten in. My partner had her gun drawn, but neither of us had a shot, especially since a mystic knife might not even have to cut Lucy to kill her.

I could feel the calming emotions Mandi was sending out at the stalker, but the propathic stuff didn't always work so well with the crazies.

"You two can leave us. My girlfriend and I would like to spend some quality time together," said the stalker.

"Can't do that," said Mandi. "Federal Agents."

"Let go of the knife and move away from Lucy," I ordered.

"We just want to be alone. Why can't you see that?" the stalker said.

"I'm not sure Lucy is with you on that," I said.

"That's why I brought this." Stalker was indicating his knife. "One stab into the dead and they rise to obey me. If I use it on the living, they become a zombie, too. Lucy will have to love me then. I'll make her."

"Actually, I think Lucy really does like you," said Mandi. Stalker looked at Lucy, wanting to believe her, but not able to take trembling in terror as a sign of affection. "It's just all the dead animals scared her. We girls are kind of frightened of dead things. You know how it is."

"I guess," conceded the stalker, distracted enough by the conversation to let me get behind an appliance island. He couldn't pick up that Mandi was putting out enough trust to let a known crooked politician get re-elected.

"I'm sure Lucy would be interested if you'd just take it slower," suggested Mandi. "Wouldn't you, Lucy?"

Lucy was terrified but she wasn't dumb. "I might be." The words might have been more convincing if she hadn't stammered.

"Most women want traditional courting. Poetry, flowers, that kind of thing," hinted Mandi, her eyes subtly darting to a nearby counter.

Stalker looked up to see the flowers my partner had stolen a look at. He got a half smile and reached up for them, loosening his grip on his hostage. I leapt over the counter, landing with my knees on the stalker's chest. I had holstered my gun while I hid, and used my free hand to grab his wrist. This loser had normal human strength, so it wasn't hard to pull the knife away from Lucy's throat.

"Move!" I yelled. Lucy did. I smashed the hilt of my blade into the stalker's nose. There was a satisfying crunch as the cartilage broke and I was able to pull the zombifying blade free.

"You're under arrest. You have the right to remain silent…" I started to say but was distracted.

"Winnie?" said Lucy. The zombie that once was her daughter stood in the smashed in doorway.

"I thought you might want to start a family again, sweetheart," said the stalker, with a very nasal tone from his crushed nose. Lucy's eyes were so clouded with grief, hope, and the sight of her fondest wish come true that she hadn't noticed the traces of degeneration around her daughter's face, or the open wounds on her knuckles from punching her way out of the trunk. The lack of eyeglasses probably didn't hurt either.

"Let me go or I'll order her own daughter to kill her," said the stalker.

"Not a chance," I said. "Besides, I'm the one with the knife now." This clown had no magic of his own that I could sense. Everything came from the knife. Without it, there was a good chance he was powerless, and I could control her since I had the blade.

"The one who used the blade has the power, not the one who holds it," he said. "Winnie, kill Mommy, honey. We'll raise her like you later."

The little girl moved toward her mother. So much for my neutering theory.

I put my knife against the stalker's throat. "Tell her to stop or I'll kill you."

"A Fed kill a suspect in cold blood? Right," he said.

I already had too many dead and it might not stop him. Plus, spilling blood when necromancy was in progress was never the best of ideas. It's actually listed as a no-no in the DMA handbook. If this loser did succeed in making Winnie kill her mother, my principles might just go out the window.

Mandi was lining up an explosive round aimed right at Winnie's chest.

"No!" I shouted and put myself between mother and zombie daughter. "Winnie, don't do this. This bad man wants to hurt your mommy. You don't want that, do you?" I knew Winnie's spirit had long since moved on, but the body held some of those memories. Hopefully, it would be enough. Lucy didn't need to endure the sight of us blowing up or slicing her daughter's body to pieces: it's a memory that would never fade, and would make the ones I had forced her to carry that much worse.

I made a foolish mistake. In my efforts to protect Lucy, I had taken my eyes off her stalker. So had Mandi. He used our distraction to grab a kitchen knife and then use it to again grab Lucy.

"Winnie, get them and rip their limbs off," he ordered.

I was no mage, but I held the zombie-making blade in front of me and focused every ounce of will I had into it. "Winnie, don't."

The little zombie girl in the pink dress stopped. I felt a surge of power from the black blade. Something was happening.

"Kill them, I said!" screamed the stalker.

"Winnie, do the right thing," I said.

The little zombie girl turned and moved toward her raiser, who was her mother's stalker. With a burst of speed that even I had trouble following, she broke the man's arm that held the knife as she flipped him down to the ground. With a stomp of her left foot, she crushed the stalker's right knee. With both hands, she grabbed his left shin and twisted, ripping the hip asunder as easily as if it were the leg on a baked chicken. The stalker's screams were loud, shrill, and inspired absolutely no pity in me.

"Winnie, that's enough," I said, whispering into the hilt of the zombifying blade as if it were a microphone. The little girl zombie looked up at me. Looking in those dead eyes, one of *my* dead's eyes, made me more disgusted than I've ever been in my new life.

Lucy had watched everything as if in shock, but she finally started to move, her eyes blinking. "Winnie, is that you?"

I spoke softly into the hilt. "Nod."

Winnie shook her head.

"I've missed you so much," said Lucy, opening her arms.

"Gently hug your mother," I whispered.

Winnie complied. Lucy held her little zombie daughter and wept. "I love you so much, Winnie."

"Kiss your mommy goodbye and wait outside," I said. Winnie complied.

"Baby, wait! Come back!" Lucy pleaded.

Mandi stepped in. "Ms. Paxton, your stalker raised your daughter as a zombie, planning to use her to hurt you. We were just lucky—"

"That your daughter's love for you was so strong that she was able to disobey the evil man who did this to her," I said. Mandi gave me a look and a smile.

"Can't I see her again? Can't she stay with me a little while?" begged Lucy.

"I'm sorry, Ms. Paxton, but there is no telling when the magic animating her will wear off. She'll collapse back into how she was before. You've been through enough. You don't need to see that." No parent should ever have to see their child die once, let alone twice.

"Her love was really strong enough to break the evil spell?" asked Lucy, looking to Mandi for reassurance.

"Yes. I've never seen anything like it. You have one very special daughter," said Mandi.

Lucy began weeping, a mix of joy, grief, and pride, with a smattering of hope that her daughter lived on in a world beyond, then collapsed into Mandi's arms.

We called an ambulance for the stalker, whose name was Horace Cuomo. He had to undergo twelve hours of surgery to get his hip turned back around. The doctors would later tell us he'd never walk right again. However, he wouldn't give up who had given him the zombifying blade. He was more afraid of them than he was of us. We gathered the animal zombie pieces I had cut off and the ones Mandi had shot up and put them in canisters for the locals to cart off. The dog head I had put in the tree had fallen and using the opening and closing of its jaw managed to crawl to the fence where the torso was impaled, but wasn't able to climb the pickets to reattach itself. Dante Amato, a necromancer from the DC office of the DMA, was coming in to deanimate them.

We told Lucy I was going to lay her daughter back down to rest. She ran into her daughter's room and came out with a stuffed raccoon. "Please give this to her, in case that bastard took the one she was buried with. Winnie could never sleep well without at least one of her coons."

"I will," I said, and walked outside. My partner followed.

"I'm going to stay with the victim for a little while," said Mandi. Her powers were helpful when it came to cleaning up the emotional wreckage. "Do you think Winnie's spirit really saved her mother?"

I shrugged.

"You don't, do you?"

"I'd like to, but no," I said.

"Then what did it? It wasn't because you were holding the blade." Mandi had tested the theory by trying to tell the little zombie to go around the side of the house so her mother wouldn't see her again. Winnie ignored her.

"Necromancy was used to bring her back. Who would have more power over a zombie—the one who raised her or…"

"The one who killed her," finished my partner with a sigh. Mandi knew I wasn't much for physical contact. It brought back too many of the bad things I did because of my demonic hitchhiker. Yet she leaned forward and kissed me on the cheek.

"Why'd you do that?" I asked. I wasn't complaining. Mandi's the only real friend I had in the world these days. It felt good.

"You could have stopped the zombie, but instead risked your own neck to help give the mother closure," said Mandi.

"I risked yours, too," I said.

"It was worth the risk," she said.

"No insult or dig?" I said.

"Not this time, partner. I'm too damn proud of you," Mandi said. "You want company taking Winnie back? At least until Dante gets there to deanimate her?"

I shook my head. "I need to do it myself." Mandi handed me the car keys. "Don't need them."

Mandi looked confused. "You never even asked the mother where they buried her daughter. You know, don't you?"

"I do." I pointed. "About a mile and a half that way. I know where all my dead are buried." After I got a new chance at life, I visited the graves of each one of my dead. It didn't begin to make amends, but it was something I had to do.

Mandi nodded. The sun wouldn't rise for a few hours. I walked around to where Winnie stood waiting in the bushes and put out my hand. The zombie took it.

"This is from your mother. She loves you very much." I handed the dead girl the stuffed animal. "I'm very sorry for what I did. I'd give my own life to undo it." The little girl zombie looked at me, unblinking. I wasn't really expecting an answer or forgiveness. I wasn't worthy of either. All I could do was go on and do the best I could and, after Dante turned her back into a corpse again, bury for a second time the little girl I had once killed.

TAG TEAM MATCH WITH HELL

by
Patrick Thomas, C.J. Henderson,
and John L. French

We were back in Manhattan and my partner, Mandi Cobb, was none too happy about it. Not because Manhattan isn't a nice place to visit or anything. In fact, Bulfinche's Pub, the only bar I trust myself to drink in, is there. But we weren't on a social call. We were there because a woman by the name of Lai Wan had called in her marker. That was all right by me, because—to be honest—I like the woman. I guess in a sense I could relate to her. She was tortured by memories, too. At least in her case, they weren't her own.

We met up with this Lai Wan when she helped rescue Mandi's nephew. Then, after helping us with that, she went the extra mile and went to bat for us with Sarge Winston. That made her okay in my book—and in Mandi's. But, it didn't mean my partner was fond of her.

Now, it's not that I have a swelled head, but I'd gone in making the assumption that whatever Lai Wan needed was something Mandi and I would be able to handle on our own. So, I was surprised to find another woman waiting when we got to the psychometrist's home. In fact, both Mandi and I did a double take.

"Karver," asked the woman on the couch petting a large black dog.

"Miss Jones," I said. The muscles in her shoulders tensed up at what I guess she perceived as a slight. Holding back a grin, I added, "Sorry, *Detective* Jones. Good to see you, Bianca."

"You two know each other?" Mandi was justifiably surprised. We'd been partnered since very early on in my federal law enforcement career and since I didn't go out or socialize much, it was reasonable for her to figure very few people outside the DMA knew my new face.

This was true. Bianca Jones was one of them.

"Unfortunately," answered Bianca, but I detected a small trace of a smile on the corner of her mouth.

"Miss—" I paused long enough for her mouth to open to protest, then cut her off. "Detective Jones and I briefly went to the Department of Mystic Affairs Academy together." A look of understanding crossed Mandi's face.

"You must be your department's paranormal specialist then," said Mandi.

Bianca shrugged, waving a hand absently as she said; "Mostly shit happens and I have to clean it up."

"And you went to the academy with Karver?"

Bianca assumed a slightly sheepish look as she said, "Sort of."

The DMA made a habit of opening up the academy to local law enforcement to better train them to deal with mystic threats. They did this mainly because they have a very limited number of agents and quite simply, we can't deal with everything that comes down the road. Sam's goal was to have at least one paranormal expert in every major local law enforcement jurisdiction in the country. The problem is that the attitude of most departments towards magic and monsters ranges from skepticism to disbelief. Funny thing, but most people don't want to consider vampyres and the like as a real possibility until they're knee deep in them and being bitten on the ankles.

Not so in Baltimore. There's been a supernatural protector of one sort or another in that city since before the Great Fire of 1904. Lately, however, Baltimore's had more than its share of mystic crimes, with Bianca in the middle of most of them. So the DMA made her the offer.

"You 'sort of' went to the DMA Academy," asked Mandi. "Ever been a little bit pregnant?"

It was my turn to smile. "Bianca left before graduation. The pregnant thing, I have no idea."

"That's because I was partnered with you, Karver," said Bianca.

"Karver, I never even got a cigar," said Mandi.

"At the academy," Bianca added with more than a touch of irritation in her voice. "I've never been pregnant."

"Well, that explains it then. I can understand why a woman partnered with Karver would want to head for the hills. I've often thought of doing it myself," said Mandi.

"Except back home where you come from all the hill people are related to you and it would have cramped your recreational activities," I said. "Or maybe it wouldn't."

Bianca was now staring, first at me, then at Mandi, unable to tell if we were hurling good-natured digs or mean spirited ones.

"Never a bad idea to keep it in the family," said Mandi joking back. "Although, I will admit to being a little upset to find out that you had a partner that I didn't know about."

"It was at the academy and just one case," I said.

Mandi started to ask details, but was cut off as Lai Wan came into the room. On seeing his mistress the black dog jumped from the couch and trotted to her side. The psychometrist took a moment to both stroke the fur on his back and give the top of his head a scratching. As she did so, you could actually watch the tension lines that had been straining the flesh around the corners of her eyes relax, then fade.

"Good boy, Stranger," she said to the dog. Her tone lost its friendly lilt as she addressed us.

"I am certain this trip down memory lane is just lovely for the three of you, but I did not summon you here to reminisce." Holding up a DVD with a gloved hand, she added, "This is why I brought you here."

"You dragged me all the way up here from Baltimore to have movie night?" asked Bianca. "And with no popcorn?"

I felt the wisecrack was halfway decent but judging by the lack of movement on Lai Wan's face, I surmised she did not agree.

"What is on this disc is not a laughing matter. You will understand once you see it."

Going over to the TV, Lai Wan pushed a button on the DVD player. A tray slid open and she inserted the disc. A minute later the screen went from blue to tacky. Very bad music that sounded like it was from some horrid garage bands from the 70s or 80s blasted out and a movie with extremely poor production value started to roll from the point of view of the driver of a car.

"You invited us here to watch bad porn," asked Bianca. Lai Wan's face remained immobile as she answered, "Yes, the absolute worst." The scene changed from the view of the driving car to a coed little league game. Where it went from there made even my stomach turn.

"Why the Hell are we watching child porn?" I demanded.

"Because," answered Lai Wan, "despite what you believe you are seeing, that is exactly what it is not."

"If I wanted riddles, I could've gone to our psychic department," snarled Mandi. "I'm guessing you want us to help stop the people who are making this filth, but how does kiddie porn involve the DMA?"

"The people who made this movie," said the psychometrist, her eyes unblinking as she spoke, "are the people starring in it."

"The children are producing it?" I asked. Lai Wan shook her head.

"They are not children. None you see before you is younger than fifty years of age."

Doing her best Ricky Ricardo impersonation, Bianca said;

"Lai Wan, you got some splaining to do."

"When this was brought to my attention I made the mistake of touching the disc."

Lai Wan's ability to see various aspects of an object's history was necessarily unpleasant, but as far as I was concerned, this had to be one of the worst things ever she'd had to deal with.

"These seeming children have made a deal with Hell, selling their souls for centuries of eternal youth. As is often the case in these matters, it appears they did not bother with the fine print."

"So," I offered, "literal eternal youth?"

The psychometrist nodded, then continued, telling us, "I called Detective Jones here because she has a history of stealing souls from what you all perceive as 'Hell.' Also, these false children are operating in her city. I asked you here Agent Karver because of your experience in dealing with demons as well as your talent for sensing the use of 'Hell' magic."

"Why did you ask me," asked Mandi.

Allowing herself the barest of smiles, Lai Wan shrugged her shoulders, offering, "It was your debt that I had to call in to get Agent Karver here. I assumed while doing the heavy lifting for us, he might require someone to pick on." Picking up a slip of pink paper, the psychometrist added, "I also thought you could make yourself useful performing menial tasks. Perhaps while we work to clean away this mess, you could fetch my dry cleaning and then prepare afternoon tea."

I had to smile. Lai Wan has a real gift for getting under my partner's skin. Proving my point, Mandi snarled, "You want a mess to clear away, I'd be happy to—"

I put my hand on her shoulder as Mandi started to rise up out of her chair. Giving her a playful squeeze that diverted her attention away from Lai Wan for the moment, I said, "Sure we could go that way and have her do that, but you might not want to drink the tea. Mandi tends to mix bodily fluids with beverages when she is upset. Sometimes they're not even hers. She saves them from previous romantic encounters in case she ever needs to plant forensic evidence."

"It was only that one time. And we couldn't get that guy for that triple homicide, but damn it he spent four days in jail for jaywalking thanks to those fluids."

Lai Wan's been exposed to our banter before, but it was easy to see in her face that Bianca wasn't sure exactly how seriously to take what we were saying. Finally, though, she said, "Wow. I had to see this or I never would have believed it. Karver actually grew a sense of humor. He was the biggest stone face I'd ever met back in the day. I was lucky to get a dozen words out of him in a row."

She wasn't wrong. My time in the academy was right after my recruitment by the Department of Mystic Affairs. As many issues as I have now, they were ten times worse back then. I wasn't exactly known for cracking smiles. Mandi is a good influence on me in that respect.

"Well then, if we are not to have tea," said Lai Wan, "then perhaps we should leave for Baltimore."

I've never been a fan of road trips even before what happened to me. With Mandi I don't mind it quite so much; however, with the distinctly different personalities headed for our DMA issued sedan, I didn't exactly predict a fun trip. I like Bianca and Lai Wan, but Jones is a little too much on the independent side—to the point where she rarely questions her own correctness. That can be a dangerous thing for a cop. It's a testament to just how good she is and perhaps a little bit how lucky, too, that she's done as well as she has so far. She should have finished the DMA academy. If nothing else it would've given her a lot more knowledge to do what she does.

Lai Wan generally comes across as aloof, perhaps even a bit superior. Because of her gifts, she usually is at least one up on whoever she's dealing with. For some people that can make her aloofness annoying, but to me it's justified. Though it's probably the main reason she rubs Mandi the wrong way. Still, despite everything, including the fact that she tends to use her abilities in exchange for currency, she did right by us, so she's fine in my book.

Getting out of Manhattan by car involved taking the Holland Tunnel to the New Jersey Turnpike. Not an easy trip on the best of days and, as it happens to almost everyone attempting the journey at nearly any time of day, we hit traffic. It was easy to see it was going to add a couple hours to our trip.

"Anyone up for a round of ninety-nine bottles of beer on the wall," asked Mandi from the passenger seat. I was driving. We could both see Lai Wan's frozen glare in the rear view mirror.

"It always seemed a waste of perfectly good beer to me," said Bianca.

"And an exercise for simpletons in repetition," said Lai Wan.

"Well, with the obesity problem the country is having, even the simpletons need their exercise," Mandi said.

We still had hours to go before we even got close to Baltimore and I wasn't about to let these two start an argument that would last longer than our trip.

"So Bianca, how is wedded life going for you," I asked.

"Remarkably well."

"Thinking about starting a family?" All three women in the car looked at me simultaneously like I was an idiot. I wasn't, but I figured this was the quickest way to change the subject. I think Bianca realized what I was doing, but she gave me a real answer anyway.

"Joe and I have talked about it, but with what I do—the creatures we fight against would not hesitate to target my child just to get at me. Maybe when Baltimore has its own version of the Department of Mystic Affairs instead of just me. So what about you and Mandi? You two going to have any little Karvers?"

"Me and Karver? Just thinking about it is giving me morning sickness," said Mandi.

"How do you know that it's not real morning sickness?" As she growled at me, I added, "Of course with Mandi the problem would always be finding out who the father was. The cost of paternity testing in any given month would be enough to bankrupt a small country."

My partner grinned. "Hey, when you give good service, word gets around."

"And so does my partner. Of course there is a difference between good service and one that's free and easy."

"True, but at least I can give it away, unlike some people I could mention and am sitting next to," said Mandi.

"Are they always like this?" Bianca had turned to look at Lai Wan who was next to her in the backseat.

"Unfortunately," answered Lai Wan. "Although I will admit I find Agent Karver amusing. Unfortunately his partner cannot keep up with his repartee." This time it was Mandi giving out the glares.

"I don't know," said Bianca. "I think Cobb is giving as good as she gets."

"She usually does," I said. "It's part of the reason she is so popular."

"This is going to be a long trip, isn't it," sighed Bianca.

Lai Wan nodded, adding quietly, "I believe by the end of it we will all have a new appreciation for the true meaning of eternity."

The road trip actually got better from there, but all attempts at humor stopped once we hit the Baltimore city limits. Besides the ages of the participants, Lai Wan could tell us only certain things about the video. It had been made in Baltimore, of that she was certain. As for the setting, all she could feel was that it had been filmed in something large and empty like a warehouse.

"I can also tell you in what country the disc itself was made. And in what city the DVDs were copied. But beyond that ..." The psychometrist merely shrugged, which meant it was time to stop Marpling and get down to some real police work.

Bianca had made a few phone calls to find out where the most likely vacant warehouses might be. Several of them were within a mile radius of each other so that's where we headed. Mandi took over driving so I could concentrate on searching for any Hell or demonic based magic. It was hardly an exact science. It's not as if I can just close my eyes and say "two miles northeast, that way." In reality it's more like putting a glass up against a door and listening for people whispering on the other side. Maybe you can hear something, maybe not.

After the first search area came up empty we mapped out an inspection grid and began driving back and forth across the city in hopes that either Lai Wan or I would be able to pick up some mystic clue. We were two hours into our grid pattern when suddenly my stomach flipped upside down like there was a nest of hornets trying to get out from the inside—my vision got much sharper. I felt the urge to beat something to a bloody pulp. I've had a lot of practice controlling not only my emotions, but that of my onetime demon hitchhiker, so this was only a medium blip on my emotional radar. Still, I told the others, "Something is nearby. And from the feel, it's not just one person or something else from Hell entirely."

"Sounds like our suspects," said Bianca. "Which way is it to the well, Lassie?"

"Guess I'm not the only one that thinks you're a bit of a dog," said Mandi.

"I would feel a little bit better about that if you weren't always trying to put that collar and leash on me," I said.

I pointed towards a half finished apartment condo building. Mandi slowed then parked across the street, as I confirmed, "Whatever it is, it's in there."

"We'll need a warrant," said Bianca. "I know a friendly judge. His teenaged daughter unknowingly had a date with a werewolf. The shifter got a little fresh and when daddy went to the rescue, things did not go well. It would have been worse, but I got there in time. I should be able to get the warrant in twenty minutes."

I didn't see how we could get a federal warrant any sooner, so I nodded. Lai Wan shook her head, sighed and simply got out of the car and walked inside the building.

"What is she doing?" asked Mandi.

"Lai Wan's a civilian, remember? She don't need no stinkin' warrant," answered Bianca.

"We can't let her go in there by herself," Mandi offered.

"I think Lai Wan can handle herself without our help," said Bianca.

"I don't think it is going to be an issue." The others looked at me confused. I told them, "Wait for it."

After a few minutes, a fourth floor window conveniently opened within our line of sight. That action was followed by Lai Wan leaning out and shouting in mock terror, "Help, oh help."

"Oh look," I said, my sincerity as genuine as the psychometrist's, "We have reason to believe a person is in danger. No warrant needed for that. I'll take the back, you two go in the front. We don't want any of them getting away after this."

"I agree," said Bianca. "But, what exactly are we going to do with them when we catch them?"

I shrugged, answering with more assurance than I actually felt. "We'll think of something. We usually do. Maybe we can get them for trespassing and loitering."

"Or maybe vagrancy and general mopery."

"There you go. That's the spirit."

We split up as planned. On my way in, I discovered a fuse box, which wonderfully had everything in the building labeled clearly on masking tape. Thanking the fates for the first real break they'd granted me in months, I hit the switch to shut down the elevators, making sure that anyone inside wouldn't be going anywhere except by the stairs.

As I made my way up the stairs, I pulled out my gun, securing it in one hand, one of my blades in the other. At the fourth floor landing, I opened the door and found the ladies waiting for me. One look told me that so far they hadn't found anything — including Lai Wan. I made a move toward a nearby door that was ajar, but Bianca beat me to it.

"Cover me," she said. Mandi and I obliged.

As the door opened all the way we could see the psychometrist standing in front of what looked like a 'tween boy waving a metal pipe. Bianca pointed her gun between his eyes.

"Police. Drop the pipe and move away from the lady." The 'tween chuckled and smacked the pipe into its opposite palm.

"Or what? What're you gonna do? Shoot a little boy? Now that'd make great TV. Hell, let's film it. Get an upload to YouTube. I mean, everyone wants to be a star—right?"

Bianca paced off a tight half-circle, keeping her gun straight-lined toward the pipe wielder, positioning herself between it and Lai Wan. In a low snarl, she ordered; "Last warning – Drop ... the ... pipe."

"Make me."

As good as Bianca is, she's still only human. She had no way of knowing what the thing before her really was. It ripped an amulet off its neck and the cloaking spell was broken.

As Lai Wan and I both screamed warnings, pipeboy blurred, grabbing both of Bianca's wrists, then lifting her over its head. A good trick since they were both about five feet tall. Bianca had stopped growing long ago. The 'tween, however, grew until it was a good seven and a half feet tall, sprouting horns and a layer of red scales.

Bianca cursed and the demon laughed. Lai Wan stepped forward. I had no idea what the psychometrist had planned against a demon, but I cut her off by shooting the demon in the kneecap. The Pit escapee laughed, but only until the pain kicked in.

We'd come into things knowing we were dealing with Hell magic, so Mandi and I had switched over to blessed ammo with holy water loads—very effective against demons.

I stepped in and stabbed my charmed blade into the wound, at the same time shooting the wrist of the hand it was holding Bianca's gun hand with. As it howled and let go, she shot its other wrist and dropped to the floor free. Bianca carries her own blessed ammo— courtesy of the Vatican, I believe.

She and Mandi fired into the demon. The ammo hurt it but it's hard to kill demons. Gunshots will slow them down, but they're not enough to stop them. Once the ladies had emptied their clips, I moved in, a blade in each hand. While they reloaded, I did a stab-and-slice, then stepped away to give them the opportunity to empty another eighteen shots into it.

During their second barrage, I managed to get around behind the damned thing and sink my left blade six inches into the side of its neck. With it firmly embedded, I used that knife to pull myself far enough up to where I could position my other blade in front of its throat. Since our nasty playmate was sentient, the regs forced me to give it a warning.

"DMA—Stand down or be destroyed."

Its response was to reach back, grab the neck of my suit and pull me over its head. I was tossed across the room, but I managed to slice through its throat as I went. The demon's hands went to its jugular to try to stop the flow of whatever it is exactly that keeps it and its kind going. Mandi and Bianca fired at the new wound, bringing it to its knees.

"Clear," yelled Mandi, tossing a DMA standard issue portable ward, which fell nicely around the demon. As soon as the circle touched ground she intoned the activation words and it flared to life. The demon smashed out at the translucent shield. It held, but flickered with each blow. Not a good sign. Still, while it held, the four of us gathered together, catching our breath.

"I've got to get me one of those," said Bianca.

"You can put in for one," answered Mandi, "but they're stingy with them. Very expensive, apparently. After we used our last one it took us almost two months to be issued a new one."

"And, they're one use only," I added. "If he'd managed to somehow stop any part of it from making contact with the floor, it wouldn't have worked."

"Will it hold?" Bianca asked.

"With him wounded, it should hold long enough for us to get a containment team here to transport him to Eastern State Penitentiary," I said.

The demon started going berserk, coming at the ward with everything it had in a frenzy that could've torn apart a small herd of elephants and made the ward flicker like a strobe light. Anyone who believed demons were cool had never witnessed anything like this.

"And exactly how long until that containment team gets here," asked Bianca.

"I'll tell them to put a rush on it," answered Mandi.

"An excellent idea," offered Lai Wan, adding quietly, "hopefully a timely one as well."

The rest of us turned and saw what the psychometrist had, namely a group of scantily clad, deceptively young-looking folks huddled together, staring at the demon and us from the set of their latest nasty flick.

"None of you move."

"We didn't do anything," said one boy, looking about nine.

"We're just kids," piped in a girl, playing on an innocence long ago lost.

"You haven't been kids in years, not since you signed away your souls," I said.

"That not against the law, is it?" asked another boy, a poster child for spoiledbrat.com if I'd ever seen one.

"No, but cavorting with a demon who just attacked two Federal Agents is," said Mandi.

"*And* a Baltimore City detective," added Bianca, a touch indignant at being left out of the mix.

"You can all be charged as accessories," I told them. The lot looked shocked. "The federal government has special courts to deal with magic crimes."

"So what? We do a couple of years, if that. You'll have a tough time convincing a jury we're not kids."

"Fine. Take that route," said Mandi. "As children who are 'victims' of child pornography you become wards of the state until you 'grow up,' which won't be for a hundred years or so. Claim you're adults and we get you on the cavorting charge."

The youngest looking of the group laughed quietly.

"We all know that ain't going to do a thing. We'll get a good lawyer and come off looking like the victims. We're adults who share a rare growth defect making a living as best we can. How were we to know that that, 'demon' you called it, wasn't one of us?" Pointing at Bianca, he added, "He fooled her, didn't he? So walk out now and we won't press charges for unlawful entry." I started to argue the point when Bianca stepped forward.

"I have a deal to offer," she said, addressing the group of overaged children. "I've stolen souls from the Devil. I've saved people who have had contracts with him. I'm offering all of you the same opportunity. Give up this life and I will do everything I can to redeem your souls."

The boy laughed, but one girl spoke up.

"What would we owe you?" Bianca focused all her attention on the girl.

"What's your name?"

"Jenna."

"Jenna, you wouldn't owe me a thing. You'll have to stop making these movies; even without a contract they give the Devil a claim on your soul."

"I look like I'm eight. How will I make a living?"

"There are enough people within New York City who would hire you on my say so," offered Lai Wan. "The work would not be anything glamorous, but it would be honest."

"Beyond that," added Mandi, "The DMA has a fleshsmith. He can remold your body so you'd look older."

"So, you interested?" asked Bianca.

"Yes," the girl whispered, a glimmer of hope shining in her eyes.

"Jenna, you can't quit. You're our star. If you leave, you're hurting the rest of us. We'll just find you and bring you back."

"No," I said, "you won't."

"How're you going to stop me? The big bad DMA agent going to beat up a little boy?"

I smiled and the 'little boy' took a step back. Behind me, Lai Wan had pulled Mandi aside and was whispering in her ear. Out of the corner of my eye I saw my partner nod.

"As you have pointed out," the psychometrist said, "it is possible you are beyond the reach of mortal law, a concept for which I hold as much contempt as you, yourselves. Still, I have my reasons for what I say next. I will now give you one chance to stop making these films."

"Bite me, bitch," said the boy.

"Are the rest of you in agreement with him?" When the faux kids nodded, Lai Wan said, "Very well. Detective Jones, if you would please take Jenna outside." Bianca nodded and left with the girl.

"Karver, you might want to leave, as well."

"I'm not leaving my partner," I said, looking at the raging demon that looked like it might burst out of its warded cage any moment.

"Karver—"

"Not open to debate, Mandi," I told her.

"What are you going to do? You can't touch us," said the boy, his voice finally breaking, revealing a hint of nervousness.

Lai Wan didn't answer him. The entire room went cold as it dawned on everyone that as far as the psychometrist was concerned, the soul sellers before us had used up their last chance in her eyes. Not even bothering to look at them, Lai Wan removed one of her gloves, then she and Mandi joined hands. Mandi used her empathic powers to link to Lai Wan and then her propathic abilities to project the psychometrist's vision into the faux kids' minds.

It wasn't pretty, but then, they'd asked for it.

I'd wondered up until that point what had caused Lai Wan to get involved. She's not one to take up a cause, to get involved in something without some kind of monetary reward in sight. But this, this had proven to be different.

She'd come in contact with one of the group's DVDs through a totally random chance—touched it by accident without knowing what it was. Her powers are so strong she usually guards against such things, but well, anyone can have an accident. When her bare fingers had brushed that first DVD she'd shown us, she had seen everything connected to the soul sellers' enterprise. She'd seen it *all*.

Every film they had made had become instantly imprinted within her mind. But far beyond that, she experienced the full depravity of those who watched the films for pleasure. All their lust, all their desire to abuse children, to feel the young bodies they saw, to rub them, lick them, rape them. In that instant, she felt their hands touching her, smelled their sweat and rotting breath and the stale fluids dried on the carpet before their televisions. Every bit of the depravity every viewer felt, from every viewing of every film made, wrapped around her body, stitched to her soul.

And more.

In that terrible, blinding moment she also felt the damage the soul sellers' movies had done to their audiences' families. The divorces, the men who'd used them as inspiration to get up the nerve to escalate their sick fantasies into the real thing. She'd experienced the pain of their victims and their families. From that one accidental touch, her soul had been over-brimmed with a hundred thousand vile tendrils of rotting poison she would never be able to remove from her mind and memory.

And in consideration of the notion that it's better to give than to receive, she gave the soul sellers the same experience, letting them see exactly what their moneymaking enterprise had done to the face of the world. In less time than it takes to blink, the lot of them ended up curled on the floor, drooling and babbling incoherently as their minds shut down from experiencing the full damage they inflicted on others.

Mandi had to go through the same thing she inflicted on them, but she had had decades of practice shielding herself. Still there was only so much that she could do. The only advantage she had was that it wasn't she who had inflicted the pain, so the pain wasn't attacking her except as collateral damage, saving its worst for those who created it. Regardless, it was still enough to bring Mandi to her knees.

"You okay, partner," I whispered when it was all over.

"No," she told me sadly, shaking her head. "But I will be." Turning away from me, she forced herself to meet Lai Wan's eyes, asking, "You get that every time you touch anything?"

"Yes," the psychometrist answered in an even voice. She began to say more, but her words were cut short by the demon. The thing had finally managed to tear through our binding ward, the mystic equivalent of running through a plate glass window. The sharded ward ripped its flesh, turning parts of it into hamburger. It was enough to drive it to the floor, but not enough to keep it down for long. And we didn't have the firepower to do much about it.

"Mandi," I shouted, "get everyone moving. Each of you see if you can carry one of the perps out. I'll hold off our playmate."

"Yeah, right," snapped Mandi. "You could carry two or three of those little weasels. It makes more sense for me to stay."

"You expect me to believe you when you tell me something makes sense? I have the better chance. Go," I shouted, adding quietly, "Please?"

"Not leaving my partner."

Our eyes met. It would rip what was left of my heart out if anything happened to Mandi. I knew damn well she wouldn't go, but I had to try. Her eyes told me she felt the same way. Stepping up to my side, Mandi trained her gun on the demon. The thing had lifted its eyes to glare death and things far worse at us.

"Lai Wan," I tried, "get outside. Tell the containment team what's happening. Hopefully they'll arrive before he gets past us."

"They will not," she answered.

"You're insane. It'll rip you to pieces. You don't even have a weapon!"

Removing both gloves, Lai Wan reached out, taking both our hands as she said, "I require no other weapon when I have the two of you."

The demon had risen to its feet, but I barely noticed. Instead, I was reliving my life as The Carver, feeling the damage the demon that had once lived within me had done with my body, not only to our victims but their families. It was harsh, but I lived with a lesser degree of it every day, so it didn't cripple me. Mandi had taken everything the child pornographers did and only lost her footing. She was vomiting before we were halfway through my dead.

Lai Wan was tough and barely blinked, choosing instead to stare down the demon. She bombarded the thing with all the pain I had caused during my years of possession, but the monster just laughed.

"Thank you," it sneered. "This is wonderful—delicious." The

demon savored every drop of both my suffering and that which had been caused with my hands. The only plus I could see in what we were doing was that it had stopped to enjoy, instead of attacking.

Mandi and I were both on the ground, my partner curled into a ball. I started to hate Lai Wan for putting her through this. I hated her more when I realized. Mandi would never be able to look at me again without remembering this. I damn well hoped we at least stopped the demon and that doing so proved worth the loss of my best and only real friend.

And then, something changed in the vision. Lai Wan went past the pain and horror I had inflicted, feeding our enemy my possessor's exorcism, my recruitment to the DMA. My time in the academy followed, the case Bianca Jones and I handled together — my partnering with Mandi. Suddenly Lai Wan's plan became clear to me. We had saturated the demon with the past evil I had lived through, suckered it into dropping its defenses, opening itself to all the psychometrist had to show it.

Unable to stop the flow, the thing felt the effect on those whose lives I had saved since I became a Federal Agent, the effect that had on their families. Joy and gratitude swamped over the thing, it experienced the tears of parents reunited with their children, the thrill of innocents spared damnation. The peace of a mother who believed her dead daughter had defeated dark magics to save her from a stalker. In its eyes, I could see the mounting horror as emotions such as kindness and simple human decency poisoned its black soul.

Mandi uncurled as I stood, but the demon had dropped to its knees, cursing and screaming, beating its trembling fists against the floor – begging for mercy. We had none to give something so evil. My partner and I stood with Lai Wan between us, showering the demon with the burning horror of virtue until the containment team arrived and Bianca led it to us. They got the demon in a much stronger and more portable version of the ward we had.

Only when the thing was trapped beyond any hope of escape, did Lai Wan release her grip on us and don her gloves once more. I stood unmoving until I heard someone calling my name.

"Karver, are you okay," said Bianca. I stared at her, more than a little confused. I must have looked it too because she added, "You're crying. Are you hurt?"

I simply shook my head. It was all I could manage. I was too overwhelmed to do anything else.

"Agent Karver has had a chance few ever do," Lai Wan said, "to see firsthand the evil and the good that he has done. Karver now knows that the good he has done carries far more weight than he had ever suspected."

"Thank you."

Lai Wan simply nodded. She wasn't ignoring me. Instead she was giving me the chance to notice that Mandi still hadn't moved. When I asked if she was "okay," she turned toward me, her face pale, hands shaking. Mandi had always been aware of what I'd done when possessed, but now she knew exactly what that meant. I turned away, unable to meet her eyes.

"Karver, look at me," she ordered. I forced myself to comply. "I can feel what you are feeling, remember? So stop it. You know me better than that. Pretty pathetic flashback. I wasn't even in it until the end. And no women. I knew your love life was pathetic, but I didn't realize it was that bad."

"Not all of us need stadium seating to accommodate our lovers," I replied.

"Hell, you couldn't even fill a loveseat," she shot back.

"What'd I miss?" Bianca asked Lai Wan in a whisper.

"Nothing," answered the psychometrist. "And everything."

"Mandi, are we—" My partner covered my mouth with her hand. There were tears in both our eyes.

"Don't insult me by asking," she said. Then she pulled down my head and kissed my forehead.

Seeing that Mandi and I could both use a change in subject, Bianca asked, "So what's going to happen to tall and scaly?"

"He'll be arraigned and jailed to await trial. The ambassador from Hell will undoubtedly try to arrange his release, arguing he is a political prisoner."

"Hell has an ambassador?"

I nodded. "Human too. Same guy for the US and the UN. A real scumbag, but effective. I think we'll be okay."

"Will you get in trouble for pulling the mojo on the porn peddlers?"

"Probably. We're not supposed to attack citizens who don't pose an immediate danger, especially human ones. Since they were pushing kiddie porn, though, I think we might just get a slap on the wrist. Thanks for the assist."

"Hey, they were working my town," she said. "Happy to get rid of them." Cracking a smile, Bianca added, extending a hand, "You know, when we first met, I didn't think you had the makings of a cop. Glad to see I was wrong."

"Me too," I said, taking her hand and shaking it.

There wasn't much more after that. No one had realized just how much her stunt had drained Lai Wan. Mandi actually had to help her back to the car. Bianca laughed at the sight. When I gave her a look, she said, "I am so glad I'm in my own town."

"What do you mean?"

"Give me a break, Karver. Getting between you and a demon is one thing. Getting back in that car is another." Bianca flashed me an evil grin. Understanding her meaning, I defended Lai Wan and my partner, saying, "Oh, I think those two are all bickered out."

Bianca was about to say something when Mandi came back from the car, grabbing my shoulder as she snapped, "We *have* to go. Say goodbye, Karver."

"But, I ..." The grip on my shoulder tightened.

Say *goodbye,* Karver."

"Goodbye Karver," I replied.

"I wish to be returned to my home and away from this one as soon as possible," said Lai Wan from the backseat of the car. "Please use the siren the entire way."

"Help me," I whispered to Bianca as I was pulled away.

Bianca just laughed and waved.

THE TALL MAN COMETH

Something brown and squishy had apparently not only hit the fan, but crushed and pulverized it. Anytime more than four DMA agents are called in on a case, it's a bad sign. We had eleven working this one, if you counted the four agents down or missing.

Two days ago the Department of Mystic Affairs got reports that no one who went in to the town of Idaho, Colorado was coming out again and that included an FBI team. That's when the DMA sent in a pair of agents—Rose Tower and Donna Winks. Tower is a jinn, Winks the victim of one. Winks had found a bottle and made a bad wish. Now no one who's not holding a DMA badge can remember Winks exists. The only reason the badge helps is Tower put in special amulets and charms along with the standard ones. To the rest of the world the poor kid's functionally invisible.

Tower had been wished to help protect America by a bottle holder, but signed up for the Department of Mystic Affairs on her own.

Winks is fairly new to the game, but Tower's as experienced an agent as they come and damn powerful. They disappeared off the grid soon after they went in. That made the powers that be nervous, especially since right after that happened, all contact with the outside world ceased from inside the town. Worse, people started forgetting the town existed. Except those of us with DMA badges, which was more than likely thanks to Tower's charms.

The next strategy they tried was to send in the World Wide Spyder. The kid survives as sentient electrons, able to travel through anything that has or can carry electric current. He practically lives on the net. Given enough time he can find anything that's stored electronically.

Spyder couldn't get into Idaho, which should have been impossible. Even an electromagnetic pulse couldn't do that. It would knock out the power, but the delivery systems would still be intact and Spyder should be able to ride in on anything that conducts electricity. He couldn't find any way into the town – not phone wires, power lines, cables, or even cell phone towers. It wouldn't be the first time real estate has been moved into another plane of existence, so they went to satellite surveillance. All the images show that the town is still there and it's even lit up. That meant the town was getting power, but nobody could figure out from where.

A second team was sent in. Mox Monroe, lava and fire demigoddess and Hunter, Celtic god of the hunt. They haven't come out either and the latest satellite surveillance showed a small, active volcano on the main street. At least that meant Mox was probably still alive.

So the DMA came to Idaho, Colorado in force. We tried to get backup from the military, but kept getting told the town didn't exist. Arguing with the military on a good day was a losing proposition, so we just accepted we were on our own. We set up a command post just outside of town.

Nobody wanted to go in blind a third time, so we turned to a blind man. Andy is a visionary whose lack of sight is only a minor inconvenience. A lot of DMA agents have dark pasts. Andy's no exception having had his eyes gouged out by his own mother when he was a child. The guy doesn't believe in hiding his disability behind dark sunglasses. He broadcasts it by putting messages on his glass eyes. When he arrived in Idaho, the right eye read *If you worked here* and the left *I'd have a headache by now*. He enjoyed the effect it had on people.

Andy took one look at Idaho and fell over in a fetal position screaming. He didn't stop even when the EMT's sedated him and took him away.

The next wave was ready to go in. It included Trevor, a vampyre who was born before the Civil War, and his partner Gus. The shapeling didn't talk much in his natural form. Today he was shifting shapes between four of the Marx Brothers and Karl Marx, although he was insisting his name was Commo Marx in that form.

Both Deputy Directors of the DMA were present—Sarge Winston and Gregory Zachs, which said something about how serious things were. I wouldn't say they hated each other only because the word was too mild.

Zachs could tell you to shove your foot where the sun don't shine and you'd put it in up to the ankle. A binders' word can overcome your natural resistance and common sense.

Sarge had assessed the situation. Normally Sarge looked annoyed, angry, but rarely worried. He was downright nervous. It was not a good sign.

"Sarge, any idea what's going on?" I asked.

The old man nodded. "Some sort of ancient darkness trying to come here and roost."

"How do you know?" I asked.

"An educated guess." Sarge touched the crimson gem that was fused to his chest. "Someone has been very talkative, offering to open portals to paradise for Emmy and me." Emmy was Sarge's wife. "Give me all the power I ever wanted."

Which was unusual. The symbiote was a creature of ancient darkness itself that got trapped in the jewel. It got fused to Sarge back in WWI. Their lives are bound together, but the symbiote is notoriously stingy with giving Sarge any more power than the old man can tap into on his own.

"Not a good sign," I said, which brought the total up to at least three.

"Nope. Sparky is scared." The gem glowed a deeper crimson. The creature hated when Sarge called him Sparky. "He knows what's in there, but is afraid to name it or even hint at what it is."

"What's the plan?" I said.

"The five of us go in and try to fix this mess," he said.

"I may not be a mathematician, but I count six of us," I said. That was including my partner Mandi and me.

"You're not going in Karver," said Sarge.

"And why not?" I said.

"I need someone out here to coordinate with any other agents who arrive and frankly we are going to need firepower in there. Your contribution would be limited."

Sarge isn't one to pull punches. Neither am I.

"We could tell Spyder and he could coordinate," I said.

"Unless it extends the radius of whatever is preventing communication with the outside," said Sarge. Taking me by the shoulders, he looked me straight in the eye. "This isn't a snub. I need someone fast on their feet to do this. Our lives and those of everyone in that town may depend on whoever I leave out here."

"You're the boss," I said and walked toward my partner. I wasn't happy, but I respected Sarge. If Zachs had been the one giving the order, that would have been a different matter. Zachs headed up Black

Ops. My soul is black from things I was forced to do. His went dark voluntarily. I didn't trust Zachs as far as I could throw him. Thanks to the revamping of my physique by the demon that once possessed me, it'd be about ten feet with a good tailwind.

"Looks like you're the fourth wave," said Mandi.

"All by my lonesome," I said, flexing my arms.

"Sarge wants me to try to anchor everyone's emotional sanity when we go in," said the empath.

"Kind of like having a deaf man take you to a concert," I teased.

"It won't be that hard. I'll just shoot for the opposite of your mental state," Mandi said.

"Sounds like a good plan to me," I said, only half joking. "You be careful in there. I don't want to have to get a new partner."

"You? I don't want to have to train another rookie. I barely have you housebroken."

"Hey, I've only missed the newspaper once this week," I joked, but Mandi hit a chord. I was a Hell of a lot less broken now than I was when I started in the DMA and most of that was due to Mandi. These days most of the agents don't cringe when they have to talk to me, but it was another matter when I started. Former serial killers, even those once possessed by demons, tend to give most people the creeps. Mandi never treated me badly and it made all the difference.

"You know where my letters…"

"I know," I said cutting her off. Every few months she updated her will and posthumous letters to her family and friends. We have a dangerous job. I only had two letters written. One was to Sarge and all it said was *Thanks*. My letter to Mandi was a bit longer.

My partner looked at me and I realized my emotions were leaking. "Bart, you know the feeling's mutual, right?"

In all the months we'd been partnered, Mandi has never once called me by the name I used before I was supposedly executed for the demon's crimes.

"You're a propath." Meant she could project emotions as well as sense them. "I know. You're getting all deep and emotional." Bad sign number four. "Things are that dark, huh?"

"Worse. I'm feeling the emotions from the town. I'm only getting two flavors. Madness is coming from I couldn't tell you how many. When I filter that, all that's left is sadistic glee or something close to it. Hard to say since it's coming off something not vaguely human."

"So you're thinking about asking him out on a date then?" I teased.

"Why waste all that time on small talk? If I'm lucky there'll be an empty restroom stall nearby and he'll be all tentacles," said Mandi, wiggling her eyebrows, but the smile was as fake as they get.

"Maybe that will distract it so the others can take a shot," I said.

"None of the guys swing that way. And even if Sarge did, he'd die before he'd cheat on Miss Emmy," joked Mandi.

"I meant a shot at taking him down," I said.

"Oh, that'd work too," she said smiling, this time only a little more convincing.

"People, we're moving out," ordered Sarge.

Mandi and I exchanged a glance that said more than words could, at least the words we'd let ourselves say. Then she grabbed and squeezed my hand. I squeezed back. Gus was currently looking like Groucho as he walked bent over into the town.

"Gus, take this seriously, damn it!" yelled Sarge. The old man liked to yell under stress. It helped him cope, same as Gus' goofy shifting, and Mandi's and my banter.

Gus shifted into the Duke, complete with cowboy hat and six shooters. Sarge was a big fan.

"Now that's more like it," said Sarge smiling.

Gus nodded at the deputy director, but turned back to wink at me. The Duke had suddenly sprouted a greasepaint moustache and eyebrows.

I watched them go in. I manned the command post for two hours, checking in every fifteen minutes with Spyder. It didn't get rid of the sick feeling in the pit of my stomach when I wondered what was happening, but it gave me something to do.

None of them came out. It was time to call in the Director of the DMA, Uncle Sam himself, but I couldn't get a signal – very unusual and bad sign number six. I guess Sarge's prediction came true. Whatever it was expanded the zone.

I could go out and report back to Sam, but nothing had changed since my last report. Spyder would have called him as soon as I missed my check in. Sam would figure out something happened with or without me. That left me with my second option—going in.

Really not much of a choice. Sarge engineered breaking me out of death row and exorcizing the seriál demon. Trevor and Gus helped him do it. Hell, Gus took my place in the chair. I owed them. I couldn't leave any of them behind. Going without Mandi wasn't even a consideration.

I'm told I come across as a tough guy and I wouldn't argue the point, but I was nervous as I walked right into the town. The agents that were already in there had enough raw power to take over a small country. All I had was a little more strength and speed than the average guy, a gun, and a pair of charmed blades. What was I going to do to something that took out gods, a jinn and a guy like Sarge who could throw a tank?

I'd do my best, that's what. Whether it'd be enough was another matter. The scales of my life had my dead on the far side and what I did as a DMA agent on my side. They would never even get close to balancing, even if I died helping someone. I owed my dead too much to let fear keep me on the sidelines.

It would have helped if I had more of an idea of what to expect. There were a lot of things born from ancient darkness – all of them powerful, most of them hating humanity for supplanting them. Very hard to kill a creature of ancient darkness, but I knew a thing or two about killing. I just hoped it would be enough to do some good.

From Andy's reaction and Mandi's words I knew that there was madness gripping the locals. I just didn't realize what that really meant until then.

There were so many bad signs I gave up counting.

People were everywhere. The majority had curled up into little balls, occasionally whimpering or drooling. I tried to wake some of them, but it was useless. Even the ones that I was able to get to open their eyes would only let out a shriek and collapse again.

It wasn't the majority that was the problem. It was the minority.

People can do some evil and nasty things to each other. I speak from personal experience, both as the doer and doee. What demons can do is even worse. This was different.

The first active person I came across was crouched down in the middle of the street, gnawing on a dog's leg and the dog wasn't dead yet – worse, I think it was the woman's pet. I realized the rest of the team was in danger and strategically this was something minor, but

I couldn't walk by. If we beat this, she'd wake up knowing what she did and those memories will haunt her for a long time. I cold cocked the woman from behind. I liked to think she might one day thank me, but I knew it was a long shot.

The dog was bleeding badly. There wasn't enough flesh left on the paw for a surgeon to do anything with. The quick and logical thing to do would be put him out of his misery. Logical was never my style. I got the poor pooch passed out drunk on scotch I commandeered from a liquor store then taped the dog's jaws shut so it wouldn't wake up and bite me. I amputated the leg with one of my rune encrusted blades. The magic helps them cut through most things, in this case the pooch's leg. I then cauterized the wound using an acetylene torch from a deserted hardware store; I poured more of the scotch over the wound and wrapped it. After putting a makeshift cone on its leg so it couldn't chew on the wound and untaping his mouth, I locked the dog in a closet in the hardware store with food and water. If things returned to normal, I'd be back to get it. If not, starvation was better than becoming a living unhappy meal.

Things continued to march from bad to worse. I found a naked guy who had apparently been standing next to the aforementioned fan when all things brown and squishy hit. He was covered from head to toe. There was far too much of it to be just his own and I wasn't going to go looking for where he got it. Poop Man was writing on a wall with the feces.

> *Mankind is unable to bend him*
> *He goes where the outer gods send him*
> *Unlike his masters, he's never been bound*
> *Either beyond the stars or in the ground*
> *He is chaos crawling on a perpetual bender*
> *One day he'll put mankind's balls in a blender*
> *Why he came to Idaho I don't know*
> *But we shall all reap what he dost sow*

Not exactly a poet, but Poop Man wasn't hurting anyone, so I let him be. I didn't want to touch him without hosing him down first either. Outer gods fit in with Sarge's theory of ancient darkness rising.

Three times I had to stop crazies who were trying to prey on the fetal people and I had to work to keep my anger from getting the better of me, like an outside force was egging my psyche on. By the third, I was out of cuffs and what he was doing to the fetal people was too horrible for me to leave him free. I had to break his legs and tie him to a lamppost in hopes that it would stop him from eating the unconscious. If the cannibal had been acting on his own volition, I'd have shot him, but there was mind control at work here. He wasn't fully at fault and I knew how that was. In all honesty, I would have preferred having all my limbs broken or even a bullet in my head than my sixty-three dead.

Soon after I found the first member of our team. Winks was unconscious on a bus stop bench. I tried to wake her, but she had fully joined the fetal position people. All I could do was lock her indoors to protect her in case the madness infecting the town would let the crazies see her. Normally it's her fondest wish, but I doubted she'd consider someone smashing her brains in or worse a dream come true.

Around the next corner was a body on fire. I'd like to say the smell of burning flesh made me gag, but the demon had altered more than my body. My mouth involuntarily started to salivate as it remembered the taste of cannibal barbeque. Then my mind kicked in and I had to swallow down the vomit trying to make its way up.

My first thought was a crazy had poured gasoline on one of the fetals. That wasn't what happened to the vampyre lying near a brick building. A shadow was half covering Trevor. It was the uncovered half where the sunlight hit him that was making him combust like someone had doused him in lighter fluid. The body fire had just started, probably from the sun moving across the sky.

Normally Trevor wears a DMA issue skinsuit in daylight. The mystic garment fit right over his clothes, magically adhering to any garments and his skin, protecting him from the deadly UV rays. The vampyre had been wearing one when he went in earlier, but apparently had lost it or it was taken along the way.

Running all out, I grabbed the vampyre's flaming body and brought him inside the brick building, which was a convenience store. Using my coat in the shadows of the storeroom, I tried to put out the fire, but it burned deep inside the tissue. I emptied two fire extinguishers and five bags of flour. The blackened flesh still glowed in places like embers. I put Trevor in some super-sized trash bags hoping the vacuum would put out the flames.

It worked, stopping Trevor from completely combusting, but he was burnt badly. The skin on the exposed flesh looked more like charcoal than meat, but he was still alive or what passed for it with the undead. There's only one kind of first aid that does any good for vampyres and it's not one I wanted to perform. What I wanted hadn't mattered much so far in this life so I sliced open a vein in my left forearm that I knew was a bad bleeder, and let the blood pour into his mouth. Trevor was so out of it, he wasn't drinking it. I had to work his throat to make him swallow.

It seemed to help after a while. The charred flesh began to throw off the ash and became oozy. I hoped it was a good sign. It was about time there was one of those I could count. Although the fact that this perp could take out a century and a half old vamp balanced things out by adding another mark to the bad signs column.

The storeroom had a full-sized freezer without any glass, which seemed like a good coffin substitute. It should keep him safe from sunlight and slow any further tissue deterioration until he could get real medical attention.

By the end of the next hour, I was exhausted physically and emotionally and I still hadn't found what was behind anything. Worse, I had no idea if Mandi or Sarge or anyone else was even still alive. I futilely tried to save people from themselves and each other. It was a losing battle. The only reason I even had a chance at all was because the crazies were few and far between.

That changed rather quickly and it took me a moment to get moving again.

Idaho had a town square, complete with a huge white gazebo. Probably used it in the summer for concerts for local bands, town picnics and the like.

It almost looked like a town meeting now. There was a crowd of crazies gathered. Some were going at each other like gladiators to the point where they were broken and bloody. Three men were taking turns raping a bronze statue of a horse carrying what was probably a bronze likeness of the founder of the town. The horse was not anatomically correct, so it had to hurt. That didn't diminish the horse rapers' enthusiasm one iota.

The center of the gazebo had an apparatus that would have looked at home in any old black and white Frankenstein movie. Electricity danced back and forth between a pair of spheres on the top of metal towers on the lightning machine. Three women kept trying to throw themselves into the sparks. Fortunately for them they were too slow to catch the lightning, although one had two obviously broken arms.

At least I knew what happened to the rest of the team. Sarge was chained to one of the towers, his head lulled down. The gem on his chest was dark. Tower was trapped in a soda display case that had been brought up from some nearby store. The doors looked like they had been fused, making it a modified bottle. Tower was conscious and struggling. Jinn physiology must be different enough from human for her to still be awake when everyone else was out.

Hunter was out for the count. He normally wore a DMA cap on duty. He didn't have one on now. A pair of antlers that any stag would be proud of extended above his head. He had charmed the hat to bend space to hide them. A hole had been punched through the top of the gazebo and Hunter's head shoved through it so he was trussed out like a trophy deer head on a hunter's wall.

Above the gazebo, suspended in air, was a man that was half Chico, half Commo. Poor Gus was drawn between a pair of trees by iron cables attached to his ankles and wrists.

The volcano the satellite had picked up wasn't hard to find in the middle of the park. The pictures missed the goddess who lay naked in the center of the pool of lava except for her badge, holster and gun. The heat of the magma had incinerated the rest of her uncharmed clothes.

A few yards away, Zachs head stuck up above the lawn. The rest of him was presumably buried beneath the ground.

Lastly there was Mandi. My partner was in a straight jacket, hanging upside-down by her ankles from a flagpole.

At the center of the gazebo was a tall man, nearly seven feet with skin the color of dried olives. He had black hair and the area in the center of the whites of his eyes was black like one huge pupil. The Tall Man was egging on the crazies by dangling a wailing infant, clad only in a diaper, above them. Whenever one of them would jump to try and grab it, he'd pull it out of reach like a child might do with a ball of yarn and a cat.

Made me remember one particular infant that… let's just say it's the worst nightmare my time with the seriál has left me with.

I pulled my gun and trained it on his head. The Tall Man kept playing with the baby. I didn't have a clean shot without risking hitting the infant or one of the jumping crazies so I moved closer.

"Gently put down the baby," I ordered. "DMA Agent."

The olive-colored man turned and had a look of surprise on his face that clearly got across that he was one who wasn't used to surprises happening to him.

But he recovered quickly. "There certainly are a lot of you DMA folks visiting my private Idaho today. I knew they were coming. Why didn't I know about you?" The Tall Man was scratching his head with the baby. The baby was crying.

"Maybe I just forgot to RSVP. Now gently put the baby down," I said, training my sights between his dark eyes.

The Tall Man laughed. "You think you can order me around…" His brow scrunched in concentration as he pulled my name out of I didn't know where. "Agent Karver?"

"Yep," I said, moving closer. "I will shoot you if you do not comply."

"Look around at what I did to the other agents. Do you think bullets are going to hurt me?"

I cocked the hammer on the automatic. The Tall Man raised an eyebrow. With a careless toss, he threw the baby into the crowd. I was too far away to even try for a catch. Instead, I unloaded my entire mixed clip at the Tall Man as I rushed toward the baby. The mixed rounds included bullets made from iron and silver, doused in holy water, and a couple of explosive rounds. I didn't stop to see what effect they had, as I plowed through the crowd toward the infant. I was a little rough on the crazies, but saving the baby took priority.

The poor little guy was being treated like a football, with all the crazies trying to grab him. A young woman won and brought him up like she was going to blow on his belly, only her mouth was open and her teeth bared. I broke her nose and a couple teeth, but I got the baby.

Problem was now all the crazies had their attentions focused on me and I was outnumbered over a hundred to one. The gazebo was the only part of the park that was relatively crazy free, so I made my way there. I had no choice but to hurt anyone who got in my way, but I was careful not to cripple them.

Once I stepped in the gazebo, none of the crazies followed, but the Tall Man was there to greet me.

"Nicely done, Agent Karver. As you can see, your bullets had no effect."

"Had to try. You'd never believe how many bad guys use that line to try and bluff their way out of a situation." And our bullets aren't the run of the mill variety. "I assume you didn't expect me to lie down and die because you said bullets wouldn't hurt you."

"I don't want your death when breaking you would be so much more enjoyable. Now I'd like you to slit that baby's throat with one of those sharp knives on your back." My coat was pretty much fried after trying to put Trevor out, so I hadn't bothered to put it back on. My machete-sized blades were in plain sight.

I reached for one and had my hand on the hilt before I realized what I was doing. The vision of me cutting another innocent's throat made me furious. I had fought the demon. I'd fight this.

Breaking mind control is more than mental or emotional. It's physical and it hurts probably like being dunked in Mox's lava pool. That's why it's so much easier to give in. I barely was able to keep my feet, but I told Tall Man to screw himself, only not quite so politely.

The Tall Man's eyebrows creased. "Interesting. I can't reach the part of your soul I need to take control of you – to share my madness. Something is already there. Something...demonic. Someone exorcized it, but its mark is still there waiting for a reunion. I suppose it is the lesser of two evils, but it does make a problem for me."

So the bad guy can't take me over because his entry point is already taken by what the seriál did to me. About time something good came out of that. It also explained why what was happening kept escalating. The Tall Man tapped into each agent's power as he took them over. He had tried to use Zachs' power to make me kill, but I had already been there, done that and apparently got a mark on my soul. I would have preferred a t-shirt.

"Not for me. You can save us both some trouble and surrender now," I said.

"Bravado is admirable, but mostly useless wouldn't you say? If I can't drive you mad, I'll simply use your friends to kill you."

"Too much of a wuss to be able to do it yourself? Figures. So what's your name, coward?"

The Tall Man laughed. "So does that ever work? Do people

actually get so very angry at such a minor insult that they blurt out a name you can use to bind them with?”

I shrugged and unloaded a string of curses, both human and demonic.

“Excellent. Much better. You can call me Nyarlathotep. That is the name I’m best known by and it is one of my true names. Unfortunately for you, I have 999 aspects and to bind me you’d have to say all of them in the order I first assumed the forms, all before I kill you. Not all of them have even been seen on Earth.”

“Yeah, all of you ancient evil ones are the same. Too damn cocky, but someone always seems to knock you back to the darkness,” I said.

“Actually, I’ve never been banished or forced to sleep. I always have my freedom. Ask Cyetrole,” said the Tall Man, glancing at the crimson gem in Sarge’s chest.

The symbiote in the gem responded and for the first time when it glowed I could understand it.

“I have spent nearly a century trapped and bound to this human’s life without revealing my true name and you give it up as a point of conversation with a human, Crawling One?”

“Is it enough to make you angry or brave enough to fight me like our battle of old?” The gem glowed and I could hear the psychic equivalent of a growl, but nothing else. “I thought as much.”

“Why do this to these people?” I asked.

“Why not?”

“That’s not much of an answer,” I said.

“It wasn’t much of a question,” said the Tall Man.

“Is there something you want?”

“Nothing you have the power to give me. I await a day that will not arrive for ages. In the meantime, I do what I must to amuse myself. And to be honest, you’re not that amusing.”

Translation—since he couldn’t take me over, it was time to kill me.

“You sound like my partner. You and I are going to settle up for what you did to her, but first…” I put another clip in, pointed my gun at the soda case/makeshift jinn bottle and fired at the top of the glass. It shattered, freeing Tower.

I moved over and pulled the jinn out, made her meet my eyes. “Look at where the demon possessed me. That’s how he’s controlling you. Cut him off."

Tower couldn't talk but she nodded, then had such a look of concentration on her face she could have been having a bowel movement.

"Thanks," she said, standing and moving toward the Tall Man. "That thing made me relive…." Tower's face became very angry. "He's so dead." A jinn and a creature of Nyarlathotep's power duking it out would wipe out the town and probably most of the county — maybe even the state, although the mountains might help contain the destruction.

I grabbed Tower's arm. "No. I'll handle him." She looked at me like I was an idiot. I handed her the baby. "You get all the innocents to safety." I told her about the dog. "Bring Trevor here."

"Trevor?" she asked.

"Yes," I said and told her where the vampyre was. The crazies started vanishing.

"This won't do you any good…" started the Tall Man. I shut him up by shoving one of my blades into his gut up to the hilt. "You ignorant little thing of flesh. That hurt."

I smiled. One of the runes is an Elder Sign. Hurts even those born of ancient darkness.

I leapt off the gazebo to the flagpole, gripping my other knife. Holding on with one hand, I sliced the rope holding Mandi's feet with the other. I jumped down and caught her before she hit the ground. Straitjackets held bad memories for her, so I sliced her out of it as quickly as I could.

"Mandi, wake up!" Nothing. I tried slapping her. Her pupils widened slightly. Mandi's powers are heightened by physical contact, so she mostly avoids it. We have that in common; only with me it brings back the horrors that were done using my flesh. I needed to grab her mind back from the Tall Man's control. Even a moment might be enough for her to take back control. I did something I hadn't done since I started my new life. Normally it would have gotten me decked by my partner, but there were both desperate times and measures in play.

I kissed Mandi. Her pupils went so wide her eyes looked as black as the Tall Man's. As my tongue touched hers, I felt it respond. Mandi once told me her first kiss formed such a strong bond with the boy she was lip-locked with that his emotions briefly superseded her own. It took her a month to break the link to him. She hadn't learned to shield yet at that young age. She's never really been comfortable with the physical intimacies of dating because of it. It's one of the reasons I tease her about being a loose woman because she is anything but.

Right now, I figured she was as unshielded as she was then and I was hoping for the same effect.

It worked. "Karver, what's happening?" Then she started to fade again.

I took her face in my hands. "Link yourself to the mark the demon left on my soul. The Tall Man can't get past it. Use it to shield yourself, then link Sarge and the rest to me."

Mandi nodded and gently touched my face with her hand. "Only one way to do it."

"Go for it. At least now I get to find out if you're as good as that fraternity claimed," I teased.

The Tall Man had been struggling with my blade since I stabbed him. He almost had it out.

"I'm better," she bragged and kissed me. Her emotions washed over me and I could feel what she felt. For that moment, I forgot everything. What the demon had done, what the Tall Man was trying to do. I even forgot about my dead. It was the greatest kiss in the history of kissing, at least for me. It seemed to last for an eternity and was over far too soon.

Mandi pulled away, with a sad smile on her face. "It's done."

The Tall Man had my blade free and was moving toward us. He wasn't laughing now.

"Link the rest," I said, holding my other blade and putting myself between Mandi and Nyarlathotep.

Mandi wasn't ever going to be the damsel-in-distress-type. She put a clip of explosive rounds in her gun and opened fire on the Tall Man's gaping abdominal wound. It slowed him down. "Already done."

Gus had shifted into his gray form, stretched out his limbs and dropped free of the cables. Sarge snapped his chains and smashed the lightning machine. Hunter smashed the wood around his neck. Mox rode a wave of lava to the gazebo. Zachs started yelling for someone to free him. Mox waved a hand and lava burned a trench around him, with a five-foot cushion of dirt between him and the magma. The molten fluid disappeared back into the earth and Zachs pushed the dirt off him and climbed out.

Tower reappeared with her partner Winks and Trevor in tow. The vampyre had a new skin suit on and was looking much better than when I saw him last.

The Tall Man wasn't happy and moved faster than I could, swinging my own knife at my neck. It was an appropriate way for me to go, but apparently it wasn't my time yet.

Sarge moved just as fast, catching the Tall Man's wrist.

"What the Hell is going on and why do I feel like I want to have sex with Karver?" demanded Sarge.

"I do too," said a naked Mox, lava moving to cover parts best not shown in public.

I looked at Mandi and raised an eyebrow. My partner pointed a single finger at me. "Not a single word."

"Sarge, my knife," I said. His chest gem shot out a ruby beam of power, smashing the Tall Man through the air, but Sarge managed to hold onto the blade and throw it to me. I handed it off to Trevor.

"What am I supposed to do with this?" Trevor asked.

"There's the bad guy's blood on it. You're a vampyre. Do I need to draw you a diagram?" I said.

Trevor grinned. Vamps can take on some of the power of those they drink the blood of. Trevor started licking my knife like it was a cherry popsicle, then started vomiting.

"This is horrid," he said, as four tentacles sprouted from his back.

Meanwhile Mox had covered Nyarlathotep and his lightning machine in flowing magma. Zachs was ordering him to give up. Hunter, Winks, and Gus were unloading every bit of ammo they had at the Tall Man.

"He's fighting me," said Mandi.

"I think I can do something about that," said Trevor, handing me back my knife. He looked at me. "And these tentacles better go away."

"You're probably the first vampyre on your block to have them," I said. "And now you have a better shot with Mandi."

Trevor reached out with his mind and I could feel the madness pouring off him. It reached out and intersected with what was coming off the Tall Man and slowed it down.

"This is keeping him busy, but how do we stop him? The machine obviously wasn't the source of his power," said Sarge. "Probably the other way around."

I told Sarge the bit about the thousand names less one. "How are we supposed to learn that many names?"

"Sparky knows," I said.

I heard the psychic growl. Having heard Sparky's true name once apparently allowed me to eavesdrop because I heard Sarge think, *"Is this true?"*

"The human is an idiot. I will not betray one of my one."

"Sparky won't betray his kind," said Sarge, not realizing I could hear.

I knew from observation that Miss Emmy talked to Sparky through physical contact with the gem. I reached out and looked to Sarge for permission. He nodded and I touched the jewel.

"This joker would have killed you," I said.

"It was part of the game. Eventually he would have given me this body to play with as I wished."

"Excuse me?" said Sarge.

"You aren't that stupid," I said to Sparky.

"I will not help you. Nyarlathotep meant me no real harm."

"Really? I seem to remember him telling me something that could very well have caused you harm. In fact, if I had to choose between saving all of us and sharing…" I let it hang there.

"You wouldn't."

I didn't say a word, only smiled.

"Think about it. Turnabout is fair play," I said.

I felt power surge through my hand. Judging by the look on Sarge's face, Sparky had just shut him out of the conversation.

"If I do this, you will keep my name to yourself?"

"I will." He could now hear my thoughts.

"Your word? Benjamin appears to believe you are a creature of your word."

Sarge's real name was Benjamin? *"I will not mention it unless it need be mentioned. That's the best I can do. I won't ever allow you to hurt someone, especially Sarge."*

"Don't be a fool. If he dies, so do I."

"We have a deal?" I asked.

"We do."

The power flow blocking Sarge from the conversation dissipated.

"What the Hell is going on?" yelled Sarge.

"He'll tell you the names," I said, handing him my bloody blade. Blood helps with a binding. "Go get him, Benjamin."

"Sparky!" Sarge yelled.

"No, time Benjamin. You need to start now. There are so many names to say to bind him. Repeat after me. Nyarlathotep, Zyeltypte,…"

Sarge did after wiping some of the blood on his fingers.

The Tall Man noticed and started screaming and laughing manically simultaneously. Everyone tried to keep him busy. It didn't work. A moment later the Tall Man simply vanished.

"Did it work?" I asked.

Man and symbiote spoke in sync.

"No."

"No."

"The Crawling One didn't call my bluff."

"Bluff?" thought Sarge.

"We have a past. I learned most of his names in preparation for a future battle. I currently know the first five hundred and thirteen in order. I know four hundred and eleven of what remains, but am not certain of the exact sequence."

Sarge mentally cursed.

"However the danger is past. For now."

Sarge repeated what Sparky told him.

"Everyone okay? Sound off," Sarge said.

Each agent did. Zachs complained about having dirt in his underwear. Gus was now Harpo and put his leg in Sarge's hand.

"I'm fine, but I still want to sleep with Karver," said Mox, looking at me. The lava covering her chest became much larger in an hourglass shape.

"Me too. Why is that?" asked Sarge.

Mandi explained.

Tower came up to me looking rather sheepish. "You freed me from imprisonment. According to the rules, I owe you three wishes."

"Can you undo my past or bring back my dead?" I asked.

"Not as they were before. I can create an illusion that would make you believe it," said Tower.

I looked over at the quasi-invisible girl. "Can you fix Winks?"

"She's my partner. Wish or no wish, I would have done it by now if I could."

"Then let's not worry about it for now. If I ever want to collect I'll say so. Otherwise, I don't want any," I said.

Tower smiled. "Fair enough."

Mandi came over by me. "Since the danger is past, I'll undo the link."

Sarge came over. "I'll arrange for your usual room in Ringvue."

"Wait a second. Why does Mandi need to be in an asylum?" I asked.

"Nyarlathotep messed with my mind. The emotional residue from that ancient evil is still there. It's going to be in all of these people for a long time, but it's a thousand times worse for me. I'm only conscious because of the link with you. Once I let that go, it's going to make me comatose for a while until I can rebuild my shields on my own."

"Then keep the link with me. I don't care," I said.

"I can't because sooner or later one of us will dominate the other, subjugate them," said Mandi.

"You know better than anyone that I would never do that to anyone else, especially you," I said.

"It's not a matter of want. It's just how it is," she said.

I turned to Tower. "Could a wish fix this?"

Before the jinn could answer, Mandi said, "No. I need to do this myself. Having someone else fix me will make me weaker and then the next time will be worse."

"What do you need me to do?" I asked.

"Nothing, Karver. Although visiting me once in a while would be nice. It may be a while before I notice you, though," said Mandi. "See you soon partner."

With that, I felt her break the link. She screamed once and fell. I caught her before she hit the ground and carried her out of the town.

Sarge got us air transport to Ringvue in New York City. It's not far from the better known Bellevue, except it specializes in mental disorders from mystic trauma.

The government funds a federal ward there. Andy and Mandi had rooms across from each other. I visited Andy a few times a day. The visionary was still in a coma from whatever it was he saw in Idaho.

I even looked in on Brody Bodach, who had become quite attached to my partner and me. The kid geezer was very upset about what happened to Mandi and actually brought her hand drawn get well cards every day. Other than that, I basically camped out in Mandi's room. The nurses tried to get rid of me after visiting hours, but the director, an older black man named Gabriel, shooed them away. He was an odd duck – walked around in jeans, played trumpet in his office – pretty good too.

"Stay as long as you like," Gabe said. "As a matter of fact, you can take part in therapy for yourself."

"I'm not sure…"

"Hush, boy. I can see what the seriál did to you. You've done an amazing job on your own, but just know we are here to help you every bit as much as we are trying to help your partner."

Then he laid a hand on my shoulder and I didn't even cringe. In fact, for a brief instant the small black man in front of me glowed and I would have sworn I saw a pair of brilliant ivory wings on his back. Then Gabe pulled his hand away and the vision was gone.

The vision unsettled me. I went outside for a walk on the Lower East Side of Manhattan. I stopped to pick up flowers for my partner and Andy, when someone came up behind me. For a moment I thought it was Gabe, but a quick look told me it wasn't.

"Agent Karver, let me get that for you," said the tall black man, a brimmed hat on his head and a pair of sunglasses on his nose. He had no hair, even where his eyebrows should have been.

"Sorry, agents aren't allowed to accept gifts," I said and looked at the man closer. I was sure I had never seen him before, but something about him was very familiar. "Do I know you?"

He took off the dark glasses revealing black eyes. "You don't remember me? One would think I was Agent Winks."

I recognized him and my blood ran cold. "Hello Nyarlathotep."

"Well, at least you can be pleasant. I just came by to say "hi" and tell you to give Agent Cobb my best. I'd visit, but even I could not enter Ringvue unless invited. I much prefer Arkham Sanatorium. How is your partner doing?"

"Well, given the circumstances," I answered, pulling out my cell phone as discretely as I could.

"I must say, you were impressive marshalling your forces to

defeat me. Well, almost. And almost has almost never been done. You should be proud of yourself," Nyarlathotep said.

"Couldn't have done it without your help," I said.

"In retrospect, I suppose it was foolish to taunt Cyetrole and give a human power over him. Well, another human." Nyarlathotep laughed. "What a horrible existence he must have. I thought he would have welcomed oblivion – a miscalculation on my part."

"Anything else?" I said, hitting 1 on my speed dial.

"Yes. I'm going to destroy you. And every last DMA agent, starting with those that opposed me," Nyarlathotep said. "But not today. Soon, but only I will know the hour. You know two of my faces, but I have 997 more. You'll never see me coming. The waiting should make your life that much more enjoyable. I have a demon aspect. Perhaps I could seek out your Arkham Sanatorium and help your seriál find you again and reconnect. With that mark, he'd have little trouble taking you again."

"That's fine. That demon will never get me again, even with your help, but he's welcome to try." The thought terrified me, but the idea of stopping the seriál, maybe even giving it a little payback had a certain vengeful appeal. "Of course when you try for any DMA agent, you attack us all. You'll only ensure your own destruction."

Nyarlathotep laughed. "The lot of you couldn't defeat me in force. How do you propose to do it now?"

"Easy," I said, holding up the video screen on my phone to face the Tall Man in a different form. "Say hello, Spyder."

"Hello Spyder," said the kid. He had been listening to our conversation and he was smart enough to play along. I had no doubt a squad of agents was headed to New York City right now, but they'd be too late to help me unless I could bluff my way out of this.

"You threaten me with a freak of electricity?"

"Who you calling a freak?" shouted Spyder, turning his aspect into a tentacled monster.

Nyarlathotep laughed.

"Don't let him get to you, Spyder. You got everything ready?" I asked.

Even though Spyder had no idea what I was talking about, he answered, "You know I do."

Nyarlathotep tilted his head. "What are you two babbling about?"

"We recorded your names. All 999, in order, with the correct pronunciations. I've got to tell you some of the alien ones were tough to say correctly. I helped with the demon one. We then sped up the recording so it can be played back in an instant, binding and destroying you," I said.

"You are bluffing or you would have done it already," Nyarlathotep said.

He called my bluff, so I raised. "I would have, but Sparky made me promise to give you one chance. He called it a peace offering. And he has more than a little pull with Sarge."

"Cyetrole's human prison."

"The day you are both waiting for will probably come long after Earth is a barren rock, so we can afford to be generous."

"It's probably best for your sanity if you keep believing that," said Nyarlathotep.

"Here's the deal. We let you walk. You forgive any grievances against Sparky and the DMA and you agree to butt out of human affairs. In return, we don't use it."

"How fast is it?" Nyarlathotep said, taking a step towards me.

"I could have used it a hundred times in the span it took you to make that step," said Spyder.

"That's impossible," Nyarlathotep said, but he stopped short.

"Technology can do some wonderful things. You have a taste for technology I hear, so you know what I'm talking about. You are always looking for new ways to use it toward your own ends, like the power amplifier in Idaho," said Spyder. At least an amplifier was everyone's best guess on the matter. "I can feel you trying to take control of me now. Don't waste the effort. I'm broadcasting remotely. If you don't take the deal, I send out the recording to any and all interested parties."

Nyarlathotep frowned. "I make no vow. We will see how it goes."

"So long as you realize the consequences of your actions," I said.

"As long as you do, Agent Karver," said Nyarlathotep.

"So we have an agreement?" I said.

"More of an understanding," said Nyarlathotep. "Good day, gentlemen." And with that, the second face of the Tall Man walked off, losing himself in the teeming masses of Manhattan.

I faced the phone.

"Remind me never to play anything but electronic poker against you Karver," said Spyder.

I smiled. "How about we take care of that recording for real?"

"How? Sparky knows nine hundred plus, but only the first five hundred or so in order."

"Call Tower and tell her I'm calling in a wish," I said.

Spyder shifted back to his real face and grinned. "I'll conference call the two of you with Sarge."

I told them my plan and according to the jinn it was very doable. We'd have a working recording by day's end.

Everyone else disconnected, but Sarge. "Karver, you did good. And Sparky says thanks."

"Tell him he's welcome," I said. Apparently my eavesdropping ability only worked in person. "Sparky is DMA like the rest of us." I may have blackmailed him, but he did the right thing in the end. "We take care of our own, whether they are former serial killers or creatures of elder darkness."

Sarge laughed. "And as a bonus I won't dock you for your time visiting your partner."

Sarge was kidding. He wouldn't have docked me. He had already arranged it so I was on the payroll to guard Mandi and Andy.

"Give Mandi and Andy my best," said Sarge.

"Will do," I said. I hung up and finished paying for the flowers. I did a brief search of the surrounding streets just in case the Tall Man was lingering, but found nothing. Of course, in another aspect I'd likely not recognize him, so I spent a lot of time checking people's eyes.

All in all, I was gone a couple of hours. Once I got back to Ringvue, I stopped by Andy's room first and put the flowers in a vase.

"Everyone sends their best," I said to the unmoving form.

"What, they couldn't visit themselves?" Andy said, suddenly moving.

"Andy, you're awake," I said.

"Karver, you're not usually one to state the obvious," said Andy. "Who put these eyes in?"

The others needed to be changed. They had gotten dirty when he went fetal. "The nurses, but I picked them." The right said "Gone", the left "Fishing."

"Nice choice."

"Thanks. How are you feeling?" I asked.

"Have you ever taken a gallon of psychedelic, mind-altering drugs, had creatures crawling around your brain which had just been dipped in honey and then added fire ants, all while nursing a hangover?" asked Andy.

"Can't say that I have."

"I'm a little better than that, thanks to Mandi's help bringing me out," said Andy.

"Mandi's awake?" I said.

"I figured you knew," he said.

I didn't bother to reply as I ran across the hall. Mandi was sitting on the side of the bed.

"You okay, partner?" I asked.

"I'd be better if there had been someone here waiting for me when I woke up," Mandi said.

"Sorry about that," I said.

Mandi chuckled. "I didn't think you'd admit to camping out here. Gabe told me that this was the first time you left the building." She saw the flowers. "Are those for me?"

"Nope. There's a cute woman down the hall in a coma. I thought the flowers might impress her. But I suppose I have known you longer." I handed her the bouquet.

"Thanks." She sniffed the flowers and put them on her lap.

"Seriously, how are you?" I said.

"Better than in the past when I've come out of madness induced comas," said Mandi.

"Practice makes perfect," I offered.

"I don't want any more practice. I'm good enough," she said.

"Yeah you are," I said.

We looked into each other's eyes and everything was quiet. The moment lasted far longer that it normally would have.

Mandi motioned me in with her index finger. I leaned my face toward hers when her hand snapped up and slapped my cheek.

"Trying to take advantage of me in my weakened state, are you?" Mandi said.

"If I was going to do that, I would have done it while you were knocked out. Probably would have caught an STD," I said.

"Caught? Any disease in its right mind would run away from you," said Mandi.

I laughed. "At least things are back to normal."

Mandi looked in my eyes. "Normal is good."

"Yeah, it is."

"We normal?" asked Mandi.

"Compared to everyone else? No. For us, we couldn't be anything but," I said.

"We should talk about what happened," said Mandi.

"We will. But it doesn't have to be now," I said, climbing into the bed. I motioned her to slide in next to me. Mandi put her head on my shoulder and I put my arm around hers. I didn't cringe a bit. Neither did she.

Darkness fell. Picking up all the pieces this time would just take a little longer than usual.

PATRICK THOMAS – With over a million words in print, PATRICK THOMAS keeps busy writing the popular fantasy humor series Murphy's Lore (Tales From Bulfinches Pub, Fools' Day, Through The Drinking Glass, Shadow Of The Wolf, Redemption Road, Bartnder Of The Gods, Nightcaps, and Empty Graves) as well as its After Hours spin-offs (Fairy With A Gun, Fairy Rides The Lightning, Dead To Rites, Rites Of Passage, and Lore & Dysorder). His Mystic Investigators series has grown to include Bullets & Brimstone and From the Shadows both with John L. French and Once More Upon a Time and the upcoming Partners In Crime both with Diane Raetz. Patrick's syndicated humorous advice column Dear Cthulhu has been collected in Have a Dark Day, Good Advice For Bad People and Cthulhu Knows Best. Laurence Fishburne's production company Cinema Gypsy Productions has taken a film and television option on Patrick Thomas' urban fantasy Fairy with a Gun. Stop by his website at www.patthomas.net.

JOHN L. FRENCH worked for over forty years for the Baltimore Police Department as a crime scene investigator and has seen more than his share of murders, shootings and serious assaults. As a break from the realities of his job, he writes science fiction, pulp, horror, fantasy, and, of course, crime fiction. Since 1992 John has been writing stories partly based on his experiences on the streets of what some have called one of the most dangerous cities in the country. His books include The Devil of Harbor City, Past Sins, Souls on Fire, Here There Be Monsters and Paradise Denied. He is the editor of Bad Cop, No Donut, Mermaids 13: Tales of the Sea and To Hell in a Fast Car: On the Road to Death and Disaster.

Beloved cult figure **CJ HENDERSON** is the creator of both the Piers Knight supernatural investigator series and the Teddy London occult detective series. Author of some 70 books, including such diverse titles as "The Encyclopedia of Science Fiction Films," "Black Sabbath: the Ozzy Osbourne Years" and "Baby's First Mythos," he has also written hundreds of short stories and comics and thousands of non-fiction pieces. Possibly the most profound thinker of our time, possibly simply a bourbon-soused sot, his work has been published in some thirteen languages and enjoyed around the world by those desperate for words ringing with truth and freedom, and perhaps too much time on their hands. For the chance to comment to the man himself on his stories in this collection, to read more of his prose or to simply learn more about this tortured nut-job, log on at **www.cjhenderson.com**.

DOWN THESE
MEAN STREETS
of Magic & Monsters walk the

MYSTIC INVESTIGATORS

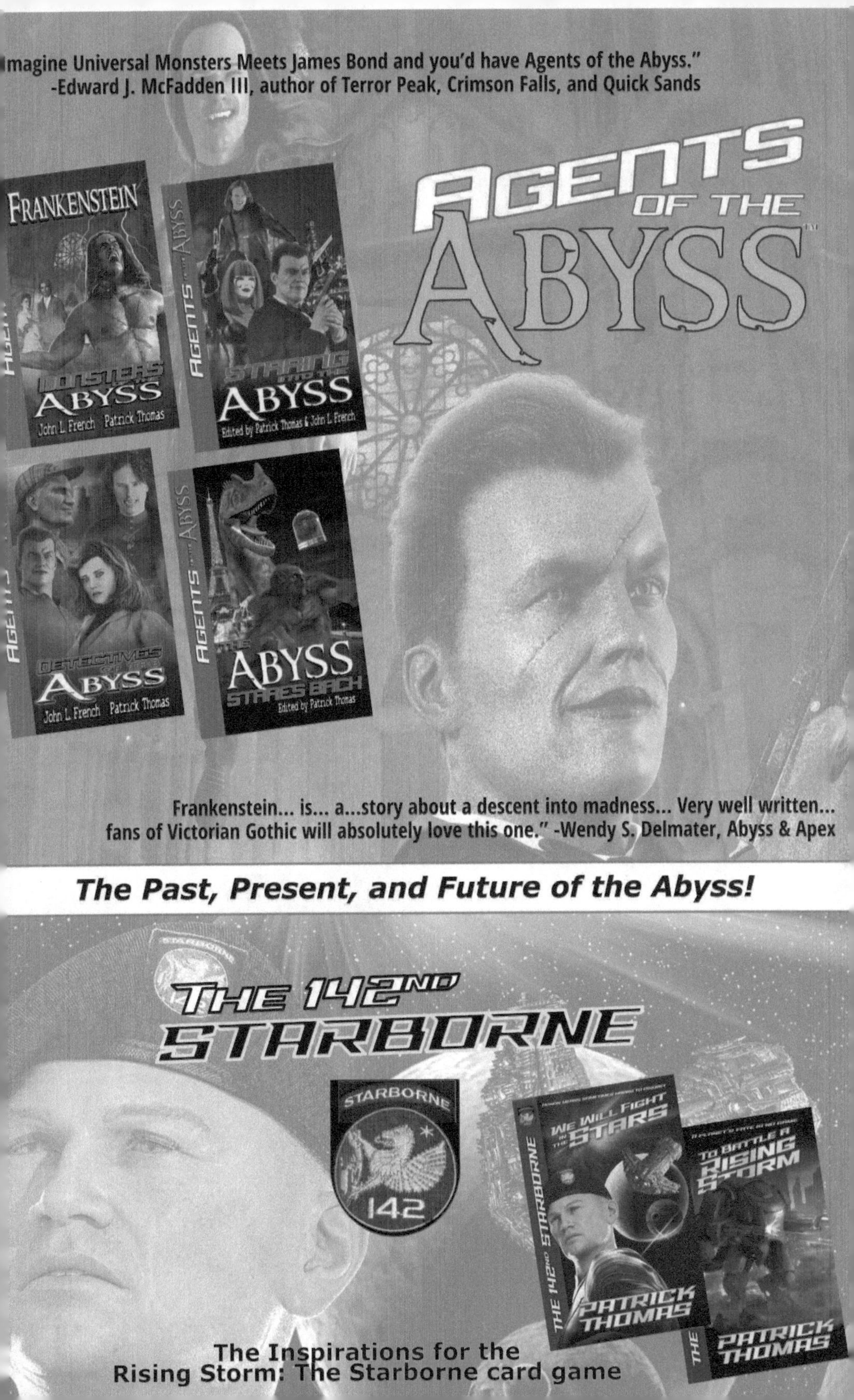

"Imagine Universal Monsters Meets James Bond and you'd have Agents of the Abyss."
-Edward J. McFadden III, author of Terror Peak, Crimson Falls, and Quick Sands

AGENTS OF THE ABYSS

Frankenstein... is... a...story about a descent into madness... Very well written...
fans of Victorian Gothic will absolutely love this one." -Wendy S. Delmater, Abyss & Apex

The Past, Present, and Future of the Abyss!

THE 142ND STARBORNE

The Inspirations for the
Rising Storm: The Starborne card game

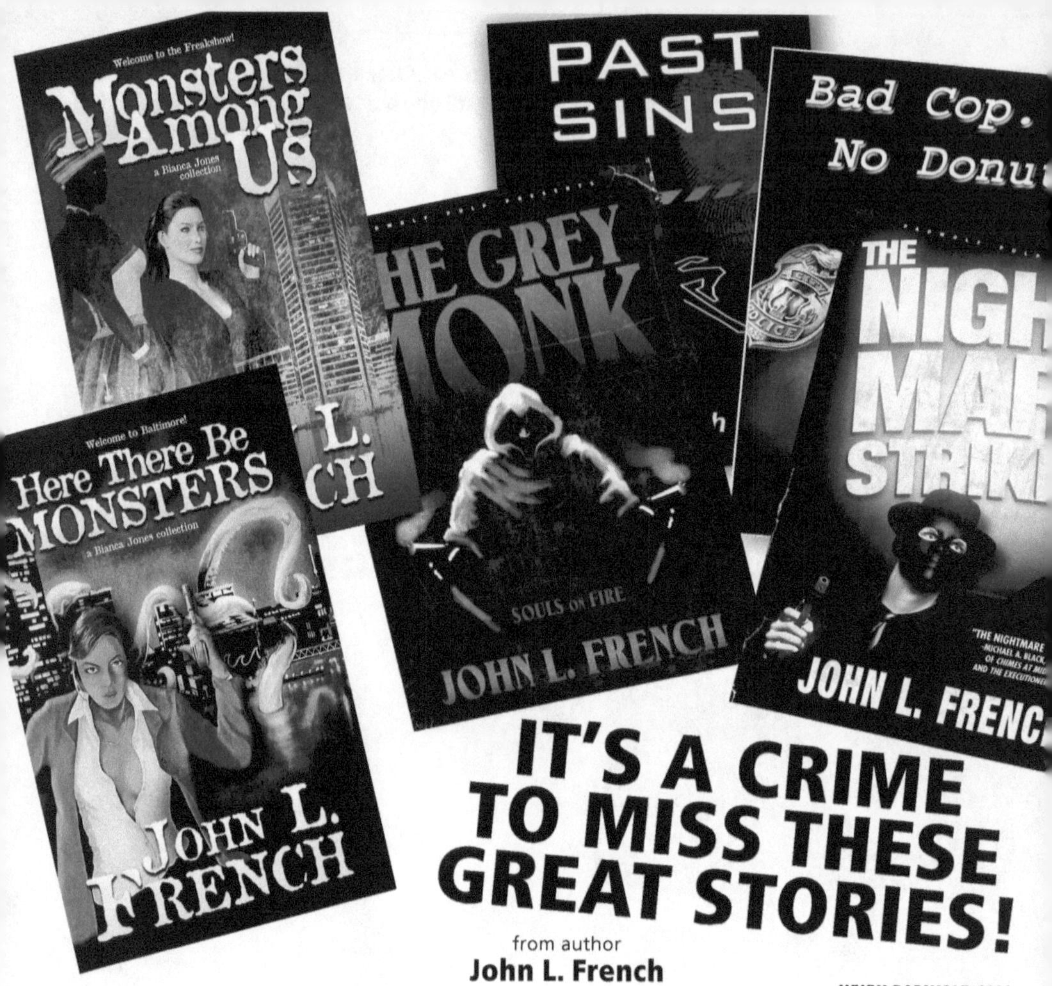

You can't
get better
than 13!

trick Thomas is... so believable it's unbelievable."
-Ida Vega-Landow, The Journal of the Lincoln Heights Literary Society

DEAD TO RITES
Patrick Thomas
C.J. Henderson

rites of Passage
John L. French
Patrick Thomas

When Darkness Falls
The Department of
Mystic Affairs
Picks up the pieces

From The Murphy's Lore Universe of
PATRICK THOMAS
www.patthomas.net

Find us on Facebook!

Even the things that go Bump in the night
will learn that you DON'T mess with...
Terrorbelle

Fairy Rides the Lightning
PATRICK THOMAS

Fairy With A Gun
PATRICK THOMAS

More

TerrorBelle
the Unconquered
PATRICK THOMAS

"Thomas certainly brings the goods to the table
when it comes to writing urban fiction...I promise, you will love...
Terrorbelle: Fairy With a Gun. Who doesn't love a well-stacked,
ass-kicking, gun-toting, woman with bullet-proof, razor-sharp win
that investigates all manner of supernatural spookiness? I know
and Thomas's humor shows through in every tale. Jim Butcher an
Laurell K Hamilton have nothing on Thomas." The Raven's Barro

From The Murph   re Universe of
PATRICK THOMAS

hape up...
You only get
NE Warning

By Invocation Only
Hex Factor
PATRICK THOMAS

rkness CURSED
Hex marks the spot
TRICK THOMAS

Hell's Detective

No One Is Above The Lore...
Even In Hell

LORE & DYSORDER
PATRICK THOMAS

SHADOWS
PATRICK THOMAS
JOHN L. FRENCH

CASE OF THE MOON MANIAC

"Dark... and charming."
- Ellen Datlow,
The Best Horror of the Year Vol. 4

One Last Chance to Save
Happily Ever After

Can a group of heroes including Goldenhair, Red Riding Hood and Rapunzel help General Snow White and her dwarven resistance fighters defeat the tyrannical Queen Cinderella? And will they succeed before a war with Wonderland destroys everything?

Their only hope to stop Cinderella's quest for power lies with a young girl named Patience Muffet who carries the fabled shards of Cinderella's glass slippers.

Roy Mauritsen's fantasy adventure fairy tale epic begins with *Shards Of The Glass Slipper: Queen Cinder.*

"Fantastic...
A Magnificent Epi[c]
-Sarah Beth Durst autho[r]
Into The Wild & Drink, Slay, L[o]

"The Brothers Grim[m]
meets
Lord Of The Rings!
-Patrick Thomas, author
of the Murphy's Lore series

"Shards is a dark, lus[h]
full-throttle fanta[sy]
epic that presen[ts]
a bold re-imaginin[g]
of classic characters
-David Wade, creator [of]
319 Dark Stre[et]

"Roy Mauritsen'[s]
enchanting epi[c]
comes at a tim[e]
when fairy tale[s]
are back in th[e]
forefront o[f]
our collectiv[e]
imagination.
-Darin Kennedy[,]
short fiction autho[r]

PADWOLF
PUBLISHING

In paperback & e-bo[ok]
Find out more
shardsoftheglassslipper.c[om]
padwolf.c[om]

Bikini Jones

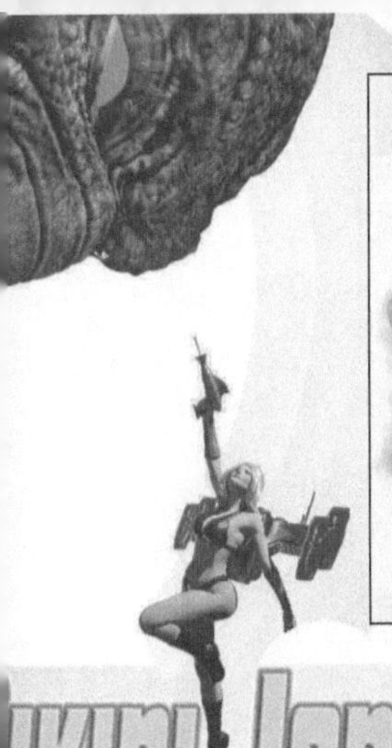

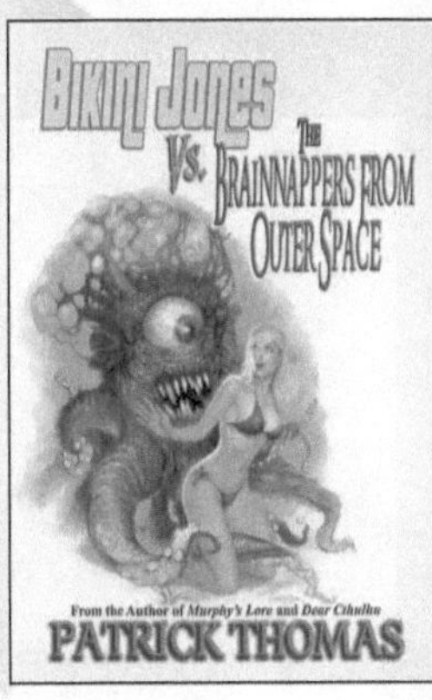

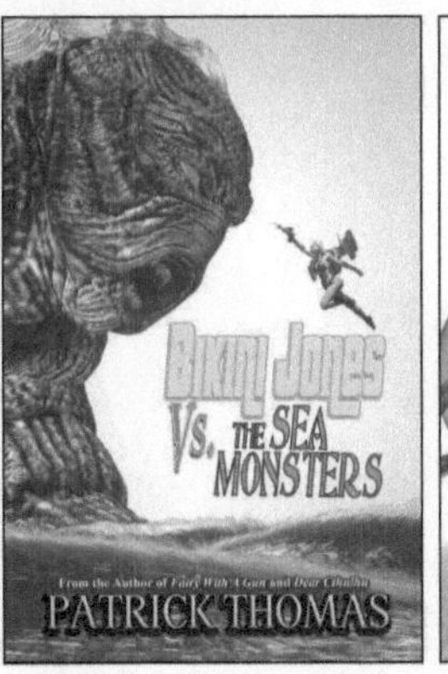

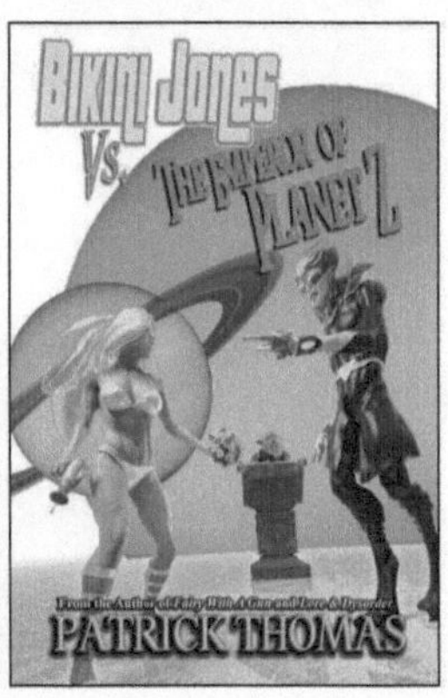

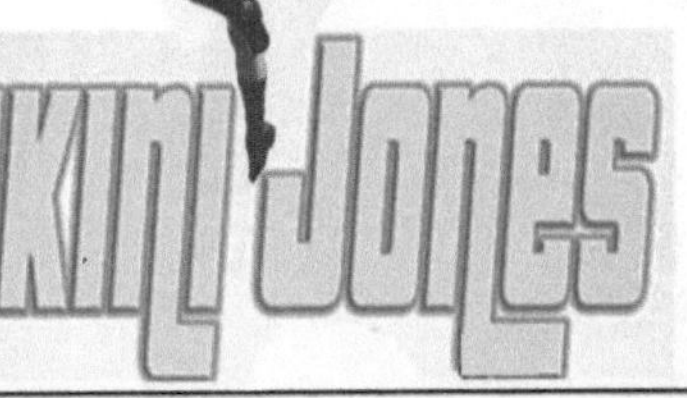

Being *CURSED* to wear a bikini
Won't stop this Hero
From *SAVING* the world

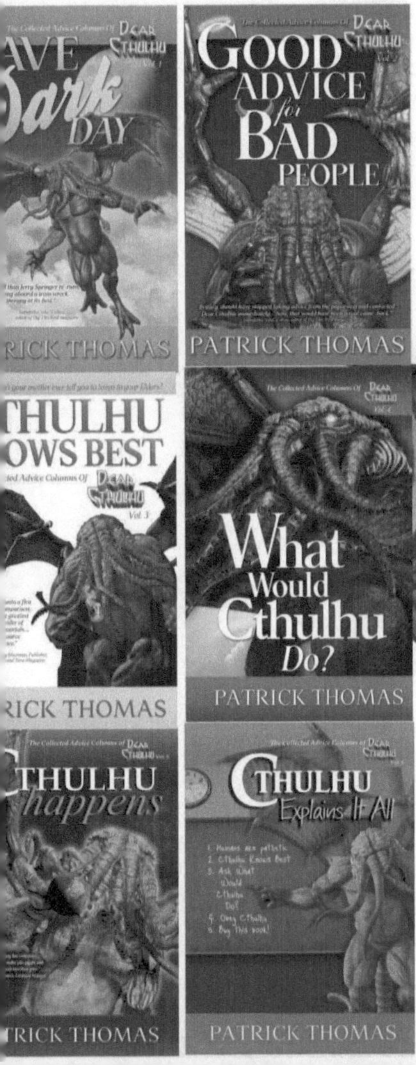

Dear Cthulhu

THE ADVICE
COLUMN TO
***END* ALL**
ADVICE COLUMNS

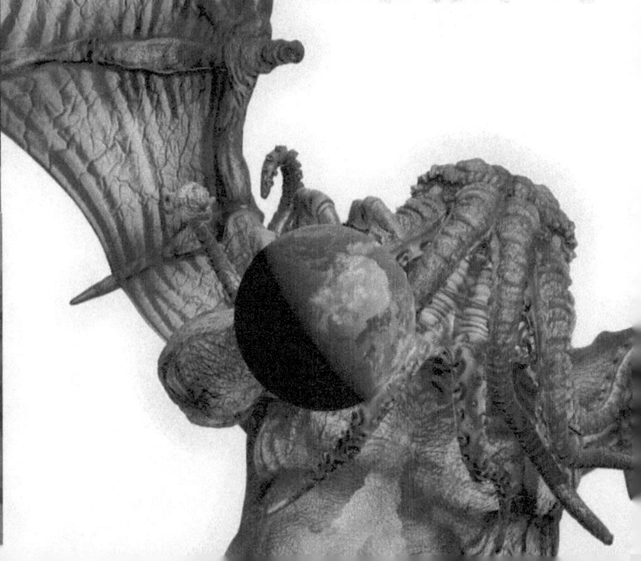